JANE BETTANY is the author of the DI Isabel Blood crime series. The first book in the series, *In Cold Blood*, was Jane's debut novel. It won the Gransnet and HQ writing competition in 2019.

Jane lives in Derby and has an MA in Creative Writing. She enjoys walking in local beauty spots and loves to explore Derbyshire's many tourist attractions, shops, and cafés.

Also by Jane Bettany

In Cold Blood
Without a Trace

Last Seen Alive

JANE BETTANY

ONE PLACE. MANY STORIES

HQ
An imprint of HarperCollins*Publishers* Ltd
1 London Bridge Street
London SE1 9GF

www.harpercollins.co.uk

HarperCollins*Publishers*
1st Floor, Watermarque Building, Ringsend Road
Dublin 4, Ireland

This paperback edition 2022

1
First published in Great Britain by
HQ, an imprint of HarperCollins*Publishers* Ltd 2022

ISBN: 9780008494834

MIX
Paper from
responsible sources
FSC **FSC™ C007454**
www.fsc.org

For Mum
with love

Chapter 1

It was after midnight and the clock in the corner sounded too loud, almost portentous.

Tick. Tock. Tick.

Counting down to the witching hour.

Tock. Tick. Tock.

Was she being unreasonable? Worrying unnecessarily?

Lauren stared out through the uncurtained window, scouring the darkness for approaching headlights. Benedict lay next to her on the sofa, supported by pillows and sleeping like the five-month-old baby he was, his chubby arms splayed either side of his head. She reached out and stroked his round, peachy cheek.

'Where's your mummy, eh?' Her voice was soft and lilting and tinged with concern.

She turned and glared at the face of the clock, urging the minute hand towards the time when she should, *must* do something. One o'clock. That's when she'd make the call. At one o'clock, Anna would be exactly ninety minutes late – Anna, who was never knowingly late for anything, and *always* on time to pick up her son.

Leaving Benedict on his temporary bed, she moved closer to the window, willing a car to appear. The pitch-black night was lit only by a smattering of stars. *She'll be here by half past twelve,* Lauren told herself. *She'll walk in with that wide, endearing smile, full of apology and still wide awake from the party – and I'll forgive her in an instant. There's been a delay, that's all. Or her car has broken down.*

But if that was the case, why hadn't she called? Why was her phone switched off?

The clock continued its relentless, steady ticking, each second a heartbeat in which Lauren grew increasingly afraid.

Chapter 2

PC Will Rowe wasn't a big fan of the night shift. He operated best on sunny days – on noisy, crowded streets. He was a townie, born and bred in Bainbridge, and happiest working within the confines of its urban, bustling centre. The dark hours of early morning were alien to him; an alternative underworld populated by furtive, shadowy people. Driving alone at night through the town's rural, outer edges made him feel unplugged and disconnected.

He was currently three miles north of town, on a remote country road, heading to the home of Lauren Talbot. At one a.m., she had called 999, concerned about her friend, Anna Matheson, who had failed to pick up her son, whom Lauren was babysitting. The force control room had dispatched Will to gather more information and assess whether the Matheson woman had gone temporarily AWOL, or was an at-risk missing person.

He leaned forward, steering his patrol car along the winding, narrow lane and scanning ahead for signs of the address he'd been sent to: Bellbrook House. Tall hawthorn hedges towered either side of the road and, in the darkness, it felt as though they were closing in on him.

He almost missed the turn. Swearing under his breath, he slammed on the brakes, reversed a couple of yards and swung right, through an open gate, and onto an upward-climbing driveway.

Bellbrook House stood on the brow of the hill, an ill-defined outline against a sky dotted with a handful of fairy-light stars. The house itself was in darkness, blending in with the moonless night.

As he got out of his vehicle and strolled towards the property, a sensor lamp burst into dazzling life. Startled, Will held up a hand to shield his eyes from its glare. As he stood there, squinting, the front door opened and a tall female figure looked out from the front step.

'I'm PC Will Rowe, responding to the call you made,' he said peering through his fingers. 'I assume you're Lauren Talbot?'

'I am.' The woman leaned against the doorjamb and folded her arms. 'I saw your car coming up the lane. I didn't want you to ring the bell in case it woke the kids.'

'Is it OK if I come in, Lauren? Am I all right to call you Lauren?'

'Of course,' she said. 'Yes to both of those things.'

Will followed her through a hallway that smelled of rose-scented potpourri and on into a spacious, unlit living room on the left.

'Would you mind switching the light on?' he said, peering at her through the gloom.

'Sure.' She reached down and turned on a table lamp. 'I've been sitting here in the dark, watching for headlights, hoping to see Anna's car come belting up the road.'

The lamp cast a warm glow across a chimney breast covered with heavily patterned wallpaper, but threw out little in the way of real brightness.

'Is that OK?' Lauren asked. 'I'd rather not turn on the main light in case it wakes Benedict.' She nodded towards the other side of the room.

Will turned, noticing the sleeping child for the first time. He was lying on a makeshift bed on the couch, arms stretched, his mouth open.

'That's Benedict?' he asked. 'Your friend's son? The child you've been babysitting?'

Lauren nodded, her face tense. 'I've got my own kids asleep upstairs as well.'

'Other than the children, are you here alone?'

'Yes, my husband's in Liverpool for a few days. A work seminar.'

A pair of matching armchairs stood on either side of the fireplace. Will pointed to them.

'Can we sit down?' He smiled. 'I need to ask some questions about your friend, and I wouldn't mind taking the weight off my size thirteens.'

Lauren placed a hand on her forehead. 'Of course. I'm sorry, where are my manners?' She sat down and invited him to do the same. 'My mind's all over the place. This isn't like Anna. She's normally so reliable. Always has been.'

'Have the two of you been friends for long?'

'Most of our lives …' Lauren smiled. 'Best mates since junior school.'

'And you rang 999 because you're concerned about her?'

She pressed her lips together and nodded. 'Anna's a single mum, so I regularly help out with childcare. Tonight … or rather, last night, I was looking after Benedict while she went to a party. She was supposed to collect him at eleven-thirty, and when it comes to picking up her son, she's never late. Never.'

'A party, you say? Is it possible she's met someone there? Lost track of time?'

Lauren hunched forward, clutching her stomach. 'It's not really a party in the true sense, more of a work do. Anna organised the whole event as part of her job. I'm pretty sure she'll have spent the entire evening making sure everything goes to plan.'

'And where does Anna work?'

'She's the marketing manager at Allwood Confectionery. The factory's celebrating its sixtieth anniversary this year, and the owners decided to throw a bit of a bash for their employees.'

'Where's the party being held?'

'At the factory, in the works canteen,' Lauren said. 'Anna would have preferred somewhere more salubrious, but the CEO didn't want to book a proper venue in case the lifting of the lockdown restrictions was delayed again.'

'Regardless of the location, I'm sure the staff will enjoy themselves.' Will smiled. 'I think we're all overdue a spot of revelry, eh?'

She gave him an uncertain nod.

'Any idea what time the party was due to finish?'

'Midnight, I think, but Anna was going to leave early.'

'Is it possible she's stayed longer than planned?'

'She would have rung if she was going to be late. Anyway, even if she'd hung around until the end, she would have been back by now.'

'And you've tried calling her … without success?'

Lauren released a hiss of air and dragged her fingers through her long blonde hair. 'Several times,' she said. 'Her mobile's switched off, and that in itself is unusual. Anna's always messing with her phone … I'm constantly telling her off about it. She's either looking something up online, or ringing someone, or texting them, or posting something on social media. She never switches off from her job, and it'll have been exactly the same tonight.'

Will smiled wryly.

'The party's meant to be a chance for Anna to let her hair down,' Lauren continued. 'But I know what she's like. She'll have been checking on the catering, taking photos, organising the speeches and awards. I bet everyone else has had a whale of a time, but not Anna. She won't have had a minute to relax.'

'When you organise an event like that, I suppose you're bound to feel a sense of responsibility,' Will said. 'I can understand why she'd want everything to go with a swing.'

'I'm sure there's been nothing for her to worry about. Anna's

6

good at her job and her organisational skills are second to none. She puts the rest of us to shame.'

'Have you checked with Anna's colleagues or family members? Perhaps one of them will know where she is.'

'I thought about trying to get hold of her mum,' Lauren said. 'But I don't have her number … and even if I did, it's the early hours of the morning. She's bound to be in bed and I don't want to worry her unnecessarily. As for Anna's colleagues, I wouldn't have a clue how to get in touch with them. She often talks about the people she works with, but I've never met any of them.'

Will extracted a notebook from his top pocket and turned to a fresh page. 'Can you give me any names?'

Lauren thought for a moment. 'The CEO is Faye Allwood, and her son, Ross, is the head of sales. There's also someone called James Derenby, who's the general manager. Anna works closely with him. He has a thing for her, actually.'

'*Thing?*' Will paused, tapping his pencil on the open page of his notebook. 'You mean he's attracted to her?'

Raising an eyebrow, Lauren smiled. 'He must be – he's asked her out enough times. Anna always turns him down though.'

'I take it she doesn't like this bloke then?'

'She likes him well enough.' Lauren wrinkled her nose. 'But she doesn't fancy him. And anyway, Anna has a rule about not dating anyone she works with.'

'Doesn't like mixing business with pleasure, is that it?'

'Exactly.' Lauren nodded. 'I wouldn't be surprised if Ross Allwood has got his eye on her as well, although Anna *definitely* won't be going out with him.'

'Doesn't she fancy him either?'

'No, and more to the point, she has very little respect for the man. Apparently, he's rubbish at his job. Anna reckons he'd have been sacked ages ago if he was an ordinary employee.'

'As opposed to the boss's son, you mean?'

'Oh, he's more than that,' Lauren said. 'When his father died

7

last year, Ross Allwood became the co-owner of the factory. His mother, Faye Allwood, owns the rest of the company.'

Will made a note of the information. 'Is there anyone else from Allwoods that I should know about?' he said. 'The sweet factory employs a lot of people. Anna must have mentioned more than those three colleagues?'

'She's talked about a few others, but only in a casual way. I can't remember their names. Sorry.'

'I'll need the name of Anna's mum as well. I do think we should let her know what's happening.'

'It's Christina. Christina Matheson. She lives in Milford, on Hopping Hill. I'm not sure of the house number.'

'We'll find her, don't worry,' Will said. Shifting his weight, he leaned forward. 'If Anna was planning to pick Benedict up at eleven-thirty, what time would she have needed to set off from the factory?'

'It doesn't take long to drive here from town,' Lauren said. 'It's a five- or six-minute journey, as long as the roads are clear. Anna would have set off in plenty of time. Providing everyone was well fed and watered, she said she was planning to leave straight after the speeches and awards, which were due to finish at eleven-fifteen.'

On the sofa, the baby stirred. Will watched his little legs and arms stretch as he moved into a new position.

'Do you think Anna will have had a drink at the party?' Will asked.

'She rarely drinks these days,' Lauren replied. 'And she never drinks if she's driving. She has sole responsibility for her son, so she likes to stay within the limit, in case there's ever an emergency.'

'What's the situation with Benedict's father?' Will said. 'Is he still on the scene?'

'No, never has been.' Lauren pulled a face, implying that she didn't altogether approve of his absence.

'Any particular reason?'

She lifted her right shoulder. 'I've no idea. I've never met the man. In my opinion, Anna should let him be part of Benedict's life, but she won't hear of it. It's one of the few things we disagree on. We've come close to falling out about it a couple of times.'

'You've argued about it?'

'We did in the early days, during her pregnancy and immediately after Benedict was born, but I try to steer clear of the subject now. Anna's adamant she doesn't want Benedict's dad involved … that the baby is *her* responsibility and no one else's. Personally, I think she's wrong, but it's her son, her choice.'

Will detected a note of peevishness in Lauren's voice, an unwillingness to accept her friend's decision.

He licked his thumb and turned to a fresh page in his notebook. 'We may need to get hold of Benedict's dad,' he said. 'Can you give me his name, please.'

'I'm afraid I can't. I don't know his name. Anna's never told me who he is.'

Will frowned. This didn't sound good. Why keep the man's identity under wraps? In his experience, people with secrets usually had something unpleasant to hide.

'As far as I'm aware, she hasn't told anyone who he is,' Lauren added. 'Not even her own mother.'

'Any chance Anna could be with this man now?' Will asked.

'I doubt it, but who knows? I haven't a clue where she is. That's why I rang 999.'

Will referred to his notebook. 'What about this colleague of hers? James Derenby? Is it possible she's finally given in and gone for a drink with him?'

'What? At one o'clock in the morning?' Lauren scoffed. 'I shouldn't imagine so. There's nowhere in Bainbridge open at this time of night.'

'Might she have gone back to his place for a drink?'

'*No.*' Lauren's face twitched impatiently. 'She's not interested in a relationship with James Derenby, or anyone else for that matter. Right now, Anna's focusing on her child and her career – in that order. Anyway, she wouldn't go off with someone without speaking to me first.'

'With respect,' said Will, 'she is a grown woman. She doesn't need your permission.'

Lauren thrust out her chin. 'I'm not saying she does, but I *am* looking after her son, and Anna's not the sort of person to take advantage. She'd let me know if there'd been a change of plan.'

'Fair enough,' Will said, conceding the point. 'Can you tell me if Anna has any health issues we should be aware of?'

'No, on the contrary, she's fitter now than she has been for years.'

'What about her mental health? Has she ever suffered from depression or anxiety? Has anything been worrying her recently? Any signs of postnatal depression, perhaps?'

'No, none of those things.'

'Any other reason she might have wanted to take off and have some time on her own?'

Lauren narrowed her eyes. 'You don't have children, do you, PC Rowe?'

'No, I don't.'

'I didn't think so.' She smiled mockingly. 'When you do, you'll appreciate the joy of occasionally having some time to yourself. Being responsible for a child twenty-four-seven can be exhausting. Given half a chance, most of us would take a break if we could. However, there's no way any half-decent parent would take off without making proper arrangements for their child – and, as a parent, Anna is more than half decent. She's an excellent mother. She lives for Benedict. He's her world. Trust me, she'd never bugger off and leave him. That's why I'm so worried. Do you think she could have had an accident?'

Will held up his hands. 'There's no evidence of that,' he said. 'There have been no RTAs reported this evening … road traffic accidents … and the control room has already checked with the hospitals. No one matching your friend's description has been admitted.'

'I suppose I should find that reassuring,' Lauren said, 'but, actually, it has the opposite effect.'

The sleeping baby's soft, exhaling breaths drifted across from the other side of the room. It was a normal, ordinary sound. Soothing. Comforting. Benedict was warm and safe and content, but Will couldn't help but wonder how the child's mother was faring in comparison.

He had a bad feeling about this. A really bad feeling. It was time to call it in.

Chapter 3

Bainbridge was in the middle of a heatwave, and DI Isabel Blood was in her back garden, making the most of the good weather. With a cup of strong black coffee in one hand and a slice of buttered wholemeal toast in the other, she lifted her face towards the early morning rays and felt herself relax. The dog was asleep at her feet, stretched out on the hot paving slabs. On the opposite side of the patio table, her husband, Nathan, was tucking into a bowl of breakfast cereal and reading the *Sunday Times*.

'What's the plan for today then?' Isabel said, breathing in the aroma of her coffee before taking a sip.

Nathan glanced up from his paper. 'Does there have to be a plan? It's Sunday. Can't we just relax and let the day unfold?'

She shrugged. Nathan's laissez-faire attitude was, as always, at odds with her own penchant for planning every minute of a day off – but for once, she didn't mind. It was only eight-thirty, but already the sun was burning fiercely in a cloudless, cyan-blue sky. The temperatures were set to sizzle over the next few hours and, sooner or later, Isabel knew she'd end up retreating inside to the dining room, which was the coolest room in the house. Her days of sun-worshipping were over. The older she got, the less tolerance she had for baking in the midday heat.

'I might do a spot of gardening when I've finished reading the paper,' Nathan said. 'Unless you've got another job lined up for me?'

Isabel smiled and closed her eyes, bathing briefly in the warmth of the morning sun. 'It's going to be way too hot for gardening, Nathan.'

'In that case,' he replied, folding his paper and placing it next to his empty cereal bowl, 'maybe I'll just chill.'

'We could go out somewhere for lunch, if you like.'

'Do you have anywhere in mind?'

'A country pub? Or we could try and get a table at the Feathers.'

'Just you and me?' he said. 'Or are we taking the kids?'

She opened one eye and took another swig of coffee. 'I'll check with Ellie … see if she wants to come, although I think she's got plans to spend the day at Lily's house, assuming she can drag herself out of bed.'

'What about Bailey?'

Isabel lifted an eyebrow. 'He's old enough to buy his own lunch, or he could try cooking something for a change.'

Their son had moved back into the family home the previous summer, following a year of travelling with his girlfriend, Sophie. The pair had ended their journey in New Zealand, where Sophie had found a teaching job in Christchurch. She'd fallen in love with the lifestyle out there and announced that she wanted to stay on. Bailey had wanted to come home.

Ultimately, the stubborn pair both got their own way – at the expense of their ten-year relationship. Broken-hearted, Bailey had flown back to the UK alone and had taken up residence in his childhood room on a temporary basis. That had been almost a year ago.

'He's regressed to being a morose teenager again,' Isabel said. 'He spends all his time watching television and slobbing around. It's winding me up.'

'Give the lad a break,' Nathan said. 'He still hasn't got over his split with Sophie.'

'Lad? He's nearly thirty. He's a grown man, Nathan. He can't mope around forever, nor can he stay with us indefinitely. You need to have a word with him.'

'*Me*? Why don't you talk to him?'

'Because he'll think I'm nagging again. It's your turn to give him a verbal kick up the arse.'

Nathan pulled a face. 'I'll give it a go,' he said, 'but I'm not convinced he'll listen to me.'

'I think he will,' Isabel said. 'You're the easy-going one. If you say something, he'll realise he's pushed his luck as far as he can. He's been back for nearly a year. He needs to stop freeloading and get himself a job.'

'In fairness, the last year hasn't been the best time to look for work.'

'I appreciate that, but he hasn't been trying very hard either. He needs to get his act together. He's well qualified. There must be something he can do.'

'If we took him out for lunch, we could talk to him together,' Nathan said.

Isabel drained her coffee cup and leaned across the table. 'Wouldn't that send the wrong message?' she said, keeping her voice low. 'Plying him with a free meal at the same time as telling him he should get a job and start paying his way? It would be kind of ironic, don't you think?'

'I suppose you're right.'

Isabel laughed. 'I usually am.'

Nathan stuck out his tongue and refilled his mug from the cafetiere on the table.

'On reflection, it's probably best if we stay put today,' he said. 'In a couple of hours it's going to be too hot for driving anyway.'

She gazed at him incredulously, an amused expression on her face. 'It's 2021, love. We do have air-conditioning in the car.'

14

He smiled. 'You know I only use that in an emergency.'

Isabel drummed her hands on the table top. 'If we're staying home, I'll go in and grab a book and catch up on some reading. Shall I make more coffee?'

He gave her a thumbs up and returned to his newspaper.

***

By nine o'clock Isabel had slathered sunblock on her bare arms and donned a pair of sunglasses. Armed with a fresh brew and an Elly Griffiths novel, she was reclining on a lounger in a shady corner of the garden. As she turned to a fresh chapter, her phone rang. She glanced at the screen. The caller was Detective Superintendent Valerie Tibbet. *Shit!* A phone call from her boss on a Sunday was never good news.

'DI Blood,' the Super said, when Isabel accepted the call. 'Sorry to disturb you at the weekend, but we have a situation … a missing woman. She attended a party last night, but failed to turn up to collect her son from the babysitter.'

Isabel swung her legs off the lounger and sat up, immediately alert. 'What do we know so far?'

'The misper is Anna Matheson, aged thirty-six. She's employed by a local company, Allwood Confectionery, which is where the party was held. She was last seen at approximately eleven-fifteen last night. Operators are reviewing footage from the factory's CCTV cameras, as well as those in the surrounding area. Matheson's car has been located in the staff car park at the factory – so if she did leave the premises, it wasn't in her own vehicle.'

'Do we know which officers are involved in the inquiry?' Isabel asked.

'Sergeant Bostock is the uniformed supervisor. The on-call detective was also contacted last night.'

'That would be DS Fairfax,' Isabel said. 'He's on duty this weekend.'

'Uniformed officers are continuing to make inquiries, and the PolSA is on standby in case a full search operation becomes necessary, but as of this morning, CID have taken ownership of the investigation. I've asked DS Fairfax to co-ordinate the inquiry – supervised by you, of course. Sergeant Bostock and yourself will need to work together to oversee the investigation and any searches.'

'I'll be at the station in ten minutes,' Isabel said.

Chapter 4

'OK, everyone, simmer down. We need to crack on. There's a lot to get through.'

Isabel was in the operations room, standing in front of the hastily garnered team tasked with tracing the whereabouts of Anna Matheson. A briefing was essential to get everyone up to speed, but she was determined the emphasis would be on the *brief*. Eleven hours had already passed since the last confirmed sighting of the missing woman, and they couldn't afford to waste a minute. The next twelve hours were crucial. Their actions during that time could spell the difference between life and death for Anna Matheson. Isabel knew only too well that the chances of finding a missing person alive and well grew slimmer with each passing hour.

The key to solving any misper case was to trace the person's last known movements and work out why they had disappeared. Officers had already made initial inquiries, but plenty of unanswered questions remained. Technology would provide them with more information, and even statistics would play a part in key decisions, but there was no way of second-guessing human nature.

Isabel found it deeply disconcerting that a seemingly sensible,

17

responsible woman could vanish without a trace. The possible reasons for Anna Matheson's disappearance ranged from innocuous to deadly. The best-case scenario was that she would turn up of her own accord, wondering what all the fuss was about. Worse case, she could already be lying in a ditch somewhere, dead and cold and lost forever.

'As you know,' Isabel began, 'thirty-six-year-old Anna Matheson has been missing since last night. A 999 call was received at one a.m. from a concerned friend, Lauren Talbot. Lauren had been babysitting Anna's five-month-old son, and was expecting her to pick him up at 23.30.'

She glanced over at PC Will Rowe, who was easy to spot. At six foot four, he towered over everyone else in the room. 'PC Rowe, you responded to the 999 call … what can you tell us?'

'The missing woman had been attending a party at her place of work, Allwood Confectionery,' he said. 'It was a celebration of the factory's sixtieth anniversary, and Anna Matheson was responsible for organising the event as part of her job. According to Lauren Talbot, Anna is unlikely to have consumed any alcohol during the evening, primarily because she was driving and isn't much of a drinker, but also because she would have wanted to keep a clear head to oversee proceedings. Her vehicle, a red Ford Focus, was still in the staff car park at the factory at two a.m., when officers did a sweep of the premises.'

'I assume someone's checked the local hospitals?' said DC Zoe Piper.

'The control room did that shortly after receiving the 999 call,' Sergeant Adrian Bostock confirmed. 'No one matching the misper's description has been admitted, and there were no serious accidents or road traffic emergencies reported last night. We've requested security footage from the factory and the surveillance cameras in the surrounding area, although CCTV is pretty sparse at that end of town. The missing woman's next of kin is her mother, Christina Matheson. PC Rowe visited her a few hours ago to inform her of the situation, and we'll send a FLO there as soon as one's been allocated.'

Isabel turned to Zoe, who had recently completed her training as a family liaison officer. 'DC Piper, I'd like you to be the FLO on this one? Think you can handle it?'

Zoe smiled, clearly pleased with the request. 'Not a problem, boss. I'll head over there as soon as the briefing's finished.'

Isabel wandered across to the whiteboard and stared at the photograph of Anna that had been pinned there. It was a corporate shot, downloaded from Allwood Confectionery's website. Anna was staring into the camera lens, wearing an expression that was both serious and professional. Her oval face was framed by wavy, shoulder-length hair, and there was a half-smile on her lips. She wasn't conventionally pretty, but there was nevertheless something striking about her. She had a distinctive face; the kind you remembered.

'Anna Matheson is single, described as approximately five foot five, slim build, with dark, curly hair,' Isabel continued. 'That's her physical description, but what else do we know about her? Is this the first time she's gone off without telling anyone where she is? Or has she done this kind of thing before?'

'Not according to her friend,' Will said. 'Lauren described Anna as steady and reliable … someone who takes her duties as a mother extremely seriously.'

'We know she's single,' said DS Dan Fairfax. 'But is there anyone on the radar who's caused problems for her in the past? What about the father of her child?'

'No one seems to know who he is, which strikes me as odd,' said Will. 'From what I can gather, her relationship with Benedict's father was probably a casual thing … but why keep his identity a secret, especially from her best friend?'

'Let's see what we can do to track him down,' Isabel said. 'What about other partners? Are we absolutely certain Anna isn't in a relationship at the moment?'

Will shook his head. 'Lauren Talbot says not.'

'OK.' Isabel steepled her fingers. 'What about the other guests at the party? Has anyone spoken to any of them yet?'

'Pretty much the whole workforce was there, by all accounts,' Adrian Bostock said. 'So far, we've only managed to contact three or four of them. One of my officers spoke to the head of the company, a Faye Allwood, and her son, Ross. They last saw Anna at about 23.10, and they were shocked and surprised to hear she hadn't turned up to collect her son.'

'We'll be speaking to the Allwoods again later this morning,' said Dan. 'We'll also be talking to the person who works closest with Anna – her colleague, James Derenby. When the factory reopens tomorrow, we'll arrange for a couple of officers to talk to the rest of the workforce. In the meantime, I assume we'll be making a public appeal?'

'We're going to have to,' Isabel said. 'The best possible outcome would be for Anna to turn up safely but, as we all know, that possibility becomes increasingly unlikely with every hour that slips by. We'll review the situation this afternoon, and if her whereabouts are still unknown, we'll hold a press conference.'

Turning to Sergeant Bostock, Isabel added: 'What about her phone? Have we been able to trace it?'

'Sadly not,' Adrian replied. 'It's turned off, and unless it gets switched back on again, there's no way to track it. We've applied to the service provider to get the historical phone data, and we'll be doing some cell site analysis. We should have all that by tomorrow.'

'The fact that her phone is switched off is a concern,' Isabel said.

'Maybe she's with someone and doesn't want to be disturbed,' Dan suggested.

Isabel was unconvinced. 'If Anna was going to roll home with a hangover after an all-nighter, I think she would have appeared by now. Let's dispatch officers to conduct another, more thorough search of the factory and the surrounding area. It's unlikely she's still in the vicinity, but we need to be sure.'

'We've got someone checking with Anna Matheson's bank to see if there's been any activity on her card,' said an officer sitting at the back of the room. 'We should have that information within the hour. We've also checked the missing woman's social media accounts, but there have been no recent posts or updates.'

Isabel released a long, slow breath, anxiety weighing heavy on her chest. 'What about the baby? If Anna didn't pick up her son, where is he now?'

'Still with Lauren Talbot,' Will said.

'Do you think Christina Matheson will want to take charge of the baby until Anna turns up?' Zoe asked.

'I'd say Benedict is better off in Mrs Talbot's care for now,' Will replied. 'She has kids of her own, so she has all the kit and plenty of experience of child rearing.'

Isabel stifled a smile. 'You make it sound as though she's running a farm, Will. People rear pigs and hens. They *look after* children. Raise them. Nurture them.'

PC Rowe stroked his beard self-consciously. 'If you say so, ma'am. Sorry … I don't have kids myself, so I'm not au fait with the lingo.'

Isabel turned to Zoe. 'As the family liaison officer, it'll be up to you to determine whether Christina Matheson wants to look after the baby until her daughter's been found.'

Zoe nodded. 'I'll get going in a minute and ask her when I get there.'

'Remember, your role isn't just about offering tea and sympathy,' Isabel said. 'As the FLO, you have an important part to play … you're the primary link between the investigating team and the family. See what information you can gather – about Anna's relationships with family, friends, colleagues and any other associates. Was anything bothering her? Find out if the mother has any thoughts on why she might have gone missing.'

'Do you think her disappearance could be connected in some way to her job?' Zoe asked.

'I don't know,' Isabel replied. 'But as she disappeared from the staff party, we do have to consider that possibility. On the other hand, this might be nothing to do with her work, so let's not jump to conclusions. Someone needs to talk to Lauren Talbot again. Based on what Will's told us, it sounds like she and Anna are close. Having had more time to reflect, Lauren may have remembered something that could help direct the search.'

Isabel glanced over at DC Lucas Killingworth, who had maintained an uncharacteristic silence throughout the briefing. 'Lucas, I'd like you to liaise with the comms team. We need to get some information out on social media, please, and an initial statement for the press. Zoe, when you speak to Anna's mother, find out if she'd be willing to do a media appeal if and when the press conference goes ahead. Let's get the details out to as wide an audience as possible. Someone must have seen Anna, or know something about her disappearance.'

Lucas shuffled uncomfortably, looking unusually subdued. 'Actually, boss, I wouldn't mind a word, after the briefing. If that's all right?'

Isabel studied him through narrowed eyes before nodding her assent. 'My office in two minutes,' she said. 'Everyone else, please keep DS Fairfax, Sergeant Bostock and myself updated on any new developments. You've all got your actions and you know the drill. Let's do our best to find Anna Matheson, and keep our fingers crossed for a positive outcome.'

Chapter 5

Lucas knocked on the door to her office a couple of minutes later.

'Come and sit down,' she said. 'Are you OK, Lucas? You were very quiet in the briefing, and it's not in your nature to be a shrinking violet.'

His shoulders drooped as he flopped into the chair across from her desk.

'I'm not sure I should be involved in this investigation, boss.' He rubbed the back of his neck. 'The thing is, I have a family connection to the owners of Allwood Confectionery. If I was asked to interview Ross or Faye Allwood, it might be awkward.'

'Awkward how?' Isabel squared her shoulders. 'What exactly is this family connection?'

'Ross Allwood is my cousin,' he said, scratching the top of his head and roughing up his red hair. 'Ross's dad and my mum were brother and sister.'

'Were?'

'Barry Allwood, my uncle, died last year. My mum and him fell out years ago, when I was a toddler, so I never knew him.'

Isabel leaned back and put her hands behind her head. 'I didn't realise your mum was an Allwood. They're quite a prominent family in Bainbridge. The factory is one of the town's biggest employers.'

Lucas shrugged. 'My grandad set up the company in the Sixties. Barry joined the firm in the Eighties with a view to taking over one day, and my mum worked there for a while as well. It's where she met my dad. He maintained the machinery on the factory floor. From what I've been told, my grandad and uncle weren't too impressed with my mum dating one of the workers.'

Isabel flashed a smile. 'She obviously didn't take any notice.'

'Nah, Mum makes up her own mind about things. Always has done. There's no way she'd have given my dad the heave-ho because her family didn't approve of him.'

'Was it her relationship with your dad that caused the rift with her family?'

Lucas curled his lip. 'No, she married him despite their objections, and Mum and Dad carried on working at Allwoods for a few years after they were wed. Mum left two months before she had me, and Dad handed in his notice the following year.'

'Why did your dad leave?'

'He was offered a job at Rolls-Royce, on twice the pay.'

Lucas leaned forward and placed his forearms on his knees. He looked nervous, unhappy about the conversation they were having.

'So when did your mum cut ties with her family?'

'When my grandad died. I was two or three at the time, so I've got no memory of what happened. All I know is, he passed away unexpectedly. A heart attack, I think. His will left the factory and all of his property to Barry. My mum got a small amount of money, but nothing else.'

'Bloody hell. That doesn't sound very fair. Did she challenge the will?'

'Not officially,' Lucas replied. 'She did talk to her brother though … tried to appeal to his sense of fairness. They were on the verge of making an arrangement when Barry's wife stepped in. According to my dad, Faye Allwood wore the trousers in that relationship, and she was determined Mum wasn't going to get a penny more than she'd been left in the will. That was when the Allwoods and the Killingworths fell out and broke off any contact.'

Isabel paused for a moment, thinking the situation through. 'To clarify,' she said, 'you've grown up not knowing your uncle, or your cousin?'

'Yep, that's it in a nutshell.'

'Have you ever run into Ross Allwood? At school, or elsewhere? I'm guessing the two of you are a similar age?'

'Ross is a year older than me, but our paths never crossed,' Lucas said. 'He was sent away to a private school, so we never mixed in the same circles.'

Isabel rolled her eyes. 'The local comp not good enough for him?'

'Obviously not.'

'Are you sure you want to step down from the case?'

Lucas waggled his head. 'It's not a case of wanting to. I just thought you should know about the connection so that you can make a judgement. The missing woman is employed by the Allwoods and was last seen at the works party. If there's even an outside chance her disappearance has something to do with her employers, my involvement in the investigation could jeopardise the case.'

Isabel placed her hands on her desk and drummed her fingers against its surface. 'You've done the right thing, Lucas. It certainly wouldn't be appropriate for you to interview the Allwoods or spend too much time down at the factory, but that doesn't necessarily mean I have to remove you from the case. You're an important part of the team and there are plenty of other ways you can contribute to the investigation.'

He grinned. 'Cheers, boss.'

'You don't know the Allwoods personally, and at this stage, there's nothing to link either of them to Anna Matheson's disappearance, but I'll assign you an office-based role so that you don't

25

have to deal with them directly. It does mean you're likely to end up viewing a lot of CCTV footage over the next few days.'

'I'm OK with that,' Lucas said.

'I'll need to make the Super aware of your connection, and I'll keep the situation under review in case the circumstances change. I'll also document my decision and the rationale behind it in the policy file. That way, both of our backs are covered.'

'I appreciate it, boss. Do you want me to tell the others, or do you want to talk to them yourself?'

'I'll mention it to Dan,' Isabel said. 'He can filter the news down to the rest of the investigation team.'

'What about the social media appeal?'

'Ask Theo to sort that,' she said. 'It'll be good experience for him.'

Lucas stood up.

'I appreciate you being up front about this, Lucas.'

He smiled. 'I'll shoot off to the ops room, get cracking with the CCTV checks.' He rubbed his hands together, feigning excitement. 'Think I'd better grab myself a strong coffee on the way.'

'One more thing,' said Isabel.

He paused. Turned.

'I'm sure I don't need to tell you this, but please don't discuss the case with your family.'

Lucas pulled an imaginary zip across his lips and made his way out of the door.

Chapter 6

When Dan poked his head into Isabel's office ten minutes later, he was wearing an eager, open-eyed expression that raised her hopes.

'Has Anna Matheson turned up?'

'No. Sorry, boss,' he said, dousing Isabel's nascent flicker of optimism. 'We do have something on the security footage from Allwoods though.'

His enthusiastic tone suggested he was about to impart some important information.

'The cameras picked up Anna Matheson leaving the party at 23.11. Come and take a look.'

She strolled into the outer office and followed Dan to his desk.

'There are nine CCTV cameras in key positions around the factory,' he told her. 'Responsibility for security of the site falls within the remit of the general manager, James Derenby. An officer contacted Derenby first thing this morning, and apparently he was very helpful. He sent over all the footage from last night, along with a diagram showing the layout of the factory and offices, including the location of the cameras.'

Dan handed her a printed diagram, which showed that the front portion of the factory site was made up of a reception area, meeting rooms and various offices, including a large space designated as the CEO's office. The reception area was centrally located at the front of the building. To the right and rear of reception were the administrative offices, and to the left were two meeting rooms and a boardroom. Behind the meeting areas was a large space marked as the staff canteen. The huge factory production area was located at the rear, and stretched across the full width of the building.

'Last night's party was held here, in the canteen.' Dan jabbed a finger at the diagram. 'According to James Derenby, the space was opened up to include this area here …' He pointed to the boardroom. 'There's a purpose-built partition between the boardroom and the canteen … a soundproofed folding wall system. It can be opened up to create a bigger space for events, such as the one held last night. The two smaller meeting rooms next to the boardroom were used as cloakrooms for the party.'

'And where are the CCTV cameras?' Isabel asked.

'Internally, there are a total of six. Three here, in the main production area.' He pointed to three triangular symbols on the diagram. 'There's also a camera in reception, a wide-angled camera in the staff canteen, and another in the packing and dispatch zone.'

'What about externally?'

'One out front, at the corner of the building.' He tapped the bottom left-hand side of the diagram. 'Again, it's wide-angled, so it covers both the staff and visitor parking areas, and the main entrance gate. There are also cameras at the rear of the factory … one here, where supplies come in, and another above the loading bay where goods go out.'

'Which camera captured the last sighting of Anna Matheson?'

'The one in the corner of the staff canteen,' Dan said. 'It shows her initially crossing from the corner of the room where the speeches were made, over towards the meeting rooms that were being used as cloakrooms.'

Isabel studied the layout, imagining the staff canteen and boardroom merged into one combined space.

'Correct me if I'm wrong,' she said, 'but someone accessing either of the meeting-slash-cloakrooms would have been out of range of the camera. So, how do you know that's where she went?'

'Because, she reappears a minute later carrying a jacket,' Dan said. 'She's putting it on as she walks across the canteen at 23.11, and out of the door on the right. That was the last sighting of her on camera.'

'And that door leads to this area here ...' Isabel scrutinised the diagram, running her finger along a central corridor at the heart of the factory complex. 'Do we know what happened to her from there?'

'Not exactly.' Dan folded his arms. 'We do know she didn't go out through the front entrance, because there's a CCTV camera in the reception area, and there's no sign of Anna leaving through the main door.'

'How else could she have exited the building?' Isabel said. 'Come on, Danny boy. Talk me through it.'

'From the central corridor, she had direct access to her own office. It's possible she called in there before leaving for the evening. Like a lot of the admin areas, Anna's office has two doors. As well as the one from the corridor, there's one on the other side that leads into the space used by the sales team ... which is a central, open-plan area. From there, she'd have been able to access all of the other offices. The finance office is at the front of the building, and leads onto the reception area – so we can rule that out. If Anna had gone out that way, her movements would have been picked up by the camera in the main reception.'

'What's to say she didn't go along the central corridor straight into the production area and exit the building from there?' Isabel said, directing a fingernail along her proposed route.

Dan shook his head. 'There are three cameras covering the

production area. It's a vast space, but one them would have recorded her presence.'

'So how *did* she get out?'

'My best guess is that she went through the sales area and into Ross Allwood's office, which has two additional doors leading off it. One opens into the production area, and the other leads directly to the outside of the building.'

Isabel consulted the plan, identifying the exterior door in question. It provided access to a cut-through at the far side of the factory. A little further along, offset from the rear of the building, was a gate that opened onto a goods road heading away from the site.

'Where does the goods exit come out?'

'On a slip road to the bypass, on the other side of the hill,' Dan explained. 'Lorries are loaded around the back, and they leave via the goods road to ease the flow of traffic. There's a camera directly above the loading bay, but the rear gate isn't in its range.'

'So Anna Matheson could have gone out through that gate without anyone seeing her?'

'Gone out, or been taken out,' Dan said. 'There's no sign of her on any of the external cameras – so my theory is, she exited the building through Ross Allwood's office. She may have arranged to meet someone on that side of the factory, possibly someone with a car.'

'And then what?' said Isabel. 'That vehicle drove through the rear gate and up to the bypass?'

Dan held up his hands. 'It does seem like the most obvious explanation.'

Isabel sat down and pulled the diagram closer.

'Two things,' she said. 'First of all, if Anna did meet someone in a car, wouldn't their arrival have been picked up by the camera at the main gateway?'

'We're checking that,' Dan said. 'The vehicle could have arrived at any time, before or during the party. Someone may even have left their car at the side of the building the previous day. We're going to have trawl through a lot of footage to establish that. Another possibility is that the car avoided the main entrance altogether, entering through the rear gate.'

'Isn't the goods road one-way? Exit only?'

'It's supposed to be,' Dan said, 'but as we all know, not everyone follows the rules of the road.'

Isabel frowned. 'If someone did come in that way, it would have meant turning the wrong way into the slip road from the bypass … a tricky manoeuvre, and dangerous too. I don't suppose there are any cameras near there?'

'Unfortunately not.'

'Typical,' she said, pulling a disgruntled face. 'Aside from the cameras, what other security measures were in place at the factory? If the firm was throwing a party, wouldn't they have locked up the offices?' She pointed to the bottom right corner of the diagram. 'The finance office is here, as is the personnel office. There's no way the management would risk someone wandering into those areas uninvited.'

'It couldn't happen, boss. According to James Derenby, access within the building is controlled by electronic key card. Only people authorised to enter those offices would be able to do so. Someone from the factory floor, for instance, wouldn't be able to gain access.'

'What about Anna Matheson?'

'I'll need to check. It's possible she has an all-areas electronic pass.'

Isabel's eyes lit up. 'This is good news, isn't it? The security system will have recorded which passes accessed the doors last night.'

'It *should* have done,' Dan said, 'but it didn't.'

'What do you mean?' She scowled. 'Why the hell not?'

'There was some sort of glitch,' Dan said. 'When James Derenby tried to download the key card data, he discovered it hadn't been saved.'

'Hadn't been saved, or was deleted?' Isabel felt a knot of unease tighten in her chest.

Dan shrugged. 'I don't know. James Derenby is looking into it. If the data was deleted, he may be able to recover it. If it was never recorded in the first place, there's no way of confirming anyone's movements around the factory last night.'

'Shit!' Isabel said. Tipping back her head, she closed her eyes. 'I don't like the sound of this, Dan. It bothers me. *Really* bothers me. If the data's gone missing, we should assume the worst. If someone has abducted Anna Matheson, it stands to reason they'd want to cover their tracks.'

'Shall I get someone from Digital Forensics onto it?' Dan said.

'Yes, and do it straight away. Lauren Talbot said that James Derenby has a thing for Anna. If any harm has come to her, he'll be a prime suspect. He's in charge of security at the factory, so he'd have no trouble switching off the key card tracking.'

'Or destroying evidence,' Dan grimaced. 'I'll get the CSIs down there now.'

'While you're at it, find out who else has access to the system. There must be other employees who know how to disable it, or delete the data.'

'Will do, boss, although it's possible the loss of data is exactly what James Derenby described it as … a computer glitch.'

Isabel sneered. 'I don't buy it, Dan. Security systems are massively robust these days.'

'Maybe it's an old system. I mean, Allwoods make kets. It's not as if they're manufacturing valuable, high-end products.'

'Kets?' Isabel said. 'Isn't that a drug? Ketamine … Special K?'

Dan laughed. 'Nah. I mean jelly sweets and penny chews and stuff. Kets. Do you not say that down here in Derbyshire?'

'You mean tuffies?' Isabel smiled. 'You're right. I don't suppose lemon sherbets and chocolate limes have much in the way of street value.'

'Regardless of how tight security is at Allwoods, the disappearance of the data is definitely suspicious,' Dan said.

'Talk to James Derenby,' said Isabel. 'Bring him down to the station if necessary. We need to question him about the security system. Is it high-tech or hopelessly out of date? And ask him about his relationship with Anna … at work and socially.'

'Will do, boss.'

'We also need to get the appeal out on social media.'

'I'll check with Lucas and find out what's happening,' said Dan. 'Where is he is, by the way?'

'In the ops room,' Isabel replied. 'I'm giving him an office-based role on this one. Turns out that Ross Allwood is Lucas's cousin.'

'What? No way!'

'Way,' Isabel said. 'And until we know more about Anna Matheson's whereabouts, Lucas won't be talking to any witnesses. DC Lindley can crack on with the social media appeal and help with the interviews. Keep your eye on him though, Dan. Young Theo is a bright lad, but he's not long out of uniform and he's inexperienced. You might need to take him under your wing.'

Chapter 7

In some ways, Zoe didn't want the journey to Christina Matheson's house to end. What was that famous saying? *To travel hopefully is a better thing than to arrive.* This was definitely one of those occasions.

The personal statement on her application to train as a family liaison officer had included a string of weasel words aimed at grabbing the DI's attention and guaranteeing her stamp of approval. Zoe had claimed that being a FLO would *widen her experience* and give her a *deeper understanding*. She'd welcomed an opportunity to gain *an insight into the psyche of families whose loved ones were missing, or the victims of crime.* Glib answers – all the things she knew her senior officers would want to hear.

What Zoe hadn't revealed were her real reasons for choosing to train as a family liaison officer. The truth was, she wasn't good with people. She was fine with desk-based investigations, but dealing face-to-face with the victims of crime wasn't something that came naturally to her. It was a weakness – one she'd so far managed to hide – but she knew her inability to engage in a meaningful way could scupper her ambitions for promotion, or even wreck her whole career. Becoming a FLO, pushing herself out of her comfort zone, was Zoe's way of addressing the problem – but now that it was happening for real, she felt nervous. Anxious. What if she couldn't do this?

Ignoring an overwhelming urge to turn the car around, go home and curl into a ball, Zoe pressed on to her destination. The misper's mother lived in Milford, in a property located at the end of a row of old mill cottages, on a hillside overlooking the River Derwent. Deep blue delphiniums and pink cosmos lined the stone walls of the small front garden, and a Montana clematis trailed across the full width of the house.

When Christina Matheson came to the door, Zoe's first impression was that she was too young to be the mother of a thirty-six-year-old. Christina was tall and willowy, with long, shiny hair the colour of horse chestnuts. Her cropped jeans exposed slender ankles, and a collection of silver bangles jangled on elegant wrists. She nodded politely as Zoe introduced herself, and then led her into a beamed living room that smelt of wood smoke and joss sticks, through to a sunny kitchen at the rear of the cottage.

As they stood in the glare of the room's bleaching summer light, Christina's face revealed its true age. Zoe could make out tiny lines on her forehead and around her grey eyes.

'I don't suppose you've heard anything from Anna?' Zoe said.

Christina placed a hand across her mouth and shook her head. 'I'm worried sick,' she said, speaking through her fingers. 'I have been since early this morning, when the police officer called round.'

'That was PC Rowe, I believe,' Zoe said. 'A tall guy … broad, with a beard?'

'Yes … he was very kind … but what he told me has left me feeling drained and on edge. I can't concentrate. I need to know that Anna's all right.'

'Given the circumstances, I'd say that's a perfectly natural reaction,' Zoe said. 'As your family liaison officer, I'm here to offer support, answer your questions, and keep you updated on progress in the search for Anna.'

'Is there any?' Christina asked. 'Progress, I mean. Have you any idea where she might be?'

'Not yet,' Zoe replied. 'Officers are in the process of talking to Anna's colleagues, but all we've established so far is that she was last seen at around eleven-fifteen last night, at her works party. Her car is in the staff car park, so she obviously didn't leave there under her own steam.'

'Do you think she could still be there, at the factory? She could be ill, or she might have fallen and hit her head … knocked herself out.'

'Officers have completed an initial search of the site,' Zoe said. 'There's no sign of Anna.'

Christina Matheson's face fell. Another glimmer of hope crushed.

'Is there anyone your daughter would have called? Someone who might have arranged to meet her, or pick her up?'

Christina put her hands on her head and sighed. 'Not that I can think of,' she said. 'Anyway, why would she need a lift when she had her car?'

'Maybe she'd had one too many glasses of bubbly,' Zoe suggested.

'No.' Christina shook her head insistently. 'Anna doesn't drink these days, and she's always on her mettle at work. She's determined to make the right impression … so she tends not to relax her guard in front of her colleagues.'

'She's told you that?' Zoe said.

'Not in so many words, but she's hinted at it. I know my daughter, DC Piper. She puts on a good show but, deep down, she lacks confidence. She's always been like that. I've done what I can over the years, to boost her self-esteem, but it's never made any difference.'

'Does she discuss her job with you?'

'Not very often. These days our conversations tend to revolve around Benedict. He's given us something to talk about.'

Zoe was learning how important it was to pick up on the things people *didn't* say. Rather than state something directly, witnesses often dropped hints, or implied things by omission.

'Are you saying you and your daughter don't have much in common, apart from the baby?'

Christina mustered a smile. 'Anna and I aren't on the same wavelength. We rarely agree on anything. Benedict provides neutral ground for conversation. Where is he now, by the way? Is he OK?'

'He's still with the babysitter. Lauren Talbot.'

'I'd rather he was with me,' Christina said, a small crease forming on her brow. 'Can you arrange for someone to bring him here?'

'Yes, if that's what you want,' Zoe replied, 'but wouldn't it be better to leave your grandson where he is for now? If Anna hasn't come home within the next few hours, we'll need to hold a press conference and we'd like you to make an appeal … if you're willing?'

Christina nodded nervously. 'I'm willing,' she said. 'Whether or not I'll be *able* is another question. If you want me to speak in front of a load of journalists, I may need to resort to some Dutch courage.'

She turned and opened the fridge, took out a half-empty bottle of Chardonnay and held it up to the light. 'I'd offer you one,' she said, waving the wine in Zoe's direction, 'but I don't suppose you're allowed to drink while you're on duty.'

'You're right, I'm not,' Zoe said. 'But even if I wasn't working, it's too early in the day for me.'

Christina glanced guiltily at the clock on the stone wall at the end of the kitchen. Ten past eleven. Almost twelve hours since Anna had last been seen.

After giving the wine bottle one last, longing look, Christina returned it to the fridge.

'Is that what you're here for? To keep tabs on me? Make sure I don't drown my sorrows?'

Zoe sat down at the kitchen table, wondering how best to answer. 'It's one of the reasons, yes,' she said, deciding to be honest. 'You're bound to be worried about your daughter, but you need to keep a clear head if you're going to make an appeal to the media. Drinking wine isn't a good idea … especially if you're going to be looking after Benedict later on. I can put the kettle on instead, if you like.'

Christina held up a hand and shuddered. 'Please don't. If I have to drink another cup of tea, I think I'll throw up.'

She pulled out a chair and lowered herself into it. 'I'm not sure how much longer I can stand this. It's the waiting I can't bear, and the wondering. Where is she? Why is her phone switched off? You must admit, that isn't a good sign.'

'There are all sorts of reasons why your daughter might have switched off her phone,' Zoe said. 'But I'm not going to lie to you. We are concerned, especially as this seems so out of character for Anna.'

'It *is* … totally out of character,' Christina agreed. 'Although I'm puzzled as to how you've come to that conclusion. You've never met Anna. How can you make a judgement about someone you don't know?'

'Our assessments are based on a number of factors,' Zoe said. 'We're monitoring the situation constantly, in light of any new information we receive and any changing circumstances.'

'Do you think she's in danger?'

'It's still early days, Mrs Matheson,' Zoe said, determined to avoid words like *risk* and *danger*. 'The odds are still in favour of Anna turning up safe and well, so try and think positively. At this stage, I'd rather not alarm you by dwelling on other possibilities, although we may need to consider them eventually.'

'Please don't feel obliged to sugar-coat things for my benefit, detective. I'm pragmatic. I realise something may have happened to Anna. As for telling me not to worry … you're wasting your breath. I'm her mother. I fret if she's twelve minutes late, never mind twelve hours.'

Zoe sat back and placed her hands on the table. 'I'll level with you,' she said. 'The longer your daughter is missing, the more our concerns grow. If she was in the habit of taking off on her own, we'd be a lot less worried, but Lauren Talbot has told us that Anna is usually very reliable.'

The mention of Lauren's name seemed to unsettle Christina. 'For once, Lauren and I are in agreement,' she said, her tone hostile. 'Although I don't usually set great store by anything that girl has to say. I don't trust her.'

Zoe sat up, wondering what had caused this lack of trust. 'It's our understanding that Anna and Lauren are best friends, and have been since childhood,' she said. 'Mrs Talbot is looking after your grandson … surely Anna wouldn't leave Benedict with someone she doesn't trust.'

'I didn't say Anna doesn't trust her, I said *I* don't.' Christina folded her arms. 'Lauren was a spoilt brat as a child, and adulthood hasn't improved her any. She's a social climber with a huge sense of her own worth. Her ego is exceeded only by the size of her house.'

'I see. Anything else you want to add to her list of faults?'

'Don't get me started,' Christina said. 'Everything about that woman annoys me.'

'Care to be more specific?'

'She drives an expensive, gas-guzzling four-by-four for starters, and her children want for nothing. Her husband has a well-paid job and, unlike Anna, the Talbots have no financial worries.'

'It's hardly fair to hold that against her,' Zoe said. 'Being rich isn't a crime.'

'I know,' Christina said, momentarily abashed. 'I suppose I've never understood why the two of them hang out together. Lauren is the antithesis of my daughter. Why would someone like her want to be friends with Anna?'

'Perhaps they enjoy each other's company,' Zoe said, shocked that Christina had such a poor opinion of her daughter's worth as a friend. 'Some of the most successful friendships are often the most unlikely.'

'In theory, maybe, but I've seen how Lauren speaks to people. She's bossy … likes to be in control, and she can be very patronising. On the face of it, she's magnanimous. She's given Anna loads of stuff …'

'Stuff?'

'Hand-me-down baby clothes, pieces of furniture, last season's designer handbags … all of her cast-offs. She treats Anna like a charity case.'

'Have you considered that perhaps Lauren is just being kind?' Zoe said. 'If she knows Anna doesn't have much money, maybe it's her way of being generous to an old friend.'

Christina wrinkled her nose. 'If you ask me, Lauren does it to make herself feel good, and to make Anna feel beholden. She's trying to get the upper hand. When they were at school, my daughter always outshone Lauren academically. For all her fancy upbringing, Lauren was never able to get the good grades that Anna achieved.'

Her words carried a hint of pride.

'When Anna got a place at university, Lauren stayed behind in Bainbridge and set up a *business*.' Christina lifted her fingers, putting quotation marks around the word. 'It was something to do with beauty products, all done on the internet in the days when online selling was starting to take off. The whole venture was funded by Lauren's dad. I believe it was moderately successful for a while, but it couldn't have been hugely lucrative because Lauren packed it in when she married Eddie.'

Zoe made a mental note to talk to Will Rowe. It would be interesting to compare his impression of Lauren Talbot with the version being peddled by Christina Matheson.

'Let's go back to considering where Anna might be,' Zoe said, deciding to steer the conversation away from Lauren Talbot. 'Is it possible she's with someone? Someone she's in a relationship with, or who she's been involved with in the past?'

'She's not in a relationship,' Christina said.

'You sound very certain about that.'

'I am. As far as I know, Anna's never had what I'd call a serious boyfriend. Not a long-term relationship. In that respect, she's a lot more like me than she cares to admit ... wary of getting involved with the wrong bloke.'

'What about Benedict's father? What do you know about him?'

'Nothing,' Christina said. 'I've asked plenty of questions, but Anna refuses to talk about him.'

'She must have told you something,' Zoe said, finding it hard to believe that Anna hadn't confided in her mother. Then again, perhaps her reticence said more about her relationship with Christina than it did about her relationship with Benedict's father.

'All she's ever said is that it was a casual thing. I think she viewed the encounter as little more than a sperm donation. Not that she was planning on getting pregnant ... that was serendipity, a happy outcome.'

'She was pleased then? When she found out about the baby?'

'Once she got over the initial shock.' Christina smiled. 'My daughter's always loved kids. I knew she wanted at least one of her own, but I think she'd begun to give up on that dream.'

'Why was that?'

'Isn't it obvious? She was in her thirties and single, and she'd lost faith in finding *the one*. Time was running out for her.'

Her explanation rattled Zoe, who was thirty-one and single, and also hopeful of having children one day.

'It can't be easy for her, bringing up a child on her own,' Zoe said. 'Do you help her out?'

'When I can,' Christina replied. 'I work six days a week though, so I'm not usually available for babysitting duties, which is why she lets Lauren Talbot step in.'

'Six days a week?' Zoe whistled. 'That sounds like a heavy

41

schedule. Even police officers get more than one day off a week … officially, at least.'

'I run a shop in Matlock Bath,' Christina said. 'During the peak tourist season, I open six days a week, sometimes seven. Things are easier in the winter. I usually close the shop down completely between January and Easter. That's when I get some serious time off.'

'Are you sure I can't make you a brew?' Zoe said, thinking the shop could be the thing that would help her connect with Christina. 'While the water's boiling, you can tell me about your business.'

Without waiting for an answer, she stood up and switched on the kettle.

'It's called *Magical Mysteries*,' Christina said, half-heartedly. 'I sell healing crystals, essential oils … anything to do with the mind, body or spirit.'

Zoe had a vision of dreamcatchers and zen jewellery and joss sticks like the ones she'd caught a whiff of in Christina's living room.

'It's obvious from the expression on your face that you're a sceptic,' Christina said.

'I wouldn't say that—'

'Don't worry about it.' Christina wafted her hand dismissively. 'You're not alone. A lot of people view the stuff I sell as mumbo jumbo. Thankfully, they're not my target audience.'

'I can't say it's a subject I've ever explored,' Zoe said.

'Perhaps you should,' Christina said. Standing up, she opened a drawer and pulled out a chunk of golden-yellow crystal.

'Here, take this. It's citrine.' She handed it to Zoe. 'It acts as a manifesting stone. It encourages optimism, reduces negativity and can aid digestion.'

Zoe lifted an eyebrow, wondering if Christina Matheson had psychic powers.

'Citrine generates light,' Christina continued. 'Carry it in your pocket … hold it in your hand occasionally. It'll boost your creativity, visualisation powers and your confidence.'

Zoe smiled. 'Do I look as if I need a confidence boost?'

'Yes,' Christina said. 'Quite frankly, you do. Hang on to it. Who knows, it might help you work out where my daughter is.'

Chapter 8

'Theo's sorted the social media appeal, boss,' Dan said, when Isabel returned to the CID room after a swift bite to eat in the canteen.

'Nice one, Theo.' She smiled at the young detective, whose corner desk was neat and orderly – a positive trait, as far as Isabel was concerned. A clear desk was something she aspired to herself, but rarely managed to achieve. 'Where's it been posted?'

'On Twitter and Facebook, ma'am. Plus, Allwoods has a special Facebook page for their employees – we've done a separate post for that. We've asked anyone who saw Anna at last night's party to get in touch immediately. The control room's already had a few calls.'

'Sounds promising,' Isabel said. 'At least we're getting the word out there. The press conference has been scheduled for four o'clock this afternoon. Hopefully, it'll generate some new information. Comms have confirmed that the local papers and radio, and the BBC regional news channel have agreed to attend. Christina Matheson is going to make an appeal, and I'd like you to sit alongside her please, Dan.'

'Wouldn't you prefer to do it, boss?'

'No, I'll observe. With the television cameras there, you're a better choice than me. I've got more of a face for radio.'

Dan shook his head and laughed.

'You never got around to showing me the CCTV footage of Anna leaving the party,' Isabel said. 'We got side-tracked with the diagram of the factory.'

'I've got the clip on my computer if you want to take a look now.'

She wandered over to Dan's desk and waited for him to find the relevant video file.

'Here you go.' When he pressed play, Anna Matheson appeared on screen, crossing the empty floor of the canteen before walking out of range of the camera.

'Pause it a minute, Dan, and tell me what's happening. It's after eleven o'clock … why is everyone sitting at tables? Why aren't they on the dance floor? I assume they had music at this party? A DJ?'

'They did, but there were speeches at eleven o'clock, and they'd only just finished.'

'Who delivered the speeches?'

'From the CCTV footage, it looks as though Faye Allwood did most of the talking, with Anna acting as MC. The main speech lasted for six minutes, although I've no idea what was said. The usual twaddle no doubt. There were a couple of presentations made as well. Long service awards, maybe? Let me fast forward a couple of minutes …'

Isabel watched the images on the screen move at high speed. When the timer reached 23.11, Dan pressed play once again.

'Take a look now,' he said. 'By the time Anna Matheson reappears carrying her jacket, the dance floor has filled up. The music must have started again while she was fetching her coat.'

Isabel leaned in and stared at the screen, watching as Anna walked beneath the camera and exited through a door on the right. Dan's observation was spot-on. While Anna was out of view of the camera, dozens of people had moved onto the dance floor, their bodies crammed together, swaying to the rhythm of an unknown song. Isabel peered at the screen and squinted.

'What *is* everyone wearing?' she said. 'Is it me, or are there loads of people with hippy hair?'

'According to social media, the party had a Sixties theme,' said Theo. 'Staff were encouraged to wear Sixties-style clothing, and the DJ was primed to play music from that era.'

Isabel, who was born in 1963, wasn't sure she liked Theo's use of the word *era*. It made it sound like a lifetime ago … a different aeon. Perhaps it was.

'I guess that fits in with the factory celebrating its sixtieth anniversary,' said Dan.

Isabel remembered what Lucas had told her about his grandfather setting up the factory in the 1960s.

'Apparently, the staff were provided with a job lot of wigs and John-Lennon-style specs,' Theo said. 'It's going to make it difficult to identify people. We'll have to go through the footage with a fine-tooth comb. No pun intended.'

Isabel smiled. 'You're right,' she said. 'It'll be hard to pick out who's who if everyone's wearing the same long wigs and glasses.'

'Thankfully, not everyone is,' Theo said. 'I've been looking through some of the images posted on the Allwood staff Facebook page. They must have brought in one of those photo booths for the event. A few shots of Anna Matheson with some of her colleagues have already been uploaded.'

'What? Online?' Dan said.

'Yep, they must have been taken earlier in the evening.'

'Download them,' Isabel said. 'Let's have a look at who she was hanging out with.'

'And when you've done that, you can come with me, Theo,' said Dan. 'We need to talk to James Derenby, and then we're going to pay a visit to Faye and Ross Allwood.'

Chapter 9

On the journey to Allwood Confectionery, Dan took the opportunity to get to know Theo Lindley a little better. He was still a relatively new DC, having joined Bainbridge CID eighteen months after Dan's own transfer from the north-east. Theo was a Derby lad, born and brought up in the suburbs and far more used to life as a uniformed officer in the city than working as a detective in a small market town. His move to Bainbridge had been driven by his desire to join CID, but Dan got the impression that DC Lindley was missing his home patch.

'So, how are you finding things, Theo?' he said.

'What? Being a DC, you mean?'

'Aye, and being based in Bainbridge as opposed to Derby.'

'It's different,' Theo said, shrugging in the passenger seat. 'But I guess human nature's the same, no matter where you are. There are fewer drug-related crimes here in Bainbridge, but still a lot more than I was expecting.'

'Don't let the rural, laid-back charm of the place fool you. Drugs are an issue in every town. What about this case?' Dan asked. 'Is it the first misper case you've worked on?'

'I was involved in a search for a guy with dementia … back in Derby. He'd wandered off, down by the river, but we found him within a couple of hours. This case is a whole different ball game. What's your gut feeling about it, sarge?'

Dan turned down the corners of his mouth. 'It's not looking good. It's over twelve hours since Anna Matheson was reported missing. If she were a teenage runaway, I'd be more inclined to think she'd buggered off on a whim, but she's a thirty-six-year-old mother. The fact that she's been out of contact for so long is bad news.'

'In that case, why aren't we carrying out a full-scale search?' Theo said.

'There are plenty of officers looking out for her,' Dan replied. 'Her description's been circulated to all units ... plus, we've got people trawling through CCTV, seeing if they can spot her.'

'But no strong leads?'

'No, not yet. Which is one of the reasons we need to speak to Anna's colleagues.'

They drove on in silence, past the community hospital, out towards the town's main industrial estate. Despite it being a Sunday, the A6 road was unusually busy, cars and bikes heading up to Matlock Bath and the Peak District.

'We're meeting James Derenby first, yeah?' Theo said, as they drove towards the huge, one-storey building that housed Allwood Confectionery.

'We are,' Dan said. 'An officer spoke to him this morning to request the CCTV footage from the factory – but that was in Derenby's capacity as the guy responsible for security at the site. We'll be talking to him as Anna Matheson's colleague and potential admirer.'

'If it turns out something untoward has happened to her, I'm guessing Derenby will be a suspect?'

'Let's wait and see, eh?'

'Has the factory has been checked for signs of foul play?' Theo asked.

'Yes, there was no sign of anything untoward. The PolSA will get a team in later for a more thorough search … assuming Anna hasn't turned up by then.'

Once they'd pulled into the visitor car park at Allwood Confectionery, Dan rang James Derenby, who was already waiting for them inside the building. He promised to come out and let them in through the front door.

Dan and Theo waited by the main entrance, standing in the full glare of the sun. Theo was in his shirt sleeves, but Dan sweltered within the confines of his jacket.

A tall, bespectacled man – presumably James Derenby – approached on the other side of the glass and pressed a release button. There was a buzz, and Dan pushed open the door.

'James Derenby?' he said. 'I'm DS Fairfax and this is my colleague, DC Lindley. Thanks for agreeing to meet us.'

'Not a problem,' James said. 'Anything to help find Anna.'

'We need to ask you some questions,' Dan said. 'Is there some-where we can talk?'

'We're the only people in the building.' James spread out his hands to emphasise the empty offices around them. 'Take your pick. We have the place to ourselves.'

'Shall we go to the canteen?' Dan suggested. 'I'd like to see where the party was held.'

'Certainly. The place is still a mess after last night, but there's a drinks machine in there and plenty of room to sit.'

They followed him into the central corridor at the rear of the reception area, and entered the canteen through a set of swing doors on the left, the same doors through which Anna had exited the previous evening.

The vast canteen reminded Dan of the assembly hall at his old secondary school. There was a polished wooden floor, a lingering smell of food, and tables and chairs scattered around the perimeter.

On the far side, across the back wall, was a servery with a selection of empty display cabinets. A stack of wooden trays waited at the end of a metal rack. The layout was that of a self-service supermarket restaurant, or a department store coffee shop.

Dan glanced at the CCTV monitor fixed high up in the corner of the room, at the camera that had captured Anna Matheson's exit at 23.11.

'How about you begin by telling me about the security system here at the factory?' he said. 'Do you know when it was installed?'

'The original system was put in way before my time,' James replied. 'Although, there was an upgrade about eight months ago.'

'Did that include the security system on the doors? The key card system?'

'Yes, there'd been an attempted break-in, so Barry Allwood insisted on a complete overhaul. Mr Allwood was the CEO at the time. He died, last December.'

'And the current CEO, Faye Allwood … she's his widow?'

'That's right. She was appointed after Barry's death, and she's now the company's co-owner, along with Ross.'

'Did Mrs Allwood work here before her husband died?' said Theo.

'Oh, God, yes. She's been here for years. Prior to becoming the CEO, she was the head of sales. Ross has taken on that role now, although he's not as good at the job as his mother was.'

They crossed the wooden floor, still strewn with streamers from the previous night's party, and sat down at one of the tables.

'I'm sorry about the mess,' James said, pushing aside a paper napkin and a couple of empty plastic glasses. 'The cleaners would normally have been in by now to tidy up and put the tables back in position, but one of your officers told me to put them off until later.'

'It's likely the police search team will want to make a more thorough inspection of the premises,' Dan said. 'You can arrange for the cleaners to come in once they've given you the all-clear.'

'You don't think Anna could still be here, do you? Somewhere in the building?'

'I doubt it,' Dan said. 'Nothing was found during the initial search this morning, but we will need to take a more detailed look if Anna doesn't show up soon.'

James took off his glasses and rubbed a hand across his eyes. 'I hope she's all right. I don't know what I'll do if anything's happened to her.'

'Are the two of you close?' Dan asked.

'We work closely together, but we aren't in a relationship, if that's what you mean,' he said, immediately on the defensive. 'Everyone relies on Anna, including me.'

'She's good at her job, then?' said Dan.

'Absolutely brilliant. She's got a real head for business, and she's a natural leader. Allwoods was struggling before she joined the company.'

'But it's doing all right now, is it?'

'Yes. Thanks to Anna, we've got more orders than we can cope with.'

Theo stuck out his bottom lip. 'Sounds like she's turned things around,' he said. 'How did she manage that?'

James slipped his glasses back on and pushed them onto the bridge of his nose. 'She's created some massively effective promotional campaigns,' he said. 'She also came up with the idea for our new gift and colleague boxes. We've been selling them online, directly to corporate customers. They've been enormously successful – so much so, we've had to increase production. We even managed to buck the trend during the lockdown.'

'The top brass must be pleased with her,' Dan said. 'How long has Anna worked here?'

'Just over two years. She was recruited as a marketing officer, but Barry Allwood promoted her to marketing manager after three months.'

'She obviously made the right impression then?' Theo said.

'Definitely. I think Barry was sceptical when Anna first arrived, mainly because she didn't have much marketing experience, but she soon proved her worth.'

'Why did she lack experience?' Dan said. 'Anna's thirty-six, isn't she? It's not as if she came here straight out of university.'

'She'd had a career change,' James explained. 'When Anna left uni, she went to work in London, in finance. She became quite the high flyer, from what I can gather. Well paid too.'

'Why would she want to give that up?' said Theo.

'Burnout.' James shrugged. 'She told me that working in the City was intense … stressful, you know? I'd imagine the lifestyle that went with it was taking its toll as well.'

'Lifestyle?' said Dan.

'Apparently, there's a heavy drinking culture in the industry. Anna told me that she and her colleagues would unwind at the end of each day by having a few drinks together. Some of her workmates used cocaine as well, although Anna was never into that. Anyway, she told me she woke up one day feeling like shit after a particularly heavy drinking session and realised she had to make some changes. She handed in her notice, came back up here to Bainbridge, got her diploma in marketing, and started looking for another job.'

'And has she given up the booze?' Theo asked.

'She has,' James said. 'Once she resigned from her job in the City, the stress disappeared, and she no longer felt the need to drink to unwind.' Frowning, he added: 'I probably shouldn't be telling you this. Anna told me in confidence.'

'Your colleague is missing,' Dan reminded him. 'Now isn't the time for discretion. It's possible that Anna's in trouble, or danger … the more information you can give us, the better. It will help us understand where she might be, or why she's disappeared.'

James placed a hand over his mouth and nodded, tears brimming in his eyes. Dan decided to give him a minute to pull himself together before continuing with the questions.

'Can we go back to something you mentioned earlier?' he said, when James had recovered his composure. 'You said you don't know what you'll do if anything's happened to Anna. If you're not in a relationship with her, what did you mean by that?'

James leaned back and let out a long, shuddery breath. 'When Anna joined the firm, I'd been working here for almost a year,' he said. 'Back then, I wasn't enjoying my job … I didn't feel in tune with the people I worked with, particularly the senior management. Quite honestly, I hated coming into work every day … and then Anna arrived and everything changed.'

Theo was making notes. 'Changed for you?' he said. 'Or do you mean Anna has changed the people you work with? Made them more amenable?'

'A bit of both, I suppose.' James smiled. 'I feel as though I've found an ally in Anna. She and I have the same work ethic and a similar sense of humour, and we both like the same books and TV programmes. We often have coffee or lunch together. Her company makes coming to work tolerable … enjoyable.'

'So, you'd class yourselves as friends?' said Dan.

'Without a doubt. Anna is someone I've come to rely on. She's talented and innovative … a consummate professional.' He spoke with undisguised admiration. 'The marketing ideas she's implemented have forced certain changes in production and packaging – things I'd been trying, unsuccessfully, to persuade the senior managers to consider.'

'She's made your job easier then?' Dan said.

'I suppose she has. Unlike me, Anna is eloquent and persuasive. She's wrought the changes that I failed to make happen, and the ideas she's come up with have played to the company's strengths and sense of history. One of her biggest successes has been a campaign to promote our traditional line of sweets. We're now marketing them to adults by tapping into their sense of nostalgia and the current trend for all things retro.'

Dan acknowledged Derenby's words with a nod. 'It sounds as though Anna knows her stuff.'

'She does,' James replied. 'I have complete respect for her business acumen.'

Dan scratched his chin. 'If you don't mind my saying, it also sounds as though you're fond of Anna ... on a more personal level.'

Derenby's face flushed red, and Dan knew he'd hit a raw spot.

'Your admiration for Anna,' he persisted. 'Does it extend beyond the workplace?'

James stared fixedly at the table top, trailing well-manicured fingernails across its surface. 'I've made no secret of it,' he replied. 'I like Anna. I like her a lot, and I've asked her out several times ... She even said yes, once, in the early days. We went to the cinema together. It'd be a stretch to call it a date, but I did hope it might lead to something ... that she might be willing to go out with me again.'

'But she wasn't?'

'No.' He glanced up, looking at Dan from beneath lowered lashes. 'It wasn't through a lack of trying on my part. Then, when I found out she was pregnant, I realised she must already have been in a relationship, but hadn't wanted to tell me.'

'Why do you think that was?'

'I don't know,' Derenby said, with a shrug. 'But she must have had her reasons for keeping it quiet.'

'What do you know about Benedict's father?' Theo asked.

'Nothing at all. She's never talked about him. After she had the baby, it was clear he was no longer in the picture – which got my hopes up again. Call me a glutton for punishment, but last month, I asked her out for dinner – I wanted her to be sure I was offering a proper date.'

'Turn you down, did she?' Dan said.

'Yep, it was same old story, except this time, she told me politely not to ask her again. She said I was sweet, but made it clear she's not interested in a relationship with me.'

'You must have been disappointed?' said Dan, knowing that the last thing any bloke wanted to be called was *sweet*.

'I'd be lying if I said I wasn't, but I tried not to take it personally. I think Anna's putting all her energies into her career at the moment.' There was a hint of self-deceit in his tone. 'She's certainly been very focused on her job lately, preoccupied even. She told me last week there are going to be some big changes over the next few months.'

'Do you know what she meant by that?' Dan said, leaning in and paying close attention to Derenby's reply.

'I assumed she was talking about a new website or branding or something … but thinking about it now, maybe there's something more radical in the pipeline … possibly new product lines, or some kind of restructuring. I'm sure Faye Allwood will be able to fill you in on the details.'

'We'll be sure to ask her about it,' Theo said, writing in his notebook.

Dan glanced at his watch, conscious that time was ticking. They were due at the Allwood house in half an hour, but there were still questions to be asked, here at the factory.

'It sounds as though you and Anna are good buddies,' Dan continued. 'But how is she with everyone else? Is she friendly with the rest of her colleagues?'

'Most of them,' James said. 'Anna isn't what you'd call a gregarious person, but she gets on with most people …' He held out a hand and rocked it from side to side. 'With a few exceptions.'

'Could you tell us who those exceptions are, please?' said Theo.

James screwed up his face in a show of reluctance. 'I don't want to speak out of turn.'

'As I say …' Dan reminded him, 'with Anna missing, you can't afford to withhold any information, no matter how trivial it might seem.'

James paused, choosing his words carefully. 'Anna's had a few run-ins with Ross Allwood. He's head of sales, but he's not popular with his team. There have been complaints about him … about his leadership qualities, or lack of.'

'Are you saying people have complained to Anna?'

'Unofficially, although Anna's hardly in a position to do anything about it. She has spoken to Ross though, told him his team aren't happy, and she's also raised the matter with Faye Allwood – but there's no sign that the problem is being addressed. I know it's a source of irritation for Anna.'

'Would you say there's conflict between Anna and Ross Allwood?' said Theo.

'Yes, I believe so. You'll need to speak to him if you want the full story.'

Dan made a mental note to do just that. 'I'd like to ask you again about Benedict Matheson's father,' he said, fishing for information. 'Is there nothing you can tell me about him? No clues to his identity?'

James shook his head. 'I'm afraid not. I've never met the man and Anna never mentions him.'

'Don't you find that odd?' said Dan.

'A little, but it's none of my business, is it?'

'Have you ever asked Anna about him?'

'I did once. She shut me down immediately … told me it was nothing to do with me. She said she didn't want to discuss it.'

'And how did that make you feel?' Dan said.

James shrugged. 'Snubbed. Hurt. I thought it might do her good to talk about it. As her friend, I hoped she might want to confide in me, but it was obvious from her reaction that nothing could have been further from the truth.'

'What conclusions have you drawn from Anna's reluctance to discuss Benedict's father?' Dan said.

James paused to consider the question. 'She's obviously determined to keep the man's identity a secret. To me, that infers he's someone she shouldn't have been with, or someone she regrets having a relationship with. The baby, though … having Benedict … that's something she *definitely* doesn't regret. Anna dotes on her son.'

'I know you've already told us that you and Anna aren't involved in a personal relationship, but I'm obliged to ask this …' Dan shuffled awkwardly. 'Is there any possibility you could be Benedict's father?'

James smiled wistfully. 'I wish,' he said. 'There's nothing I'd like more.'

'But you're not the kid's dad?' Theo clarified.

'I thought I'd made that clear.' James shook his head. 'There's no way I can be. It's simply not possible. Anna and I have never slept together.'

Chapter 10

Before leaving the factory, Dan wanted to take a proper look at the office layout within the building.

'There's something else you can help with,' he said, when Derenby had finished answering their questions. 'I need to confirm how Anna Matheson managed to leave the factory without the CCTV camera on the front gate picking up her departure.'

'There's a simple enough explanation,' James told him. 'She must have left through the rear gate.'

It was the conclusion Dan and the DI had come to when they'd studied the site diagram, but he wanted clarity on the route Anna had taken. Had she planned her exit carefully, intending to disappear without a trace? Or had someone else made that decision for her?

He wandered over to the corner of the canteen and pointed upwards. 'The last recording of Anna during the party was captured on that camera,' he said. 'She walked out, into the corridor at 23.11.'

'You can get directly into Anna's office from the corridor,' James said. 'Perhaps she spent some time at her desk before she left.'

'Can you show us Anna's office?' Dan said.

'Sure.'

They exited the canteen and entered the corridor, where James pointed at two doors.

'That's my office,' he said, indicating the one on the left. 'This one's Anna's.'

He presented his pass to a panel above the door handle.

'Does your pass open every door in the building?' Dan said.

'Yes,' James replied, as he stepped into the office and turned on the light. 'But only because I'm responsible for security. Not many people have an all-access pass.'

'Can you tell me who does?' said Theo, who had followed in behind them.

'All of SMT … the senior management team.'

'And who does that include?' Theo said, as he retrieved his notebook from a back pocket.

'The CEO, obviously, and the other heads of department. Ross Allwood is head of sales, Roy Morris is head of production, Nicola Warren is head of personnel, and George Amberton is head of finance.'

'What about you?' Dan said, as he prowled around Anna Matheson's office. 'Are you classed as a senior manager?'

'No, but I do report directly to the CEO.'

'You're the general manager, right?' said Theo. 'What exactly does that entail?'

James smiled caustically. 'All the things that nobody else wants to do. I'm a jack of all trades … a sort of project manager. Most of my time's taken up with tendering and procurement. If the factory needs a new piece of machinery, for instance, it's up to me to track down the right piece of kit at the best price. I negotiate and maintain the contracts for everything from security, to cleaning and haulage. I also act as Allwood's link with the community and local charities … that's my favourite part of the job.'

'Does the company have an affiliation with any charity in particular?' Theo asked.

'It changes each year. The employees vote annually on which

good cause their various fundraising activities will support.'

'I'd have thought liaising with charities would fall under Anna's remit,' Dan said, as he continued to inspect the office. 'It sounds more like a PR thing … something a marketing officer would do.'

'Manager,' James corrected him. 'Anna is the marketing manager. She and I tend to work together on the charity stuff.'

'But Anna's not a senior manager?' Theo said. 'I take it she doesn't have an all-areas pass?'

'No. Like me, she's not a member of the inner circle. Her pass gets her into most of the administrative offices, but not the production area. Access to the factory floor is restricted for health and safety reasons.'

'OK,' Theo said. 'And what happens if Anna needs to go into the factory?'

'Roy Morris or one of his team members will let her in, and accompany her.'

'But, other than the production area, Anna has full access to the offices?' said Dan.

'To the admin areas, yes, but not the senior managers' offices. If Anna has a meeting with a member of SMT, the PA will let her in, or the manager will buzz her in – although, during the working day, their doors are usually wide open anyway. SMT makes a big thing of maintaining an open-door policy.'

'Why does each office have its own security?' Theo said, a puzzled frown wrinkling his brow. 'I can understand there being a key code or electronic pass keys on the main doors, but it seems like overkill to have them on individual doors.'

'It was something Barry Allwood insisted on when the security system was upgraded last year,' said James. 'He was convinced someone was stealing information and passing it on to competitors.'

'An employee?' said Dan.

'That's what he thought, but nothing was ever proven.'

'You're responsible for security,' Dan said. 'He must have

discussed the situation with you … shared his thoughts on who might have been behind the leaks?'

'As a matter of fact, he didn't, and it pissed me off at the time. I came to the conclusion I must have been on his list of suspects.'

'What were *your* views on the security breach?' Dan said. 'Do you think Barry Allwood was right? Could someone have been passing on confidential information?'

'He never backed up his claims with any proof,' James said. 'At the time, I thought he was being overanxious, possibly even paranoid – but who knows? There may have been some truth to it. What is it they say? *Just because you're paranoid doesn't mean they aren't after you.*'

Dan smiled. 'Did the problem go away after the security upgrade?'

'It was never mentioned again,' James said. 'Then again, Barry died a few weeks after the new system was installed, so maybe the problem disappeared because he wasn't around to follow it up.'

'Going back to the question of door access,' Theo said. 'You're saying only the senior managers and their PAs have access to the SMT offices?'

James nodded. 'Yes, and myself, of course.'

Theo bounced the end of his pen against the open page of his notebook. 'I don't wish to labour the point, but the head of personnel, for instance – she has access to *all* the SMT offices?'

'That's right?'

'What about her PA?'

'The PAs only have access to their own boss's office. Not to the offices of other heads of service.'

Having completed his visual assessment of Anna Matheson's work space, Dan concluded that it was typical of offices up and down the country. A pale beech desk stood at one end, with an electric-blue, ergonomic office chair tucked beneath it. A desktop computer occupied the left-hand side of the desk, and a full stack of trays stood beside it. Next to that, was a framed photograph of a chubby-cheeked baby. Benedict Matheson, he assumed. At the other end of the room were two filing cabinets, an upright chair, and a bookshelf.

A glazed partition wall provided the only natural light in the room. At its centre was a second door. Dan pressed the green release button to open it, and walked through into the open-plan office beyond. It was furnished with four desks and an informal seating area.

'Who uses this space?'

'The sales reps,' James said. 'They're out on the road most of the time, but they call in at least once or twice a week.'

'Four desks,' Dan said. 'Does that mean there are four reps?'

'No, there are at least twice that many, covering several different regions, but they hot-desk. It's unusual for them to all be in at once.'

Dan swivelled his body, taking in the layout that he remembered from the site diagram. 'Help me out here, Mr Derenby,' he said. 'As we know, Anna's final appearance on the CCTV system shows her exiting the canteen. Talk me through how she could have left the building without triggering the camera in reception.'

'There are only two other ways to exit the building from here. The first option would be through there,' said James, nodding towards one of the doors leading off the sales reps' area. 'It leads to the ladies' and gents' toilet block, which can also be accessed from the other side, directly from the factory.'

'In other words, the toilets are on a corridor,' Dan said. 'With a door at either end?'

'That's right. In theory, Anna could have gone past the loos, and out the other side, into the production area. From there … again, in theory … she could have exited through Roy Morris's office, which has a door that leads out to the side of the building.'

'But only in theory?' said Dan.

'I told you, her pass wouldn't have opened the door to the factory production areas, nor would it have opened the door to

Roy Morris's office. More to the point, there are security cameras in the factory that would have picked up Anna's movements.'

'So we can discount that option then. What other route could she have taken?'

'The other way out would be via Ross Allwood's office, which also has an exterior door to the side of the building.' He inclined his head, indicating the relevant door. 'If Anna left that way and exited through the rear gate, she'd have been out of range of any security cameras – although the same thing applies – Anna couldn't have accessed Ross's office with her pass.'

'Unless he let her in,' said Theo. 'Or someone else did.'

James nodded. 'That's a possibility.'

'But because of the data glitch, there's no record of whose pass might have been used?' Dan said.

'No, I'm sorry about that. I realise it makes things difficult for you.'

'You can say that again.' Dan scowled. 'And in light of Anna's disappearance, the lack of data isn't merely inconvenient, it's also highly suspicious. Is it unusual for the system to go down? Is it normally reliable?'

'I've never known it happen before,' James said, looking distinctly uncomfortable. 'Of course, there is another possibility.'

'And what's that, Mr Derenby?' said Theo.

'That someone disabled the data recording temporarily,' James said, his voice cracking. 'I hope that's not the case, because it would suggest someone was covering their tracks, and that can only mean one thing … that something bad has happened to Anna.'

Despite having come to the same conclusion, Dan was careful to keep his expression neutral. He was acutely aware that for all his show of anxiety, James Derenby could well be the person responsible for turning off the door monitoring.

'Aside from yourself, who else knows how to disable the system?' he asked.

'Anyone who has access to the app,' James replied. 'If you know what you're doing, it's easy to switch things down. It's similar to the kind of app you might use to control your central heating at home. Most of the time you leave it alone, but you can override the settings remotely if you need to.'

'Can you confirm who has access to the app?' said Theo.

'All of the senior managers,' James said. 'And me.'

'And is there any way to determine whether the problem was caused by a glitch, or because someone closed the system down or deleted the data?' Dan said.

'I'd have to check with the software company,' James replied. 'All I can tell you right now is that there is no data available for the period between 10.45 p.m. yesterday and 3.08 a.m. this morning. The system either failed, or someone switched it off.'

Chapter 11

As they made their way along the sweeping driveway to the Allwood residence, Theo let out a long, low whistle. Looming in the distance was an enormous Victorian house.

'Bloody hell!' Dan said. 'It's massive.'

'Certainly nothing like the house I grew up in,' said Theo.

'You and me both. It's in a grand setting all right, but it's bloody remote. I'm not sure I'd want to live out here in the middle of nowhere.'

'I reckon I'd forego the bright lights of the city to live in a house like that,' Theo said. 'It must be worth a small fortune. Who'd have thought there was so much money to be made from boiled sweets?'

The three-storey property was built in the Gothic style from local grey limestone, giving it a façade that was bleak and dour. Two black Mercedes-Benz cars were slewed on the large gravelled turning circle at the end of the driveway, directly in front of the house.

Given the gloomy atmosphere of the place, Dan half-expected the door to be answered by a decrepit, liveried servant, but it was a casually dressed Ross Allwood who let them in.

'Any news on Anna?' Ross asked, as he led them through a vast hallway, past a winding staircase, through to the back of the house.

'Not yet, I'm afraid,' said Dan. 'We're hoping you can provide us with information that will help us work out where she is.'

Faye Allwood was waiting for them in a sunny reception salon that looked out over the rear garden. The room was extravagantly furnished and bigger than Dan's entire flat.

'This is my mother,' Ross said.

Mrs Allwood was in her late fifties, slender and elegant, and slightly haughty-looking. The expression on her high-cheek-boned face suggested she found their visit an intrusion, but when she spoke, her voice was friendly and welcoming enough.

'Please, sit down, gentlemen,' she said. 'We're obviously very concerned. Tell us what we can do.'

'Can you confirm when you last saw Anna?'

'I've already given that information to one of your officers, but I'm happy to go through it again,' she said. 'I was with Anna during the presentations. I made a brief speech at about eleven o'clock, and handed out a couple of long service awards. Anna left a few minutes after that, but I can't be precise about the exact time.'

'Anna took photos of the award presentations,' Ross added. 'I spoke to her afterwards, but only briefly. She seemed to be in a hurry. I assumed she was heading straight home.'

'What about you, Mrs Allwood?' Dan said. 'You didn't speak to Anna again before she left?'

'No.' She shook her head. 'The last proper conversation we had was right before I made my speech. I asked her to sort out the presentation slides on the laptop. I'm not very technical, and I was worried I'd mess it up.'

'Did she mention whether she was meeting anyone after the party?' Dan asked.

Faye shrugged her bony shoulders. 'She didn't say anything like that to me. I was under the impression she was in a rush to pick up her son. To be honest, I was rather annoyed that she wasn't staying until the end of the party. The whole event was supposed to be a PR opportunity, and PR *is* Anna's responsibility.'

'PR?' Dan said. 'I thought the party was for the staff ... to celebrate the factory's anniversary?'

'Well, yes, that as well.' Faye flicked a hand, looking slightly shamefaced. 'But it wasn't just employees at the party. Some of our key retailers were also invited.'

Dan turned to address Ross. 'As head of sales, I'd imagine you were looking after those guests?'

'Yes, I was. There were a couple of tables set aside for the retailers, and I spent most of the evening wining and dining them. People started to circulate a lot more once the speeches were over, and quite a few gravitated towards the dance floor. The booze had been flowing, and everyone was letting their hair down by then.'

'We've checked the factory's security footage,' Dan said. 'Anna didn't leave through the front entrance, and her car is still parked at the factory. We believe she must have left from the other side of the building, along the rear exit road. She may have been on foot, but more likely she left in another vehicle.'

'The gate wasn't locked, so that's certainly a possibility,' said Ross.

'As Anna's exit wasn't recorded on any of the security cameras,' Dan added, 'we believe she may have gone out through your office, Mr Allwood. I gather it's out of range of the CCTV surveillance.'

'That's right, it is,' he replied, his voice hesitant. 'My office has a door that leads onto the side of the building. From there, Anna would have been able to leave through the rear gate without her movements being picked up on camera.'

'The only problem we have with that theory is that Anna's door pass doesn't give her access to the SMT offices.'

'In that case, someone must have opened the door for her,' Ross said. 'That's something that can be easily checked.'

'Ordinarily, yes,' said Dan. 'But mysteriously, there's no record of which electronic passes were used last night.'

Faye Allwood arched an eyebrow. 'What do you mean, *no record*? Are you saying the data's been deleted?'

'Either that, or it was never recorded in the first place,' Dan said. 'We understand the system can be overridden using an app.'

Ross glanced at his mother, a baffled expression on his face. 'There is an app,' he said, 'but why would someone switch off the system?'

'Presumably to hide their movements within the building,' said Theo. 'We believe someone either turned off the system or deleted the data to hide the fact that they were with Anna.'

'If we can digress for a moment,' Dan said, 'perhaps you can explain why each door is monitored. Why the need for that level of security?'

Faye rolled her eyes, looking embarrassed. 'That was my late husband's idea. He had a bee in his bonnet about someone leaking information to our competitors.'

'Were his fears justified, do you think?' Dan asked.

'No, he was being ridiculous, and I told him so,' Faye said. 'We'd developed a new range of sweets that he thought would make us a fortune overnight. When they failed to bring in revenue as quickly as he'd hoped, Barry started to fret about rival firms manufacturing copycat products.'

'Is that what was happening?' Dan asked.

'There were a few products launched that had a striking similarity to ours … perhaps with a few tweaks to colour or flavours … but that kind of thing happens. We've been guilty of it ourselves, in the past.'

'So, unlike your husband, you weren't concerned about a possible security breach?' Dan said.

'I wasn't concerned in the least,' Faye Allwood replied. 'Instead of commissioning a security upgrade, Barry should have kept his money in his pocket and exercised a little patience. It can take months, even years, for new products to take off. Those same products are now beginning to bring in a huge amount of revenue for us … it's a shame Barry isn't here to see it.'

Ross reached across and placed a hand on his mother's shoulder, squeezing it gently.

'It sounds like the business is doing well, then?' said Dan.

'Better than it's ever done,' Faye replied.

Despite the confidence of Mrs Allwood's response, Dan decided he would check Allwood's financial position for himself. For now though, he decided to move on to a different question.

'Can I ask what time the two of you left the party last night?' he said.

'I left shortly after midnight,' Faye replied. 'I went through the main reception and out the front door.'

'Did you get a taxi?'

'No, I drove myself home, via the rear gate.'

'And you saw no sign of Anna, as you drove along the goods road?'

'No. Of course not,' Faye replied. 'I would have said.'

'What about you, Mr Allwood?'

'I left around twelve-thirty. Officially, the party ended at midnight, but there were a few stragglers, and I felt obliged to stick around. I was one of the last to leave.'

'How did you get home?' Dan said.

'I got a lift … from a colleague, Evie Browell. She works in personnel.'

'And did this Evie Browell take you straight home?' Theo asked.

Ross laughed. 'Yes, she did. She dropped me here around one o'clock, and then she went home to her cat, and her husband of thirty-five years. Evie is one of the employees who received a long service award at the party.'

Dan didn't like the condescending smirk Ross Allwood was giving them, as though he and Theo were a couple of clowns.

'Just so that you know, we'll have officers at the factory first thing tomorrow,' Dan said, making it clear he was telling, rather than asking. 'They'll be questioning anyone who was at the party, who may have seen or talked to Anna. We'd also like to post a message on your staff intranet to encourage people to engage with us. And, if you have a tannoy system at the factory, we'll use that to make an announcement.'

'We can arrange both of those things,' Faye Allwood said. 'I'll ask Nicola Warren, the head of personnel, to liaise with your officers in the morning.'

'The best-case scenario is that Anna turns up safe and well in the next few hours,' Dan said. 'If she does, we won't need to trouble you.'

Faye smiled. 'I'm sure that's what we're all hoping for, detective.'

Theo shuffled forward and cleared his throat. 'Would you say that Anna takes her job seriously? Is she happy at work? Has she had any problems recently?'

'She's very efficient,' Faye said, somewhat begrudgingly. 'She's also very ambitious. She came to us with no experience, but she's demonstrated a natural gift for product promotion and marketing.'

'Were you responsible for recruiting her?' Dan asked.

'No, it was my husband who took her on. Barry employed Anna on a temporary basis initially, but he was extremely impressed with her abilities, so he decided to take her on permanently.'

'And what about you, Mrs Allwood?' Dan said. 'Were you equally impressed?'

'I wasn't as enthralled with her as my husband appeared to be,' she said. 'Anna can be rather opinionated at times, and a little too forthright in her views. Having said that, I have no complaints about her work.'

'Anna's devised some very successful marketing campaigns,' Ross said, as if making amends for the paucity of his mother's praise. 'I've worked with her on promoting our line of retro sweets, and we're getting some fantastic results from that.'

'A strong campaign must have made your job a lot easier,' said Dan.

'Definitely.' Ross stared at Faye defiantly. 'Unlike my mother, I have no objection to Anna having strong opinions. She makes sure her ideas are heard, and that's all to the benefit of Allwoods.'

'Are there any major changes afoot within the company?' Dan said. 'We heard that some kind of announcement is imminent.'

'Announcement?' Faye said, dismissing his words with a huff. 'Who told you that?'

'That's irrelevant, Mrs Allwood. I just need to know if it's true. Is something happening at Allwoods? A takeover maybe?'

'Absolutely not,' said Ross. 'I'm not sure who you've been talking to, but whoever it was has given you some duff info.'

Dan felt a prickle of frustration. Who was telling the truth here? The Allwoods, or James Derenby? Or was it Anna who'd been spreading false rumours?

'Our employees are constantly speculating about something,' Faye said. 'Last year there was talk of an American company taking over. All nonsense, of course, but the gossip still persisted.'

Dan did his best to smile. 'Tell me about Anna's relationships at work,' he said. 'Is there anyone she's particularly close to?'

'She's very pally with James Derenby,' Faye said.

Ross shook his head argumentatively. 'Anna's friendly with everyone, Mum. She's well liked at work, although I don't think she's made many *close* friends. She can be standoffish at times … She tries too hard to be professional, to make a good impression.'

'She's definitely very career-centric,' Faye said. 'If I had to describe Anna, I would say she's *single-minded* – less so, perhaps, since becoming a mother, but she's still extremely driven. It's as though she has something to prove.'

'We understand Anna had a disagreement with the two of you recently,' Dan said.

'Disagreement?' Faye repeated. 'What kind of disagreement?'

'I was hoping you'd fill us in on the details,' Dan replied. 'We believe there have been complaints … about Mr Allwood, from members of his team.'

'Oh, for pity's sake!' Faye threw back her head. 'There are *always* negative elements in every team, especially in sales. I ran that department for years. The reps are walking egos. They're racked by jealousy and petty rivalries, and they *all* think they know best.'

Dan turned to Ross, who was pulling nervously at the collar of his polo shirt.

'Would you agree with that assessment, Mr Allwood? Is it a straightforward case of employee dissatisfaction, or is there more to it?'

Ross glanced at his mother before answering. 'They don't like the way I run the team,' he said. 'They say I don't motivate them.'

'Ross …' Faye spoke sharply, her voice a warning for caution.

'I'm not going to lie about it, Mum. I know you've done your best to brush the whole thing under the carpet, but we both know I'm not cut out to lead a sales team. Anna knows it, and so do you – you just won't admit it.'

'Rubbish!' Faye snapped. 'You're more than capable if you put your mind to it. If you'd prefer *not* to do the job, that's something else entirely, but it's not a topic we should discuss now.' She glared at him pointedly.

'Does Anna have an opinion on the matter?' said Dan.

'Anna has an opinion on everything,' Faye said. 'However, her views on this issue are irrelevant. She's the marketing manager. It's not her place to decide who should run the sales team. As I've already mentioned, she pontificates about things that are nothing to do with her. My son and I *own* Allwood Confectionery. *We* have the final say on what happens. Anna would do well to remember that.'

'Let's hope you get a chance to remind her of that,' Dan said.

Faye Allwood crossed her legs and folded her arms. 'Is there anything else you need to ask?' she said, abruptly. 'Only we do have things to do this evening.'

'One final question,' Dan said. 'Anna's son is only five months old. Why isn't she still on maternity leave? Did she choose to come back to work early?'

'Yes,' Faye replied. 'She could have taken more time, but she told us she didn't like being out of the loop. I think she wanted to come back so that she could keep her finger on the pulse, so to speak.'

'Did anyone fill in for Anna while she was off?' said Dan.

'We recruited a graduate on a temporary contract,' Ross told him.

'Name?' Theo asked.

'Fenella Grainger,' Ross replied. 'She was nowhere near as good as Anna, but she kept things ticking over. We kept her on for a few weeks after Anna returned to work, but we had to let her go in the end. I think Anna was glad to see the back of her, to be honest. She and Fenella didn't exactly hit it off. I suspect there was a touch of professional rivalry.'

'It was a shame,' said Faye. 'Fenella showed great promise, and she still hasn't managed to get a full-time position.'

'Does she keep in touch then?' said Dan.

'Not really, but I had a chat with her last night, at the party.'

'Fenella Grainger was a guest at the party?' Dan said.

'Yes,' Faye said. 'And if Anna doesn't turn up for work tomorrow, we may need to call on Fenella's services for a second time.'

Chapter 12

'What did you make of the Allwoods?' Dan asked, as he and Theo drove back into the centre of Bainbridge.

'They were exactly as I expected them to be.'

'Up their own backsides, you mean?'

'Something like that.' Theo smirked. 'A bit *entitled*.'

'Entitled?' Dan said. 'I'm not sure about that. I think they're nouveau riche.'

'Yeah, that much was obvious from the interior décor.'

'You do know that Ross Allwood is Lucas Killingworth's cousin?' Dan said.

Theo pulled back his head and stared at him from the passenger seat. 'Seriously? Are you joking me.'

'No, straight up. Ross's dad and Lucas's mother were brother and sister. Lucas is being given office-based actions on the case for now, in case there turns out to be any connection between the Allwoods and Anna Matheson's disappearance.'

'Blimey, I'd never have pinned Ross Allwood as Lucas's cousin. There's not even a passing resemblance.'

'Well, our Lucas is a one-off,' Dan said. 'And he takes more after Mark, his dad.'

'You've met his dad?'

'Yep, at Lucas's barbecue, last summer. He managed to squeeze one in, between the bad weather and the lockdowns. Mark was in charge of the cooking. He seemed nice, as did Mrs Killingworth. Very down to earth, the pair of 'em.'

'That's what I'd expect,' Theo said. 'Ross and his mother might live in that great big house ... but Lucas? He certainly doesn't come across as being from a posh family.'

'According to the DI, Lucas's mum and Barry Allwood fell out a long time ago. Lucas doesn't actually know the Allwoods, even though they're related.'

'Fancy,' Theo said. 'Our very own DC Killingworth related to a boiled sweet magnate.'

'Don't you get saying anything to him,' said Dan. 'If he wants to talk about it, that's fine. Otherwise, keep it under your hat.'

Laughing, Theo turned to gaze out of the passenger-side window. 'Are we heading straight back to the station?'

'Aye, I need to get back for the press conference,' Dan said. 'I was hoping we wouldn't have to do it ... that Anna Matheson would have turned up by now.'

'It's nearly sixteen hours since she went missing,' Theo said. 'It doesn't look good, does it?'

'No, it doesn't,' Dan said. 'My gut's telling me this isn't going to end well.'

***

The press conference was scheduled for four o'clock, but Zoe arrived twenty minutes early with Christina Matheson in tow. Dan introduced himself, doing his best to reassure the missing woman's mother that the press conference was nothing to worry about, even though he felt sick with nerves himself.

'Thank you for providing us with a photograph of Anna,' he said. 'I take it we have your permission to make it available to the media?'

'Of course,' Christina said. 'If you think it will help.'

'I'm sure DC Piper has already briefed you on what to expect,' Dan continued. 'But to confirm, I'll begin by making a short statement, and then you'll make your appeal. The media have been told not to ask questions, but you should expect a lot of cameras, including a TV camera.'

Christina was kneading her hands. 'Now that I'm here, I'm not sure I can do it,' she said. 'What if I make a hash of things?'

'You'll be fine, Christina,' Zoe said. 'Do your best – that's all anyone can ask.'

'If you'd rather not deal with the media yourself, we can always ask a trusted family member or a friend to act as a spokesperson,' Dan said. 'It's not too late to do that.'

'There's no one else I can ask,' she replied.

How had someone of Christina Matheson's age ended up with no friends or family to turn to? Dan thought. It was sad, and slightly odd.

'What about Lauren Talbot?' said DI Blood, who had joined them to oversee the appeal. 'Perhaps she'd be willing to say a few words.'

Christina Matheson's reply was quick. Too quick. Contemptuous even. 'No, I'll do it,' she said. 'I'm Anna's mother. If anyone's going to speak to the press, it should be me.'

'If you're sure,' said DI Blood, nodding swiftly.

Christina reached out and gripped the DI's forearm. 'Where do you think she is? What's happened to my daughter?'

'I wish I knew,' DI Blood replied. 'We're not sure why Anna has disappeared. She may have had an accident, she could be the victim of a crime, or it could be something else entirely – but a public plea like this will generate new leads that we can investigate. In all missing persons cases, it's essential to get the message out to as many people as possible. We've already launched a social media appeal, and this press conference will spread the word even further. Hopefully, we'll have some answers for you soon.'

At one minute past four, with DI Blood watching from the back of the room, Dan led Christina Matheson out in front of the press. As they settled down behind a long, narrow table, cameras clicked and reporters switched on recording devices. There was a good turnout, which would generate plenty of coverage for the news story.

Dan began with a prepared statement.

'We're here today to appeal for help in finding Anna Matheson, who was last seen at eleven minutes past eleven yesterday evening, at a works party at Allwood Confectionery. She had arranged to collect her five-month-old son from the babysitter at eleven-thirty, but failed to turn up. Anna is white, approximately five foot five inches tall, of slim build, with shoulder-length dark curly hair. When last seen, she was wearing a short-sleeved, emerald-green, knee-length dress and a short black jacket. We're urging anyone who has any information regarding Anna's whereabouts to contact the police by calling 101, or you can get in touch through our social media channels. Christina Matheson, Anna's mother, would now like to say a few words.'

He turned to Christina, who appeared to have frozen. Dan slid a glass of water in her direction. She picked it up and took a sip, and then another. Looking directly into the television camera, she began to speak.

'My daughter is one of the most reliable people I know,' she said. 'The fact that she failed to collect her son from the babysitter fills my heart with fear. She is a wonderful and loving mother, and she would never let her son down. She certainly wouldn't abandon him.'

She took another swig of water before continuing. 'I hope and pray that Anna is all right, but deep down I'm worried that something has happened to her. It's not in her nature to disappear. Somebody somewhere must know where she is, or have an idea of what might have happened to her. If you're one of the people she works with and you were at the party last night, I'm asking you to please get in touch. If anyone out there knows anything … *anything at all* … that will help find Anna, please talk to the police. Did you see Anna last night, or in the early hours of this morning? Did you see something suspicious at the party or out on the roads? Please, please call if you have information that will help bring Anna home safely. And, Anna? If you *are* watching this, please get in touch. I love you so much, and I'm worried about you, darling. Your little boy needs you. Please come home if you can.'

At the sight of tears welling in Christina Matheson's eyes, the sound of camera shutters rattled through the conference room.

'Do you think Anna's still alive?' yelled one insensitive reporter.

'We won't be taking questions today,' Dan said. 'All I will say is that we're keeping an open mind about what may have happened, and doing everything we can to locate Anna. As Ms Matheson has already stated, Anna's disappearance is out of character. Obviously, the longer she remains missing, the more concerned we are about her safety, which is why we're asking you to spread the word and help us gather the information we need to find her. Anyone who thinks they may have seen Anna should contact us immediately – and, of course, if Anna herself is able to contact her family or the police, we'd urge her to do so. Thank you.'

Dan stood up and Christina Matheson followed suit. Despite being reminded there were to be no questions, a couple of journalists shouted at their retreating backs. Ignoring them, Dan ushered Christina Matheson out of the room.

'You did brilliantly, Christina,' said DI Blood, who had abandoned her position at the back of the press conference and hurried around to meet them. 'Let's wait and see what information the appeal brings. In the meantime, we'll continue to do everything we can to find your daughter.'

'I'd like to see my grandson now,' Christina said. 'It's not right that he's still with Lauren Talbot. I want him home with me, so he'll be there when Anna comes back.'

'Of course,' said DI Blood. 'We can arrange that.'

Dan nodded at his boss to acknowledge the request. Getting Benedict Matheson over to his grandmother's house was something that could be easily accomplished. As for Anna coming home, he thought that was far less likely.

Chapter 13

Zoe was in the passenger seat of a patrol car, sitting alongside PC Will Rowe, who was driving her over to Bellbrook House to collect Benedict Matheson.

'You'd better ring ahead,' Will said. 'Check that Benedict has a car seat over at the Talbots', otherwise he won't be able to travel in the car with us.'

Zoe made the call and told Lauren Talbot what was happening.

'Why is Christina insisting on taking care of Benedict, when he's perfectly safe and happy here?' Lauren said. Her voice was angry and strident, forcing Zoe to hold the phone away from her ear.

'She's the child's grandmother. In the absence of his mother, it's understandable that she wants to take charge of the little boy.'

'He's better off here, with me,' Lauren insisted. 'Christina's skills as a mother have always left a lot to be desired. I doubt her skills as a grandmother are any better.'

'I'm not ringing to ask your permission,' Zoe said. 'Merely to ascertain whether there's a car seat available for Benedict, so that we can transport him to Mrs Matheson's.'

'Transport him? For goodness' sake, he's a child, not a piece of furniture to be manhandled. And it's *Miss* Matheson. Christina has never been married. Heaven forbid she would ever do anything so conventional.'

Zoe gritted her teeth, feeling the heat of a red rash spreading across her neck. 'Do you have a car seat that we can use? Yes or no?'

'Yes. I assume you'll know how to fit it?'

Zoe hadn't the foggiest, but she wasn't going to admit that to Lauren Talbot.

'We'll be with you in approximately five minutes,' she said instead. 'Please gather Benedict's belongings together and have him ready to go when we arrive.'

As she stabbed at her phone to end the call, Will smiled from the driver's seat.

'*She's* full of herself,' Zoe said. 'It doesn't sound as though she wants to let Benedict go.'

'I think she's fond of the little lad,' Will said. 'That's no excuse for being rude, though.'

Zoe slipped her mobile into her pocket and shrugged. 'Her friend's missing. I suppose I ought to cut her some slack.'

Will smiled. 'You're a nice person, Zoe.'

She shot him a sideways look. 'Do you know how to fix the car seat? I hope you're not expecting me to do it.'

'Don't worry, I'll sort it,' Will said. 'I'm a dab hand.'

Zoe was surprised. 'I thought you said you don't have kids,' she said.

'I haven't, but I've got two nephews. It's amazing what you learn when you're on uncle duties.'

Zoe leaned against the headrest. 'I'm an only child, so nephews and nieces are never going to be an option for me.'

'You'll have to wait until you've got children of your own then.' Will smiled. 'It'll be a steeper learning curve for you, that's all.'

She half-turned in her seat to look at him. 'That's rather presumptuous, isn't it? Assuming I'm going to have kids.'

He pulled a face. 'Sorry. Have I touched a nerve? Don't you like children?'

'I'm sure they're lovely, but I'd rather not tempt fate. I'd be putting the cart before the horse if I started thinking about having a family. I'm not even in a relationship.'

'I'm sure that won't be the case for long.' He grinned.

Against her better judgement, Zoe allowed herself to smile back. 'PC Rowe, I get the distinct impression you're trying to flirt with me,' she said, peering at him through wary eyes.

'Maybe.' He winked playfully. 'Yeah, I think I am.'

***

As they pulled up in front of Bellbrook House, Will nodded at the moonlight blue Porsche Cayenne and the black Nissan 370Z parked under the double carport.

'The Talbots obviously aren't short of a bob or two,' he said.

'Flash cars don't impress me,' Zoe said.

'Why doesn't that surprise me.' A smile tugged at the corners of his mouth. 'The fact that there are *two* cars on the drive suggests that the husband is back. He was at a work seminar in Liverpool when I came up last night. Might be worth talking to him … see if he has any ideas on where Anna might be.'

It was Edward Talbot who came to the door. He was tall, smooth and devastatingly good-looking. When Zoe held up her warrant card, he gave her a smile that rendered her temporarily flummoxed.

'My wife's in the kitchen, getting Benedict ready,' he said. 'Any news on Anna?'

'Nothing yet,' Zoe said. 'We've just come from a press conference, so that might generate some new information.'

'Disappearing like this is *so* not her,' he said, as he led them down the hallway to the back of the house. 'I'm trying to stay positive for Lauren's sake, but I can't help but think something untoward must have happened.'

'Do you have any thoughts on where Anna might be?' said Will. 'Any ideas on what may have happened to her?'

Edward Talbot shrugged. 'I wish I did.'

They turned right into a large, sleek kitchen. Lauren Talbot was standing at its centre, holding one of the cutest babies Zoe had ever seen. At the far end of the room, two little girls were sitting together, watching a wall-mounted television. Presumably these were the Talbots' own children.

'Hello, Benedict,' said Will, smiling at the baby. 'You look wide awake today.'

'He's due a nap, actually,' Lauren said, her voice snippy and peevish. 'He'll probably fall asleep in the car. The seat's over there.' She nodded towards a small table, on which a grey car seat had been placed.

'I hope you're going to keep me updated,' Lauren said. 'I realise I'm only in the loop at the moment because I've been looking after Benedict. Now that I'm handing him over, I'm sure I'll be left in the dark as to what's happening.'

'Don't fret, we'll keep you informed,' Will said. 'You're the one who reported Anna missing, after all.'

Zoe turned to Edward Talbot. 'I understand you were away last night.'

'That's right,' he said. 'I've been in Liverpool, attending a conference.'

'When did you find out that Anna was missing?'

'When I got home, earlier this afternoon. That's when Lauren told me.'

Zoe widened her eyes. 'I'm surprised your wife didn't ring you last night, or text you.'

Lauren interjected. 'I thought about it,' she said, 'but it was late and Eddie was too far away. There was nothing he could have done, so I decided not to disturb him.'

'You should have rung me, Lauren. If I'd known what was happening, I would have left Liverpool earlier.'

'It wouldn't have made any difference, would it? Here ...' She thrust the baby into her husband's arms. 'Hold Benedict for a minute. I put some of his clothes in the wash last night … I need to get them out of the tumble dryer.'

Edward took the child reluctantly, holding him stiffly.

'Hurry up,' he said, as his wife disappeared into the adjacent utility room. 'I've still got my best shirt on. I don't want him throwing up all over me.'

'Would you like me to hold him?' Will offered.

Looking relieved, Edward handed the baby over.

'Are you and Anna close?' Zoe asked. 'Good friends?'

'She's more Lauren's friend than mine,' Edward replied, 'but I do like Anna. Always have. She's very down to earth, keeps my wife grounded.'

'I heard that,' Lauren said, as she returned to the kitchen, folding a tiny blue sweater and a miniature pair of jeans. 'You've got that the wrong way round, Eddie. If anything, I'm the one who keeps Anna's feet firmly on the ground.'

'Have you had any more thoughts on Anna's whereabouts, Mrs Talbot?' Will said, as he entertained the baby with a spot of gurning.

'I've thought about nothing else,' she replied. 'Last night you asked whether Anna could be with Benedict's father, and I'm beginning to think that would make sense.'

'Are you sure you're not grasping at straws?' Edward said. 'You don't even know who Benedict's father is.'

'*I* don't, but Anna does,' Lauren said, clearly annoyed that her husband was challenging the theory. 'As for grasping at straws, that's all I've got. There's no logical explanation as to where Anna might be, so I'm trying to think laterally. What if this bloke is demanding to see Benedict? What if he's abducted Anna and is refusing to let her go unless she allows him to see his son?'

Edward Talbot screwed up his face and placed a hand on the back of his head. 'Now you're being ridiculous,' he said. 'Stop being so dramatic, Lauren, and let the police do their job. And for God's sake, don't send them off on a wild goose chase.'

'I'm worried about her, Ed,' Lauren said. 'I'm scared. What if something's happened to her?'

'It's pointless me trying to tell you not to worry,' Zoe said, 'but rest assured we will keep you informed when we know more.'

'Let's get this little chap to his grandma's house, shall we?' said Will.

Smiling forlornly, Lauren leaned in to stroke the baby's head and kiss him goodbye.

Chapter 14

A creeping sense of anxiety accompanied Isabel as she left the office that evening. Every member of the investigation team was busy following procedure, doing their best to find Anna Matheson, but without any real clues as to what might have happened, there was no guarantee their efforts would pay off.

Officers had finished a second search of the factory, as well as a sweep of the surrounding area, but there was no sign of the missing woman. There had been no activity on her credit or debit cards, and no sightings of Anna on any of the CCTV footage checked so far.

It was now seven o'clock, almost twenty hours since Anna Matheson had last been seen. On the drive home, Isabel steeled herself, preparing for the worst.

She found her family in the living room, slumped in front of the television, watching an overhyped quiz programme featuring celebrities and a lot of shouting.

'Evening,' Nathan said, glancing fleetingly in her direction before refocusing on the unfolding action on TV. 'You're late. Are you OK? Have you eaten?'

'I had a meal at work,' Isabel said. 'I'm pretty knackered though. It's been quite a day.'

'We saw the appeal on the news about your missing person,' said Bailey, who was stretched out on the settee with their dog, Nell.

Isabel pushed her son's legs onto the floor and sat down beside him. Nell immediately shifted her allegiance, snuggling into the crook of Isabel's arm.

'As press conferences go, it's not been massively successful,' she said, as she stroked one of the dog's velvet-soft ears. 'There's been very little response so far.'

'Maybe this woman has decided to take off for a while,' Bailey said. 'Sometimes, all people need is some space … time to clear their head.'

'I hope you're right,' Isabel said. 'Trouble is, from what we know of her, she's not the kind of person who would do that. As you'll have heard on the news, she's got a five-month-old baby. She's a responsible parent, and she also takes her job very seriously.'

'It said on the telly she was last seen at Allwood Confectionery,' Bailey said. 'Is that where she works?'

'Yeah, she's their marketing manager. Come to think of it … didn't you and Sophie work at Allwoods one summer, back when you were students?'

At the mention of his ex-girlfriend's name, Bailey released a melancholy sigh. 'That seems like a lifetime ago,' he said. 'It was the summer before our final year at uni. Sophie worked on the production line, and I ended up in the packing department. The pay was crap, but you could eat as many sweets as you liked.'

Isabel chortled. 'I'll bet the local dentists love Allwoods employees.'

'Surprisingly, the novelty of eating sugary sweets wears off after a couple of days,' Bailey said. 'In fact, working there put me off tuffies for life. Sophie loved it though … a job in a sweet factory was her idea of heaven. I hated every minute of it.'

'I didn't know you felt that way about it,' Isabel said. 'You never said anything at the time.'

Bailey shrugged. 'It was no big deal. We knew we'd only be

there for a few months. It was just a way of earning some money. Mind you, it was hard work.'

A roar of applause burst from the television screen.

'By hard work, I assume you mean physically demanding? I can't imagine it would be mentally taxing.'

'It was physically demanding *and* mind-numbingly boring. Plus, you had to ask permission if you wanted to go to the loo. It made me feel like a kid at school.'

Isabel looked across at her daughter, who was responding to a crescendo of quiz-show excitement by slapping her hands together like a performing seal.

'Talking of school,' Isabel said. 'Have you had your reading lists for the new term yet, Ellie?'

'Most of them,' she replied, without taking her eyes off the screen. 'I'll show you when this has finished.' She used her toe to point at the television, where a group of celebrity contestants were spinning round on some kind of rotating wheel.

'We've got hundreds of channels to choose from,' Isabel said. 'Is there nothing better to watch than this?'

The question was met with a chorus of objections.

'Sorry, love,' Nathan said. 'Looks like you're outnumbered.'

***

Before Isabel went to bed, she set her alarm for six a.m. The intention was to go for an early run before work – but fate had other plans. Five minutes before the alarm was due to go off, her phone rang, waking her from a deep, dream-filled sleep.

The caller was Sergeant Bostock, the uniformed supervisor on the misper case. The fact that he was ringing so early didn't bode well. Isabel braced herself as she accepted the call.

'Morning, ma'am,' he said. 'Sorry to bother you so early. I'm afraid we've had word that a woman's body has been found. It matches Anna Matheson's description.'

Nathan was asleep, sprawled next to her. Isabel sat up slowly, trying not to wake him.

'Where?' She took a deep breath and leaned against the headboard.

'Up in Brightcliffe Woods, off the Enderdale Road. An elderly man found the body … He was out walking.'

'Bit early for a walk, isn't it?'

'It is for us, but this old guy is a twitcher, on the lookout for some rare breed of bird. He spotted more than he bargained for this morning.'

'Poor chap,' Isabel said. 'But if he's found Anna Matheson, he's succeeded where we failed.'

She felt something heavy settle in the pit of her stomach. Sadness? Guilt? Regret?

'Do we know if there are signs of foul play?' she said.

'According to the officer who attended the scene, it's definitely a suspicious death.'

'Shit!' Isabel closed her eyes and dragged air into her lungs. 'This isn't how I wanted this to end, Adrian.'

'No. I know. Me neither.'

'Do me a favour will you? Get in touch with DC Piper. Ask her to head over to Christina Matheson's house. Someone needs to break the news that a body's been found, and it may as well be Zoe.'

Chapter 15

Brightcliffe Woods covered a steep hillside on the west bank of the River Derwent near Cromford. In medieval times, the ancient woodland had been part of a royal hunting forest. More recently, the area had been designated a site of special scientific interest.

Every May, when their kids were young, Isabel and Nathan had taken them to the woods to see the bluebells. They had always followed the main trail – which, in early summer, was carpeted on either side with the richly scented flowers. Weaving sideways up the hill, it led to an ancient yew, purported to be almost two thousand years old.

Carrying her murder bag, Isabel followed the same trail now. It was cooler here, beneath the trees, away from the heat of the early morning sun. A chorus of birdsong echoed from the highest branches. The sound was loud and eerie, almost primeval.

A short distance along the path, she encountered the young uniformed officer who was on scene guard.

'It's down there, ma'am,' he said, pointing beyond a line of tape, towards a section of the woods that was thickly populated with birches.

Isabel signed the crime scene log, opened her bag and pulled on the full body suit, shoe covers, gloves, and face mask that were stashed away in readiness. Leaving the main path, she proceeded along the approach path set out by the CSIs, chosen by them as the route least likely to have been taken by the perpetrator. Balancing carefully on a series of ridged metal stepping plates, she headed towards the white CSI tent in the distance. The location of the body was in a dip, roughly a hundred yards off the trail – deep enough in the woods for it to have lain undiscovered for days, had it not been for the intrepid birdwatcher.

A technician wearing a body suit was scouring the area, searching for evidence. Another was crouching near a tangled patch of brambles, examining something on the ground. Raveen Talwar, the crime scene manager, was inside the tent, leaning over the body.

'Hello, Raveen,' Isabel said, her voice quietly reverent.

He nodded. 'Morning, DI Blood.'

'Is it Anna Matheson?'

'Take a look for yourself.' He stood back, revealing the slender, supine form of a woman, her green dress startlingly bright against the earthy tones of the sylvan setting.

Suppressing a shiver, Isabel inhaled deeply and took a step closer.

There was no doubt in her mind that the victim was Anna Matheson.

She was lying face up, her eyes open, staring lifelessly at the roof of the tent. Her curly hair formed a brown halo around her head, a stray tendril spiralling across her left cheek onto the collar of her jacket. The emerald-coloured shift dress she wore was made from raw silk, giving it a shiny, jewel-like quality. The scoop neckline exposed a harsh, red welt around Anna's throat.

Isabel closed her eyes and turned away.

'Strangulation?' she said, once she'd stepped away from the confines of the tent.

'It sure looks that way,' Raveen said, as he followed her into the open air. 'But it'll be down to the pathologist to confirm the official cause and time of death.'

'When do *you* think she died, Raveen? I'm sure you've already formed your own opinion.'

He smiled. 'You know me too well, DI Blood. I'd say she's been dead for twenty-four hours at least, probably longer – but Emma's the pathologist. I wouldn't want to pre-empt anything she has to say.'

'Have you uncovered any other forensic evidence?'

'Nothing unusual so far, but we're still looking. I've clipped and swabbed the victim's fingernails. We might get lucky and find a trace of DNA that isn't the victim's.'

'Anything else you can tell me?'

'It looks like the body was dragged here.' He pointed to a trail of disturbed undergrowth leading off the path. 'The floor of any wood or forest is covered in vegetative matter … leaves, branches and bark all decompose above the soil – but there's hardly any sign of those kind of deposits on the victim's clothing.'

'Which means?'

'I'd say the victim was wrapped in some kind of fabric … something strong, like a heavy-duty canvas tarp. It would have made the task of dragging the body to this position much easier.'

'Do you think one person, acting alone, could have managed it?'

'It wouldn't have been easy,' Raveen said. 'But it's possible. I think if two people had brought the body here, they're more likely to have carried it through the woods. The drag marks from the main trail … broken-down bracken and twigs … that suggests one person pulling the body behind them.'

Relieved to be out of the tent and back under the whispering canopy of trees, Isabel filled her lungs with air. Tipping back her head, she stared upwards, watching the gentle sway of the leaves in the branches high above.

'Are you OK?' asked Raveen.

'No, I'm not,' she said. 'On days like this, I wish I could be made redundant.'

Raveen regarded her quizzically, his brow furrowed.

She looked at him and gave a half-hearted smile. 'If I was redundant, it would mean I was living in a world free from this kind of needless loss of life,' she explained. 'The UK would be a place where senseless violence had been eradicated, and police officers were no longer required.'

Raveen touched her arm. 'It's never going to happen, Isabel.'

'I know. It's wishful thinking, that's all.' Her gaze drifted into the distance, where a shaft of sunlight had pierced the cover of the trees. 'I struggle when I'm working on a case like this. When a life is taken for no good reason, I find myself asking how much longer I can keep doing this.'

'What? Be a copper?' He studied her intently. 'You're not thinking of retiring, are you?'

'There are days … like today … when I think about nothing else,' she admitted.

'Just because something is hard, doesn't mean you should give up.'

'I know.' Isabel nodded. 'I'll keep going. For now.'

'Glad to hear it,' Raveen said. 'Because when something like this happens … the world needs people like you, to put things right.'

Isabel pushed her hands into her pockets, listening to the machine-gun rattle of a magpie somewhere above them.

'If we're lucky, we'll track down the killer,' she said. 'We aim for justice, Raveen, but justice doesn't always put things right. This woman's child will grow up without a mother. There's nothing I can do to right that wrong.'

Chapter 16

The thing that Zoe had been dreading had come to pass. As the family liaison officer, it was down to her to break the devastating news to Christina Matheson that a woman's body had been found. Although they were still awaiting official confirmation, there seemed no doubt that the victim was Anna. Overnight, the investigation had gone from a missing persons case to a full-blown murder inquiry.

Zoe lingered at Christina's doorstep, running through in her head what she was going to say. She wanted to be kind, to phrase things delicately, but there really was no gentle way to tell someone that their child had been murdered.

Being the FLO meant she'd be responsible for practical matters – such as arranging for Christina to formally identify Anna's body – but she would also be expected to gauge Christina's reaction to the death, and note any comments that the terrible news might provoke. Zoe felt a huge sense of duty, and the weight of it made her nervous. She so wanted to get this right.

Lifting her right hand, she rapped her knuckles against the squat wooden door and waited.

***

94

In the end, Zoe didn't need her carefully rehearsed words. The expression on her face must have spoken for her. When Christina opened the door and took in Zoe's demeanour, she placed a hand over her mouth and gave a startled cry.

'She's dead, isn't she?'

'A body was discovered this morning,' Zoe said, speaking as softly as she could. 'I'm sorry to have to tell you, but we believe it's Anna. We're now treating the investigation as a murder inquiry.'

Letting out an animal-like howl, Christina doubled over, her body folding at the waist. Zoe reached out to steady her.

'Come inside and sit down,' she said, guiding the weeping woman across the living room, to the armchair furthest from the window. 'I'm so very sorry for your loss. I realise you're in shock, and I appreciate you'll need some time to take in what's happened, but I will need to ask you some questions.'

Christina sank into the chair and continued to weep pitifully. Zoe held her hand and allowed her to cry.

'I knew something awful must have happened,' Christina said eventually, her voice shuddering with sorrow. 'I'm shocked, of course I am, but from the minute I heard she was missing, I think I've been expecting this … dreading it. I don't understand. Who would do something like this? *Why?*'

'We don't know yet,' Zoe said, 'but rest assured, there's an investigation team working out what happened, and who was responsible.'

Folding her hands across her midriff, Christina began to rock back and forth, gently nursing her grief. 'How was she killed?'

'Initial reports suggest she was strangled,' Zoe replied. 'I'm truly sorry, Christina. I know how hard this must be for you, but can you think of anyone who might be capable of doing this to Anna?'

'No.' She moaned softly. 'Why would anyone want to kill my lovely daughter?'

Unable to provide an answer, Zoe instead asked another question. 'Was there anyone your daughter was scared of? Or someone she didn't get on with?'

'If there was, she didn't talk to me about it,' Christina replied, pressing the fingers of her right hand against her temple. 'Was she … attacked? Sexually assaulted?'

'We don't believe so, but we won't know for certain until the pathologist has had an opportunity to examine Anna properly.'

Christina began to weep again, her cries rising to anguished, gulping wails.

Feeling utterly inadequate, Zoe went into the kitchen to fetch some water. By the time she'd filled the glass and returned to the living room, Christina was beginning to compose herself.

'In view of what's happened, we'll need to conduct forensic and police searches at Anna's home,' Zoe said, as she handed over the water. 'Do you have a key to her house?'

In between shuddering breaths, Christina nodded. 'In that dresser over there. It's the one with the feather keyring.'

Zoe yanked open the drawer Christina had pointed to. Among the jumbled contents, tangled up with other odds and ends, Zoe spotted an iridescent blue feather. As she retrieved the keyring, she heard the sharp cry of a baby from somewhere upstairs.

Christina stopped rocking and glanced at the ceiling. 'He'll know something's wrong. Babies sense these things.' She looked at Zoe imploringly. 'Would you go up to him? I'd go myself, but if he sees that I'm distressed, it'll upset him even more.'

Zoe gripped the keyring in her palm, the feathers tickling her fingers. She knew nothing about babies – how to hold them, or soothe them, or speak to them. Feeling ill-prepared, she found herself wishing that Will Rowe was here. He'd know what to do.

The crying intensified.

Knowing it wasn't acceptable to baulk at such a request, Zoe took a step towards the stairway. She was the family liaison officer, and sometimes families included crying babies. This was the first time she'd faced this kind of situation in her new role, but it wouldn't be the last. If she wanted to succeed as a FLO, she'd have to learn to cope with such practical challenges.

Pushing the key into her pocket, Zoe took a deep breath and began to climb the stairs.

Chapter 17

The murder investigation had been assigned the operational name Zebra. The discovery of the body had, if anything, instilled an even greater sense of urgency within the investigation team. Beset by a sense of failure, Isabel was feeling stressed and disheartened.

'DC Piper has obtained a key to the victim's house from Christina Matheson,' she said, addressing the officers who had gathered in the ops room for the latest briefing. 'There's absolutely nothing to suggest that Anna Matheson was killed in her own home, but Forensics are examining the property and a police search will be carried out once the CSIs have finished. At the very least, we should be able to get our hands on the victim's laptop and other devices. I've asked Digital Forensics to prioritise the analysis of the victim's internet history, and we're expecting the phone data from the service provider sometime today. That will tell us who the victim has been communicating with recently.'

'What do we know about how she died?' Dan said. 'Do you think she was killed in the woods, or was her body dumped there?'

'Initial findings suggest the primary scene was elsewhere. She was killed – strangled – and her body was moved,' Isabel replied. 'We'll know more once the post-mortem's been carried out.'

There was a moment of respectful silence. A reverential pause before Isabel continued.

'DC Lindley and PC Rowe are at Allwoods right now, talking to employees as they arrive for work. The last sighting of Anna Matheson was at the factory. If she disappeared from there, or was murdered there, it's likely the killer has a connection to Allwoods and was at the party.'

'James Derenby has provided us with a list of attendees,' said Dan. 'The majority of the guests were factory employees, but not all of them.'

'Get someone to run the full list of names through the PNC,' Isabel said.

'That's a lot of names, boss.'

'Do it anyway,' she said. 'And if you find anyone with so much as a speeding fine, I want to know about it.'

'We've had a few calls following yesterday's press conference,' Sergeant Bostock said, 'but unfortunately, nothing of any real significance – at least not so far. We'll make a further statement to the press shortly, letting them and the public know that this is now a murder investigation.'

'One of the lines of inquiry I'd like to prioritise is tracking down Benedict Matheson's father,' Isabel said. 'The fact that Anna kept his identity a secret is a red flag. What was she hiding? Is it possible the baby's father is someone she worked with, or someone she'd been having an affair with? Could Anna have been threatening to expose the relationship? Let's see what we can find out.'

'I'll get Zoe to talk to the victim's mother again,' Dan said. 'She might be able to shed some light on who the mystery bloke might be.'

'I'd also like someone to interview the people Anna worked closest with,' Isabel said. 'We need to quiz James Derenby and Ross Allwood again … ask them about their relationship with Anna. I know James has already denied being the child's father, but if he was involved in Anna's murder, he'd have every reason to lie. Lauren Talbot hinted that both Derenby and Allwood were interested in establishing a relationship with the victim. Check with Anna's colleagues to see if there's any truth in that. Find out what the gossip is around the water cooler.'

'We could ask for voluntary DNA samples from Derenby and Allwood,' Dan suggested. 'By comparing them against Benedict Matheson's DNA, we'd know for certain whether either of them is the father.'

'We can ask,' Isabel said. 'Although I'm not sure how willing they'll be.'

'If they've got nothing to hide, why wouldn't they want to co-operate?' Dan said. 'If the little lad isn't theirs, a DNA test is their chance to prove it, once and for all.'

'We should certainly put in a request,' Isabel said. 'However, the paternity question may have nothing to do with the crime we're investigating. The motive for Anna's murder could be something else entirely … something connected to a different aspect of her personal life, or possibly her job. Perhaps Anna discovered something unsavoury about someone at the factory, or about the company itself. Let's do some digging. Allwoods is celebrating its sixtieth anniversary this year, but *is* there cause for celebration? Find out if the company is profitable, or up to its eyes in debt.'

'In terms of building a profile of the victim,' said Adrian Bostock, 'we've received conflicting reports. For instance, Lauren Talbot's description of her relationship with Anna is at odds with Christina Matheson's version of the friendship. On top of that, James Derenby has indicated that Anna had a problem with alcohol in the past, but no one else has mentioned it. Why is that? We need to get to the truth of what Anna Matheson was really like.'

'If she was a recovering alcoholic, she might not have wanted that information to be common knowledge,' Isabel said. 'But if she told Derenby, I'd imagine she would also have opened up to her mother. Let's check with Christina Matheson and some of

Anna's other colleagues to find out how much – if anything – they knew about her drinking habits.'

'In terms of the victim's movements,' Adrian Bostock said, 'we're running her car reg through the ANPR to try and establish where she went in the days leading up to her death. I'm hoping that might throw up something of interest.'

Isabel sighed. 'It seems to me we're juggling a huge number of questions. What we need now are some answers.'

Chapter 18

Will Rowe was standing at the main gate at Allwood Confectionery, shoulders back, muscular arms folded. DC Theo Lindley was standing a few metres away with his hands in his pockets.

The company's employees had begun to arrive at eight o'clock. There had been a trickle of people at first, few enough for Will and Theo to manage between them. They'd been stopping everyone on their way in, asking three key questions. *What is your name? Were you at the party on Saturday night?* and *Did you see or speak to Anna Matheson?* Those who replied in the affirmative to the last question were also asked *when* they had last seen Anna and what, if anything, they had talked about.

The main shift started work at 8.20 a.m. and by 8.10 a.m. the trickle of workers coming through the gates had turned into a steady stream – far too many people for two officers to deal with.

'Let's go inside,' DC Lindley said, when the last of the employees had scurried past them. 'Nicola Warren's going to make an announcement at nine o'clock. Anyone we haven't managed to speak to at the gate will be asked to come and see us in the canteen.'

'Have you learned anything useful from anyone?' Will asked.

'Not so far,' Theo said. 'Most of the people I've spoken to saw Anna at the party, and some of them even talked to her, but no one remembers seeing her after the speeches. What about you? Any joy?'

''Fraid not,' Will said. 'The ones I stopped had a similar story to tell. Most of them remember seeing her at some point during the evening … one guy even sat on the same table, but he said Anna was flitting around a lot, taking photos, setting things up for the speeches and so on.'

'Let's head inside and find the HR woman,' Theo said. 'After that, we can go to the canteen to wait for the announcement. With any luck, we'll be able to get something to eat.'

***

Any remaining signs that a party had taken place in the staff canteen had been cleared away. The tables had been moved back, and the aroma of fried eggs and bacon was lingering in the air. There was a small queue of people at the counter, ordering hot drinks and takeaway breakfasts.

Will and Theo joined the line. They bought sausage butties, which they ate at a table close to the door.

'This cob's bloody lovely,' Theo said, wiping his fingers on a napkin. 'I wish they did grub as good as this in the station canteen.'

When the hands of the clock on the wall reached nine a.m., the sound of a clear female voice boomed from the tannoy system.

'*Good morning, everyone. This is Nicola Warren. As most of you will already have heard, our marketing manager, Anna Matheson, went missing after the sixtieth anniversary party on Saturday. It's my sad duty to report that Anna's body has now been found, and the police are treating her death as a murder inquiry. I realise this will come as a huge shock to you all, and I know you'll join with me in offering heartfelt condolences to Anna's family and friends.*

'*Many of you will have seen the police officer and detective who were at the main gates this morning, and I know some of you have already spoken to them. DC Lindley and PC Rowe will be in the*

103

staff canteen all morning. If you haven't talked to them yet, and you saw or spoke to Anna Matheson on Saturday night, please visit the canteen during your break and answer any questions they may have. Anna was a well-liked and much-respected colleague who made an enormous creative contribution to Allwood Confectionery over the last few years. Her loss is tragic, and I'm sure many of you will want to find a way to preserve her memory, perhaps by setting up some kind of fundraising effort in Anna's name. For now, we ask that you do everything you can to co-operate with the police. If you have any information that could help their investigation, please share it with them as soon as possible. Thank you.'

Theo patted the corners of his mouth with a fresh napkin. 'Sounds like we'll be here all morning, waiting for people to wander in during their breaks,' he said. 'Trouble is, if someone has something to hide, or information they don't want to disclose, they'll be sure to avoid us. All they have to do is stay at their work station.'

'We're checking people's names off against Saturday's guest list,' Will said. 'So at least we'll have a record of who we've spoken to.'

'True enough,' Theo said. 'Let's see how the next couple of hours go. If there are people who haven't come forward to talk to us, we'll make it our business to go and find them.'

They were sitting facing the door to the corridor. It swung open, and the head of personnel marched towards them. Nicola Warren was barely five feet tall, with a sharp, inquisitive face, framed by a short pixie haircut. Will stood up, towering over her as she approached.

'Hello again, gentlemen,' she said. 'I take it you heard my announcement?'

'Yes, thanks for that,' said Theo. 'Let's hope it prompts a positive response. What time do your employees take their breaks?'

'The first wave should come through in about ten minutes,' she said. 'Break times are staggered, so don't expect a stampede.'

'No worries,' Theo said. 'We'll catch people as they come in.'

'We haven't taken a statement from you yet, Mrs Warren,' Will said. 'Did you see Anna on Saturday night?'

'I was at the party,' she replied, 'and I did speak to Anna, but only briefly regarding the long service presentations. Other than that, she and I spent very little time together.'

'Can you remember when you last saw her?'

'About eleven o'clock, or just after. The CEO was making her speech, and Anna was standing close by with her camera. I didn't notice her again after that. I'm sorry I can't be more helpful.'

The door opened again, and two female employees wearing white overalls and blue hairnets made their way into the canteen. Nicola Warren made her excuses, leaving Will and Theo to ask their questions.

***

Disappointingly, the first dozen or so members of staff they spoke to divulged nothing of interest. Most of them had seen Anna during the evening, but none were able to offer any insights that might crack open the case.

Their luck turned at eleven o'clock, when a woman in her fifties wandered in. Dressed in a black, knee-length skirt and a bright blue blouse, she bustled towards them purposefully. Her round, rosy face was half-covered by the face mask she was wearing. As she lowered her plump body into the chair directly opposite Will and Theo, she gazed at them expectantly with eyes the colour of sultanas.

Will had never been altogether comfortable with the wearing of face masks. He could see the sense in them, and had been fully on board with them during the lockdown. He also understood why so many people continued to wear them, even though they were no longer mandatory. Nevertheless, masks left him feeling at a disadvantage. He often struggled to read people's expressions when the lower half of their face was covered. He did his best to watch their eyes, to gauge their mood and determine whether they were telling the truth – but even though eyes were supposed to be the windows to the soul, he didn't find it easy.

'My name's Lynne Foxley,' the woman said, placing a chubby hand on the table between them. 'I work in the finance team, have done for the last thirty years.'

'And were you at the party on Saturday, Lynne?' Will said.

'Yes, duck, I was. I saw Anna there too, so I thought I'd better come and talk to you.'

'Did you and Anna have a conversation?' Theo asked.

'We exchanged a few words. I complimented her on her dress. She looked absolutely stunning. Most people were wearing silly glasses and tacky Sixties-style fancy dress, but Anna's frock was chic and sophisticated. It was a short, classic shift dress, typical of the Sixties, and it was made from the most beautiful, emerald-green fabric. Gorgeous, it was. Such a lovely colour. It made her stand out from the crowd, if you know what I mean. Made her easy to spot.'

'Does that mean you noticed her more than once during the evening?' said Theo.

'Yes, I struggled to keep my eyes off that dress,' Lynne replied. 'I have an appreciation of fashion and styles, you see. I'd love to be able to wear something like that myself, but I'd need to shed a couple of stone first.' She laughed self-deprecatingly.

'Did you happen to notice who Anna Matheson talked to during the evening?' Will said.

'She talked to loads of people,' Lynne said. 'She was taking photographs and chatting, so she circulated a lot. Unlike the rest of the management, Anna's always been able to make people feel at ease.'

'She was well liked at Allwoods was she?' said Will.

'Oh, definitely. Very popular. She'll be missed, that's for sure. She did seem out of sorts on Saturday, mind you. Not quite her usual chirpy self, if you get my drift.'

'In what way?' Theo said.

'It was her smile. Anna has … had a lovely smile, but on Saturday it didn't quite reach her eyes. I got the impression she was anxious about something, or impatient for the party to be over.'

'She was the organiser of the event, wasn't she?' Will said. 'Perhaps she was worried things wouldn't go to plan.'

Lynne frowned. 'Maybe, but I suspect something else was bothering her. She seemed uncharacteristically bad-tempered … even had cross words with a couple of people during the evening, and that wasn't like her.'

'You witnessed this?' said Theo.

'Only from a distance. I didn't hear what was said, but she looked fuming, as though she was trying to keep a lid on her temper.'

'Who was she talking to at the time?' Theo asked.

'James Derenby was one of them,' Lynne replied. 'He and Anna had quite a spat early on in the evening, and I also saw her have a go at Ross Allwood. She also had a snappy exchange with Faye Allwood as they were setting up the presentation. They were keeping their voices low and hoping no one would spot them, but … as I say, my eye was drawn to Anna in that dress, so I couldn't help but notice.'

'Any idea what they were discussing?' Theo said.

'No, sorry, duck. They were too far away for me to hear. It's no secret that Anna and Faye don't get on though … there are plenty of rumours as to why that might be … but they usually put on a good show in public. That's why I was so surprised to see them sniping at each other on Saturday.'

Will leaned forward, encouraging her to confide. 'Why don't they get on?' he said. 'You mentioned rumours. Can you tell us what's been said about Anna and Faye?'

Lynne sat back and folded her arms. 'I'm not sure I should. It's probably all tittle-tattle anyway, and I'm not one for spreading office gossip.'

Will swallowed down a smile. Not for a second was he taken in by Lynne Foxley's protestations. In fact, he wouldn't be surprised if she was the one who started the rumours in the first place.

'Now's not the time to be coy, Mrs Foxley,' he said. 'Anna Matheson has been murdered. Nobody's going to think you're being vindictive by telling us what you've heard. On the contrary, it's your duty to share that information. You'll be helping our inquiry and saving us time.'

'Well, I suppose when you put it like that …' Lynne hiked her mask higher onto her nose. 'The whispers began when Anna let it be known she was pregnant. No one knew who the father was, so people started to speculate.'

'And did they have a candidate in mind?' said Theo.

'A lot of people thought it might be James Derenby, but I wasn't one of them. He's a nice enough bloke, and I know he and Anna got on well, but there's never been any chemistry between them … no romantic spark.'

'Who was your money on then?' Theo said.

'Mr Allwood,' Lynne said. 'Not *Ross* Allwood, as some might have you believe. In my opinion, the baby's father is Mr Allwood senior. The late Barry Allwood.'

Will sucked in a deep breath and sat back, running some quick calculations through his head. Benedict Matheson was now five months old, and Barry Allwood had died the previous year. Depending on *when* in 2020 he had died, he could, theoretically, be the child's father.

'When did Barry Allwood pass away?' he asked.

'Last December,' Lynne replied. There was an air of smugness about the way she folded her arms. Clearly, she was enjoying being in the know. 'Right before Christmas it was. By my reckoning, Anna Matheson would have been about five or six months gone by then. There's no doubt about it, Barry Allwood could have fathered her baby.'

'Are you just guessing here, Mrs Foxley?' Theo said. 'Or do you have evidence to back up the claim?'

She fixed him with a stare. 'I don't know for certain, but I'm pretty good at picking up on these things … a sixth sense, you know?'

'And what was your sixth sense telling you?' Theo asked.

'That Mr Allwood and Anna were close.'

'And how did you come to that conclusion?' Will said, doing his best to hide his scepticism.

Lynne shrugged. 'Body language … the familiar way they interacted. Barry Allwood was usually standoffish with his employees, but that wasn't the case with Anna. They were always chatting and joking whenever I saw them together.'

'And that's it, is it?' Will said. 'Apart from your instincts and observing them together, you have no actual evidence that Anna Matheson and Barry Allwood were having an affair?'

'Well, no …' Lynne said, sounding irked. 'Obviously they were keeping it a secret. They were hardly going to be open about their relationship, were they? The rumours grew though, after she'd had the baby.'

'What kind of rumours?'

'I heard that Anna was given a massive salary increase when she came back to work after her maternity leave. Of course, Mr Allwood senior had passed away by then, but people were saying the pay rise was intended to keep her sweet … hush money, if you like.'

Theo nodded. 'We'll check that out,' he said, the firm tone of his voice bringing the conversation to a conclusion. 'Thank you for your time, Mrs Foxley. We appreciate you talking to us and we'll follow up on the points you've raised.'

Even though Will couldn't see it for the mask, it was apparent from her smiling eyes that Lynne Foxley was wearing a cat-who-got-the-cream grin. He could almost hear her purring. Having shared her theories, she stood up, moved over to the servery, bought a takeaway coffee, and left the canteen with a friendly wave.

'Interesting,' Theo said. 'If you dig deep enough, there's always treasure to be found.'

'The question is,' Will said, 'have we just hit pay dirt, or uncovered a hoard of fool's gold?'

Chapter 19

Dan was leaning against the door to Isabel's office, his arms folded.

'Anna Matheson's laptop has been recovered from her home address, boss,' he said. 'Digital Forensics are analysing her internet search history and looking for anything else of interest.'

'I don't suppose there was any sign of a mobile phone at the home address?' Isabel said.

'Nah, 'fraid not. I've just spoken to Theo. He's down at the factory, and he said several people have reported seeing Anna with her phone on Saturday night, so the killer must have taken it. It's probably been destroyed by now. We're obtaining phone data from the service provider, and we're doing some cell site analysis to find out where the phone's been over the last few weeks, including the day she was killed. Together with any hits we get from the ANPR, that should give us a handle on Anna Matheson's movements in the run-up to her murder.'

'Have the lads learned anything else of interest at the factory?'

'Apparently they've been talking to a woman called Lynne Foxley, who said she witnessed Anna having cross words with James Derenby, Ross Allwood and Faye Allwood on Saturday night.'

'All at the same time?' Isabel said. 'Some kind of mass argument?'

Dan smiled. 'No, separate incidents. This Foxley woman has also suggested that *Barry* Allwood might be Benedict's father. She reckons Anna and Barry were close.'

Isabel raised her eyebrows. 'Seriously? No one else has mentioned that.'

'No, but in fairness, we haven't been asking about Anna's relationship with Barry Allwood, have we? He died back in December, so technically, he could be the child's father.'

'Ask Zoe to talk to Christina Matheson again,' Isabel said. 'Let's get her view on whether Barry Allwood could be Benedict's father.'

'Will do. I'm about to head up to Allwood Confectionery myself … thought I'd poke a stick at the hornet's nest, see what I can stir up.'

'Be careful you don't get stung,' Isabel said.

Dan grinned. 'Don't worry, I'll be careful. I don't suppose you fancy coming with me?'

Isabel was tempted, very tempted, but she was also aware of the stack of paperwork in her in-tray, and the huge backlog of emails in her inbox.

'I'd better not,' she said. 'The Super's made it clear she wants me to oversee things. According to her, DIs should sit back and let their team do all the leg work.'

'I know that's what you're *meant* to do,' Dan said, 'but it's never stopped you before. I thought you enjoyed getting your hands dirty?'

Dan was right. There was nothing Isabel liked more than being involved in the nitty-gritty of an investigation, even though she wasn't supposed to. She relished the prospect of talking to witnesses and suspects – it was the best way to sniff out the truth and properly assess the evidence. Overseeing investigations, juggling budgets and delegating actions was all well and good, but it was boring. *Incredibly* boring. Isabel wasn't cut out for sitting at a desk. It was one of the reasons she'd never pursued a higher promotion.

Then again, if she allowed herself to get too hands-on with this case, she'd incur the wrath of the Super and, right now, she didn't need the grief.

'Don't tempt me, Dan. Much as I'd love to accompany you, I'll let you get on and do some digging on your own. Super's orders.'

Dan folded his arms. 'Fair enough,' he said. 'I've obviously misjudged you.'

'*Misjudged* me? In what way?'

'I was under the impression you made your own rules,' he said, holding up his hands. 'That you liked to follow your *own* path.'

She was aware that he was goading her, that his words were meant as a challenge. Pursing her lips, she peered at him thoughtfully, carefully contemplating how she would respond.

'You know what, Dan?' she said, eventually. 'You're absolutely bloody right. The day I start dancing to Val Tibbet's tune is the day I should jack all of this in.'

She spun away from her desk and peeled her jacket from the back of her chair.

'Come on,' she said. 'What are we waiting for?'

Chapter 20

Their first stop at Allwoods was to check in with DC Lindley and PC Rowe. The constables were stationed in the canteen, which was filling up with the lunchtime rush.

'Thanks for passing on the info from Lynne Foxley,' Dan said. 'Has anyone else disclosed any other gems of wisdom since our last phone conversation?'

'Nothing major,' Theo said. 'We've now spoken to nearly everyone who attended the party on Saturday. There are a few names on the list we've yet to connect with, but they're part-time workers who won't be in until later in the week.'

'We need to speak to them ASAP,' Isabel said. 'Ask the personnel team for their contact details, and don't let them give you any flannel about data protection. This is a murder investigation.'

'A few of the guests at the party weren't staff,' Will said. 'James Derenby has provided us with contact numbers for the other guests, so we'll be giving them a call this afternoon.'

'In that case, you may as well head back to the station and make the follow-up calls from there,' Isabel said. 'Dan and I are going to have a word with a few of the administrative staff, and the senior managers, if they're around. We'll also follow up on the information Lynne Foxley gave to you, particularly in regard to a possible relationship between Anna and Barry Allwood. And we'll find out if there's any truth in her receiving a recent pay rise.'

'Tread carefully, ma'am,' Theo said. 'Despite her protestations to the contrary, Mrs Foxley looked like the sort of person who enjoys a nice bit of juicy gossip. Her theories may be pure speculation.'

'Thanks. I'll bear that in mind,' said Isabel. 'But we can't afford to ignore what she said. At the moment, any lead is welcome, however dubious.'

***

Nicola Warren's PA wasn't pleased to see them.

'You should have rung ahead and made an appointment,' she said. 'Nicola's about to go into a meeting.'

'We won't keep her long,' Isabel said. Without waiting for permission, she moved past the PA's desk and gave the open door behind her a cursory knock.

'Nicola Warren?' Stepping into the office uninvited, Isabel held up her warrant card and introduced herself and Dan. 'We have some questions for you regarding Anna Matheson.'

The head of personnel was lifting a jacket from a coat stand in the corner. 'I can't talk now, detectives,' she said. 'I'm expected at a meeting that's due to start in three minutes.'

'Perhaps you could ask your PA to send your apologies?' said Dan.

'I'm sorry, but I can't do that,' Nicola said, shrugging herself into the jacket. 'I'm chairing the meeting, so my attendance isn't exactly optional.'

'If you're the chair, you have the authority to postpone the start time,' Isabel said, her voice firm. 'We don't intend to keep you long … fifteen minutes tops.'

Nicola sighed impatiently and brushed past them. 'Let me talk to my PA.'

While a whispered conversation took place at the PA's desk, Dan and Isabel sat down and made themselves comfortable.

'So, how can I help you?' Nicola said, once she'd returned to her office. 'What's so urgent that it can't wait?'

Isabel found the woman's attitude offensive. 'One of your employees has been murdered,' she reminded her. 'We're treating the matter as a high priority. I assumed you and the rest of the senior management team would want to do the same.'

Nicola leaned back in her chair and let out a sigh. 'Of *course* we do. We're all very distressed about what's happened, but that doesn't alter the fact that my colleagues and I are busy people. However, we're more than willing to co-operate in any way we can. What is it you want to know?'

'Let's start with the recruitment of Anna Matheson to Allwoods,' Dan began. 'Did you interview her for the job?'

'No, as a general rule, I only sit in on interviews if we're recruiting for a senior role. When Anna was taken on, it was as a marketing officer, but only on a temporary contract – so the usual screening process didn't apply.'

'Are you saying she wasn't given a proper interview?' Isabel said.

'The personnel officer spoke to her and did some reference and qualification checks, but there wasn't an interview panel, as such, because – technically – there wasn't a permanent job to fill.'

'If there was no job,' said Dan, 'why was Anna taken on?'

Nicola Warren propped her elbows on her desk and steepled her fingers. 'Two years ago, Allwoods was losing market share. We needed someone who could rewrite our marketing plan and strategy, and implement some new product and promotional ideas. Anna Matheson was appointed specifically to take on that task, as a one-off project. At that stage, we didn't expect the role to continue in the longer term.'

'So how *was* Anna selected?' Dan asked. 'Was it through a recruitment agency? I understand she had no track record of working on similar projects?'

Nicola pressed her lips together. 'No, she didn't. At the time, Anna had only just completed a diploma in marketing, and didn't have any previous practical experience.'

'In that case, why was she appointed?' Isabel persisted.

'As I recall, someone recommended her. I can't remember the details. All I know is, we needed someone and her name came up. We were told she was very bright and innovative, so the personnel officer brought her in and talked to her.'

'And you can't remember who made the recommendation?' said Dan.

'I'm afraid not. It didn't come to me directly.'

Isabel raised a questioning eyebrow. 'Oh? Who did it come to?'

Nicola Warren drummed her fingers together impatiently. 'Barry Allwood. I'm sure he would have remembered who gave him Anna's name, but of course there's no way of asking him now. As I'm sure you're aware, Barry died last year.'

'Yes, we're aware of that,' Isabel said. 'He was your CEO at the time, I understand.'

Nicola Warren nodded.

'Did Mr Allwood put pressure on you to recruit Anna?' said Dan. 'Is it possible he already knew her?'

'On the contrary,' Nicola replied. 'Barry was rather under-whelmed by her initially. He put forward her name, but it wasn't until after she'd been taken on and he got to know her … know her work … that he began to respect her.'

'They had a good working relationship then?' Isabel said.

'Yes, I would say so. Barry became more and more impressed with Anna. Her revised marketing strategy soon began to pay dividends, and consequently Barry asked us to offer her a permanent contract as a marketing manager.'

'A promotion, then? As well as a permanent contract?'

'Yes, and a salary increase to match – but everyone agreed that Anna was worth every penny.'

'Someone told us that Anna also received a hefty pay rise

more recently,' Dan said. 'After she came back from maternity leave. Is that true?'

Nicola pressed her lips into a thin line. 'Who gave you that information?'

'That's irrelevant,' Dan replied. 'Please, answer the question.'

Nicola nodded begrudgingly. 'Yes, she did receive another pay rise. Given the circumstances of Anna's death, I don't suppose I'm breaching any confidentiality rules by confirming that.'

'Did Anna *ask* for more money?' said Isabel. 'Or was the increase instigated by someone else?'

'It was put forward as a proposal at an SMT meeting. All the senior managers valued Anna's contribution to the business, and we wanted to ensure she came back after her maternity leave.'

'Can I ask how much we're talking about?' Dan asked.

Nicola paused before giving him an answer. 'I'm not sure how it's relevant, but she was given an extra ten thousand a year.'

'Ten thousand pounds?' said Dan. 'Blimey. That's one hell of a pay rise. I wish the police force was that generous.'

Isabel turned to her sergeant and gave him a disapproving half-frown.

'We were aware that Anna would be bringing the baby up on her own,' Nicola Warren explained. 'Our concern was that she'd be tempted to look for a job with a more generous remuneration package. Ten thousand pounds seemed like a substantial enough increase to retain her, here at Allwoods.'

'Can you recall who put forward the proposal for the pay rise?' Dan said.

'No, I can't, but it may be in the minutes. I'll ask my PA to dig them out and let you know.'

'Going back to Anna's relationship with Barry Allwood,' Isabel said. 'Do you have any reason to believe it might have been more than a working relationship? Is it possible it had developed into something more personal?'

Nicola Warren stiffened. 'If you're implying that's the reason she was given a permanent contract, I'm surprised at you, DI Blood.'

'I'm not implying anything,' Isabel replied. 'I'm well aware that women get promoted on merit these days – or, at least, they should do. However, you can't deny that relationships do sometimes spring up in the workplace. It happens. So, I'll ask you again, was Anna in a personal relationship with Barry Allwood?'

Nicola Warren glared. 'Not that I'm aware of,' she said. 'Barry liked Anna, of that I'm sure, but there was never any suggestion of anything improper between the two of them. As far as I know, they were nothing more than colleagues. Barry was happily married, and his wife has worked alongside him for the last thirty-five years. If he was going to have an extramarital affair, I doubt he would have chosen to conduct it right under Faye's nose.'

'One of your employees thinks otherwise,' said Dan. 'They've gone as far as to suggest that Barry Allwood fathered Anna Matheson's child. What's your view on that?'

'I'd say it's complete claptrap,' Nicola replied, a crease appearing down the centre of her forehead. 'I don't know who told you that, and it's probably better that I *don't* know, but whoever it was, was talking rubbish.'

'Are you saying that because you're certain there was no relationship between Anna and Barry Allwood?' Dan asked. 'Or are you trying to defend the reputation of a dead colleague?'

'Neither,' said Nicola. 'I'm saying it because there's not one shred of evidence to back up such a wild accusation. I don't know who Benedict's father is. Anna never told me and, as it was none of my business, I didn't pry.'

'Surely you understand why we'd like to know?' Isabel said. 'The fact that Anna chose to keep the identity of her baby's father a secret does suggest she had something to hide … and that *something* could be connected to her murder. If someone knows Anna had a clandestine relationship, they might also know why she was murdered. They may even be the perpetrator.'

'Barry Allwood has been dead for eight months,' Nicola said. 'Even if he was Benedict's father, he obviously isn't responsible for Anna's death.'

'What about Ross Allwood?' said Dan. 'And James Derenby? We understand both gentlemen may have pursued the possibility of a relationship with Anna at some point, or may even have had a relationship with her in the past.'

Nicola Warren released a sharp huff of air. 'I thought the police were supposed to deal in facts,' she said. 'This is pure speculation.'

'At the moment, there are very few known facts in this case,' Isabel said, defending Dan's question. 'Sometimes we're forced to work our way through rumour and guesswork in order to get to the truth.'

Nicola leaned back. 'I'll admit there was plenty of conjecture when Anna announced her pregnancy,' she said. 'The office gossips had a field day. The rumours had begun to die down in recent months but, clearly, Anna's murder has stirred things up again.'

Isabel persevered. 'Are you able to confirm whether Anna had a relationship with either James Derenby or Ross Allwood?'

Nicola Warren tapped the arms of her chair. 'Here at Allwoods, we try to discourage workplace relationships. We're not naïve enough to suppose these things never happen, but they can become problematic when people work together. Romantic involvements tend to cloud people's judgement, and if that relationship subsequently breaks down, it can create ill feeling and resentment – which is why work romances are best nipped in the bud.'

'You still haven't answered the question,' Dan said. 'Did Anna Matheson have a relationship with either James Derenby or Ross Allwood?'

Nicola gave a tight smile. 'Not that I'm aware of,' she said. 'As head of personnel, that kind of situation would have been brought to my attention. On the other hand, if the parties concerned were discreet, it's possible it could have happened without anyone knowing. James and Ross are the only ones who can provide you with a definitive answer. You'll need to talk to them.'

'Don't worry,' Isabel said. 'We intend to.'

'Good.' Nicola pushed back her chair and stood up. 'In that case, I'll let you go and find them. I take it you've finished with me now?'

'We may need to talk to you again at some point,' Isabel said, 'but we'll leave it there for the time being. You can go to your meeting now.'

'Thank you,' Nicola replied, her voice tart. 'Better late than never.'

Chapter 21

Dan and the DI had split up, to save time. His next port of call was to see Ross Allwood.

Ross's PA, Connie Slade, was drinking a cup of tea, and a pack of Shrewsbury biscuits lay open on her desk. 'You're out of luck,' she said, rubbing biscuit crumbs from her fingers. 'Ross is out of the office. He's gone to Northampton ... a meeting with one of our retailers.'

'Is he coming back later?'

'He is, but he won't be returning to the office until tomorrow. Sorry.'

'No problem,' Dan said. 'I'll try and catch up with him then.'

Or, more likely, I'll call in and see him at home this evening, Dan thought, deciding not to share this plan with the PA in case she tipped off her boss. Dan wanted his visit to be a surprise.

'Have you spoken to one of our officers about the last time you saw Anna Matheson?' Dan asked. 'I'm guessing you were at the party on Saturday night.'

'As a matter of fact, I wasn't,' Connie replied. 'It was my sister's thirtieth birthday on Saturday, so I went out for a meal with her and the family instead. The last time I saw Anna was on

Friday afternoon. She was running around like a headless chicken, making last-minute arrangements for the party.'

'Did you know Anna well?'

'Only in a work capacity.'

'I understand she'd been dealing with some complaints … about your boss.'

The PA picked up a paperclip and began to unfold its metal loops. 'It's all something and nothing,' she said, flippantly. 'A couple of the sales reps have been whinging, and Anna got caught up in the crossfire.'

'Do you know what the reps have been whinging about?'

Connie pulled the straightened-out paper clip between her thumb and index finger.

'They don't like the way Ross does business,' she said. 'Most of the reps have been with Allwoods for years, so they're far more familiar with Mrs Allwood's style of management. When she was head of sales, she was a lot more hands-on. Ross leaves the reps to get on with things. He believes in autonomy, which means he's not constantly pecking at them, reminding them of their targets.'

'I'd have thought the reps would welcome being left to get on with their jobs,' Dan said. 'Why would they complain about being given more freedom?'

'I think some of the older ones resent being managed by someone as young as Ross,' Connie said. 'There have been a couple of confrontations … let's call them personality clashes.'

'Between Ross and the reps?'

'Yes, but don't ask me any more than that, because I've not been privy to all the ins and outs. If you want to know the details, you're better off speaking to the reps directly.'

'Can you give me the names of the people who've been complaining?'

'Ryan Reed and Pete Pilkington are the two main instigators.' She opened a drawer and pulled out a couple of business cards. 'Here are their contact details if you want to get in touch.'

'I'll do that,' Dan said. 'Thanks.'

'You're welcome,' she said. 'Although, in my opinion you're wasting your time. You're mistaken if you think a dispute over office politics could have anything to do with Anna's death. I'll admit there were plenty of things Ross and Anna didn't agree on, but they weren't sworn enemies if that's what you're hoping to hear.'

'What about Anna's other colleagues? Was there anyone she didn't get along with?'

'Not that I know of …'

Dan waited, noting the hesitation. It was obvious Connie was keeping something back.

'Have you spoken to James Derenby?' she said, after a moment.

'Yes, he and I have spoken a couple of times. I was under the impression that James and Anna got on well.'

'He liked her a lot more than she liked him.'

Dan folded his arms. 'If you've got something to say, Connie, you should just come out and say it. Is there something you want to tell me about James Derenby?'

She reached for another biscuit and dunked it in her tea. 'I'm probably being unfair,' she said. 'I hardly know James.'

'But?'

Connie looked in both directions, presumably to check whether anyone was within earshot.

'A friend of my cousin's went out with him years ago,' she continued, once she was satisfied no one was listening in. 'After she broke it off with him, he wouldn't leave her alone. She said he used to follow her, like he was obsessed.'

'You mean he stalked her?' said Dan.

'I wouldn't say that, but I know he made her feel uncomfortable.'

'Did she report him to the police?'

'I don't think so.' She shrugged. 'Like I say, it was a friend of my cousin's. I don't know her very well.'

'But you know her name?'

'Hayley.'

'Last name?'

'I can't remember, but I can find out. I'll ring my cousin and ask her.'

'Give me a call as soon as you have the information,' Dan said, handing over his card.

'Will do. I'll ring her now and let you know.' She chewed the side of a fingernail. 'I do hope I've not said the wrong thing. I don't want to get James in trouble.'

'You were right to mention it,' Dan said. 'It's probably nothing, but we'll follow it up. Thank you. You've been very helpful.'

Dan considered joining the DI, who had gone to talk to James Derenby – but it was too soon to start asking questions about Connie's cousin's friend. He'd hold back until he'd heard Hayley's side of the story.

Chapter 22

Isabel had wandered through the sales office, out to the front desk. From there, the receptionist had taken her into the central corridor and pointed out James Derenby's office.

She found him at his desk, looking sleep-deprived and spaced out.

'I'm DI Blood, Bainbridge CID,' Isabel said. 'Mind if I come in?'

'Sure. Come and take a pew.'

'How are you?' Isabel asked, as she sat down.

James shrugged. 'I've had better days,' he said. 'I've been sitting here, thinking about Anna … I still can't believe what's happened. I came into the office today to keep my mind off things, but I'm not sure I'll get much work done. I can't concentrate.'

'That's understandable. You're in shock. I believe you and Anna were friends. It's a perfectly normal reaction, given the circumstances.'

James took off his glasses and rubbed his hands up and down his face, as if trying to rub some colour into it.

'Why are you here?' he asked. 'You do know I've already spoken to the other detective?'

'I have a few more questions,' Isabel said. 'And there are a couple of things I'd like to go over with you again. About your relationship with Anna.'

Sighing, James sat back and spread his hands across the desk. 'If you're hoping I'll give you a different answer to the one I gave DS Fairfax, get ready to be disappointed. My relationship with Anna was as a colleague, and as a friend. I would have preferred us to be more than that, but we weren't.'

'And there's no way you could be the father of Benedict Matheson?'

'No.' He folded his arms. 'I thought I'd already made that clear.'

'Would you be willing to provide a sample of your DNA, so that we can confirm that?'

'Is my word not good enough?'

'As I'm sure you'll appreciate, given the circumstances of Anna's death, we can't afford to take anyone at their word. If you provide us with a DNA sample, it will allow us to rule out certain lines of inquiry and focus our efforts in all the right places.'

'I'm not stupid,' James said. 'I know I'm under no obligation to give you my DNA.'

'That's true,' Isabel replied. 'It's purely voluntary at this stage. However, given that Anna was your friend, I hoped you'd be willing to co-operate. Your DNA would only be used for comparison purposes. It won't be stored on the police database.'

James locked his hands behind his head and stared up at the ceiling. 'If it will help find Anna's killer and get you lot off my back, then, yes … I'll do it. And once you get the results, I hope you and your team will stop pestering me about my non-existent romantic relationship with Anna and concentrate instead on finding her killer.'

Proving that James Derenby wasn't Benedict Matheson's father would remove one possible motive for murder. What it wouldn't do was rule him out as a suspect – but Isabel thought it best not to mention that.

'Thanks for your co-operation, James,' she said. 'I appreciate it. You can come down to the station to provide a DNA sample, or we can arrange for someone to come here.'

'I'll come to the station,' James replied. 'The last thing I want to do is feed the office rumour mill.'

Chapter 23

Zoe's attempts to forge a relationship with Christina Matheson had stalled. The victim's mother was becoming increasingly withdrawn and reticent, and Zoe's efforts to develop a bond were being politely but firmly rebuffed. Perhaps this was Christina's way of dealing with bereavement: her grief-induced silence driven by the overpowering realisation that Anna was gone.

Zoe's instinct was to give the woman space to process her loss, but she was under orders. Answers were needed, and the DI was expecting her to ask all of the right questions.

'Have you thought about who will take care of Benedict?' Zoe asked, as she made a pot of tea in Christina's sunny kitchen. 'Ordinarily in these circumstances, the father would step up and take responsibility, but that's not going to be possible if you don't know who he is.'

The question was her opening gambit, a way of segueing into the question she really wanted to ask.

Christina was sitting at the table, bouncing Benedict on her knee. 'I'm more than capable of looking after my grandson,' she replied, her voice resolute.

Zoe smiled tentatively at the baby, completely in awe of him. He seemed to have a fascination with everything around him. Right now, the focus of his attention was a fluffy toy rabbit. He held it by its ears, playing with it briefly before throwing it onto the floor.

'We'd like to track down the baby's father,' Zoe persisted. 'If nothing else, he might be able to provide you with some financial support.'

Benedict had moved his attentions to the string of brightly coloured beads that were dangling from Christina's neck. He reached out, pulling the necklace towards his mouth.

'We'll be all right,' Christina replied, as she took off the beads and placed them out of the reach of her grandson. 'Anna was in a pension fund at work. There'll be a lump sum, something for me to invest for Benedict's future. Quite honestly, our financial position is the least of my worries. I can live on a small income – that's what I'm used to. What I'm not sure about is whether I can live without Anna.'

'If you intend to look after your grandson, you're going to have to.'

'You're right. What choice do I have?' Christina kissed the top of the baby's head, tears welling in her eyes. 'I don't know if I'll ever come to terms with it, though. My life has never been straightforward … certainly not what you'd call easy … but Anna was always there for me. She was the one good, constant thing … the person I could rely on. It breaks my heart to think of Benedict growing up with no memory of her.'

'It will be up to you to keep her memory alive,' Zoe said.

Christina nodded.

'I appreciate how hard this must be for you, especially dealing with it on your own,' Zoe added. 'Perhaps when Benedict's father finds out what's happened to Anna, he'll come forward. How would you feel about that?'

Christina shrugged dismissively. 'I'll cross that bridge if and when I come to it. Personally, I don't think it will happen.'

Benedict was now clutching a tablespoon, examining his reflection in its curved metal bowl.

'What about Anna's dad?' said Zoe. 'Have you been able to get in touch with him to let him know what's happened?'

'Anna's father is dead,' Christina replied. 'He was never part of her life anyway. It was always just her and me. The two of us.'

'You must have had a strong mother–daughter bond then?'

'We did when she was young,' Christina said. 'Less so as she got older.'

'What did you think when Anna told you she was pregnant?' Zoe said, swinging the conversation back to the subject of Benedict's paternity. 'Were you surprised? Happy?'

Christina smiled sadly. 'I experienced both of those emotions. I was also relieved, and worried.'

'Talk me through your reaction,' Zoe said. 'Why were you relieved?'

Benedict had begun to suck the spoon, so Christina bent down to retrieve the toy rabbit. As she slipped the stuffed toy into her grandson's arms, she extracted the spoon from his chubby fingers. He watched unhappily as the spoon was confiscated and, for a moment, Zoe thought he might cry. Then, after giving his grandmother an angelic smile, Benedict resumed his inspection of the rabbit's ears.

'Anna always liked children,' Christina said. 'I knew she wanted one of her own, but she'd never had much luck with relationships. She met a few decent blokes along the way, but none of them wanted to commit to anything serious. With hindsight, it was probably a good thing. When she was living down in London, Anna's lifestyle wasn't exactly conducive to having kids.'

'This was when she was working in the City?'

'Yes. I didn't see much of her back then. A couple of times a year she'd come up here, and occasionally I'd go and stay with her in London – but she and I had very different views on certain things, which meant we didn't always get on.'

'What was the problem?' Zoe said. 'Didn't you approve of her lifestyle?'

Christina grimaced. 'I tried not to be judgemental. I like to think I have a liberal outlook, but, yes … there were aspects of Anna's life back then that I didn't approve of.'

'Her drinking, for instance?'

Christina frowned. 'How do you know about that?'

'One of Anna's colleagues mentioned she'd had a problem with alcohol in the past.'

'James?'

'Yes,' Zoe said. 'James Derenby. Have you met him?'

'Only once. He seemed very nice, and I know Anna liked him … trusted him … but she hardly ever talked about her drinking issues. To be honest, I'm surprised she confided in James.'

'What exactly were her issues with alcohol?' Zoe asked.

Christina pulled her grandson into a hug.

'When Anna worked in the City, she was constantly stressed out. She found the job a strain, and having a drink was her way of unwinding. The problem was, she came to rely on it. It had gotten to the point where she couldn't get through the day without at least one bottle of wine every night. Some of her friends had a cocaine habit as well, but Anna told me she never did drugs.'

'And you believed her?'

'I had no reason not to,' Christina said. 'She was completely up front about her drinking, so I'm sure she would have told me if she'd had a problem with drugs. Back in 2018 … it would have been around Easter time … she came to visit me and I could tell straight away she was exhausted and desperately unhappy. I sat her down and made her talk to me.'

'What did she say?'

'She told me she couldn't carry on as she was. She didn't want the life she had … it wasn't what she'd envisioned. She felt she was missing out on the chance to have a steady relationship and a family, and that it was time for her to give up the booze. The only way she could see of doing that was to remove the source of the stress that drove her to drink in the first place.'

'Her job?'

Christina nodded. 'Anna went back to London, handed in her notice, and a month later she moved back up here, to Derbyshire. She'd managed to save some money, so she rented a flat in Derby for a while and studied for a diploma in marketing. Once she'd qualified, she started to look for a job, and eventually she was taken on at Allwoods.'

'And she managed to kick the drinking?' Zoe asked.

'Yes, she went cold turkey, so it wasn't easy. Gradually though, she got into a much healthier lifestyle and a better frame of mind. She took up running and joined a gym, and she never looked back.'

'That sounds like an amazing turnaround. You must have been very proud of her.'

'I was,' Christina said. 'Once she'd sorted herself out, I hoped she might meet someone ... but I don't think she was quite ready for a full-on relationship. Keeping herself on the straight and narrow – drink wise – that took a lot of energy and effort. When Allwoods took Anna on permanently, she moved over to Bainbridge ... got a mortgage and bought herself a house. She seemed happy, and I know she enjoyed her job.'

'And then she found out she was pregnant?' Zoe said.

Christina smiled at her grandson, rocking him gently on her knee.

'It wasn't something she planned. That much she did tell me. She said she'd slept with someone ... that it was a casual thing – and, although she was shocked to find herself pregnant, she was also thrilled. From the minute she found out about the pregnancy, she knew she wanted the baby.'

Benedict laughed as Christina tickled his tummy.

'Anna must have told you *something* about Benedict's dad,' Zoe insisted.

'Only that she slept with him while her guard was down. She told me she went out last July, to celebrate the easing of the lockdown restrictions. She decided to have a drink ... a few glasses of wine, as an experiment. I think she was testing herself, checking whether she could control her alcohol consumption. The experiment must have backfired, because she got drunk, ended up sleeping with someone and regretted it immediately. What she never regretted was conceiving Benedict. Having a child, being a mother … that changed Anna. After she left London, her life was in transition. Having Benedict brought her through to the other side.'

Christina's voice cracked and tears spilled down her cheeks.

'The person she slept with,' Zoe said. 'Do you think it could be someone she worked with? James Derenby, perhaps, or Ross Allwood?'

'No!' Christina stood up and carried Benedict to the kitchen window. With their backs turned, the two of them looked out at the flower-filled garden. 'It's possible she slept with James, but I doubt it. He was Anna's friend, but she wasn't attracted to him.'

'Did she tell you that?'

'Yes. James regularly asked her out, but Anna wasn't interested in dating him. She said he was nice, and it would have made life simple if she'd fancied him – but my daughter never did things the easy way. She took after me in that respect.'

'And what about Ross Allwood?' Zoe said. 'Did she ever date him?'

'Definitely not. She would never have gone out with him.'

'Why not?'

Christina spun around and stared at her. 'Lots of reasons. One of them being he's a waste of space. My daughter loved her work, but lately, Ross Allwood had become a fly in the ointment. She said he was completely useless as head of sales. He made her job much harder than it should have been.'

'We've been told that Anna spoke to Mrs Allwood about Ross's professional inadequacies,' Zoe said. 'Apparently, people have complained about him.'

Christina turned back to face the window. 'I knew about the

complaints, but I didn't know she'd spoken to Faye about them,' she said. 'I'll bet she got short shrift from her.'

'You talk as if you know Mrs Allwood. Are the two of you acquainted?'

'I've met her,' Christina said. 'No doubt Faye would have defended her son to the hilt, whether he deserved it or not. Now, if you'll excuse me, I'm going to take Benedict upstairs for a nap. He can hardly keep his eyes open.'

Chapter 24

By two o'clock, Isabel was back at the station, sitting at her desk. A yellow Post-it Note was stuck to her computer screen, the message on it written in DC Lindley's distinctive handwriting.

Please call Detective Superintendent Tibbet.

She unpeeled the note and, holding it aloft, went out into the main office.

'What time did the Super call, Theo?'

'About an hour ago, a few minutes after I got back,' he replied. 'She was after an update on Op Zebra.'

'What did you say to her?'

'Not a lot. It was pretty obvious she didn't want to talk to me. It was you she wanted to speak to.'

'And did she ask where I was?'

'Yeah, I told her you were down at the factory, conducting interviews.'

Isabel sighed and rolled her eyes. 'Thanks, Theo.'

'What?' He pulled a sheepish face. 'Did I say the wrong thing?'

'It's OK. Don't worry,' Isabel replied. 'You know what they

say … tell the truth and shame the devil. I'll give her a call now – the Super, that is. Not the devil.'

Theo grinned mischievously. 'From what I've heard, they're one and the same.'

Smiling, Isabel went back into her office, closed the door and picked up the phone.

'I gather you're after an update on Operation Zebra,' she said, when Valerie Tibbet came on the line.

'Yes, I am,' Val said. 'I was hoping to speak to you earlier. Imagine my surprise when I was told you were at Allwood Confectionery, interviewing suspects.'

'What's so surprising about that?' Isabel said, playing it cool but bracing herself for a bollocking. 'We're in the middle of a murder case.'

'I'm aware of that,' Val said. 'But I thought I'd made it perfectly clear that I wanted you to *oversee* this investigation. You're a DI, Isabel. It's not your job to go out and gather evidence. Leave the leg work to your team. You need to take a step back, become less hands-on, and start trusting the people who work for you.'

'I do trust them.'

'Do you? It doesn't seem that way to me. And I've worked on your team, remember?'

'That was a long time ago,' Isabel said.

'True, but your management style hasn't evolved very much since then. I know from personal experience how much you like to interfere. You're a meddler.'

'Ouch,' Isabel said. 'That's a bit below the belt, even for you.'

'Is it? I'm not sure your officers would agree. How do you think they feel, having you breathing down their necks all the time? You need to start managing from a distance, DI Blood. That's not a request, it's an order.'

Isabel screwed up her nose and stuck two fingers at the telephone handset. 'Let me make one thing clear,' she said, taking a deep breath to control her anger. 'I respect my officers. I let them do their jobs and I'd never knowingly undermine them. However, I'm not – and never will be – one of those DIs who spends all their time behind a desk. Talking to suspects helps me process the evidence and solve the case. I *enjoy* getting involved.'

'We're here to do a job,' Val said. 'Not to enjoy ourselves.'

Isabel mustered a half-smile. 'How I run my team isn't something you need concern yourself with, Detective Superintendent Tibbet. You've made it plain you don't agree with my management style, but the one thing you can't deny is that my team and I get results.'

'I'll admit you have an excellent clear-up rate,' Val said, after a momentary pause. 'But I doubt that would suffer if you were to take more of a back seat. The "I" in "DI" stands for inspector, Isabel, not investigator. You'd do well to remember that.'

'Let's not forget that I'm also the SIO on this case,' Isabel said, determined to have the last word. 'The Senior *Investigating* Officer. I think that gives me the right to talk to a few suspects, don't you? Now … shall I give you an update on Op Zebra?'

***

The Super's words were still ringing in her ears when she paid a visit to the pathologist at two-thirty. The conversation with Val had riled her – mainly because she knew, deep down, she had a point. Isabel didn't like treading on anyone's toes, but sometimes she couldn't help herself. Meddling was a facet of her nature.

The sensible, well-advised thing to do would be to follow the Super's orders – but sod that for a game of soldiers. Isabel liked getting involved in the detail of an investigation – loved it, in fact. It was a deeply entrenched part of her management style. She couldn't change now, not even if she wanted to.

There was no way she was going to sit behind a desk, chasing pieces of paper or clicking a computer mouse. She liked getting out and speaking to people face-to-face – it was the reason she'd chosen to come and see Emma Willis this afternoon, rather than send some else.

'I can confirm that the cause of death was strangulation,' the pathologist told her. 'There are minute traces of blue fibre in the lesion on the victim's neck. I believe she was strangled from behind with a length of polypropylene rope ... the sort commonly used in agriculture, or for sailing or camping.'

'Have you been able to identify the brand of rope?'

'We're trying. I'll keep you posted on that.'

'What about the time of death?' Isabel said. 'Have you narrowed that down?'

'Somewhere between eleven o'clock on Saturday evening and two o'clock on Sunday morning is my best estimate. I can't be more precise than that. Sorry.'

'So, she could have been killed elsewhere, away from Allwoods?'

'It's possible,' Emma said. 'As yet, we've found no forensic evidence to tell us, unequivocally, where the murder took place.'

'My gut feeling is that she was killed at the factory, and her body was moved.' Isabel scratched her forehead. 'But what I can't get my head around is how a crime like that could happen without someone seeing something?'

'I can't help you there,' Emma said. 'It'll be up to you and your team to work out the details.'

'Cheers.' Isabel grinned. 'Is there anything else you can tell me about the victim? Any indication that she was sexually assaulted?'

'No.' Emma shook her head firmly. 'No sign at all that the attack was sexually motivated.'

'That's something, I suppose. Although it's not much of a consolation for Anna's family.'

'There were traces of fibre under one of her fingernails,' said Emma. 'I suspect she would have struggled ... reached around to try and dislodge the hands of her killer. If the perpetrator was wearing gloves – and that would seem like a safe bet – that could be where the fibre came from.'

Isabel nodded her thanks. 'All we need to do now is find the gloves, check them for traces of DNA, and we can wrap up the case.'

'Good luck with that,' Emma said.

***

'We've run the victim's car reg through the ANPR,' said Adrian Bostock. It was three-fifteen, and he and Isabel were in the incident room.

'Did she go anywhere interesting in the days prior to her death?'

Adrian adopted a disappointed expression. 'On the contrary,' he said. 'All of her journeys were local, most of them flagged on cameras between her home and place of work. The most exciting trip appears to have been a visit to the supermarket. On top of that, the cell site analysis of her phone confirms the ANPR findings. Over the last month, the victim's mobile has pinged off the signal masts closest to her home, her mother's house, her friend's house, her place of work, and the nursery that provided day care for her son. She certainly hasn't visited anywhere out of the ordinary, or too far afield.'

'Have we had the phone data?'

He nodded. 'We have. Again, it's routine stuff. We're checking, but nothing of concern has been flagged that would link in with her murder.'

'What about the PNC checks?' Isabel said. 'You had someone checking through the guest list. Has that thrown up anything interesting?'

'Apart from a few minor motoring offences, no one who attended the party has any previous convictions – with one glaring exception. Ross Allwood.'

Isabel placed her knuckles on her hips. 'Ross Allwood has a record?'

'Strictly speaking, no. He wasn't charged, but he was given

a warning for possession of drugs. Cannabis and cocaine. The quantities suggested personal use. There was no indication he was dealing, which is why he was let off with a warning.'

'When was this?'

'June 2019.'

'But nothing since then?'

'No. He seems to have been keeping his nose clean ... or should I say, powder-free.'

Isabel was sceptical. 'Just because he hasn't been caught again doesn't mean he isn't still taking drugs.'

'Do you think Anna Matheson knew about his habit?'

'It's not easy keeping a lid on something like that,' Isabel said. 'Then again, so what? Even if Anna did find out, it's not exactly earth-shattering ... hardly the sort of revelation that would lead to murder.'

'No, but it is information she could have used against him.'

'I don't think so.' Isabel shook her head. 'I agree that potentially, someone could use something like that as leverage ... threaten to tell an employer, for instance – but that wouldn't work in Ross Allwood's case. As co-owner of Allwood Confectionery, he's his own boss. He's hardly going to sack himself, is he?'

'I guess not,' Adrian said, 'although it might be worth checking with the personnel department ... see if they're aware of Ross's penchant for recreational drugs.'

'Based on the information we've gleaned so far, my main impression of young Ross is that he's used to getting his own way,' Isabel said. 'And, OK, he may have a drug habit, and be rubbish at his job – but neither of those things are a motive for murder.'

'I agree. As motives go, being exposed as a cokehead is pretty bloody weak.'

'There are a shedload of variables in this case,' Isabel said. 'And still one hell of a lot of questions. Let's get everyone together tomorrow morning for an update. I think it's time for a review.'

Chapter 25

Dan had arranged to meet Pete Pilkington at the main reception desk at Allwoods at 3.30 p.m. When he arrived, the sales rep was already waiting, leaning against the tall desk, chatting to the receptionist. He was dressed in a well-cut navy-blue suit, paired with highly polished brown leather shoes. It was a smart enough look, albeit a tad OTT for someone selling kets.

'Pete Pilkington? I'm DS Fairfax. Thanks for agreeing to meet me so quickly.'

'Not a problem,' Pete replied, his Welsh accent rich and melodious. 'I was over in Nottingham when you called, so it was just a matter of bombing up the A52. It's a rum do about Anna. She was all right. I liked her. The girl knew her stuff.'

The personnel department had offered Dan the use of one of the small meeting rooms next to the boardroom. As they settled down at a small, circular conference table, Pete Pilkington eyed Dan warily.

'This is where the personnel team hold job interviews,' Pete said. 'Is that what's happening now, is it? Are you interviewing me?'

'Do you have a problem with that?' Dan said.

In reply, the rep gave a nonchalant shrug.

'There are some things I need to ask,' Dan continued. 'About Anna.'

'That's fine. I'll help if I can, although I didn't know her all that well. In my job, I spend a lot of time on the road. I only come into the office once or twice a week, so I didn't run into Anna very often.'

'Did the two of you get on OK, when you did encounter each other?'

'Sure.' Pete nodded. 'As I said, she was good at her job. I had a lot of respect for her.'

'We've been told you spoke to her recently about Ross Allwood? More precisely about his inadequacies as the head of sales?'

Pete folded his arms and smacked his lips together. 'We did have a conversation about Ross, yes. The guy should never have been made head of the department. I mean … we all know *why* he was, but it shouldn't have happened.'

'I don't know why,' Dan said. 'Perhaps you could enlighten me.'

'Isn't it obvious? You must know he owns half of the company.'

'That doesn't explain why he's the head of sales.'

Pete Pilkington leaned back, making himself as comfortable as he could on the hard, wooden chair.

'Before Barry Allwood died, Ross was a sales rep,' he said. 'Not a very successful one either. Faye Allwood was head of sales back then. Rumour has it she'd put pressure on Barry to find a better position for their son. That's how Ross ended up as rep.'

'What was he doing before that?'

'He worked on the production line, supposedly learning the ropes. He'd been doing that for years, and Barry never seemed in any hurry to promote him. He had to give in eventually, of course. I think he made Ross a sales rep because that's where the lad could do the least harm. The worst that could happen would be that he failed to get any new business.'

'Are you sure about that?' Dan said. 'If he'd messed up, he might have lost some important accounts. I have no head for business, but even I know that would have impacted negatively on the company's profitability.'

'Barry had thought of that,' Pete said, tapping the side of his slightly wonky nose. 'Ross's remit was strictly to go looking for *new* business. Responsibility for maintaining the existing accounts was down to me and the more experienced reps, alongside closing deals with our own new clients.'

'I see. Doesn't sound like Barry Allwood had much faith in his son's abilities.'

Pete sneered knowingly. 'He'd got Ross sussed. Baz knew he was a waste of space. He told me so himself, but he felt obliged to give the lad a job ... keep him out of trouble, as it were.'

'What kind of trouble?' Dan said.

Pete smirked. 'You're the copper, mate. You'll know a lot more about that than me. What I heard was, Ross had been caught in possession of drugs. Barry was less than impressed, as you might imagine.'

'Talk me through what happened here at the factory, after Barry died,' Dan said.

'Ownership of the company passed to Faye and Ross. Fifty-fifty. She became the CEO, which left the head of sales position vacant. Being totally honest, I hoped I might get the job, as did Ryan Reed. We've both been at Allwoods for over twenty-five years.'

'You were annoyed then, when Ross Allwood was appointed?'

'Annoyed? Bloody furious, more like. They didn't even have the decency to interview me and Ryan ... but there you go.'

'That must have left you feeling bitter,' Dan said. 'Is that why you complained about Ross's performance?'

Pete Pilkington scowled. 'I try not to bear grudges ... in my experience, bitter people are usually miserable fuckers. I prefer to make the most of things. My glass is always half full, see, never half empty.'

'So if you're not bitter, why did you lodge a complaint about Ross Allwood?'

'I thought … *still* think, that his lack of leadership skills is affecting the sales team. We're achieving our targets, but that's largely down to the promotional work Anna Matheson has implemented. In theory, we should be *smashing* our targets, not just meeting them. The thing is, a lot of people depend on this company for their livelihoods, me included. I want Allwoods to thrive, not just survive. In my opinion, Ross Allwood's lack of professionalism will run the business into the ground if he's allowed to carry on long term.'

'Did Anna Matheson agree with you?'

'She did, and she spoke to Faye Allwood about it. Anna wanted Ross to relinquish his position as head of sales.'

'And what did Faye Allwood think to that idea?'

'She didn't like it … not one little bit. She and Anna had a set-to. Faye told her to back off, but Anna was a feisty little thing and she was determined not to give up. She told me she had something up her sleeve, a secret weapon, although she wouldn't tell me what it was.'

'Any thoughts on what she meant by that?' Dan said.

'Not a clue, mate. Haven't the foggiest. What I will say is that she seemed very determined, and confident too. The truth is, I've been banking on Anna coming up trumps. Won't happen now though, will it?'

'No,' Dan said. 'Sadly not.'

'Tell me to mind my own business, but why are you so interested in Ross Allwood? You don't think he had anything to do with Anna's murder, do you?'

Dan knocked his knuckles together. 'At this stage in the investigation, we're simply gathering as much background information as we can,' he said. 'There's no suggestion that Ross Allwood was involved in Anna's death, but we've been made aware of the tensions between him and Anna, so we're obliged to check the facts.'

'In terms of your investigation, you'd do well to remember

that Anna's objection to Ross was purely about his professional inadequacies,' Pete said, tugging at the cuffs of his immaculate white shirt. 'She was very proficient herself, a highly skilled and capable woman, and I think she expected everyone else to operate to the same high standards. But, on a personal level, there was never any real animosity between Anna and Ross. She did her best to get on with him. If anything, I think she felt sorry for him.'

This revelation was a surprise to Dan, contradicting everything he'd learned so far.

'And what about you, Pete?' he said. 'Do you feel the same way about Ross Allwood?'

'Me?' Pete laughed. 'No, I don't. I think he's a complete pillock. As far as I'm concerned, the sooner he resigns, the better.'

***

Once he'd concluded the interview with Pete Pilkington, Dan bought a sandwich from the factory canteen. He consumed it on his own, at a corner table, mulling over the case while he waited for Ryan Reed, the other sales rep, to arrive.

He turned up at four-fifteen in reception, a stouter version of Pete Pilkington, with the same air of cocky pride. As Dan escorted him to the same small meeting room, Ryan boasted that he'd been Allwood's salesperson of the year in 2020, and was confident of retaining the title in 2021.

His views on Ross Allwood were, if anything, even more scathing than those put forward by Pete Pilkington, although he was unable to provide any additional information of significance.

It was clear to Dan that the two top performers in the sales team begrudged Ross Allwood his position, and their resentment appeared to be justified. If their reports were to be believed, Ross was useless as a manager, and his inadequacies clearly rankled those who reported to him.

That said, he must have had some redeeming characteristics

because despite being Allwood's worst critic, Ryan Reed admitted he had nothing against Ross personally.

'It's his inability to do his job that irks me,' he said, as Dan's questioning came to an end. 'I want to make that clear.'

As Dan headed back to the station, he resolved to pay a visit to the Allwood home that evening, with the intention of getting Ross's take on the criticism levied against him. Was it all something and nothing? Office politics turned sour? Or was there more to it?

Could the underlying tensions caused by Ross Allwood's failures have somehow led to murder?

Chapter 26

Isabel arrived home to the unexpected and initially welcome news that Bailey had secured an interview for a job. However, her sense of excitement was short-lived.

'Allwoods?' she said, when Bailey told her where he was going the following day. 'You've got to be kidding. You've got an interview at the sweet factory?'

She pulled off her jacket and threw it onto the back of the settee, where Bailey and the dog were sprawled. The dog lifted her head and put her ears back.

'Why the hell would you want to work there?' she said. 'What's the job?'

Bailey sat up and folded his arms, a fixed stare hardening his face. 'It's in the packing department,' he said. 'It was you that put the idea in my head, actually. You reminded me about the place, and I thought it was worth a try.'

'Sorry?' She shook her head, unable to grasp what her son was telling her. 'You spent three years at university and a further year doing your master's … and you've applied for a job in a factory? In the packing department?'

'Don't give me a hard time, Mum,' said Bailey, pushing his hands into the pockets of his sloppy jeans. 'I thought you'd be pleased. You've been going on at me for weeks to get a job.'

'I've been *going on*, as you put it, for you to sort yourself out and get your career back on track. You were teaching English as a Foreign Language before you went off on your travels. Why don't you take that up again?'

Bailey kicked at the carpet with bare feet. 'Two reasons. First of all, in case you hadn't noticed, there's been a worldwide pandemic. No one's recruiting for EFL teachers at the moment, certainly not round here. Secondly ... and more importantly, I don't like teaching. It's too much hassle.'

'Hassle?' She glared at him. 'You want to try joining the police force if you want to know what hassle is. Besides, who ever said work was meant to be easy? That's why it's called *work*.'

Bailey stood up. 'Give me a break, will you? One minute you're complaining about me being unemployed, the next you're moaning because I'm being interviewed for a job you don't approve of. You need to make your mind up, Mum. You can't have it both ways.'

'I didn't say I don't approve of the job ... I said you could do better. You're overqualified.'

'Yeah, and I'm not the only one.' Bailey's words were loaded with anger and frustration. 'This country is full of highly educated people running around after the same few jobs. I'm trying to be realistic, Mum. I don't intend to work at Allwoods forever, but it'll tide me over until something better comes along.'

With that, he marched out of the living room and into the kitchen, Isabel and the dog following close on his heels.

'Don't walk away from me, Bailey. I'm talking to you.'

'You're not talking, Mum. You're shouting.'

Nathan was over by the window, rootling through the contents of the cupboard under the sink. He turned to see what the commotion was about.

'I suppose you know about this, Nathan?' Isabel said.

'By *this*, I assume you're referring to his job interview? I'll take it as read you don't approve?'

Suppressing the urge to scream, Isabel plonked herself down at the kitchen table and took a deep, calming breath.

'I applaud the fact that he's taking action, but it's ludicrous that a man with his qualifications has applied for a job packing sweets.'

'I agree with you,' Nathan said.

'You do?'

'Don't sound so surprised.' Nathan closed the cupboard door and stood up straight. 'I think he needs to aim higher, and I've told him so.'

'*Hello!*' Bailey said. 'I am here, you know.'

Nathan sat down next to Isabel. 'The thing is, son, you need to start building yourself a career,' he said. 'You're not a student anymore ... you haven't been for quite some time. When you and Sophie decided to go travelling, we assumed you were working through your wanderlust. We thought you'd get it out of your system and then come back and settle down.'

'Yeah, well ... so did I, and look how that turned out.'

'Are you regretting not staying in New Zealand?' Isabel asked.

Bailey shrugged petulantly. 'Not really. I do miss Sophie ... I'm not going to deny it, but that's over now. I need to move on, get a job and start again.'

'But not any old job, surely?' Isabel said. 'You need to think carefully about what you want to do with your life. If you don't want to teach, how about working in the community, or for a charity?'

Bailey looked at her, sour-faced. 'You're kidding, aren't you? The pay's crap.'

'It'd be more than you'll earn at Allwoods,' Isabel said. 'Look, Bailey, I don't want to interfere—'

'Yeah. Right.'

'All I want is for you to pursue your dreams,' Isabel continued.

'Take up a career that will mean something to you. Something you can be proud of.'

'A proper job like yours, you mean?' he replied, his tone caustic. 'Something I can commit myself to? A job that will consume me?'

Isabel sat back, stung by the verbal blow. 'Is that how you see my career with the police?' she said.

'Well, you have to admit, it does control your life,' Bailey said. 'You've always worked stupidly long hours, and you get a shedload of grief and stress, and for what? A solid pension? You've got to ask yourself whether it's worth it.'

'Hey! Don't speak to your mother like that,' Nathan said. 'She works bloody hard, and always has done. You should be proud of what she does.'

Bailey moved over to the table and sat down opposite them, flexing his fingers.

'Sorry, Mum. I know you love your job … and you're good at it … but not all of us are cut out to be dedicated career people. The truth is, I don't know what I want to do with my life. I thought a job at Allwoods might buy me some time to think things through. It certainly can't do any harm.'

'On the contrary,' Isabel said, struggling to control her temper. 'We're in the middle of a murder investigation centring on Allwood Confectionery. Having you working there isn't advisable. It could compromise the case.'

'Compromise it how?'

'Trust me, Bailey. If you were employed by Allwoods, it would complicate things. I'm asking you to reconsider, or at least think about postponing the interview until after the case has been concluded.'

'And when's that likely to be?' He stared at her, his blue eyes cold and flinty.

'I don't know,' she said, turning away from her son's anger. 'It could be a few days, or a few weeks. Or it could be months.'

Bailey let out a low growl of frustration. 'That's so typical,' he said, waving his hands in the air to emphasise his point. 'Once again, *your* career comes first. To hell with the rest of us.'

'That's a bit harsh,' she said, glancing at Nathan in a silent appeal for backup.

'Your mum's right, Bailey,' he said. 'All we're asking is that you don't make any hasty decisions.'

Bailey scowled. 'As you both keep reminding me, I'm nearly thirty. That means I'm old enough to make my own decisions, hasty or otherwise.'

'So, you're going to go for the interview anyway?' Isabel said, knowing she couldn't forbid it, but hoping sense would prevail.

Bailey stood up, the chair scraping on the tiled floor. 'I'm not sure yet,' he said. 'I'll let you know. Sod your investigation, Mum. I'll make up my own mind.'

Chapter 27

To say that Faye Allwood looked dismayed to see him would be an understatement.

'You've called at a bad time, DS Fairfax,' she said. 'We're about to sit down and eat. Ross has been out all day, so we're having a late dinner.'

'I'm sorry to disturb your meal, but I do need to come in. I'd like to talk to your son to clear up a few points.'

Faye tucked a strand of hair behind her ear. 'I'm tempted to tell you to get lost and come back later,' she said. 'However, as you're investigating a murder, I suppose I have no choice but to let you in.'

'Thank you,' Dan said. 'I appreciate it.'

He followed her through the grand hallway to a large kitchen at the back of the house. Ross Allwood was sitting at a table, eating a plate of spaghetti carbonara. As Dan breathed in the mouth-watering aroma of garlic bread, he felt the beginnings of hunger pangs. Maybe he should call for a takeaway on his way home.

'Please don't think us rude, but you'll have to talk while we eat,' Faye said, as she resumed her place at the table. 'If there's one thing I can't abide, it's cold pasta.'

'Actually,' Dan said, 'I was hoping to speak to your son on his own.'

'Oh, for heaven's sake.' Faye picked up a fork with her right hand and waved it around. 'Ross and I have no secrets. Go ahead and ask whatever you need to. I promise not to butt in.'

Dan thought about insisting on privacy, but decided he would resort to that only if Faye Allwood failed to keep her promise.

He hadn't been invited to sit down and, quite honestly, he was glad of it. Sitting at their kitchen table, watching the Allwoods stuff their faces, wasn't his idea of fun.

'I've been speaking to some of the members of your team, Mr Allwood,' Dan said. 'They don't seem to rate your abilities as head of sales, and I know there have been complaints. I also know that Anna Matheson spoke to you and your mother about the issue.'

'So what?' Faye Allwood said. 'How is that relevant to your investigation?'

Dan glared at her. 'Mrs Allwood, you said you'd refrain from commenting. If you're not able to do that, I'm going to have to ask you to leave the room.'

'Excuse me! You can't order me around in my own house. You've barged in on a meal—'

'Mother, shut up,' Ross said. 'I'm quite capable of answering for myself. I'm not twelve years old. I don't need you to speak for me.'

Pressured into silence, Faye plunged the fork into her spaghetti and began to twirl it around.

'Anna wanted me to step down,' Ross explained. 'She said I wasn't cut out for a sales role. She was brutally honest … said I'd be better off spending my days on the golf course than at Allwoods. She obviously had a very low opinion of me.'

'Of your business skills, you mean? Or you personally?'

'My business skills, mainly. Or lack of. It was a bone of contention between us, but that doesn't mean I didn't like Anna. In many ways, we got on all right. When she wasn't having a go

154

at me about my rubbish management skills, she could be quite kind and sympathetic.'

'About your drug habit?' Dan said.

Faye Allwood dropped the handle of her fork and opened her mouth to speak, but her son silenced her with a glare.

'You were found in possession of a quantity of cocaine and cannabis a while back,' Dan continued. 'I'm guessing you still partake now and again?'

'I'm hardly going to admit to that, am I?' Ross replied.

'Did Anna know you take recreational drugs?'

'Yes, I think the rumour mill at the factory has made most people of aware of that fact. You can't fart in that place without someone finding out.'

'Ross,' Faye said. 'Please don't be coarse.'

Dan smiled inwardly. Mrs Allwood had barely batted an eyelid when Dan had raised the subject of drugs, but the woman obviously drew the line at mentioning flatulence at the dinner table.

'Did Anna talk to you about your cocaine habit? Did she offer advice?'

'She told me it was a mug's game,' Ross replied. 'But she didn't lecture me … and I was grateful for that. What she did say was that I was the only person who could change things. She said I had to *want* to change, more than anything, otherwise the need for drugs would always have the upper hand.'

'Did she tell you about her own battle with alcohol?' Dan asked.

'Anna?' Ross said, sounding genuinely mystified. 'No, she never mentioned that. She did tell me that a lot of her London friends took coke. She never said anything about her own drinking though. Are you saying she was an alcoholic?'

'A recovering alcoholic. At least, that's what we believe.'

Dan turned to Faye Allwood. 'Did you know that, Mrs Allwood?'

'You're talking to me?' she said, pointing at her sternum. 'You want me to speak now, do you?'

'Just answer the question, please.'

She swept her hair away from her face. 'It's the first I've heard of it. Then again, Anna was good at keeping secrets.'

'Really? What else was she keeping to herself?' said Dan.

'Who the father of her child was for starters.' Faye shrugged. 'I don't like slyness and secrecy. I much prefer people to be straightforward and up front about things.'

'We're trying to track down Benedict's father,' Dan said. 'We'd like to talk to him.'

'Quite right too,' Faye said. 'It's time he started taking his responsibilities as a parent seriously. If my son were the baby's father, I'd certainly expect him to step up and do the right thing.'

'But you're not,' Dan said, turning back to Ross.

'No. Definitely not.'

'And would you be willing to provide a DNA sample, so that we can confirm that?'

'Are you joking? I've told you I'm not the child's father. Isn't that enough? Why would I lie?'

'People lie for any number of reasons,' Dan said. 'Covering up a murder, for instance.'

Ross stopped eating and reached for his half-empty glass of wine. 'You've got some nerve, I'll give you that,' he said.

Faye sat back, her face leached of colour. 'I hope you're not suggesting my son is a suspect in Anna's murder?'

'Not at this stage,' Dan said. 'There's no evidence to implicate Ross in Anna's death, but their recent disagreement does make him a person of interest. There's also been speculation that he could be Benedict Matheson's father …'

'That's not true … I've just told you that,' Ross said.

'Fair enough,' said Dan. 'But it's something we'd like to confirm with a DNA test.'

Ross put his hands on his head. 'This is ridiculous,' he said, his voice an angry hiss. 'I'm under no obligation to comply with your request. Give me one good reason why I should.'

'You're right,' Dan replied. 'If you do agree to provide a sample of DNA, it would be on a voluntary basis.'

'If that's the case, you can piss off. You haven't got a shred of evidence against me, so why the hell should I have to prove my innocence? Besides, what you're effectively asking me to do is take a paternity test. How's that going to help solve Anna's murder?'

Faye looked pensive, as though the cogs of serious consideration were whirring inside her head.

'Don't be too hasty, Ross,' she said. 'Let's think this through for a minute.'

The last thing Dan had expected was co-operation from Faye Allwood. On the contrary, he'd been bracing himself, waiting for her to pipe up with her objections. The fact that she was encouraging her son to comply with Dan's request was astonishing.

'You can't be serious, Mother?' Ross said. 'You honestly want me to go along with this? Give them my DNA?'

'Think about it, sweetheart. You're telling the truth. You aren't Benedict Matheson's father, and giving the police a DNA sample is the easiest way to prove that. They obviously think the child's father is also the killer, so why don't you give them your DNA and rule yourself out as a suspect?'

Although her reading of the situation wasn't strictly accurate, Dan didn't correct her. If he kept quiet and played this right, Ross Allwood might agree to co-operate.

'Shouldn't we consult a solicitor, or something?' Ross said, worry etched on his face.

'What would be the point?' Faye replied. 'Just give them the damned DNA and show them you've got nothing to hide.'

Chapter 28

'After a little persuasion, we now have DNA samples from both James Derenby and Ross Allwood,' Isabel said, at the following day's briefing. 'Christina Matheson had already granted permission for us to take a DNA sample from Benedict Matheson, so we're now in a position to make a comparison. I've asked for the results to be rushed through as a priority.'

'Both Derenby and Allwood have strenuously denied any sexual relationship with Anna Matheson, never mind fathering her child,' Dan said. 'The fact that they've volunteered a DNA sample does suggest they're telling the truth.'

'I agree,' Isabel said. 'And in light of that, I think it's time to issue another statement to the press and on social media, appealing to Benedict's father to come forward and speak to us.'

'I'll arrange that, boss,' said Theo. 'Leave it with me.'

'Apart from getting the DNA samples, are there any other developments?' Lucas asked.

'I've been given an unexpected heads-up by Ross Allwood's PA,' said Dan. 'She mentioned that a friend of her cousin's … a woman called Hayley Carter … went out with James Derenby for a while. When they split up, Derenby didn't take it well … made a nuisance of himself by all accounts.'

'Have you spoken to the woman?' Isabel said.

'Not yet, the PA's only just confirmed Hayley's surname.'

'In that case, you can let Lucas follow it up,' Isabel said. 'The PNC checks flagged up nothing on Derenby, but if he *has* formed an unhealthy attachment to a woman in the past, what's to say the same thing didn't happen with Anna Matheson? See what you can find out, Lucas. Talk to Hayley Carter, and get Derenby's version of events as well.'

Lucas nodded. 'Will do, boss.'

Zoe put her hand up.

'What is it, Zoe?' Isabel said.

'We've been focusing on the identity of the baby's father,' Zoe said. 'But how important is the question of paternity? How relevant is it to the investigation?'

'The honest answer to that is ... I don't know,' Isabel said. 'But you're right. We mustn't get side-lined by something that may have no bearing on the case. Right now, the most important question we should perhaps be focusing on is: *Why was Anna murdered?*'

'As far as I can see, there's no clear motive,' Lucas said. 'It might even be a random killing. Anna could have been in the wrong place at the wrong time.'

'I don't think so,' Isabel said. 'We can rule out the perpetrator being a sexual predator, because there are no signs of sexual assault, but I strongly believe that's Anna disappearance from Allwoods is significant. The party was for staff and special guests. Partners weren't invited. Anyone at the factory that night either worked for, or with Allwoods.'

'What do we know about the company?' Adrian Bostock said. 'Do we have the financials yet? And what about the senior management team? Did anything show up on any of the background checks?'

'The latest set of company accounts show that the business is doing very nicely,' Dan said. 'Profits have increased by around twenty per cent in the last two years. During that time, the company has also invested in several pieces of expensive machinery, pushing up the value of their capital assets. On top of that, the firm has a healthy contingency fund.'

'What about the people who run the place?' Isabel said. 'Any anomalies there?'

'The financial background checks flagged up one potential issue,' said Lucas. 'The head of production, Roy Morris, has a sizeable overdraft. However, he's recently gone through a divorce, so that would account for him being in dire straits.'

'Has anyone spoken to him?' Isabel asked.

'I have,' said Theo. 'Turns out he wasn't at the party.'

'Did he say why he didn't go?'

'He'd promised to drive his daughter down to Dorset for the weekend. She was competing in a gymkhana event, whatever the hell that is. He told me he'd have preferred to go to the party, and he did try to wriggle out of the road trip with his daughter, but Morris's ex-wife was having none of it. I checked – he was away all weekend, staying in a hotel near Blandford Forum.'

'OK … well that rules him out,' Isabel said. 'One less brick wall for us to encounter … we've got enough of those already. What we need to do now is keep an open mind, and focus on motive. Someone wanted Anna Matheson dead. Why? Was it someone who had something to hide … something that Anna knew about? This murder could have been about silencing Anna, or perhaps someone had something to gain financially by erasing her from the picture. Or was it something much more personal? We need to consider how Anna's existence might have impacted on, or threatened someone else.'

'Any further news from Forensics?' said Adrian. 'Was there any trace evidence on the victim that could be linked to the perpetrator?'

'There were tiny traces of fibre from the rope used to strangle her,' Isabel said. 'They're trying to track down the brand. Fibre traces were also found under one of Anna's fingernails, which may have transferred during a struggle. Finally, there were some partial footprints found in Brightcliffe Woods near to the dump site. Raveen believes they're from a size 8 wellington boot.'

'Men's size 8, or women's?' said Zoe.

'Men's,' Isabel replied. 'I'm reliably informed by Raveen that a men's 8 is equivalent to a women's 9½.'

'There aren't many women with feet that big,' Lucas said. 'Although Zoe's are pretty massive.'

The burst of laughter in the room brought a blush to Zoe's cheeks.

'I'll have you know I take a size 7,' she said, looking askance at Lucas. '*Women's 7.*'

Isabel smiled. 'Lucas does have a point, even if he didn't make it very well,' she said. 'We mustn't assume that the person wearing the boots was male. I wear a size 5, but if I put on a couple of pairs of thick woolly socks, I'm sure I'd be able to walk around in a pair of men's size 8 wellies.'

'On the other hand,' Lucas said, tipping his head in Isabel's direction. 'Someone with much bigger feet wouldn't necessarily be able to cram them into a smaller size. Did I make that point eloquently enough for you, boss?'

'Yes, thank you, Lucas. Very articulate.' She smiled at him. 'Now, aside from the size of the perp's feet, what other lines of inquiry do we have that need to be followed up?'

'No one's spoken to Fenella Grainger yet,' Dan said. 'She covered the marketing job at Allwoods while Anna was on maternity leave, and she was at the party on Saturday. Ross Allwood mentioned that she stayed on for a few weeks after Anna came back to work, and the two women didn't hit it off.'

'Do we know why?' Isabel said.

'Probably a case of professional rivalry,' Dan replied. 'Maybe Anna was feeling territorial, and didn't like the idea of anyone moseying in on her position. I'll follow it up with Fenella Grainger though, just in case there was more to it than that.'

'OK, let's keep plugging away,' Isabel said. 'We're looking for leads, preferably not the sort that take us up the garden path. Progress is slower than I'd like, folks. It feels as though we're no further forward now than when Anna first disappeared.'

Chapter 29

Dan rang Fenella Grainger straight after the briefing, and she agreed to come in to the station at eleven o'clock. He joined her in interview room one, where she sat gripping a cup of vending machine coffee provided by the duty sergeant.

Her hair was long, tumbling either side of her elfin face and down over her shoulders in a flaxen wave. Dan thought she looked incredibly young.

'I appreciate you coming in,' he said, once he'd run through the usual formalities. 'We know you covered Anna Matheson's job while she was on maternity leave, and that you worked with her briefly when she returned. We're talking to everyone who was at the party at Allwood Confectionery on Saturday night. Do you have any information that might shed light on what happened to Anna?'

'Me?' Fenella said, shuffling nervously. 'Why would I? I hardly knew her.'

'Did you speak to her at the party?'

'Briefly. We didn't talk for long. The thing is, Anna and I never clicked? Neither of us was interested in spending time in each other's company.'

'Was there any particular reason the two of you didn't get along?'

'I didn't say we didn't get along. We just never had the chance to establish a rapport, you know?'

Dan rested his chin on his right thumb. 'The thing is, Fenella, in my line of work you learn to read code,' he said. 'And, to me, *not clicking, not establishing a rapport …* that's code for *the two of you didn't like each other.*'

Fenella lowered her gaze. 'If there was any animosity, it stemmed purely from Anna.'

'You felt Anna was hostile towards you?'

'Yeah … she was dead nice with everyone else. It was just me she didn't like.'

'Why do you think that was?'

'She resented me doing her job, obvs,' she said, pushing a stray wave of hair from her eyes. 'She was massively protective of her role, and I know she wasn't impressed with me. I went in the week before she went off on maternity leave, for a kind of handover?'

Dan decided to overlook Fenella's irritating habit of lifting her voice at the end of a sentence, regardless of whether she was asking a question.

'She tried to show me everything?' she continued. 'There was way too much to take in all at once, and it didn't help that she raced through everything at ninety miles an hour. It was ridiculous. She tried to teach me in a few days what it had taken her two years to learn. It's no wonder I struggled to pick things up.'

'Did you enjoy the job, once you'd got the hang of things?'

'Yes, it was amazing, although I only did it for a few months – and then Anna came back. I was hoping she might take a longer maternity leave, but she seemed desperate to return to work.'

'You were kept on for a while, I understand? After Anna's return?'

'Only for a week or so. There was some talk of me being taken on as Anna's assistant, but she was having none of it.'

'Perhaps she thought she didn't need an assistant,' Dan said.

Fenella looked at him incredulously. 'Are you serious? It was a busy job. She would definitely have benefited from the help. It was me she didn't want. Simple as.'

'Had you done something to annoy her?' Dan asked. 'Aside from taking over her job for a while?'

As Fenella considered the question, an impish dimple appeared in her left cheek. 'Thinking about it, she took against me from the off. When I arrived for the handover, I was directed to her office. The door was open, so I went inside. Anna was on the phone with her back to me, so she didn't realise I was there. She was arguing with someone on the phone. She was keeping her voice down, but I could tell she was angry.'

Fenella traced a finger around the rim of her empty coffee cup.

'Anyway,' she continued, 'I waited, and eventually, when she noticed me standing there, she ended the call. She was furious. When I told her who I was, she said: "*Lesson one, Fenella. Always knock when you enter someone's office. Lesson two: it's rude to listen in on people's private conversations.*" Those were her first words to me. She was horrible, and it sort of set the tone for our relationship.'

'Do you know who she was talking to on the phone?' Dan asked.

'No. I knew nothing about Anna at that stage. It was only later, when I heard how secretive she was being about the baby's father, that I thought it might have been him she was talking to.'

Dan sat up. 'How did you come to that conclusion?'

Fenella tipped her head back, thinking, her eyes scanning the ceiling. 'It was her attitude and her tone of voice … the way she was speaking? She was almost hissing, furious in a way you can only be with someone you know well.'

'It could have been a nuisance caller,' Dan said.

Fenella dismissed that suggestion with a brief shake of the head. 'When someone deals with a call like that, their anger's a lot more guarded and impersonal … in fact, most people just end the call and block the number. The conversation Anna was having was heated. Vicious. From the things she said, I'm certain she knew the person she was talking to, and knew them well.'

'Can you recall her side of the conversation? What was said?'

Fenella was tearing off pieces of the cup holder that had been used to deliver her coffee, littering the table with tiny pieces of cardboard. Dan was tempted to snatch it from her, to yell at her to concentrate. This could be important.

'What can you remember?' he said, the sharpness in his voice making her jump.

'She was already well into her stride when I walked into the office,' Fenella replied. 'The first words I heard were: *"No way! No way!"* That's when I realised she was arguing with somebody. Then she said something like: *"There's no fucking way I'm going to let you do that."*'

In those circumstances, Dan thought, the well-mannered thing for Fenella to have done would be to clear her throat, or cough politely to make her presence known. On the other hand, he mustn't be too critical. The fact that she'd stood there, earwigging, could well provide him with some vital information.

'Anything else?' Dan said. 'Did she use the person's name at all?'

'No. I would have remembered that.' Fenella pulled at her bottom lip. 'I'm pretty sure she said, *"This should never have happened …"* No, hang on, I think it was: *"We should never have let this happen."* She then said, *"You're going to have to accept this is not your problem."* As she said that, she turned around and saw me.'

'And what did she do then?'

'Said a hurried *"got to go"*, or something similar, and ended the call. Then she stood up and laid into me for listening in to her private conversation.'

'What time of day was this?' Dan asked.

Fenella thought for a moment. 'It would have been a few minutes after ten o'clock? I was asked to report to reception at ten a.m. and, after I'd signed in, someone took me straight to Anna's office … so it would have been a few minutes past the hour?'

'And can you remember the date?'

'Not off the top of my head, but I can look back through my old emails from the recruitment agency, if you like. They sent me details of when and where to report. It would have been sometime in early February, but I can't remember the exact date. I'll check it out and get back to you.'

'Thank you,' Dan said. 'I'd appreciate you doing that as soon as possible.'

If he could confirm the time and date of that telephone conversation, he might be able to use the phone data from the service provider to track down who Anna was speaking to. It was something. Not much, but it was a start.

Chapter 30

When Raveen Talwar rang to say he had some news to share, Isabel experienced a surge of optimism. A piece of solid forensic evidence was exactly what she needed. Listening intently, she leaned her elbows against the wooden surface of her desk, grateful for its solidity.

'I'll confirm what I'm about to tell you in an email,' Raveen began, 'but the information I've just received is pretty startling, and important enough to warrant me telling you in person.'

'Go on,' she said, pressing the phone to her ear.

'We're fast-tracking Derenby and Allwood's DNA, but it's going to be at least another twenty-four hours before we get the results. When we do, we'll compare their DNA with Benedict Matheson's, and let you know if there's a match.'

Isabel rolled her eyes impatiently. 'I already know this, Raveen. Please tell me that's not why you're ringing.'

'No,' said Raveen. 'What I'm calling to tell you is far more interesting.'

'Spit it out then,' she said, her pulse quickening. 'My nerves are already on edge. Don't keep me in suspense.'

'The DNA swab from Benedict Matheson went off to the lab twenty-four hours earlier than those from Derenby and Allwood. We've just had some results back.'

Isabel released the breath she'd been holding on to. 'I see … that's good news I suppose, but you won't be able to do a comparison until you get the other results, will you? We're still going to have to play the waiting game.'

'Not necessarily,' Raveen said. 'The thing is, Benedict Matheson's DNA is a partial match for an individual stored on the police database.'

Isabel gripped her phone and leaned into it.

'Tell me more, Raveen.'

***

When their conversation was over, she sat for a moment, trying to absorb the implications of what Raveen had told her. Running the information through her head, she considered all the permutations. It pointed to one obvious conclusion.

Through the glass partition that separated her office from the open-plan space beyond, she could see Lucas at his desk, hunched over his computer. Zoe was standing behind him, twirling a strand of blonde hair around her finger as she stared at something on Lucas's screen.

Isabel got up and went out to talk to them. 'I've had a call from Raveen,' she said. 'Benedict Matheson's DNA results are back.'

'That's quick,' Zoe said. 'Any news yet on whether they're a match with Derenby or Allwood?'

'We're still awaiting those results, but there is a match with someone else … someone who's already on the police DNA database.'

Zoe's body stiffened. 'So this person has a record?'

'It's slightly more complicated than that,' Isabel replied. 'Benedict's DNA was compared against the whole system, which – as you know – includes police officer samples stored for elimination purposes.'

'Hell fire,' said Lucas. 'Are you saying the baby's father is a copper?'

'What I'm saying is the analysis flagged up a partial match to a police officer whose DNA is stored on the database.'

Zoe's eyes widened. 'Anyone we know?'

'Yes,' Isabel said, her expression serious. 'It's someone we know very well indeed.'

Chapter 31

'Tell us then.' Zoe had pinned back her shoulders, and her eyes were bright and attentive. '*Who?* Which officer is a match?'

As Isabel opened her mouth to answer, the door swung open and Dan sauntered into the office.

'I've been interviewing Fenella Grainger,' he said, as he sat down at his desk. 'She's given me a lead about an overheard telephone conversation between Anna Matheson and an unknown person who may be the child's father. I've given the details to the guys in the ops room. They're going to see if they can track down the call from the phone data.'

'That sounds like a promising lead,' Isabel said, her voice calm. 'And you're just in time to hear another startling piece of news, Dan. Benedict Matheson's DNA has been matched with an officer on the police database.'

'Bloody hell!' Dan sat up. 'Who's that then?'

Isabel felt three pairs of eyes boring into her. She folded her arms, quietly enjoying the moment of suspense. 'Benedict Matheson is a match with you, Lucas.'

'Me!' Lucas's scruffy head shot up, his face crumpling in disbelief. 'Fucking hell, you've got to be kidding. I'm not the baby's father. I've never even met Anna Matheson, never mind got her up the duff.'

Isabel cringed at his choice of phrase. 'I didn't say you were the baby's father. I said there was a match with your DNA. A familial match.'

Zoe was staring, slack-jawed. 'So, what does that mean exactly?'

'I would have thought it was obvious,' Isabel said. 'Lucas's DNA matches Benedict Matheson's because they're blood relatives. The initial analysis shows that they share six and a half per cent of their DNA, which suggests Benedict is Lucas's first cousin, once removed.'

'What's one of them?' Lucas wrinkled his nose. 'Once removed? What's that when it's at home?'

'It's either the first cousin of one of your parents,' Isabel said. 'Or, your own first cousin's child.'

'Bloody hell!' Lucas gave a low whistle. 'So, Ross *is* the baby's father.'

'We won't know for definite until his DNA has been properly compared to Benedict's, but it's looking that way. It certainly gives us grounds to bring him in for questioning.'

'Does this mean he's the killer?' Zoe said.

'I don't know,' Isabel replied. 'But it would mean the two of them had some kind of relationship … something that Allwood has strenuously denied. Let's get him in, see what he has to say for himself.'

Chapter 32

Lucas decided to get out of the station before his cousin arrived. He'd made contact with Hayley Carter and was now on his way to Derby to meet her at her place of work. The office building she worked in was close to the velodrome and Pride Park Stadium. The latter was familiar territory for Lucas, who regularly attended Derby County matches with his dad.

Hayley was employed by a firm of accountants and she met Lucas in the reception area, where they settled down for a chat in the comfortable waiting area. She was a tall, solidly built woman in her early thirties.

'I must confess I was intrigued by your phone call,' she said. 'Why do you want to talk to me about James Derenby? Has he done something wrong?'

Lucas smiled. 'It's a routine inquiry,' he said. 'Someone told us you used to go out with him. We understand James made a nuisance of himself when you split up.'

Hayley frowned. 'That was years ago,' she said. 'We were both ridiculously young at the time. We dated at school, in the sixth form. It was the first serious relationship for both of us.'

'And how long did the relationship last?'

'For about a year.'

'It was you who broke it off, I take it?' Lucas asked.

'Yes, I was conscious we'd both be going off to uni, and I didn't want to tie myself to someone from back home … I wanted to be free to see other people and enjoy life as a student. James went ballistic when I broke up with him. He took it really hard and made a complete tit of himself for several weeks afterwards.'

'In what way was he a tit?' Lucas said, smiling.

'You know … all the usual things,' Hayley replied. 'Hanging around outside my house, following me around the pubs on a Friday night, texting me, trying to call me. When I didn't answer, he called my friends and asked them to talk to me. Basically, he wanted us to get back together. I wasn't interested.'

'Did you report any of this to the police?'

'No. If it had carried on, I might have done – but it all stopped when James and I went off to uni. That seemed to bring him to his senses. I went to Bristol and he studied in York. I think the distance between us must have given him a better perspective. In my first week at uni, he sent me one final text to apologise for his behaviour. I didn't hear from him again after that.'

'Have you seen him since?' Lucas asked.

'I bump into him occasionally. We both still live in Bainbridge and it's a small town, so it's inevitable. When I do see him, it's all good. James and I are fine now.'

'This intense behaviour of his, his inability to let go of a relationship – do you think James could still be like that?'

'How would I know? It's a lifetime ago since he and I were together … people change. I'm married now, have been for nearly ten years. I never think about James. I've no idea what he's like these days. Sorry, but it wouldn't be fair for me to make a judgement based on his behaviour fifteen years ago.'

***

Lucas had never been inside Allwood Confectionery. He'd stood outside the place a few times, an outsider looking in. As a kid, he and his mates had regularly hung around the factory after dark. Security had been lax in those days. There was rarely anyone around to chase them off, or stop them throwing stones at the giant Perspex letters above the main entrance. On one occasion, they'd managed to dislodge the 'w' of Allwood. Laughing, they'd picked it up and run off with it, leaving behind the newly named *Allwood Confectionery.*

'I'm here to speak to James Derenby,' Lucas said now, as he held up his warrant card for the receptionist to inspect. The interior of the building was impressive, if a little old-school. He wondered how much it had changed since his mum and dad had worked there.

James Derenby came out and greeted him, and then took him through to his office. Perhaps it was his imagination, but as he entered the corridor, Lucas thought he could smell the faint, sugary aroma of lemon, strawberry, sour apple … all the tangy flavours Allwoods sweets were famous for.

'I've already given a statement to one of the other officers,' James said, as he sat down at his desk. 'I've spoken to several of your colleagues, actually. I'm not sure what else I can tell you.'

On his way to the factory, Lucas had received some interesting information regarding the whereabouts of James Derenby's car in the early hours of Sunday 8th August.

'We ran your car registration through the ANPR system,' Lucas told him. 'Do you know what that is?'

'Automatic number plate recognition,' James replied. 'I'm a big fan of *Traffic Cops*.'

Lucas nodded. 'If you've watched *Traffic Cops*, you'll know how ANPR works.'

'It flags up stolen vehicles, doesn't it?' said James. 'So that you can intercept them, and stop them?'

'Yep, that's pretty much how it works,' Lucas replied. 'The

cameras also record and store details of all passing vehicles, even if they're not of interest. In certain circumstances, we can access that data for investigative purposes.'

'My car hasn't been stolen.' James smiled nervously. 'And it's all properly insured and taxed.'

'I'm sure it is,' Lucas said. 'I'm not worried about that. What does bother me is why your car was driving in the vicinity of Anna Matheson's house at 1.15 a.m. on Sunday.'

James locked eyes with Lucas, but said nothing.

'What were you doing out at that time, and why were you driving near to Anna's home?'

James lowered his head and examined the backs of his hands, saying nothing.

'Can you answer the question, please, Mr Derenby?'

'Look, there's a simple enough explanation,' James replied, lifting his head and looking Lucas in the eye. 'Anna and I had a minor falling-out at the party, and I wanted to apologise.'

'At one-fifteen in the morning? Couldn't it have waited until the next day?'

James blew air through the side of his mouth. 'I knew I wouldn't be able to sleep, not until she and I had cleared the air. I tried calling her when I got home, but her phone was switched off. The only way I could put things right was to jump in my car and drive round to see her.'

'Why was it so important to you? What had you argued about?'

'I'd made a fool of myself. Again.' James leaned forward and held his head in his hands. 'Even though I told myself I shouldn't, I asked her out. One last-ditch attempt, you know?'

'And that led to an argument, did it?'

He nodded. 'She'd made me promise to stop asking. She'd already made it clear she only saw me as a friend … but I'd had a few drinks at the party, and I felt emboldened. It was stupid, and if I could take it back, I would. Anna told me to get a grip, that I was beginning to creep her out. Those were her last words to me.'

Tears flowed down Derenby's cheeks, but Lucas chose to ignore them.

'So you decided to drive round to her house, to sort things out between you?'

'Yes. I parked on her street and knocked on the door, but there was no answer. The lights were all out, so I assumed she'd gone to bed. I knocked a second time, and a third. I thought she could hear me but was choosing to ignore me. Then I got to thinking that maybe she wasn't there ... that she was with someone else. When I knocked a fourth time, the next-door neighbour stuck his head out of an upstairs window and told me to bugger off. So I did.'

'And you didn't see or speak to Anna?'

'No. Like I say, she wasn't there. Now that I know what happened to her, I'm guessing she may already have been dead.'

'Why didn't you tell us this before?' Lucas said. 'In your statement, you said you went home from the party by taxi. You said nothing about going out again almost immediately.'

'I'd been drinking ... I was over the limit. I wasn't going to drop myself in it, was I?'

'Do you find it hard when women turn you down, Mr Derenby?'

James looked bemused. 'What do you mean by that?'

'Your ex ... Hayley. We understand you made a real nuisance of yourself when she gave you the elbow. She told me you followed her around, waited outside her house, bombarded her with texts.'

'You've spoken to Hayley?' James sounded angry now. 'Why would you do that? Have you got me down as some kind of psycho, or something? Do you think it was me who killed Anna?'

'Did you?'

'No, of course I didn't ... and I'm not a psycho either. I'm thirty-three years old. I've matured a hell of a lot since Hayley and I split up. I was eighteen when I went out with her. She was my first love and I was gutted when we broke up. I behaved like an idiot; I know I did. At the time, I didn't want to accept that it was over … I was convinced I could persuade her to give it another go. I was a prat, OK? Naïve. But I'm not that person anymore.'

'But you must have felt disappointed when Anna told you she didn't want to go out with you?' Lucas said.

'Yes, but I didn't make a nuisance of myself – not with Anna. I cherished the friendship we had. I'd never have done anything to jeopardise it.'

'For the record, then. On the night of the party you're saying you got home, jumped in your car and drove to Anna's house, arriving at approximately 1.15 a.m. You knocked several times, but there was no answer and no lights on. You didn't see her, or speak to her.'

'Yes, that's what happened. You do believe me, don't you?'

Lucas jigged his head from side to side. 'On balance, yes. I'd say you're telling the truth. We'll check with the neighbour, see if he's able to back up your story – but rest assured, if you *are* lying, we will find out.'

Chapter 33

'I don't know how many times I have to say this … I am *not* the father of Anna's baby.'

It was one o'clock, and Dan was in interview room 2 with the DI. Ross Allwood had agreed to come down to the station for a voluntary interview, but he'd turned up with his solicitor in tow. No doubt Faye Allwood had insisted on it.

'You're absolutely certain of that?' Dan said.

'Oh, for pity's sake.' Ross held up his hands, one either side of his ears. 'This is ridiculous. Are you stupid, or what?'

'I'm not stupid, and neither is DI Blood,' Dan said. 'And DNA analysis is rarely wrong.'

'Well, it's wrong on this occasion. If the results of my DNA swab show I'm Benedict Matheson's father, there's been an almighty cock-up on the test.'

'As a matter of fact, we're still waiting for the results of your DNA test,' said Dan.

'In that case,' said the solicitor, 'why is my client here?'

Ross slammed his hands on the desk. 'I've never had a relationship with Anna,' he said. 'So how can I possibly have fathered her child?'

DI Blood had been sitting alongside Dan, observing silently.

When she cleared her throat, Dan knew she was about to intervene.

'To clarify, you're saying that you and Anna never had sexual intercourse?' she said.

'I think you can take that as read,' Ross replied, his voice shrill with anger. 'There's no way the kid is mine. Ergo, Anna and I have never had sex.'

'There are other ways of conceiving these days,' DI Blood said, somewhat flippantly. 'Artificial insemination. IVF.'

'For God's sake! Listen to yourself.' Ross leaned back and folded his arms. His face was red, but he seemed sure of himself. 'I can only conclude that you guys must be desperate to pin her murder on someone … *anyone* … but you ain't gonna to pin it on me.'

The solicitor grunted. 'My client has made it abundantly clear that he was never involved with the victim.'

'Even if I was …' Ross interjected. 'Even if I *am* Benedict's father, what possible reason would I have for killing Anna?'

'We know that she was putting pressure on you to step down from your role at Allwoods,' Dan said.

Ross hissed air through his teeth. 'Get real. Anna wasn't in a position to dictate who did what at Allwoods. My mother and I *own* the company. No one tells us what to do.'

'You have a history of drug use,' said DI Blood. 'Perhaps you've decided to diversify … maybe it's not just sweets you're selling these days. Did Anna find out you've been dealing drugs.'

'This is preposterous … pure conjecture on your part,' the solicitor said. 'My client doesn't have to answer—'

Ross cut him off with a scowl. 'I'll decide whether or not to answer,' he said. 'And for the record, I'm *not* selling drugs. Never have, never will.'

They were interrupted by a knock. Theo's head appeared around the door.

'What is it, DC Lindley,' DI Blood asked, through gritted teeth.

'I need to have a word with you, ma'am? You *and* DS Fairfax.'

Dan questioned the DC with a look.

'It's important,' Theo added. 'I wouldn't interrupt you otherwise.'

Dan smiled apologetically at Ross and his solicitor. 'Let's take a break, gentlemen,' he said. 'We'll resume again shortly. Interview paused at 1.06 p.m.'

***

'This had better be good,' Dan said, when he and DI Blood had joined Theo in the corridor.

'Believe me, sarge, it is. There's someone at the front desk asking to speak to the person in charge of Anna Matheson's murder. He says he's the baby's father.'

Chapter 34

DC Lindley's words had unceremoniously snapped the tenuous link they'd desperately been trying to substantiate. Isabel felt as though she had thrown a dice, landed on a snake, and plummeted back to square one.

She issued instructions that the man at the desk be taken to interview room 4. Once he'd been ushered safely inside, Dan had terminated the interview with Ross Allwood, who had sauntered out to the front desk wearing a sanctimonious, I-told-you-so grin. Isabel was tempted to kick his backside as he left.

'Let's go and see what the daddy-o has to say for himself, shall we?' she said.

'I can't wait,' Dan replied. 'A bit of a turn-up, eh?'

'I'm not sure it is,' she said, irritation pulling at her mouth. 'Perhaps we should have worked it out for ourselves, instead of wasting the budget running DNA tests on Derenby and Allwood.'

When she and Dan settled down at the table in interview room 4, Isabel took the opportunity to scrutinise the man in front of her. She watched his expression carefully, gauging his reaction as Dan cautioned him and explained that the interview would be recorded.

'We understand you've come forward as a result of the media

appeal made earlier today,' Dan said. 'The one asking for Benedict Matheson's dad to get in touch?'

'That's right.'

'So, for the tape, you're saying *you* are the father of Anna Matheson's child?' Isabel said.

'I am. That's what she told me, anyway, and I had no reason to doubt her.'

'Are you willing to provide a sample of your DNA, so that we can confirm your relationship to the baby?' Dan asked.

'Yes, although I don't think there's much doubt.'

The man's face was etched with worry. Even so, he was still a handsome bugger. No doubt about it. It was easy to see why Anna Matheson had been tempted.

'I'd like to start by asking you about the nature of your relationship with Anna,' Isabel said.

Edward Talbot wrapped his arms across his flat stomach, hunched forward and chewed his bottom lip.

'Before we start, can I ask that you keep what I'm about to tell you in confidence?'

'You can ask,' Isabel replied. 'But this is a murder investigation, Mr Talbot. We're not in the business of protecting people's reputations or their marriages, if that's what you're asking us to do.'

Edward ran a hand through his quiff of dark hair.

'This whole thing is a complete nightmare,' he said. 'It's been hard enough hiding things from my wife, but now … now that Anna's been murdered … I don't know what to think, or what to do.'

What was he expecting? Sympathy?

'Perhaps you should have thought about that before you embarked on a relationship with your wife's best friend,' Isabel said. 'As for what you should do … I'd say that's obvious. Benedict Matheson has lost his mother. He needs a parent. If you *are* his dad, you need to step up and take responsibility … unless, of course, you had something to do with Anna's murder.'

Edward flexed his shoulders, thrusting out his chest as if to deflect the accusation.

'Of course I didn't. Do you seriously think I'd be here today if that was the case?'

'Tell us about your relationship with Anna,' Dan said, steering their line of questioning back on track.

Edward's body sagged wearily. He leaned forward, his head in his hands.

'It would be wrong to call it a relationship. It was a one-off thing. A mistake. We both regretted it afterwards and agreed never to mention it again. After it happened, Anna and I tried to avoid each other as much as possible … and then she found out she was pregnant.'

'How did you respond to that news?' Dan asked.

'How do you think?' Edward said, turning his head to one side. 'I was hardly going to crack open the champagne, was I? I'm not proud of it, but I suggested she got a termination.'

'And how did Anna react to that idea?' Isabel asked.

'She refused to even consider it. She was determined to keep the baby, even though the circumstances of its conception couldn't have been much worse. Obviously I wasn't happy, but I had no choice but to accept her decision.'

'But you were unsettled by the situation?' Dan said.

Edward's response was to cast a withering glance in Dan's direction. 'Wouldn't you have been? The scenario couldn't have been more problematic if we'd tried. Anna couldn't hide her pregnancy from Lauren indefinitely, and she couldn't tell my wife the truth … not without scuppering their friendship and destroying my marriage.'

'And you didn't want that to happen?' said Dan. 'You wanted to stay married?'

Scratching his left eyebrow, Edward sighed. 'Lauren isn't the easiest person to live with, but in the main, she and I are happy. We have two daughters … a nice lifestyle. I don't want to ruin that … but, believe me, it will all hit the skids if Lauren finds out I'm Benedict's father.'

'Is it possible your wife has already found out?' Isabel said.

'No.' Edward gave an exaggerated shake of his head. 'Anna and I agreed. She wasn't going to tell anyone, not even her own mother. It was the only way to keep a lid on things. You know what it's like … you tell one person … and even if you swear them to secrecy, there's always a risk they'll blab. The best option – as far as Anna was concerned – was that she'd bring the baby up on her own. She said she didn't want any financial help from me, or any other support for that matter.'

'That must have been a relief for you,' said Isabel, not even trying to hide her sarcasm. 'Regular child support payments would have been difficult to hide from your wife.'

'I did offer, unofficially, to help out with money,' he said. 'Anna told me she didn't want it. She didn't want me involved in the baby's life at all.'

'It can't have been easy for you, not being able to acknowledge your own son,' Dan said, adopting a more sympathetic approach. 'Especially after he was born.'

Edward laced his fingers together and stared at his hands. 'Turning my back on him has been one of the hardest things I've ever had to do. The situation has been complicated by Lauren's eagerness to babysit. She's become genuinely fond of Benedict. I come home from work some days, and there he is … looking at me, with eyes that are just like mine. I've been trying to keep my distance from him. I'm scared of getting too close … of allowing myself to feel anything for him … in case I give myself away.'

'Is it possible your wife has noticed a resemblance between you and the baby?'

He gave a slight shrug. 'I don't think so. It helps that Benedict looks nothing like our own daughters. They take after Lauren's side of the family, so there's been no danger of her spotting a likeness to our own kids. Anyway, Lauren trusts me, and she trusted Anna. It would never enter her head that we might have betrayed her.'

Isabel wondered how people's lives and relationships managed to get so tangled. It wasn't only in the soap operas that these things happened. Real life was messy too.

'How did it happen?' Isabel said. 'You said it was a one-off thing?'

Edward puffed up his cheeks. 'I'd been at work. I came home late and walked in on Lauren and Anna. They were having a girls' get-together. Nibbles and Netflix, kind of thing. The lockdown restrictions hadn't long been lifted, so it was the first time they'd seen each other in a while. They were making the most of it. Lauren had opened a bottle of wine and she was trying to persuade Anna to have a glass. Anna didn't really drink. She never said as much, but I got the feeling she had a problem with booze – or may have had, in the past.'

'But she never actually told you that?'

'No.' Edward shook his head. 'But I'd seen how uncomfortable she was whenever anyone offered her a drink … always quick to turn them down.'

'But she gave in and had a drink with your wife?' Isabel said.

'Yes. Lauren can be very persuasive. Persistent. *"Go on, Anna, just one glass. We're supposed to be enjoying ourselves."'* He imitated his wife's voice. 'I left them to it in the end, but one glass must have led to another.'

'Aye, when someone has a drink problem, that's what tends to happen,' Dan said.

'Anna had come up to our house in her car,' Edward continued, 'and by the time they'd finished drinking, she was in no fit state to drive home. When I went back into the living room, they were giggling and laughing, both of them in a good mood. Lauren asked me to drive Anna home. It was agreed she'd come back to our place the following day to collect her car.'

'Wouldn't it have been easier to let her stay the night at your house?' Dan said. 'From what I've heard, you've got a big enough place. Plenty of spare bedrooms, I'd imagine.'

'It's a pity we didn't do that. If we had, none of this would have happened – but Anna didn't want to put us to any trouble, and we weren't sure whether overnight stays were even allowed at that stage in the lockdown.'

'So you drove her home,' Isabel said.

'Yes. She invited me in, asked if I'd make her a coffee to try and sober her up, and we got talking … I'm sure you can guess the rest. One thing led to another. What can I say? It was stupid. Reckless.'

Isabel tapped her fingers together. 'It could also be considered a motive.'

'A motive? For what?'

'Murder,' she said. 'You didn't want Anna to spill the beans. You've already told us you don't want to jeopardise your marriage. Was Anna threatening to tell Lauren the truth? Is that it? Did you decide to silence her?'

'Whoa! Stop right there,' Edward said. 'I didn't do anything to Anna. I had no reason to. You've got nothing on me – you can't have, because I haven't done anything wrong.'

He was breathing heavily, all the colour drained from his cheeks.

'OK. Then what about your wife, Mr Talbot?' Isabel said. 'Perhaps she uncovered your little secret and decided to take revenge … remove her disloyal friend from the picture.'

'Lauren is many things, but she is *not* a killer,' Edward said, banging the table to make his point. 'Besides, she was looking after Benedict and my daughters. Are you suggesting she committed murder with three children in tow?'

His point was a good one. Isabel had plenty of experience of looking after a gaggle of lively young kids. It made herding cats seem easy. She turned and nodded at Dan, encouraging him to ask his next question.

'I'd now like to clarify your whereabouts on the night Anna disappeared,' he said. 'Your wife told one of our officers that you were in Liverpool at the time. Have you any way of proving that, Mr Talbot?'

'Certainly, I was at a two-day business and sales seminar.'

'Friday and Saturday?' said Dan.

'That's right.'

'And what time did this event finish?'

'About four o'clock on the Saturday, but a few of us had arranged to get together afterwards.'

'For a business meeting?' Dan said. 'Or more of a social thing?'

'A little of both,' Talbot replied. 'We had a meal in a steak house at the Albert Dock. It was called Miller & Carter, I think. We were quite a noisy crowd, so I'm sure the staff there will remember us.'

'And what time did you leave the restaurant?' Dan said.

'I'm not sure.'

'Not to worry.' He made a note of the point. 'They're bound to have CCTV, so the restaurant manager will be able to confirm exactly when you left.'

'It was probably around nine o'clock,' Edward said. 'Most of the gang went on to a bar, but some of us made our way back to the hotel.'

At that time of night, Isabel estimated it would take around two hours to drive from Liverpool to Bainbridge. If Talbot had set off at nine o'clock, he'd have had time to get to Allwoods before the speeches ended.

Dan asked another question. 'Which hotel were you staying at?'

'The Atlantic Tower. It's right near the Liver Building.'

'Is there anyone who can confirm what time you got back to your room?' Dan said.

'I'm sure the hotel has CCTV as well,' Talbot replied. 'And the rooms have those key cards, so there should be some kind of electronic record.'

'Of course.' Dan smiled. 'We'll be checking that, but I thought you might have been with someone … someone who could vouch for you.'

Edward shifted his position and leaned forward in his chair. 'There is someone,' he replied, brushing an imaginary piece of fluff from his sleeve.

'Does this person have a name?'

'Rose. Rose Preedy. She and I walked back to the hotel together.'

'A colleague of yours, is she?'

'An associate. We run into each other from time to time.'

'And how long were you with her … this Rose Preedy?'

'All night.' Edward cleared his throat. 'Right through until breakfast.'

At least he has the decency to look shamefaced, Isabel thought.

Chapter 35

'Quite the womaniser, isn't he?' Dan said, as they headed back up the stairwell to the CID office. They'd left Edward Talbot in the care of the duty officer, who was arranging a DNA swab.

'Some men just can't keep it in their trousers,' Isabel said. 'Having said that, being a serial adulterer isn't a crime … and if Rose Preedy confirms she was with Edward Talbot all night, it puts him in the clear.'

'I'll ask Theo to contact her … see if she's willing to confirm Talbot's alibi.'

'His coming forward as the baby's father has put a massive spanner in the works,' Isabel said, when they reached the top floor. 'In the absence of any obvious motive, I was convinced the question of paternity would be the key to this murder.'

'You could still be right,' Dan said. 'Lauren Talbot might have uncovered her husband's little secret and arranged for someone to bump Anna off.'

'There aren't many people who'd know how to arrange to have someone killed,' Isabel said, casting doubt on the suggestion. 'And paying someone to commit murder doesn't come cheap.'

'No, but the Talbots don't seem to be short of money.'

'OK, fair point. Get someone to check their accounts. Find out if there have been any large withdrawals or payments recently. I think it's unlikely, but we'd better make sure.'

As they crossed the stairwell, Isabel paused.

'Can I ask you something, Dan?'

'Sure,' he said. 'Fire away.'

'Do you think I interfere? Get too involved in a case?'

'Blimey!' Dan grimaced. 'Of all the questions you could have asked, I wasn't expecting that one – and I'm not sure I should give you an answer. I'm on a hiding to nothing if I say the wrong thing.'

'Come on, be honest with me. Do you do think I poke my nose in?'

'I wouldn't say that. I wouldn't dare!' He grinned. 'I do think you like to keep tabs on us, but that's your style, isn't it? It's not necessarily a bad thing.'

'It is as far as the Super's concerned. She says I'm a meddler.'

'Really?' Dan laughed. 'DI Blood, aka The Meddler. It makes you sound like some kind of supervillain, one of Batman's enemies, or something.'

Isabel frowned. 'You're not taking this conversation seriously, are you, Dan?'

'I don't think I need to, boss. Far be it for me to contradict the Super, but you do a good job. I'll admit your presence does sometimes cast a long shadow, but you always know when to step back and let your team get on with things.'

She smiled. 'Thanks, Dan. In that case, I'll carry on doing what I've always done, and that includes ignoring the Super.'

***

When they entered the office, they were met by the smell of freshly brewed coffee. Someone had been over to the café.

'I don't suppose anyone thought to buy me an Americano?' Isabel said, as she breathed in the roasted coffee bean aroma.

'Sorry, boss,' Lucas said, sipping sheepishly from his favourite coffee mug. 'I would have done, but you were in the interview room. I didn't know how long you'd be. Didn't want it to go cold.'

'I could go over and get you one,' Theo said.

'Creep,' Lucas muttered, smirking sideways at his colleague.

'Thanks for the offer, Theo, but there's something I want to discuss with you all, and it can't wait.'

'What's that then, boss?' said Dan, flicking the switch on the kettle on the way back to his desk.

'If Edward Talbot *is* confirmed as Benedict Matheson's father, we're left with a glaring and screamingly urgent question: why is the baby's DNA a match with Lucas?'

'Not surprisingly, I've been wondering the same thing,' Lucas said. 'Perhaps Talbot *thinks* he's the daddy … maybe Anna Matheson *told* him he was … but DNA doesn't lie.'

'Perhaps Anna got it wrong,' Theo said. 'Or maybe, for some reason, she wanted to hide the truth.'

'Until we get the full DNA results back, the only thing we are certain of is that Benedict Matheson is Lucas's first cousin, once removed,' Isabel said.

'Which means Ross Allwood is still in the frame,' said Lucas.

Isabel felt the beginnings of a headache. This case was drifting, ever-changing, pushing them along false trails and forcing them to follow the hazy, shifting scent of shadows.

'We'll find out for definite when we get the test results,' she said. 'But that's going to take at least another twenty-four hours.'

She paused.

'Of course, there is another explanation.'

Another pause.

Lucas shuffled impatiently. 'Go on,' he said.

'If Ross Allwood *isn't* the child's father, we have to consider the possibility that Anna Matheson was *also* your cousin, Lucas.'

Lucas gripped the sides of his chair, arms rigid.

'Are you OK, Lucas?' Dan said.

He nodded.

'What do you reckon?' said Isabel. 'Is it possible?'

'Search me,' Lucas replied, his voice breathless. 'I don't know what to think anymore. I'm losing the plot, if I'm honest.'

'Does your mum ever discuss her family?' Isabel said. 'Could you talk to her? Make some discreet enquiries?'

Lucas frowned bad-temperedly. 'I thought you said not to discuss the case with my family.'

'I'm not asking you to discuss the case. Just to have a casual chat, find out if your mum knows anything about Anna. You don't have to mention the details of the investigation.'

'I'll talk to her,' he said. 'But my mum's not daft. If she gets wind that something's up, she'll give me a right grilling.'

'If that happens, tell her you're not allowed to discuss the case. Orders from the boss.'

'Is it me, or is there suddenly a whole new layer to this investigation?' said Theo. 'It seems like we're questioning the identity of *Anna's* father now.'

'It's definitely something we need to clarify,' Isabel said.

'Christina Matheson told Zoe that Anna's father is dead,' said Dan. 'We know Christina has never married, and that Anna's father wasn't around when she was growing up.'

'Is Zoe with Christina Matheson now?'

'As far as I know, boss.'

'Ring her, Dan. Ask her to talk to Christina … find out if Barry Allwood was Anna's father.'

Chapter 36

Zoe could feel the sun warming her back through the thin cotton T-shirt she was wearing. She was in Christina Matheson's kitchen, sitting by an open window. Instead of ventilating the room with a fresh, cooling breeze, the aperture was bringing in wafts of warm air from the blisteringly hot garden.

Zoe had arrived at the cottage at two o'clock. As she'd approached the front door, she'd glimpsed Christina asleep inside, stretched out on the settee. Peering through the tiny, multi-paned front window, Zoe had watched for a moment, feeling guilt-ridden about barging in and disturbing such a restful scene.

Now, suitably roused, Christina was sitting at the kitchen table, rubbing sleep from her eyes.

'How are you feeling?' Zoe said. 'I'm sorry for waking you. You looked dead to the world.'

She winced at her own choice of words, but Christina didn't appear to have noticed.

'I took a sleeping tablet and it zonked me out,' she said. 'But I can't spend the whole day asleep. It's not going to make my problems go away, is it? They're always going to be there, waiting for me when I wake up. Anna's dead. Nothing's going to change that.'

Zoe stood up and moved over to the shadier side of the kitchen.

'I'll make you a coffee,' she said, holding up the kettle and weighing it in her hand to see how much water it contained. 'That'll wake you up good and proper.'

'Thanks, but I think I'd prefer a cold drink,' Christina said. 'There's a carton of orange juice in the fridge.'

As Zoe retrieved the carton from the fridge door, she could tell straight away it was almost empty. After taking a glass from one of the cupboards, she poured out what was left of the juice. It reached less than an inch from the bottom of the glass.

'Looks like you're fresh out of orange. Do you have anything else? Squash? Any cold cans?'

Christina shook her head. 'I've got nothing in, and I don't know when I'll find the energy to go to the supermarket again.'

'I'll pour you a glass of water. Or, if there's a shop nearby, I can go and get you a few groceries.'

Christina stretched her arms and yawned. 'There's a convenience store on the main road,' she said. 'You know what? I wouldn't mind going out myself. I feel as if I've been cooped up here for days. Some fresh air would do me good.'

'I don't think the air's very fresh, actually,' Zoe said. 'It's absolutely sweltering out there.'

'Even so, I could do with a change of scene. Benedict's fast asleep, but will you listen out for him?'

Zoe found the prospect of more babysitting perturbing. She was still out of her depth when it came to looking after Benedict. How would she cope if he woke up, demanding attention?

'Are you sure you don't want me to go to the shop?' she repeated. 'It's no trouble.'

'Thanks, but I'd like to go myself. I need to get out of here, even if it's only for a few minutes.'

Christina unhooked a canvas shopping bag that was hanging on the back of the door. After opening a drawer, she retrieved her purse and headed into the living room, towards the front of the house.

'I'll get some more juice, and some cold cans,' she said, over her shoulder. 'Is there anything in particular you like? Coke? Fanta? Lemonade?'

'Coke will do fine,' Zoe said. 'Diet Coke.'

She followed Christina into the living room, watching as she closed the door and set off along the front path. Outside, a blackbird was shouting, chink-chink-chink, and there was a distant hum of traffic drifting up from the main road. Other than that, an uneasy calm filled the room. Zoe listened, straining to hear the sound of the baby stirring in his cot but, apart from the low purr of the fridge in the kitchen, the inside of the house was silent.

She wasn't sure why she'd come here this afternoon. There was very little progress to report in terms of the investigation, but she'd felt obliged to check in with Christina, even if it did mean disturbing her sleep.

When Zoe's phone suddenly burst into life, she flinched, fearful the sound would wake Benedict. Stabbing frantically at the screen, she accepted the call to silence the ring tone.

'Zoe? Are you at Christina Matheson's place?'

It was Dan.

'Yes. I got here about ten minutes ago. Why? What's up?'

'We've had a visitor to the station,' Dan said. 'Edward Talbot. He told us he's the baby's father.'

'*What?*' Zoe lowered herself onto the throw-covered settee. 'You're kidding me?'

'You know I never make jokes about an investigation, Zo. We've taken a DNA sample to be sure, but the man's adamant he's the daddy.'

'I'm guessing Lauren Talbot doesn't know about this?'

'No, and of course Talbot was keen for us to treat what he's told us in confidence.'

'I'll bet he was.'

'The thing is,' Dan said, 'if the DNA does confirm his paternity, it raises another massive question …'

'Why does Benedict Matheson have a DNA match with Lucas?' Zoe said, finishing the sentence for him.

'Exactly. We're working on the premise that Anna Matheson may also be Lucas's cousin. If she was, there's a good chance Barry Allwood was Anna's father.'

'Surely Christina would have told me, if that was the case?' Zoe said. 'Why would she keep something like that to herself?'

'Force of habit, maybe,' Dan replied. 'Whatever her reasons, I need you to talk to her about it. Now.'

'Of course. She's nipped out to the shop, but she won't be long. I'll speak to her as soon as she gets back and I'll let you know what she says.'

As she ended the call, Zoe let out a long, panicky breath. Had she messed up? Would the DI give her a bollocking for not finding this out earlier? And if Barry Allwood was Anna's father, why hadn't Christina said anything? Did she not realise the potential significance of that kind of information?

Zoe chastised herself for not questioning Christina more thoroughly, or pressing harder for information about Anna's father. If what they suspected was true, it put a whole new spin on the investigation and could completely alter their interpretation of the case.

Chapter 37

The sticky summer heat clung to Christina's arms as she walked down the hill. The air was heavy with humidity, the atmosphere charged as though a storm was building. From the main road came the noise of heavy traffic, droning in her ears. It was the holiday season, and people were driving up to Matlock Bath to ride the cable cars and eat ice creams and fish and chips.

It felt good to be out of the house, where the cloying, inescapable reality of Anna's death seemed to have seeped into the walls of every room. As she walked, Christina thought about Anna, and Benedict, and the events of the last few days. Why hadn't she told the detective everything about Anna's job, and about who her father was? These pieces of information could be important. She should divulge them. It was foolish to keep that kind of information to herself.

The thing was, she'd practised the art of silence and secrecy for so long now that it had become a way of life. There were certain facts she chose to keep hidden … not because she was ashamed of them, but because they were no one's business but her own. Or, at least, they never used to be.

But what if that was no longer the case? What if her long-held secret was the key to unlocking the answers to her daughter's murder?

DC Piper seemed like a nice enough young woman, a little unsure of herself perhaps, and a tad awkward in her approach – but Christina sensed that the girl had a good heart. She felt that Zoe was someone she could confide in. It was time to talk to her, to open up.

A bell jangled loudly above her head as she entered the shop. Behind the door, an oscillating fan blew clammy air along the central aisle where Tony, the proprietor, was stacking shelves. As she walked past him on her way to the cold drinks fridge, he gave her arm a sympathetic squeeze and offered his condolences.

Was this how it was going to be from now on? People regarding her with sad eyes and a pained expression? Everything she did tainted by shock and loss?

She stumbled to the end of the shop, pulled open the fridge door, and grabbed a large bottle of Diet Coke and two cartons of orange juice. As she passed the ice-cream freezer she stopped and lifted the lid. A blissful blast of cold air escaped. Christina plunged an arm inside and picked up two white chocolate Magnums. One for her, one for the detective.

The chilled goods cooled her body as she carried them to the checkout. She waited in silence as Tony scanned her purchases, dropping them one by one into her cotton bag.

As she presented her debit card to the contactless reader, she felt dizzy. Perhaps it was the act of doing something ordinary and routine that felt off – but all of a sudden, everything felt wrong. Horribly wrong. Being there, shopping for ice creams and fizzy drinks seemed like an inane thing to be doing. Then again, what *was* the protocol when your child had been murdered? Were you supposed to stay indoors behind drawn curtains? Were you expected to lose your appetite for ice cream?

Feeling anxious and slightly sick, Christina hurried out into the street. Beneath her feet, the pavement was soft, as though the tarmac was beginning to melt. Heat radiated through the soles of her flimsy sandals, into her legs, which felt unexpectedly weak and incapable of carrying her the short distance home.

Inexplicably, she thought back to the summer of 1985, to the day of the Live Aid concert. Anna had been a couple of months old, and Christina had pushed her in the pram to the shop to buy ice cream, ready for the concert, which was due to start at noon. As she'd wheeled the pram along the pavement, staring down into the face of her precious child, she had failed to notice the tall man walking towards her. Anna's father.

He'd stopped and talked to her for a minute, asked how she'd been, what she was up to. When he peered beneath the parasol that was shading the baby's face from the sun, he was unaware that he was looking at his own child. The way Anna had smiled back up at him had felt like a betrayal.

That was the one and only time he'd seen Anna as a child.

Christina had been under no illusion that their fleeting relationship had been anything more than a flirtation. The guy was already taken, and Christina knew she could never compete.

That afternoon in 1985, Christina had gone home and eaten a whole tub of raspberry ripple ice cream as she watched Live Aid. Anna, who had been such a grisly, sicky baby, chose to sleep for hours that day. Perhaps she sensed that her mother wanted to listen to the concert, or maybe her encounter with her father had cast a calming spell on her for a while.

Fast forward thirty-six years, and Christina couldn't comprehend that she would never see Anna, her grown-up baby, again. Gripped by an overwhelming urge to get home, she increased her pace and stumbled, dismembered by grief. Visiting the shop had been a mistake. She should have let the detective come instead.

Her heart ached as memories of Anna fluttered around in her head. As she dashed across the road, a suffocating wave of sorrow hit her at the same time as a car that was hurtling along the A6 on its way to Matlock. The impact threw Christina's body into the air. She landed with a muffled thud on the other side of the road, along with her cotton bag, which was still looped over her arm.

Its contents spilled out around her. The bottle of Coke rolled into the road, pressure fizzing within it, and the ice creams, smashed and broken, began to melt in the afternoon sun.

Chapter 38

Christina had promised she would be no more than five minutes, but she'd already been gone for quarter of an hour. If she didn't come back soon, there was a chance the baby would wake up and Zoe would have to step in again and do something ... pick him up, sing to him. Do whatever it was you were supposed to do with five-month-old babies.

From somewhere in the distance came the wail of a siren, the sound increasing as it got nearer. She listened, one ear on the siren, the other straining to hear a noise from upstairs.

What if she had to change the baby's nappy? That would certainly be a first. Not a pleasant task, but she would manage, wouldn't she? It couldn't be that difficult.

As the howl of the siren reached its crescendo, Zoe crossed her fingers and hoped Benedict would sleep through it. She waited, expecting the sound to fade as the emergency vehicle continued along the main road, below the cottage. But instead of moving on, the vehicle seemed to have stopped. Something must have happened on the busy A6. Had Christina witnessed an accident? Is that what was delaying her return?

As a police officer, Zoe's first instinct was to go out and investigate, but she couldn't leave Benedict on his own.

She listened again for any sound of movement from the cot upstairs, wondering if the siren had woken him. Nothing. Creeping up onto the landing, she peered into the small back bedroom. The baby lay with his arms above his head. Asleep. Fast asleep.

After tiptoeing back down the stairs, Zoe went out through the front door, and down the path to the garden gate. From there, she could make out the flash of a blue light. Another siren approached from the direction of Derby. Two emergency vehicles. Ambulance. Police.

As Zoe headed back into the house, worry began to burrow beneath her skin. In the kitchen, she picked up her phone from the table and rang through to the station control room. The call was answered on the second ring.

'It's DC Piper here,' she said. 'I'm in Milford, and there appears to have been an incident on the A6. What can you tell me about it?'

***

Zoe was still sitting at the kitchen table when DI Blood contacted her a few minutes later.

'I heard about Christina Matheson,' the DI said. 'Are you OK, Zoe?'

'It's really shaken me up,' she said, her fingers trembling as she held the phone to her ear. 'She went out for some cold drinks. She was only meant to be gone for a few minutes.'

'I'd like you to go to the hospital to check on her condition,' DI Blood said.

'What about the baby? I can't leave him on his own. Shall I call Lauren Talbot, see if she'll come over and look after him?'

'Given what we've learned about the child's paternity, I don't think that would be wise. I've asked a patrol car to come over to relieve you while we work something out. Anna's son may have to go into foster care until Christina recovers …'

'*If* she recovers,' Zoe said. 'The control room spoke to one of the paramedics. Christina's condition is critical, but stable. She's unconscious, with multiple broken bones and a possible fractured skull. I'd have gone down to the road to see for myself, if it wasn't for Benedict.'

'Are you OK with him?' said the DI. 'I know you haven't had a lot of experience with children.'

'He's asleep at the moment,' she said, one ear cocked to the ceiling. 'Let's hope it stays that way until the cavalry arrives.'

'Did you manage to speak to Christina before her accident? About whether Barry Allwood was Anna's father?'

'No, sorry, boss. She was pretty groggy when I first arrived. She'd taken a sleeping pill and I'd woken her up – that's why she insisted on going to the shop … to get some fresh air. Dan didn't ring me until after she'd left. I was going to ask the question as soon as she got back.'

On the other end of the line, the DI released a sigh.

'That's unfortunate. A case of bad timing I guess.'

'I'm sorry, boss. I feel as though I've let you down.'

'Not at all, Zoe. It's hardly your fault that Christina's had an accident.'

Zoe swallowed to clear her throat. 'I hope it was an accident,' she said. 'You don't think someone could have run her down on purpose?'

'No.' DI Blood's reply was firm and swift. 'I called and spoke to the officer on the scene. The car that ran her down was driven by a middle-aged man from Leicestershire. He and his wife were on their way up to Ashford-in-the-Water for a short break. They're saying that Christina walked straight out in front of them. They're pretty cut up about it, by all accounts.'

'Well, that's something of a relief,' Zoe replied. 'I was concerned it might be a hit and run.'

'Given the investigation into Anna Matheson's murder, you're right to be suspicious.'

As she listened to the DI, Zoe heard a sound from upstairs, a cross between a gurgle and a grizzle.

'Uh-oh, I think the baby's woken up,' she said, feeling suddenly inadequate.

'Don't worry, Zoe. All you need to do is pick him up and give him a cuddle.'

'You make it sound easy,' Zoe said. 'The trouble is, I'm not sure he likes me.'

'What's not to like?'

Zoe smiled, calming herself. The DI was right. There was nothing to be afraid of. People looked after babies all the time. How hard could it be?

'You'll be fine,' DI Blood added. 'Just try not to drop him.'

Chapter 39

Dan wandered into Isabel's office as she put the phone down.

'I've just been told about Christina Matheson,' he said. 'What's the latest?'

'Still unconscious. I've asked Zoe to go over to the hospital. She'll let us know if there's any change.'

'Did she get chance to talk to her, before the accident?'

'No. Unfortunately not.'

Moving aside the ever-present pile of box files from the chair opposite her desk, Dan sat down.

'I hope Ms Matheson's going to be OK,' he said. 'Otherwise that little lad will be left with no one to look after him.'

A sombre silence descended.

'You don't think …'

'What?' Isabel said.

'That she stepped out in front of the car on purpose?'

Isabel ran a finger along her right eyebrow. Strange that Zoe had been worried about it being a possible hit and run, whereas Dan was more concerned about the possibility of suicide.

'I doubt it,' she said. 'Zoe said that Christina had been asleep and had gone out to clear her head. Her mind would have been on other things, Dan, plus the temperature's pretty intense and energy-sapping today. I'm sure she was distracted, that's all. Not paying attention.'

Dan nodded, accepting her interpretation of events. 'We've been taking another look at the CCTV footage of the factory exterior. On the day of the party, Ross Allwood's car was driven in through the main gate at four-thirty in the afternoon. Faye Allwood's car arrived just before five o'clock.'

'There's nothing unusual in that, is there? They probably got there early to help set up … make sure everything was going to plan.'

'True. Anna Matheson arrived even earlier at four-fifteen. The only thing of note with the Allwoods is that they both parked their cars around the far side of the building, not in the main staff car park. I spoke to the receptionist, and she said Ross often parks there and uses the side door to get into his office, rather than coming through the main entrance at the front.'

'We know Faye Allwood drove home after the party,' Isabel said. 'Any sign of her car on camera later in the evening?'

'No. No other sign of her vehicle on CCTV that day,' Dan replied. 'She said she left the party around midnight, and that she went out through the rear exit. As you know, the cameras don't cover that area.'

'And Ross Allwood?'

'He left with one of the employees … an Evie Browell. The cameras confirm that. He and Evie left through the front entrance at 12.34 a.m., along with another woman. They walked round to the staff car park, got into Mrs Browell's car and went out through the front gate.'

'And James Derenby? What time did he get to the party?'

'At five-fifteen, in a taxi. Again, the footage confirms that.'

'So by five-fifteen, the victim was inside the factory with the Allwoods, and Derenby. Anybody else?'

'The caterers had arrived by then. The DJ didn't turn up until quarter to seven.'

'And what time did the party start?'

'Seven-thirty, at least officially, but people started to arrive from seven onwards. Most of them hung around the front of the building initially, supping cans of beer and chatting.'

'A pre-party gathering, eh?' Isabel smiled. 'Necking miniature bottles of vodka no doubt, getting themselves into the party spirit.'

'It's cheaper than buying drinks at the bar.' Dan grinned. 'And the measures are always a lot more generous.'

'Did Anna, the Allwoods or Derenby join in with this pre-party frivolity?'

'There's no sign of them on the footage. I'd imagine they were inside, finalising the last-minute preparations.'

'Having seen the guest list, I'd estimate there were around a hundred people at the party,' Isabel said. 'In theory, any one of them could be responsible for Anna's disappearance and subsequent murder.'

'Yeah,' Dan said, 'but what's your gut telling you?'

'That it was all carefully planned. The way she disappeared, the way her body was disposed of – there was nothing improvised about any of that. Someone had thought everything through in advance. The question is, who?'

Chapter 40

Lucas had sloped off early. Since finding out about the DNA match with Benedict Matheson, he'd been unable to concentrate on anything, especially those bloody CCTV images. His eyes were tired and his mind distracted – not the best combination when you're scanning hours of grainy footage.

There was no denying, he felt differently about the case now … now that he knew he and Anna were related. OK, so he'd never met her, but she was still his flesh and blood, right? It was distressing to think that someone within his family had become the victim of murder. Despite the muggy, cumulative heat of the day, he felt chilled and shaky.

Instead of walking straight home, Lucas found himself turning in the opposite direction. Bainbridge was known for being hilly, and the street he was climbing now was one of its steepest. It led up and over to the other side of town and his parents' house.

He would follow the DI's instructions and have a chat with them. A *casual* chat, being careful not to reveal any details about the case, factual or speculative.

He stripped off his jacket as he walked, hooked it onto his index finger and threw it over his shoulder. Even now, at almost five o'clock in the afternoon, the heat was stifling and the air heavy and claustrophobic. It normally took less than fifteen minutes to walk to his parents' house from the station, but the scorching temperatures slowed him down.

It was twenty past five when he finally arrived at his parents' 1930s semi-detached home, the house he'd grown up in. Five years ago, his mum and dad had seriously considered moving, but in the end they'd decided to stay put and build an extension. Lucas thought it ironic that they'd opted to enlarge the house only after he and his brother had finally moved out.

Growing up, he'd found the cramped house oppressive and overcrowded. As a teenager, the complete lack of privacy and elbow room at home, combined with his mum's mild but constant nagging, had driven Lucas out onto the streets. Regardless of the weather, he and his mates had hung around at the park, under bus shelters, or on street corners – any place that gave them the freedom to be their boisterous, stupid selves, where they could laugh and shout and sneak the odd bottle of cider. During those years, Lucas had been desperate to escape the confines of home. It was only after he left that he realised how much he missed the place. He loved going back there now: being fussed over by his mum, and sharing a beer with his dad in the man cave, aka the garden shed.

When he let himself into the kitchen through the back door, the smell of fried onions and sausages hit him like a wave, and he was unable to stop his stomach from growling loudly.

His mum was standing at the hob, pushing sizzling onions around a pan with a wooden spoon. When she heard the door open, she turned and smiled at him.

'Ey up, Lucas,' she said, her voice warm, and sweet as melted caramel. 'What are you doing here?'

'Thought I'd drop by, see if Dad was firing up the barbecue this evening.'

Karen Killingworth turned off the gas under the pan and moved it to the back of the hob. 'I was hoping he would, but he says he can't be bothered. Reckons it's too hot.'

'Too hot?' Lucas pulled a face. 'What's up with him? This is perfect barbecuing weather.'

'I agree, but you know what he's like.' She shrugged. 'I'm doing hot dogs instead, and we're going to sit outside and eat them. I must admit, it's quicker than waiting for your dad to light the charcoal.'

'Did I hear my name?' Mark Killingworth had entered the kitchen from the hallway. 'Ey up, son. What're you up to?'

'I was hoping for some free snap,' Lucas said. 'But Mum says you're refusing to light the barbie.'

Mark screwed up his face. 'It's too bloody hot to be slaving over a barbecue. I'm at melting point as it is.'

'Lightweight,' Lucas said.

'Don't worry, duck, you'll get your free snap,' Karen told him. 'We've got plenty of cobs, and I'll stick some more sausages on the grill. Grab yourselves a cold beer and I'll bring the hot dogs out in a few minutes.'

Carrying an ice-cold can of Marston's Pedigree each, Lucas and his dad stepped outside and wandered down to the far end of the garden, to the pergola Mark had built during the previous year's lockdown.

'It's not like you to turn up mid-week,' Mark said, when they'd made themselves comfortable on the outdoor furniture.

'I finished early today. Thought I'd swing by.'

'You're welcome any time, you know that,' Mark said, as he snapped the ring-pull on his beer. 'How's work?'

'All right. You know, same old same old.'

Mark narrowed his eyes and took a swig of his Pedigree. 'Is it though?' he said. 'Your mum and I were watching the news the other night … I understand a woman's disappeared from Allwoods.'

'She's since been found,' Lucas said. 'Or, rather, her body has. It's a murder investigation now.'

'Bloody hell, son.' Mark pulled a face. 'That's horrendous. What happened?'

Lucas placed the cold can against his temple. 'You know I can't discuss an ongoing investigation. The Allwoods connection has already made things awkward.'

'How come?'

'I had to tell my DI that I was related to Ross Allwood.'

'Why? You don't even know him. I hope your boss isn't keeping you off the case because you're related to that bugger.'

'I'm still on the case, just taking more of a back seat. I don't mind. I wouldn't want to do anything to jeopardise the investigation.'

'You don't think Ross could be involved, do you?' Mark said, stony-faced.

'Don't ask me questions I can't answer, Dad.'

'Can't answer because you're not allowed to? Or can't answer because you don't know?'

Lucas was saved from replying by the arrival of his mum. In one hand she was carrying a huge serving plate piled high with hot dogs, in the other she held a bowl of fried onions.

'I'll go and fetch the salad and some plates,' she said. 'Do you want mustard, Lucas?'

'You sit down, Mum. I'll go in and get the rest of the stuff.'

'Cheers, duck,' she said, rearranging a cushion on the rattan sofa. 'Can you bring some paper napkins as well, and a beer for me?'

***

Lucas came back carrying a tray. On it, he'd balanced a bowl of colourful salad, some napkins and cutlery, a squeezy bottle of American mustard, and four more cans of Pedigree. When he placed it on the table in front of his mum, he could tell from her solemn expression that she knew about the murder.

'Your dad's been telling me about the woman who disappeared from Allwoods,' she said, before he'd had chance to sit down again. 'I can't believe she's been found dead.'

Lucas bought himself some time by silently placing two of the hot dogs on a plate, piling on some onions and trailing a zigzag of bright yellow mustard across the top.

'We saw Christina Matheson making the appeal on the news,' Karen continued. 'We knew her years ago. That poor woman. I can't begin to imagine what she must be going through.'

He wondered how they'd known Christina Matheson, and what the hell his mum would think if she knew the victim could be her niece. He was tempted to say something – *very* tempted – but he'd promised the boss he'd keep his mouth shut.

'Come on, then,' Karen said. 'Are you going to tell us what's been happening down at the factory?'

Lucas sat down. 'We don't know what's happened,' he said, his voice subdued. 'Even if we did, you know I can't talk about it.'

'It's terrible though, isn't it?' Karen persisted. 'It's hard to believe something like this has happened here in Bainbridge, never mind at the factory. My dad would be spinning in his grave if he knew.'

'Your dad was cremated,' Mark said.

Karen nudged her husband's arm. 'Shush, you. It's a figure of speech. Be quiet and let Lucas tell us about Christina's daughter.'

'Leave it, love,' Mark said. 'Like he said, he's not allowed to talk about it.'

'Sorry, Mum.' Lucas sat up. 'Dad's right. But if *you* know anything useful about Christina or Anna, I'd be interested to hear it.'

'We know nothing, son,' Mark said. 'We didn't know Anna, and although we knew Christina, it was years ago, before you were born. We haven't seen her since.'

A dribble of mustard landed on Lucas's chin as he bit into his hot dog.

'Where do you know Christina from?' he asked, wiping his face with one of the napkins.

'She worked at the factory when we were there,' Karen said. 'I

213

didn't know her very well. She was on the shop floor and I was in the offices. Your dad knew her a lot better than I did.'

Mark shook his head. 'Only casually.'

Karen smiled. 'It's all right, you don't have to be coy. I know you and half the male employees were besotted with her. Christina was a lovely-looking woman. An absolute stunner.'

'Nah.' Mark winked. 'Not a patch on you, love.'

Karen gave him a disbelieving smile as she opened her can of beer. 'It's sweet of you to say so, and very loyal, but you don't have to pretend. Christina was beautiful, and I know you made a play for her. Admit it. It's absolutely fine … it's not as if we were going out with each other at the time.'

Mark was beginning to look uncomfortable. Reaching forward, he spooned onions onto a hot dog. 'I never made a play for her, as you put it. I'll admit she was a looker, but she was too airy-fairy for my liking … a bit of a hippy. Plus, I was about twenty at the time, and I didn't know how to talk to girls back then. I wouldn't have stood a chance.'

Karen laughed. 'Thinking about it, you were a bit useless, and hopelessly tongue-tied. It took you months to pluck up the courage to ask me out.'

Mark grimaced. 'That's because I was scared shitless about what your dad would say.'

Lucas had heard their romantic reminiscences so many times he knew the story off by heart. Before they launched into yet another retelling of their hilarious first date, he decided to intervene.

'Going back to Christina Matheson,' he said. 'Do you know if she went out with anyone at the factory?'

'Not that I know of,' Mark said. 'She was quite flirtatious, but I think that was just her way. In my opinion, she wasn't the sort to get involved with one of her co-workers. She was a dreamer with big ideas, at least it seemed that way to me. She upped and left one day, didn't even bother working her notice. We all assumed she'd moved on to bigger and better things.'

214

'She's aged well,' Karen said, straightening her own greying hair with her fingers. 'When I saw her on the news, I recognised her immediately. My heart went out to her. No one should have to deal with their child disappearing, let alone being murdered. It doesn't bear thinking about.'

'As a matter of fact, Christina Matheson is in hospital now,' Lucas said. 'She was involved in an accident this afternoon ... knocked down by a car.'

Karen opened her mouth, and covered it with her hand.

'Bloody hell,' Mark said. 'It never rains, does it? Is she going to be all right?'

'I'm not sure. She's still unconscious,' Lucas replied.

They lapsed into silence, each of them staring into mid-air, lost in their own thoughts. Lucas felt awkward. He'd promised the DI he'd do some digging, but he knew how reticent his mum could be when it came to talking about her family. When he and his brother were young, they'd always got short shrift whenever they plucked up the courage to ask questions. As kids, they had felt cheated by the lack of contact with their uncle – not because they were interested in him as a person, but because they would have liked access to free confectionery from the factory. Whenever Lucas had spent any of his precious pocket money on sweets, he avoided buying anything produced by Allwoods on principle. He'd refused to pay for something that, by rights, he should have got for free.

'I know you don't like talking about your family, Mum,' he said now, 'but there's something I need to ask you.'

Karen placed the hot dog she was holding back onto her plate and wiped her fingers. 'Go on,' she said.

'This question may seem like it's coming out of left field, but is there any chance Christina Matheson had a relationship with Barry Allwood?'

At the mention of her brother's name, his mum's expression closed up.

'Why are you asking that?'

'Don't clam up on me, Mum. Please, answer the question.'

'Not that I'm aware of,' she replied, pushing her plate into the centre of the table. 'But it's not impossible. Barry was always a cocky sod when it came to women, even after he was married.'

'Are you saying he had affairs?'

Karen held up a hand to fend off the question. 'I suspect so, but I don't know for sure. How would I? Barry and I were never close.'

'But you were working at the factory at the time,' Lucas said, pressing on doggedly. 'Surely you would have heard if there'd been any gossip … rumours that Barry and Christina were in a relationship.'

'*I* never heard any mention of it,' Mark said.

'Me neither,' said Karen. She looked annoyed, as though Lucas was intruding into forbidden territory. 'You never knew your uncle. He was a sneaky bastard, so if he was going to conduct an affair, I'm sure he would have been careful to keep it under wraps. Mind you, in fairness to him, he was far too young when he married Faye. If you ask me, he should have spent a few more years sowing his wild oats … got it all out of his system.'

'So why didn't he? Why did he tie himself down if he wasn't ready?'

'It was the Eighties,' Mark said. 'A lot of people married young back then. Not like you lot these days … waiting until you're in your thirties, or not bothering to get married at all.'

'He was also under pressure from your grandad,' Karen said. 'Dad was friends with Faye's father, Tom Middlechurch. Tom was rolling in it, and there was an unspoken agreement that he'd invest in Dad's business after the wedding.'

'Bloody hell.' Lucas screwed up his nose. 'Barry married Faye for money? That's a bit crass, isn't it?'

'Don't get me wrong, that wasn't the only reason he married her,' Karen said. 'The two of them were well suited, and they'd known each other since their late teens. The arrangement suited everyone, including my brother and his cow of a wife.'

Mark reached across and squeezed her arm. 'Don't get yourself worked up, love. That's all in the past.'

'That's as may be, Mark, but she was the one who did me out of my inheritance.' Pulling her arm away, Karen reached for her drink. 'I'm sure Barry would have played fair, if it hadn't have been for my self-seeking sister-in-law.'

'If Faye's dad pumped a lot of money into the factory, maybe she was trying to protect her family's investment,' Lucas said.

His mum silenced him with a glare.

'Sorry,' Lucas said. 'I don't like having to stir all this up. The fact is, I promised my boss I'd ask the question.'

'If your boss wants to know something then maybe she should ask me herself,' Karen said. 'You know I don't like revisiting the past, Lucas. There are too many emotional wounds, which is why I stepped away from it all a long time ago. If I hadn't, I'd have spent the rest of my adult life feeling hard done by and resentful. Life's too short for all that crap.'

'Is that all your boss wanted to know?' Mark asked. 'Whether Christina was having an affair with Barry?'

Lucas took a deep breath. How the hell did the boss expect him to get any answers if he wasn't allowed to share any details of the case? Sod it. If he couldn't trust his mum and dad, then who could he trust?

'She wanted to know whether they'd had an affair,' Lucas said. 'And whether there's any chance Barry could have made her pregnant.'

'What?' Karen slammed her beer can on the table top. 'Are you serious?'

'Calm down, Mum. I'm following up a line of inquiry, that's all.'

'Line of inquiry?' said Mark. 'Bloody hell, son. It's not just the sausages that are getting a grilling round here this evening, is it?'

Lucas shrugged, unapologetic.

Karen's face began to crumple as the implication of Lucas's question sank in. 'Do the police think the girl who was killed was Barry's daughter?'

He'd already said too much, but this was his mum. He'd never lied to her, and he wasn't going to start now.

'It's a possibility, yes.'

'Oh, God.' Karen put her head in her hands. 'This is unbelievable.'

'How sure are you about this?' Mark said, his face pale. 'What evidence do you have?'

'You know I can't talk about that.'

'Come on, son. Play the game. You can't come round here and drop that kind of bombshell without giving us the facts. It's not fair on your mum.'

'I'm sorry, Dad. I can't talk about it … and you mustn't tell anyone about it either. You'll get me in trouble if you do.'

Karen was nodding distractedly, staring off into the mid-distance.

'Looking back, it *was* strange … the way Christina left so suddenly,' she said. 'She was there one minute, gone the next. As far as I know, she didn't work her notice or say goodbye to anyone – but that would make sense if she and Barry had been having an affair, wouldn't it? If she got pregnant, it would have been like him to pay her off.'

'Being brutally honest,' said Mark, 'it's more likely Barry would have asked her to get rid of it … the baby, I mean. Given her money to go away and sort it.'

'What about her job?' Lucas said. 'Surely he wouldn't have sacked her, taken away her livelihood because it didn't suit him to have her around anymore?'

'Your uncle would have seen her right,' Mark said. 'He would have given her some dosh … told her to go and get a job elsewhere.'

'We don't know that,' Karen said, her tone suddenly defensive. 'Me and my brother never got on, but he's dead and it's not fair to accuse him of things he can't defend himself against. Everything we've said is pure speculation. If I had to stand up in a court of law, all I could say for sure is that Christina left Allwoods very suddenly. I wasn't aware that she and Barry were an item, and I had no reason to suspect she was pregnant. Do you agree, Mark?'

Mark shrugged. 'Yes, I guess that about sums it up,' he said. 'Sorry, son, but we're not in a position to confirm or deny anything.'

Chapter 41

Zoe had been kept waiting at the hospital for what seemed like a preposterously long time. With each minute that passed, she grew increasingly convinced that someone would march out into the corridor and give her bad news.

When she'd first arrived, she'd been told that Christina was still unconscious, having sustained a severe bang to the head – and the doctors were concerned about a possible bleed on the brain. Since then, there had been no further updates. Nothing.

Sitting on a hard plastic chair in the waiting area, she watched the creeping hands of the wall clock and thought about Will Rowe. He'd been one of the officers dispatched to relieve her of childcare duties at Christina Matheson's cottage. When Zoe had spotted him walking up the path, she'd felt a warm glow, and an overwhelming sense of relief. She told herself she was glad to see him because he'd do a good job of looking after Benedict Matheson until someone from social services took over. Deep down, though, Zoe knew there was more to her reaction than she cared to admit. She admired Will's kindness, his strength, and the warmth of his smile. Plus, there was the added bonus that he seemed to like her. Did she like him as well? Fancy him? Was that it?

By six o'clock, her thoughts returned to Benedict Matheson, who truly was the cutest, most gorgeous baby she'd ever met – although admittedly she hadn't encountered many. What would happen if Christina failed to regain consciousness? Would Edward Talbot step forward, do the decent thing and take responsibility for his son? Was there anyone else that the court could appoint as his guardian? Or would little Benedict end up being taken care of by 'the system', passed from foster home to foster home, or adopted, his name changed? Zoe reflected on how a few catastrophic moments had the potential to alter the course of a person's life forever. She found the prospect terrifying.

Hunger was gnawing at her stomach, but she didn't want to go off in search of a vending machine in case she missed the doctor when he or she finally appeared. Slipping her hand into the pocket of her jacket, she felt around for a packet of chewing gum – but her fingers closed on something else instead. Something hard and rough. The citrine crystal.

She pulled it out and examined it. The faceted tip was the deep gold of Chardonnay wine, the colour soaking into the rougher, sharper root of the rock, which was white, like compacted ice. Zoe squeezed the crystal in her palm. Was it her imagination, or could she feel it pulsating, pumping energy into her hand and up her arm? What had Christina Matheson called it? *A manifesting stone.* She'd said the stone encouraged optimism and reduced negativity.

Zoe closed her eyes and allowed herself to believe in the crystal's power. She told herself to be optimistic about Christina Matheson's recovery, visualising her back at her cottage, standing in the flower-filled garden holding a happy, smiling Benedict.

That's what she was thinking when the door on her right swung open and a doctor emerged.

Chapter 42

As she switched off her computer, Isabel glanced at her phone. She'd been hoping all day that Nathan or Bailey would get in touch, but there had been no messages. Usually, she received a regular supply of texted trivia from her husband and kids. Today – the day when she actually *wanted* to hear from them – there was nothing. Zilch.

She was desperate to know whether Bailey had attended the interview at Allwoods, and annoyed that no one had bothered to keep her in the loop. She could understand why Bailey was giving her the silent treatment, but Nathan could have updated her, couldn't he?

As she left her office, she called across to Dan, who was at his desk, putting down his phone.

'I'm going home. See you in the morning.'

'Hang on, boss, you'll want to hear this before you go.' He beckoned her over. 'Digital Forensics have sent some info over. They've downloaded Anna's electronic calendar, which was synced between her phone and laptop.'

'Her personal calendar?'

'Yep,' Dan said. 'It shows she had an appointment with a

solicitor scheduled for two days after the party. I've just got off the phone to the law firm.'

'And?'

'Anna had arranged to meet their specialist in inheritance and family law.'

'Do they know what she wanted to discuss?'

'Unfortunately not. The appointment was made through the office manager, so the solicitor never actually spoke to Anna. All the manager could tell me was that Anna was after some advice on inheritance laws. If Anna *was* Barry's daughter, she may have been planning to make a claim on the estate. She could even have been after part-ownership of the factory.'

Isabel frowned pensively. 'If she was Allwood's daughter – and that's still a big *if* – there may have been grounds for her to make a claim on the basis that she hadn't been left a reasonable financial provision. But Barry Allwood died in December, didn't he? If she was planning to challenge the will, why wait so long?'

'I don't know,' Dan said. 'But the fact that she had an appointment lined up with a lawyer two days after the works party has got to be more than a coincidence. Didn't she tell James Derenby there were going to be big changes?'

Isabel nodded. 'Perhaps this is what she meant.'

'Ross and Faye Allwood wouldn't have been happy if they found out Anna was planning to challenge the will. If she'd succeeded, they would have lost out big time.'

'Ask one of our legal eagles to take a look at Barry Allwood's last will and testament,' Isabel said. 'If the beneficiaries were named, I wouldn't have thought there'd be much scope for Anna to make a claim. On the other hand, if the wording was more general … if, for instance, Barry Allwood stated that he wanted to leave fifty per cent of his estate to his living children …' She smiled knowingly, letting Dan finish her sentence.

'Then anyone who could prove parenthood would have a claim on the estate,' he said.

'Get someone to check it out,' said Isabel. 'If Anna Matheson did have a legitimate claim, then we finally have a strong motive for her murder.'

Chapter 43

It was seven o'clock by the time Isabel got home. Nathan was in the living room, watching *Celebrity Antiques Road Trip* and drinking a bottle of lager.

'Bit early for drinking, isn't it?' she said.

Nathan held up the bottle. 'It's this heatwave,' he said. 'I needed something to cool me down. Bailey had a few mates round earlier, so he went to the offie and bought a dozen bottles. Thought I'd snaffle a couple before he guzzled the lot.'

Isabel rolled her eyes when she noticed the brand her son had chosen. *Corona Extra.*

'He could have picked a different sort,' she said. 'We don't need any extra Corona, thank you very much. We've already had more than enough to last a lifetime.'

Nathan laughed. 'He said it was on offer. Want one?'

He reached down to the side of his armchair, picked up a second bottle, and removed the top. She took it from him and sat down.

'It's not like him to buy a crate of lager,' she said. 'Is he by any chance celebrating a new job? I take it he went for the interview?'

Nathan muted the television.

'Actually, he didn't bother in the end, although he was at pains to point out that his decision had nothing to do with me or you, or with your job. He's decided to make other plans.'

'What other plans?'

'It's best that he tells you himself. He's in the kitchen.'

Isabel took a swig of lager and stood up.

'You might want a nip of something stronger than lager when he tells you what he's got in mind,' Nathan said, as he restored the sound to the television. 'Brace yourself.'

Taking a deep breath and another glug from the bottle, she went into the kitchen. Bailey was making a doorstop sandwich. Cheese and onion, by the smell of it. There were breadcrumbs on the worktop, and he hadn't put the lid back on the butter.

'Ey up,' she said, bending down to pick up a curl of onion skin that had landed on the floor. 'Your dad says you've got something to tell me.'

Bailey paused his sandwich making. 'I didn't go for the interview,' he said.

'I know. Your dad's already told me that.'

'I've decided to go to Carcassonne instead.' He sliced the sandwich horizontally. 'To stay with Grandad Corrington.'

Isabel pressed her lips together to stop herself from blurting out the first words that slipped into her head: *How is* that *going to help your career?*

She stiffened, telling herself not to interfere. 'I thought France was still on the amber list?' she said. 'It's not that long since you had your second jab, is it?'

Bailey shrugged. 'Based on the latest rules, I should be all right to travel next week.'

'I see. And you've already spoken to your grandad, have you? He's agreed to this?'

'Yes, I FaceTimed him this morning. I think he's excited about seeing me at last. He was gutted when we couldn't go over last summer, and he's not getting any younger, Mum. I want to meet him.'

Isabel pulled out a chair and sat down at the table. 'I can understand that,' she replied, keeping her voice calm. 'I'm hoping I might be able to see him again myself in a few months – but it's hard to make any long-term plans at the moment. The travel restrictions seem to be changing constantly. You do realise you could end up stuck in France if the Covid situation goes belly-up again.'

'That's all right. I plan to stay for a while anyway. At least three months.'

'*Three months?*' She was doing her best to stay cool, trying not to screech.

'I'm going to see if I can get a temporary job out there, while I decide what I want to do with the rest of my life. I know some basic French … enough to get by.'

Isabel wasn't sure why she felt so frustrated and pissed off. Perhaps it was because Bailey was choosing to run away again, rather than face up to the task of getting his career back on track.

Was she overstepping the mark? Being too judgemental? She'd joined the police force at eighteen and had stuck to one job all her life, but that didn't mean her children had to do the same. She could hardly blame Bailey for wanting to travel. It was the thing people longed for more than anything right now – but how much more wandering would he need to do before he finally settled down? Then again, where was it written that towing the line and settling down were compulsory? People had far more options these days.

'You're a grown man, Bailey. You have to make your own decisions.'

He scowled. 'You're saying all the right words, Mum, but they don't match your tone of voice. You obviously don't approve.'

'Sorry, I didn't mean to sound disapproving. All I want is for you to be happy. If going to visit your grandad is what it takes, then so be it. At least it'll get you out from under our feet.' She smiled to take the sting out of her words.

Bailey transferred his sandwich onto a plate. It looked delicious.

'I know you want me to settle down, Mum, and I will eventually … but not yet. I'm a mess. My head's all over the place. Breaking up with Sophie hit me hard. I had my future all mapped out … and every aspect of it was with her.'

'Obviously you and her weren't meant to be.'

'We were as far as I was concerned,' he said. 'I was going to ask her to marry me when we got back from New Zealand.'

Tears pooled in Isabel's eyes, her heart aching for him. 'Oh, love. I'm sorry. I didn't know.'

Bailey managed a weak smile, but his face was a picture of sadness and regret. 'Why would you? I didn't tell anyone.'

'Not even Sophie?'

He shook his head. 'Not even her.'

Isabel watched as he pressed his lips together, holding in his emotions.

'I must admit, I thought you and Sophie would last forever,' she said.

'Me too,' Bailey replied. 'I thought we were soul mates, you know? I honestly believed we wanted the same things. I didn't think anything could ever break us up … but, hey … I was wrong.'

'You were both very young when you got together,' Isabel said. 'Maybe Sophie needs to spread her wings a little … She might come back eventually. Who knows, the two of you could get back together.'

Bailey ran a hand through his hair. 'Nah. That's not going to happen. Even if she came back now, *today*, we couldn't go back to the way things were. In a way, she's done me a favour. She's made me re-evaluate things. Every day I ask myself *What do I want from life?* And every day the answer is the same. *I don't know.*'

Isabel reached out and pulled him into a hug. 'You'll work it out,' she said. 'You're still young. There's no rush.'

He frowned. 'That's not what you said the other day when you told me to get my career on track.'

'I'm hardly in the best position to give career advice, am I? Follow your heart, Bailey.'

'I am,' he said. 'That's why I'm going to stay with grandad.'

'*What?*'

They turned. Neither of them had heard Ellie slip barefoot into the kitchen from the garden room. She was wearing shorts, a cropped top and a pair of enormous sunglasses.

'You're going to see Grandad?' Ellie said. 'In Carcassonne?'

'Yeah, I'm hoping to get a flight next week,' Bailey said. 'I'm planning to stay a while … try and get some work out there.'

'Well, if you're going, then so am I,' Ellie said, folding her suntanned arms.

'We need to wait and see what happens with the travel restrictions,' Isabel said. 'Maybe you, me and Dad can go over during the autumn half-term, eh?'

'Why can't I go out with Bailey?'

'Because he's planning on staying for a while, and you'll be starting sixth form in a few weeks.'

'I could fly out with Bailey, and then come back on my own,' Ellie said.

Isabel suppressed a sigh, trying not to get cross. She loved her kids with all her heart, but they knew how to wind her up. Their constant carping was becoming a blight on their well-being as a family.

'I'm not going to book you a flight, Ellie. Not while everything is so up in the air – no pun intended. You know what things are like right now. Every time we turn on the telly there's a new rule, or a new variant to contend with. You're going to have to be patient. Besides, your GCSE results are due in a couple of days. You'll want to be around to celebrate those, won't you?'

'Why?' Ellie pulled a face. 'It's not like I've been able to take my exams or do anything properly. Everything's gone to shit this year.'

'Ellie!'

'What? It's true. Unlike most of the kids at my school, I *wanted*

229

to go to lessons and take exams. It's what people my age are supposed to do.'

'Why does it matter?' Bailey said. 'You're bound to get top marks anyway.'

'It matters to me,' Ellie said, her voice a wobbly shriek. 'I wanted to *earn* my grades. I don't want some kind of watered-down Covid grade.'

'If you do well, it's because you deserve to,' said Isabel. 'Anyway, why are you so fixated on getting straight A's?'

Ellie rolled her eyes. 'You don't know what you're talking about, Mum. It's not even A's anymore. There's a numeric system now, which you'd know if you weren't still living in the Dark Ages.'

Isabel responded with her daughter's favourite word. 'Whatever,' she said. 'You're setting yourself a high standard, Ellie. It's commendable that you want to do well, but nobody's perfect.'

'Kate and Bailey got straight A's,' Ellie said.

'At GCSE we did,' Bailey replied. 'Not at A level. The higher the qualification, the harder it gets. Just do your best. That's all anyone can ask.'

'I'd love to have had the chance to do my best,' Ellie said, her voice snappy. 'But I've missed loads of lessons this last year, and nobody in this house seems to care. It's all been about *you*, Bailey. No one's bothered about me, or how stressed I've been feeling.'

Isabel had heard enough. She plonked her beer on the table and stood up, hands on hips.

'The whole world is stressed right now, Ellie. And don't you dare say that no one cares about you, because you know that's not true. Stop looking for drama where it doesn't exist. Life's challenging enough as it is.'

She retrieved her beer with one hand and, with the other, filched one half of Bailey's sandwich.

'Come on,' she said. 'Stop whinging, the pair of you. Let's go and relax in the garden and enjoy the evening sun.'

Ellie and Bailey glared at each other.

'Or,' Isabel added, 'if you prefer, you can stay inside and watch *Celebrity Antiques Road Trip* with your dad.'

Silently, reluctantly, they followed her out into the garden.

Chapter 44

'Is the dog not out here?' Isabel said, as they settled around the patio table.

'Don't think so.' Ellie adjusted her sunglasses. 'She must be inside with Dad.'

'She's not with your dad,' Isabel said, a wave of anxiety roiling in her stomach. 'Come to think of it, she didn't run up and greet me when I got home either. She normally does, but I assumed she was out here in the garden, sunning herself.'

Bailey, who'd been munching on his half of the sandwich, paused mid-chew. Isabel narrowed her eyes, taking in his expression.

'Bailey? Why are you looking shifty? Has something happened?'

He shook his head. 'No, not that I know of.'

'What aren't you telling me?'

He shuffled uncomfortably, wiping sandwich crumbs from his mouth. 'A couple of mates came round earlier,' he said. 'I let them in through the side gate, and they went out the same way. I'm wondering … perhaps they left it open.'

Isabel stood up, fear tugging at her insides. 'Go into the house, Ellie,' she said. 'Check every room.'

As her daughter ran inside, she turned to Bailey. 'You'd better head out there and start looking,' she told him. 'And if anything's happened to that little dog, Bailey, I'll hold you to blame.'

'It's not my fault if she's run off.'

'No? Whose fault is it then?' Isabel was shaking. Anxious. 'You need to stop acting like a reckless kid and start taking responsibility for your actions. Now get out there and start looking.'

***

Once they'd established that the dog wasn't in the house or garden, Nathan joined Bailey, searching the nearby streets and yelling Nell's name. A distraught Ellie jumped into the car with Isabel and they began to scour the wider area.

Tears were running down Ellie's face. 'What if someone's stolen her, or she's been hit by a car?' she said.

'Let's not assume the worst,' Isabel replied, trying to sound reassuring, even though she was sick with worry. 'It's not as if she's a prize French bulldog or a pedigree Pekingese. I don't think Patterjacks are high on the list for dog thieves. She's probably having the time of her life … running around, enjoying her freedom. Someone's bound to find her, and she's got a tag on her collar so they'll know how to get in touch.'

Isabel had hoped her words would provide some comfort, but they seemed to have the opposite effect. Ellie buried her face in her hands and wept uncontrollably.

'Come on, sweetheart. Think positive thoughts. We'll get a phone call soon, I'm sure we will.'

Ellie shook her head. 'No,' she said, in between sobs. 'We won't. Nell isn't wearing her collar. I took it off, earlier. It was so hot … I thought she'd feel cooler without it. So, even if someone does find her, they won't know who she belongs to.'

The revelation was an emotional gut punch. Isabel steered the car to the side of the road and put on the handbrake.

'It's all right, love,' she said, pulling Ellie into her arms. 'She'll be OK. She's microchipped. We'll find her.'

**

They drove up and down and round the streets of Bainbridge, scanning pavements and gardens, hoping to catch a glimpse of Nell's cheeky little face, or her rear end scampering along a pathway.

At one point, Isabel spotted the tip of a black tail, and a flare of relief surged through her lungs – but her hopes were dashed when she realised the tail belonged to a black cat, lurking in an alleyway.

Gradually, they extended the search area, circling out to the edges of town. Ellie hunkered down in the passenger seat, quietly inconsolable.

'How far do you think she could have gone?' Isabel said. 'Do you think she might have gone up the hill to the woods?'

'Maybe,' Ellie said, sniffing miserably. 'We take her there for walks sometimes. She could be anywhere, Mum.'

'Do you know what time Bailey's mates left?'

'About half an hour before you came home,' Ellie replied, wiping her eyes with the heel of her hand. 'They're a right pair of clowns. I don't know why he hangs out with them. They obviously haven't got a clue about dogs, otherwise they'd have been more careful and closed the gate.'

'It's not fair to blame them,' said Isabel. 'Bailey's the one who should have checked the gate.'

The light was beginning to fade, but they drove on, combing the streets, looking for signs of movement. Isabel was numb with fear, and her heart was racing.

When Ellie's phone burst into life, the ring tone sounded piercingly ominous. 'It's Dad,' she said, staring at the screen.

'Answer it then.'

Ellie accepted the call, and listened, the phone pressed to her ear.

Isabel's insides turned to ice as fresh tears streamed down her daughter's face.

'What?' Isabel said. 'Have they found her?'

Ellie shook her head. 'No. There's no sign of her. Dad says we should go home and wait for her to turn up.'

They drove back in silence, a fresh layer of despair weighing heavy on their shoulders. When they pulled onto the driveway, Ellie jumped out and ran straight inside. Isabel followed on shaky legs, adrenaline pumping around her veins, along with a terrifying sense of dread.

Bailey was standing in the hallway, hands in his pockets, looking pale and guilt-ridden.

'I'm sorry, Mum,' he said. 'It's my fault, I know it is. I didn't think.'

Isabel brushed past him. 'That's the trouble, Bailey. You never do.'

Chapter 45

'I've spoken to our legal guys,' said Dan.

He was in DI Blood's office, which was stuffy and stifling. It was 9.30 a.m. on Wednesday morning, and there had been no let-up in the weather overnight. The mithering heat had drained his energy, making him short-tempered and uncomfortable.

'What did they say?' the DI asked.

Dan plonked himself onto the boss's visitor chair, which was positioned in front of an open window. The sash had been pushed up as far as it would go, and a weak waft of warm air was billowing ineffectually around the office.

'They've checked the will, and Barry Allwood's estate was left to his wife and son, to be split fifty-fifty. He specifically named Ross Allwood as his beneficiary. There was no mention of *living children*. No doubt the solicitor would have advised against that. Only a poor lawyer would draw up an ambiguous will.'

'Do you think Barry Allwood would have known ... or at least suspected that he had another child.'

'I've no idea,' said Dan. 'Even we don't know that for certain. We're still not sure Anna Matheson *was* his daughter.'

'Faye Allwood might know, but the only person who can tell

us for certain is Christina Matheson. Unfortunately, she's still unconscious. Zoe's down at the hospital again this morning.'

'No news?' Dan asked.

'The doctor had a quick word with Zoe last night. Christina's condition is unchanged, but stable. Zoe's on standby to talk to her as soon as she regains consciousness.' Isabel struck her knuckles against her desk. 'In the meantime, let's get hold of the solicitor who drew up the will. Find out if he or she can tell us anything else.'

'I'll do it now.' Dan stood up. 'Are you OK, boss? You look a bit pale.'

'I've not had much sleep,' she replied. 'The dog ran off last night, escaped through the side gate. We were hoping she'd come back overnight, but no such luck. Nathan and Bailey are going to ring round the vets this morning, and go out again to look for her. Ellie's going to wait at home in case she turns up. I feel sick … I'm scared to death something awful's happened to her.'

'Don't you want to take the day off?' Dan said. 'We can cover for you here if you want to be at home.'

DI Blood shook her head. 'That's kind of you, Dan, but I need to be here. We're at a critical point in the investigation. Nathan will let me know if there's any news.'

'Have you posted it on social media?' Dan said.

'Yes, we've put something on the Spotted: Bainbridge page, and a few other places online. My big worry is that Nell's wandered up to Calper Woods and got lost. She's an inquisitive little thing, a proper terrier. I don't know what we'll do if anything's happened to her. Ellie will be gutted. We all will.'

'I know someone who's got a drone,' Dan said. 'If she doesn't turn up soon, let me know and I'll get in touch with him. If she's somewhere in the woods, a drone would be the best way to track her down.'

The DI nodded. 'Thanks, Dan. I appreciate it.'

***

Twenty minutes later, he was back in her office with an update.

'I've spoken to Charles Gorley, Barry Allwood's solicitor. He said the will was drawn up five years ago and it was all pretty straightforward. Everything went to Faye and Ross Allwood, in equal parts.'

'There was no mention of any other children?'

'No, but what the solicitor did say was that he'd bumped into Barry Allwood more recently, at some kind of business function. Barry told him he was going to make an appointment to review a few legal matters. Gorley suggested he ring his assistant to set something up. Allwood died less than a week later. He never did get round to making that appointment.'

'Did the solicitor have any idea what Allwood wanted to speak to him about?'

'It seems not. He said Allwood was vague, and Gorley didn't press him because they were with a group of other people at the time.'

Isabel arched an eyebrow. 'Do you think Barry Allwood had found out he was Anna's father and was thinking of changing his will?'

'Maybe. Maybe not. We're flying blind here, aren't we?'

'I suppose we are, but if that's what he *was* planning, it's a shame he ran out of time.'

'It is, but his death wouldn't necessarily have been the end of the story.'

'How so?'

'Gorley said that if Anna could have proved she was Barry's daughter, she may have been able to make a claim.'

'She wasn't his daughter legally,' Isabel said. 'Someone's already checked Anna's birth record. There's no father's name on the birth certificate.'

'That wouldn't necessarily have affected the validity of her claim,' Dan said.

'You know this for certain?'

'I asked Gorley. Apparently, when it comes to being able to claim against a parent's estate, the law no longer distinguishes between legitimate and illegitimate children. However, where the parent *isn't* included on the birth certificate, the claimant has to take a DNA test to prove they're the biological child of the deceased.' He pulled a notebook from his pocket and began to read from it. '*The Inheritance (Provision for Family and Dependants) Act 1975 allows any child of the deceased to seek reasonable financial provision from the estate, even if they're not mentioned in the will. A successful claim under the 1975 Act would mean a redistribution of the estate, regardless of the will.*'

'Perhaps that's what Anna Matheson planned to do,' Isabel said.

'The solicitor also told me there's a time limit for making that type of claim.'

'How long?' Isabel asked.

Dan again referred to his notes. 'Six months from the date the grant of representation was issued.'

'Grant of representation?'

'It's the same thing as probate. In Barry Allwood's case, that was granted on 2 March, eleven weeks after he died.'

'So, if Anna Matheson was planning to make a claim on the estate, it would need to have been lodged by 2 September … just a few weeks from now.'

Dan scratched his chin. 'Why would she leave it so late?'

'I don't know,' Isabel said. 'Maybe she didn't. Maybe this little scenario is playing out purely in our imaginations.'

'But if not?'

'If not, and if we're correct, then Anna Matheson could have been on the verge of making a financial claim that would have impacted on the Allwoods. If they were aware of that, then they would have a clear motive for her murder.'

Chapter 46

Isabel had been asked to attend a late morning strategic meeting at police headquarters in Ripley. She'd tried to wriggle out of it, but the Super had insisted she go along.

'Leave Operation Zebra to your team, DI Blood,' Val said. 'They'll get in touch with you if they need to.'

Isabel was now sitting at a conference table, listening as the people around her discussed a new strategy aimed at maximising the allocation of resources and delivering a better service to the community. She usually made a point of voicing her opinions – but today she was distracted, her mind firmly on other things. Besides, she was growing increasingly cynical about the effectiveness of these kinds of meetings. They generated a lot of hot air, and not much else. No matter how imaginatively they spread their resources, there would always be too few officers. Isabel might have felt differently if they'd been meeting to discuss the recruitment of a thousand new officers for the county. Now *that* would be something worth talking about.

The one blessing was that the meeting room was air-conditioned, which made her presence there fractionally more tolerable. Her phone was on the table in front of her, switched to silent, but she was keeping a careful eye on the screen, desperate for news on the dog. Five minutes before the meeting was scheduled to finish, a text popped up on the screen.

Her heart was thumping as she angled the phone and read the message. She felt a jolt of disappointment. It wasn't news about Nell, but a short text from Dan.

The DNA results from Derenby and Allwood are back. Ring me ASAP.

She slipped the phone into her pocket and began to gather together the handouts from the meeting, ready for a quick getaway. A detective chief inspector from Matlock was rambling on about force priorities, public perceptions, and how the distribution of resources and crime prevention needed to be spread more evenly across the county. Isabel had met the DCI on several occasions – he was well known for liking the sound of his own voice. She willed him to shut the fuck up and let her get back to the station.

The meeting was due to finish at twelve-thirty, but the windbag from Matlock was still holding forth at twelve-thirty-five. Eventually, someone at the far end of the table stood up and made their apologies, explaining that they had another meeting to go to. Isabel took the opportunity to make the same excuse.

She rang Dan from the car as she drove back to the station, intrigued as to why he wanted to speak to her as soon as possible. As far as she was concerned, Edward Talbot's revelations had satisfactorily solved the mystery of Benedict Matheson's paternity. The DNA results from Derenby and Allwood were merely a formality. Irrelevant.

So why was Dan so desperate to speak to her?

He picked up on the second ring.

'Hey, Dan. I got your text. What's up?'

'Is your meeting finished?'

'Yes, I'm on my way back.'

'The DNA results for Derenby and Allwood confirm that neither of them is Benedict's father,' he said.

'You sound surprised. Isn't that what we were expecting? It certainly ties in with Edward Talbot's claim to paternity.'

'It's not that aspect of the results that's puzzling me,' Dan said. 'What baffles me is that Ross Allwood's DNA doesn't match at all. He and Benedict aren't related. He's definitely not his father, and it looks like he's not his uncle either.'

'Shit,' Isabel said, as she processed the information in her head. 'You realise what this means?'

'Why do you think I rang you? If Ross and Benedict aren't related, then neither were Ross and Anna. And if that's the case, it puts paid to at least one of our theories. Looks like we might have to rethink things.'

Isabel turned down the hill that led into the centre of Bainbridge, pressing her foot hard on the accelerator.

'I'll be back in five minutes,' she said. 'Make sure there's a strong coffee waiting for me when I get there.'

Chapter 47

Someone had been out to the Coppa Café. A paper cup of their finest blend was waiting on her desk. Dan was in her office, sitting by the window, drinking from a large bottle of water.

'Thanks for getting the coffee,' she said, as she sat down.

'I'd like to take the credit, but it was Theo who fetched it.'

'In that case, cheers to Theo.' Pulling off the plastic lid, she raised the cup and sipped the strong, rich liquid, grateful for the caffeine kick. 'You not having one, Dan?'

'It's too hot for coffee. I'm sticking with water until this heat-wave's over.'

'There's a storm forecast for later,' Isabel said. She thought of Nell, out there on her own somewhere, and hoped to God she would be found long before the thunder and lightning started.

'Let's hope it clears the air,' Dan said, distracted. 'I realise it's warm in here, boss, but do you mind if I close the door? Lucas is sitting out there, and I don't want him to hear what I'm about to say.'

'You and I are probably thinking along the same lines,' Isabel said, once the door was firmly closed. 'That if Anna and Ross weren't related ...'

Dan nodded. 'Then the DNA match between Lucas and

Benedict Matheson may have come through a different branch of his family.'

Isabel paused, sipping her coffee. 'We mustn't jump to conclusions. There are numerous possibilities.'

'One of which is that Lucas's dad is also Anna's dad,' said Dan, keeping his voice low.

'No.' Isabel shook her head slowly. 'The percentage DNA match isn't high enough. If Anna was Lucas's half-sister, he'd share around twelve and a half per cent of his DNA with Benedict. The match was only six and a half per cent, which puts him firmly in the first cousin once removed range.'

'Does Lucas's dad have a brother?'

'I haven't a clue,' Isabel said. 'Let's ask him to come in, shall we? It's preferable to us sitting here speculating.'

'And coming up with the wrong answer, you mean?' Dan stood up. 'I'll go and get him.'

'Thanks. And Dan? Bring Zoe's biscuit tin in, would you?'

***

Lucas stood in front of her desk, hands in pockets, like an errant schoolboy called to see the head teacher.

'Go and grab yourself a chair,' she said, nodding towards the outer office. 'And then sit yourself down for a minute.'

She dunked one of Zoe's chocolate digestives into her coffee while she waited for him to return.

'We've received an unexpected result from Ross Allwood's DNA test,' she said, when Lucas had settled down in front of her. 'This may sound like a weird question, but does your dad have a brother?'

Lucas shuffled. 'He did have,' he replied, a look of suspicion in his eyes. 'Uncle Simon. He died about five years ago.'

Isabel cleared her throat. 'Do you think there's any chance he could have been Anna Matheson's father?'

'What?' Lucas threw himself against the back of his chair, jerking as if he'd been shot. 'Where the hell did that question come from?'

Isabel filled him in on the details of the DNA test.

'We know there's a match between you and Benedict Matheson,' she said, summarising the situation as concisely as possible. 'And as there's no match between Ross Allwood and the baby, we're now considering whether you're related to Anna through the Killingworth branch of your family.'

Lucas held up a hand, fending off her words. 'Hang on. That's one hell of a leap. You're always telling us not to make assumptions, boss. You need to practise what you preach.'

She decided to overlook his impertinence. It was obvious from the expression on Lucas's face that she'd taken him by surprise. Maybe she shouldn't have sprung this on him.

'I only make assumptions if I'm desperate,' she said. 'And believe me, Lucas, I'm beginning to despair with this case. We've got absolutely nothing in the way of solid evidence. Assumptions are all we have right now. As I'm sure Dan's told you, there's some suggestion that Barry Allwood was thinking of changing his will. Quite frankly, when I heard that, I was bloody relieved. We finally seemed to have a motive for Anna's murder. However, if it turns out Barry Allwood wasn't related to Anna, that motive is out of the window and we're back to the drawing board.'

She could see that Lucas was struggling to breathe evenly. The atmosphere in her office was stifling, prickling with tension, the air thick.

'Maybe you're trying too hard to make the pieces fit,' Lucas said. 'Anna Matheson's murder may be nothing to do with any of this. And just because Ross Allwood *isn't* related to Anna doesn't mean he isn't responsible for her death. He could have a completely different motive. And what about Edward Talbot? Who's to say he isn't in the frame?'

'Edward Talbot is in the clear,' Isabel said. 'The woman he was with in Liverpool has confirmed they spent the night together.'

'Is there any chance you and *Talbot* are related?' Dan said.

'For God's sake, sarge!' Lucas placed his hands on the edge of Isabel's desk and pushed himself onto his feet. 'You're grasping at straws now.'

'Sit down, Lucas. Dan means no offence. All he's trying to do is work out how you and Benedict might be connected. There are all sorts of possibilities, and it's logical that we start with the obvious ones.'

Rather than sitting back down, Lucas walked over to the door. 'You know what? If you don't mind, I'd like some time alone to process what you've told me,' he said. 'Listening to these wild speculations is doing my head in. I'm going to ring my dad. I'll arrange to meet him for a drink and sound him out. He and his brother were close. If there's any chance my Uncle Simon fathered Anna Matheson, my dad will know about it.'

'Thanks, Lucas,' Isabel said. 'I appreciate it. I'm sorry to put you through this and I apologise for bombarding you with questions.' She picked up the biscuit tin and held it out to him. 'Here … stick this back on Zoe's desk as you go past. Hopefully she won't notice there's a biscuit missing. Take them away before I eat any more.'

As he took the tin from her, Lucas's mouth twitched, not quite a smile. 'Trust me, she'll notice,' he said. 'I think she counts them. If *I'd* scoffed two of her biscuits, she'd give me a right bollocking. You're all right though. She won't dare say anything to you.'

'I've only had one, Lucas. Not two.'

'That's not what I'm going to tell her.' He levered open the tin, removed a biscuit and pushed it into his mouth. Chomping and smiling at the same time, he strolled back into the main office, placing the tin of biscuits on Zoe's empty desk on his way out.

'Cheeky bugger,' Isabel said.

Chapter 48

Brushing biscuit crumbs from his shirt, Lucas headed into the stairwell, calling his dad's number as he thundered towards the ground floor.

'Ey up, Dad,' he said, when Mark Killingworth answered. 'Am I right in thinking you're on holiday this week?'

'This week and next,' Mark replied. 'Why, do you fancy doing something? I was going to call you, but I thought you'd be busy, working on the murder investigation.'

'Yeah, I am, but I've got time for a drink. Fancy meeting me for a swift one at the Kings Arms?'

'When?'

'Now.'

'It's a bit early in the day for us, son. I'm not sure your mother will be up for it.'

'Actually, Dad, I meant just the two of us,' Lucas said. 'There's something I need to ask you.'

There was a pause before Mark answered. 'Don't take this the wrong way,' he said, 'but I don't like the sound of that.'

***

Lucas ordered two pints of Marston's Pedigree as he sat in the pub garden. The drinks were delivered as he texted his dad to let him know where he was. Seeking out the shade, he'd picked a table in the corner, beneath a tree.

As he waited for his dad to arrive, he sipped his beer and reflected on how his attitude to Operation Zebra had changed. At the beginning of the investigation, he'd treated it like any other case, albeit an interesting one. His connection to the Allwoods had made things unusually complicated, but he'd tried not to let that get in the way of doing his job. He'd resolved to get on and contribute in whatever way he could to help the investigation.

Things had changed completely when he'd found out that he and Anna Matheson were related. He was gobsmacked at how much that news was getting to him. He hadn't known the woman, had never even met her, so why did he suddenly care so much? Why did it make this murder investigation feel so different? So personal? And how were the latest developments going to affect his mum and dad? He dreaded having to ask probing, uncomfortable questions about his Uncle Simon – but he needed to find out if and how he'd been connected to the victim.

He was halfway down his pint by the time his dad turned up wearing a face mask featuring a ram symbol. Mark Killingworth was Derby County through and through.

He sat down, pulled off the mask and slurped a mouthful of beer. 'Cheers, Lucas,' he said. 'I needed that. It's hotter than the Sahara out there.'

'Dad, you've never been to the Sahara.'

'Yes I have.' Mark swallowed another slug of beer and wiped his mouth. 'Your mum and me went to Tunisia in 1985. It was our first holiday together and we went on a trip to the Sahara Desert. We even had a ride on a camel. I've got photographic evidence if you don't believe me.'

'All right. Keep your hair on.' Lucas lifted his hands in mock defence.

'Are you going to tell me what's up, then?' Mark said, changing the subject. 'Why the sudden rendezvous?'

Lucas undid another button on his shirt. 'It's kind of a work thing,' he said. 'I probably shouldn't be telling you this, but the woman who was killed … Anna Matheson …'

Mark nodded.

'Turns out her relationship to me might not be through the Allwood side of the family.'

Mark spluttered, half-choking on his beer. 'You're kidding me,' he said, coughing to clear his throat. 'What do you mean by that?'

'I don't know, Dad. I was hoping you might be able to shed some light on the situation.'

His dad regarded him silently, and then shook his head. 'Search me.'

'The thing is, we still haven't established who Anna Matheson's father was.'

'Why is that so important?'

'It might not be,' Lucas admitted. 'On the other hand, it could be a crucial factor in her murder.'

Eyebrows raised, Mark put down his glass. 'I hope you don't think it's me?'

Lucas screwed up his face. 'No. The DNA match points to her being my cousin. That got me wondering whether Uncle Simon knew Christina Matheson. He worked at Allwoods for a while, didn't he?'

Mark puffed up his cheeks and ran a finger down the condensation on the outside of his glass. 'Not while Christina Matheson was there, he didn't. As far as I'm aware, your Uncle Simon never met her.'

'Would he have told you, if he had? If he'd had an affair with her, for instance?'

'Bloody hell, Lucas. I don't like this. You're treating me like I'm some kind of witness … like you're interviewing me.'

'Sorry, Dad. I need to know. I want to get the boss off my back.'

Mark wheeled his finger in a circular motion. 'Let's reel back a minute, shall we? Even if Simon was this woman's dad – and I don't for one minute think he was – what's that got to do with her murder?'

'We're trying to establish the facts,' Lucas replied. 'Work out who might have a motive. It's complicated.'

'How old was this woman … the one who was killed?'

'Thirty-six,' Lucas replied. 'Born in 1985.'

'Your Uncle Simon was already married with a couple of kids by then.'

'Come on, Dad.' Lucas gave him an old-fashioned look. 'That doesn't mean he couldn't have had a bit on the side.'

'No, no, no.' Mark objected by waving his hands. 'Simon wasn't like that. He thought the world of your Aunty Gillian. There's no way he would have cheated on her. They were devoted to each other. Anyway … why have you dismissed the obvious contender?'

'Who's that then?'

'Your fucking Uncle Barry. Being married certainly didn't stop him from playing the field.'

Lucas drained the last of his pint. 'He's pretty much been ruled out. There's no DNA match between Benedict Matheson and Ross, so Anna and Ross couldn't have been related.'

Mark laughed. 'You lot can be bloody naïve.'

'You lot?'

'You coppers. Call yourselves detectives? Has it not occurred to you that Ross might not be Barry's son?'

Chapter 49

'Sarge?' Theo said, shouting across from his desk on the other side of the CID room. 'Nicola Warren's PA has sent through the minutes of Allwood Confectionery's monthly SMT meeting for May. You wanted to see them?'

Dan glanced up from his computer screen. He'd been reviewing evidence, updating the case log and generally wrangling with the investigation. He welcomed another piece of information to add to the mix, providing it was useful.

'Have you read them?' he asked. 'Do they mention who put forward the proposal to give Anna Matheson a pay rise?'

'I've sent everything over to you,' Theo said. 'The document's called SMTMonthlyReviewMay21.doc. The pay rise is mentioned in the "marketing update" section. The wording's vague.' Theo read from the screen of his PC. '*It was proposed that Anna Matheson's remuneration be reviewed and a salary increase applied on her return from maternity leave. The motion was agreed in principle, subject to the personnel department identifying suitable job matches across different data sources and carrying out a salary comparison.* There was an action noted for Nicola Warren, but no mention of who put forward the motion.'

'Crap,' Dan said. 'I thought minute-taking was supposed to be about recording who said what?'

'Haven't got a clue, mate,' Theo replied. 'Thankfully, I've never had to take minutes. I'd rather gouge my own eyes out with a pencil than do something that tedious.'

'I don't think it's quite as bad as you're making out, Theo. You'd be good at it, actually. You have a tidy mind, and you're organised – qualities that haven't escaped the DI's notice.'

Theo stretched his mouth into a shape that was a cross between a grimace and a smile. 'Is that a good thing?'

'Definitely,' Dan replied. 'DI Blood likes people who work in a well-ordered way.'

Theo allowed himself to smile properly.

'Talk to some of the other senior managers at Allwoods,' Dan told him. 'The meeting wasn't that long ago. See if they can remember who put forward the motion.'

'You think it's relevant to the case?' Theo said.

'I don't know,' Dan replied. 'But we can't afford to overlook anything. If we can pull together enough of these seemingly unrelated pieces of information, they'll hopefully build up into a bigger picture – one that will give us the answers we need.'

Chapter 50

Zoe was back at the hospital. Waiting.

She'd been told that the doctor would talk to her when he made his rounds at 1.30 p.m. It was now two o'clock, and there was still no sign of him. As far as Zoe was aware, Christina Matheson was still unconscious.

She pulled up the top on a bottle of water, pulled down her face mask, and let the cold liquid flow down her throat. At least it was reasonably cool, here in the corridor. As she sat, she listened to the distant noises from the ward: the sound of squeaky wheels; someone shouting for a nurse; subdued laughter from the end of the corridor near the nurses' station.

At ten past two, a group of three people entered the corridor from the far end, heading in Zoe's direction.

'You're the detective?' said one of the men, presumably a doctor, but not the one she'd spoken to the previous evening.

Zoe nodded and showed him her warrant card.

'I believe you're after an update on Christina Matheson's condition?'

'That's right. How's she doing?'

'Improving. She's sustained several fractures, but she'll make a full recovery. I'm also pleased to report that she's regained consciousness.'

Zoe felt a warm glow of relief. She was thrilled that Christina was going to be OK, but even more pleased that Benedict Matheson still had his grandmother, someone who would act as his guardian and be around to look after him.

'Can I talk to her?' Zoe said.

'For a few minutes,' the doctor replied. 'I'll ask a nurse to take you in to see her, but bear in mind that Ms Matheson is still very tired. Please don't wear her out with too many questions.'

***

Christina was lying on a bed, propped up by pillows, in a sunny room off a side ward. There were dark bruises on the right side of her face, but otherwise she looked pale, and older somehow. More vulnerable.

'Hello,' Zoe said. 'It's good to see you're awake. You had us worried there for a while.'

Christina studied Zoe's face. 'I was with you, wasn't I? Before …'

'Before the accident,' Zoe said. 'Yes. You went out to buy some cold drinks from the shop. Do you remember?'

'I remember buying the drinks, and some ice creams, but nothing after that. The nurse told me I stepped out in front of a car. I've broken my leg and my wrist, and fractured my hip, and I have a concussion.'

Zoe pulled a grey plastic chair closer to the bed and sat down. 'I've spoken to the doctor. He says you'll make a full recovery.'

'Where's Benedict?' Christina asked, concern etching lines on her face.

'Don't worry,' Zoe said, trying to reassure her. 'He's being well looked after. He'll be back with you before you know it, just as soon as you're able to take care of him again.'

'He's not with Lauren Talbot, is he?'

'No,' Zoe said. 'He's being looked after by a foster family. We didn't want to leave him with the Talbots because … well, there's

254

been a development on that front. Edward Talbot came to see us. He says he's Benedict's father.'

Christina pressed her head back into the pillows and closed her eyes.

'I did wonder whether that might be the case,' she said.

Zoe put her head on one side. 'You should have shared your suspicions with us.'

Christina opened her eyes. 'I didn't want to say anything in case I was wrong. It was a guess on my part, a gut feeling. I didn't see Anna and Edward together very often, but when I did, I sensed something between them. A spark. Nothing more. I thought perhaps I'd imagined it.'

She rubbed the unbruised side of her face.

'I questioned Anna about it when Benedict was born … came right out with it … asked whether Eddie was his father.'

'And what did she say?'

'What she always said. That she wasn't willing to discuss it. That it was irrelevant.' Christina pulled herself up and stared at Zoe. 'It's not irrelevant now though, is it? Not now that Anna's dead. Do you think he'll get custody?'

'I don't know,' Zoe replied. 'It's too early to say what might happen. As far as I'm aware, he hasn't told his wife yet. I suppose a lot will depend on how she takes the news.'

'She'll throw a hissy fit.' Covering her face with her hands, Christina groaned. 'What a mess. What a bloody, stupid, awful mess.'

'It is a bit complicated,' Zoe said. 'But try not to worry. Things have a way of working out.'

Christina dragged her hands down her face and leaned forward on her elbows. 'Do you think Lauren found out? Could she be involved in Anna's murder?'

'We have no reason to believe so. She was looking after Benedict and her own children when Anna went missing.'

'What about Eddie? You don't think he …'

'No,' Zoe said, intervening quickly. 'He was in Liverpool when Anna died. That's been confirmed.'

A nurse had come in and was standing by the bed. She looked at Zoe and pointed to her watch.

'Give me two more minutes,' Zoe said. 'Please?'

'Two minutes,' the nurse replied. 'No more.'

'There's something important I need to ask you,' Zoe said, once the nurse had left the room. 'Can you tell me about Anna's dad?'

Christina stared at Zoe with startled eyes, her mouth clamped shut.

'Please, Christina. It's important. Who was he?'

Several seconds passed before she spoke. 'What difference does it make?'

'It's an important detail, information that could be relevant to the case.'

Another pause, precious seconds ticking by. Zoe was worried the nurse would come back and chuck her out before she'd had time to get the answer she needed.

Christina let out a heavy sigh. 'Barry Allwood,' she said. 'Barry was Anna's father, but he wasn't aware of it until a few years ago.'

The desire to unearth more information was making Zoe's heart beat faster.

'Tell me about it.'

Christina leaned back and gazed at the ceiling. 'I worked at Allwoods for a while, back in the Eighties. I was young, only nineteen. I've always been a free spirit, but in those days I was pretty wild. Barry was twenty-four, and already married to Faye. I don't think either of them were particularly happy. Theirs was less a match made in heaven and more a match made at the golf club. Barry's dad and Faye's dad were business associates, and the families socialised together. Barry and Faye were thrown together and the family encouraged their romance, even though everyone knew what Barry was like.'

'What was he like?'

'He had a roving eye. Getting married was never going to put a stop to his pursuit of other women. I was one of many.'

'Didn't that bother you?' said Zoe.

Christina produced a half-smile. 'Not at all. I wasn't looking for a serious relationship. I wanted some excitement, and Barry provided that. He was funny. He made me laugh. We only saw each other occasionally, a few snatched hours here and there.'

'It wasn't serious then?'

'Far from it, although we did manage a couple of overnight trips, when Barry was supposed to be away on business. I knew the relationship wasn't going anywhere though. I didn't particularly want it to. When it was over, I wasn't in the least bit upset.'

'Did you end it, or did he?'

'He did. Barry told me that Faye was getting suspicious. I'm not sure if that was true. It's more likely he was getting bored, and he used his wife as an excuse to bring things to an end. Either way, I didn't mind. It was fun while it lasted, but I had no qualms about calling it a day.'

'Did you know you were pregnant when he broke off the relationship?'

The white hospital pillowcases rustled as Christina shook her head.

'I found out a few weeks later,' she said, her expression suddenly stern. 'I went to see Barry, and he told me to have an abortion. He gave me money … cash. Quite a sizeable amount. He said it was best that I leave Allwoods, and he told me not to contact him again.'

'I take it you didn't want an abortion?' Zoe said.

'I thought about it. I even made an appointment, but I couldn't go through with it. I decided to keep the baby and bring it up on my own – just like Anna did with Benedict. She and I were more alike than she cared to admit.'

'Did you tell Barry Allwood that you were going to have the baby?'

'No. I said nothing, and I made sure I kept out of his way. I'd already left Allwoods, and our paths never crossed anyway – we didn't mix in the same social circles. I used the money Barry gave me to set up my business.'

'Selling crystals?'

'Yes. Back in the Eighties, people were really getting into all that stuff. I started off small … I had a stall at psychic events and mind, body and spirit fairs. My mum was still alive in those days, so she was able to take care of Anna when I was working.'

'And Barry didn't find out about Anna?'

'I made sure he didn't. Before my baby bump started to show, I went to stay with my mum in Derby. I lived with her until Anna was born, and moved to Milford when she was a few weeks old.'

'Milford's quite close to Bainbridge. Weren't you concerned about running into Barry?'

Christina smiled wistfully. 'I did see him once. I was pushing the pram and there he was, strolling towards me along the road, as large as life. It gave me quite a turn. My first instinct was to avoid him, but I knew he'd seen me. If I'd turned around and run away, it would have looked suspicious, so I carried on walking and stopped to talk to him. I told him I was working as a child-minder, and that the baby in the pram was my newest charge.'

'And he believed you?' said Zoe. 'Did he not put two and two together and come up with the right answer?'

Christina laughed bitterly. 'Barry was too arrogant to consider the possibility that I might have gone against his wishes. I'd told him I was going to get rid of the baby, and in his mind, that's what I'd done. He was used to getting his own way … telling his *bits on the side* what to do. He didn't realise it, but I was one of the few people he couldn't boss around – me and Faye. We were both a match for Barry in our own way.'

Zoe was conscious of the time. She'd already used up the two-minute leeway she'd been given by the nurse.

'Did Anna know who her father was?'

'I told her around the same time I told Barry … two years ago, or thereabouts. Anna was back in Bainbridge. She'd been through a hellish time in London, but she was doing her best to turn her life around. She went back to university part-time, got herself a marketing qualification, and I thought everything would be all right – but then, she couldn't find a job. She applied for loads of positions, and she got quite a few interviews, but Anna was something of an anomaly. She was in her thirties, and the companies she was applying to were looking for fresh-faced young graduates. No matter how hard she tried, she had no luck getting a job, and she began to lose heart. Depression started to creep in. I was worried she'd turn to drink again if she didn't get work. Obviously, I didn't want that to happen. I was desperate. That's the only reason I contacted Barry.'

'To try and get Anna a job?' said Zoe.

Christina nodded.

'And how did that go?'

'I rang him,' Christina said. 'I didn't dare go and see him face-to-face, because I knew he'd be furious.'

'And was he?'

'Oh, yes, and then some. When I told him about Anna, he raged at me. He shouted so much I thought my phone was going to burst into flames. I tried to calm him down … told him that I had no intention of telling anyone that he had a grown-up daughter. All I wanted, I said, was for him to give Anna some work. She needed marketing experience. A temporary job for a few months was all I was after. A leg up. Something she could put on her CV to give her the track record she needed.'

'And he agreed to that?' said Zoe.

'Eventually, but only after I'd said a few things that I shouldn't.'

'What kind of things?'

'Nasty, spiteful things. I told him if he didn't do as I asked, I *would* talk to Faye. In return for my silence, I asked him to give Anna a three-month contract. He agreed … reluctantly.

Not because he wanted to help his daughter, but because he was covering his own arse. He said I'd given him no choice.'

'And when did you tell Anna that Barry Allwood was her dad?'

'After she'd been working there for a few weeks. If anything, she was even more furious with me than Barry had been. I told her one Friday evening, after she'd received her first salary payment from Allwoods. She came round with a bottle of wine to thank me for pulling strings with my old friends.'

'So she knew you were acquainted with Barry Allwood?'

'She was aware I'd worked there when I was young. Initially, I told her Barry was an old friend, but suggested she keep quiet about it. I told her it wouldn't look good if people thought she'd got the job through nepotism.'

Christina reached towards the water jug on top of her locker, and Zoe stepped in to help.

'Go on,' she said, as she poured water into a glass and handed it over. 'You need to finish telling me before the nurse comes back and throws me out.'

Christina sipped her drink. 'After I told her that Barry was her father, Anna and I spent the whole weekend arguing. We'd had plenty of barneys over the years, but never one quite like that. She said I'd put her in an impossible situation and refused to accept that I'd done it to help her. Anyway, to cut a long story short, she went back to work on the Monday morning, and talked openly to Barry. They agreed she'd work out her contract, and that neither of them would say any more about their relationship – either to each other, or to anyone else.'

'How did you feel about that?'

'Relieved,' said Christina. 'It sounds selfish, but I wanted to keep Anna to myself. I wasn't keen on her establishing a relationship with her dad.'

'But that's what happened, is it?'

'Yes,' Christina said, as she swallowed another gulp of water. 'In many ways, Anna and Barry were very alike. They each had the ability to put their emotions aside and focus on the job in hand, and Anna was brilliant at what she did. Her lecturers on the marketing course called her *remarkable* and, despite his anger at what I'd done, Barry couldn't help but be impressed by Anna. I think, in his own way, he was proud of her. Her professionalism and skills were top-notch. Barry's son was useless in comparison. Anna said Barry had very little respect for Ross's capabilities.'

'Your daughter must have appreciated getting some recognition from her dad, even if it was only for her work.'

'You're right. She did.' Christina smiled. 'As Anna's contract drew to a close, Barry offered her a permanent job and a decent salary. They agreed it would be purely a business arrangement. On a professional level, the two of them were getting along like a house on fire, but neither of them was ready for a parent–child relationship – but towards the end of last year, I think that situation began to change. Given time, I believe Barry would have acknowledged Anna as his child ... but he died, so that never happened. Perhaps it was never meant to be.'

Zoe frowned. 'Why didn't you tell us all this from the off, Christina?'

'Because keeping quiet about it has become second nature to me,' she replied. 'I said nothing for decades. It's hard to break that habit. Besides, I didn't think it was important, or relevant. Barry's dead, and no one knew about Anna's connection to him.'

'Maybe they did,' Zoe said. 'And now, Anna is also dead. Have you considered that her connection to Barry might be the reason she was murdered?'

Christina waved a hand to stop her from talking.

'Don't say that. Please. If it's true, it means Anna's death is my fault.'

Zoe touched Christina's arm. 'None of this is your fault,' she said. 'And we shouldn't jump to conclusions. The investigation team is considering several different angles. The connection between Anna and Barry Allwood is just one of them.'

261

Christina's eyes had filled with unshed tears. 'The thing is,' she said, 'I think Anna was up to something. In the weeks before the party, she was unusually quiet, almost furtive. When I asked her if she had something on her mind, she said it was nothing she could discuss with me at that point. Then, soon after that, she told me about the complaints against Ross. I put two and two together and assumed she was planning some kind of action against him – but who knows, maybe it was something else.'

'Do you think Ross knows that Anna was his half-sister?' said Zoe.

'I'm pretty sure he doesn't. Anna certainly didn't tell him.'

Behind them, the door opened and the nurse came in, her sensible, rubber-soled shoes squeaking on the shiny floor.

'Time's up,' she said. 'I'm going to have to ask you to leave now.'

Chapter 51

Isabel had been to see Raveen in the Forensics Unit. As she left the building, she checked her phone. Still no news from home.

She tapped out a message to Nathan.

Have you found her?

His reply pinged back immediately.

Not yet. I'll let you know as soon as there's any news. 🤞 *xx*

Worry was suppressing her appetite, but she knew she should eat something. It looked as though she'd be working late again, so she needed to keep her strength up.

She took a detour to the café and bought a ham sandwich and a bottle of Buxton water. As she strolled back to the station, the sun burned fiercely on the back of her neck. Placing the plastic bottle of chilled water against her hot skin, she rued the lack of an air-conditioned office to return to. At Bainbridge nick, you were lucky if you had a window that opened.

She usually walked up the stairs, but today her feet felt heavy and overheated, so she took the lift. Emerging on the top floor, she stepped into the warm miasma that had risen through the building and become trapped in the CID room. Rather than diving into her own office, she went and sat at Lucas's empty desk.

'Are you all right, boss?' Dan said.

'Fine,' she replied. 'I need a minute to cool down. It's roasting out there. I wish the storm would break.'

Conscious of her red face and neck, she switched on an electric oscillating fan that was sitting next to Lucas's computer.

'How come Lucas has a fan and I haven't?' she asked.

'He bought it himself,' Zoe said. 'I told him he should get it PAT tested, but you know Lucas … he never listens to anything I say.'

Isabel lifted her face to the billowing stream of cold air and closed her eyes.

'Any news on your dog, boss?' Dan asked.

The compassionate tone of his voice made her feel unexpectedly vulnerable and overwhelmed. Rendered speechless by her emotions, Isabel shook her head, keeping her eyes closed to hold in the tears that were welling up behind her eyelids.

'I've just come from the hospital,' Zoe said. 'Christina Matheson's regained consciousness, and she's confirmed that Barry Allwood was Anna's father.'

Isabel opened her eyes and listened intently as Zoe relayed the details of the conversation she'd had with Christina Matheson.

'Good work, Zoe. That's very interesting, especially in light of the news I have to share. I've been over to see Raveen … I asked for some more direct comparisons with the victim's DNA, and he's had the results.'

She got up, went over to the whiteboard and grabbed a marker.

'Lucas and Anna Matheson share twelve per cent of their DNA, which means they're definitely first cousins.'

She wrote the information on the board.

'However, when Anna's DNA was compared to Ross Allwood's, there was no match at all. In light of what Christina Matheson has told Zoe, that can only mean one thing.'

Dan exhaled. 'Ross Allwood isn't Barry's son.'

Theo, who'd been sitting quietly at his desk in the corner, rested his temples on the heels of his hands. 'This investigation is messing with my head,' he said. 'How can people function when they lead such complicated lives?'

'The convoluted relationships in this case have definitely made things harder,' Isabel agreed. 'But now that we've peeled back the layers, we have a much clearer picture. If we focus on the interactions between the persons of interest, we should be able to ascertain the truth.'

'Can I throw something else into the mix?' Theo said.

'By all means,' Isabel replied. 'Every scrap of information is welcome.'

'I've just been informed that Ross Allwood's car was picked up on traffic cameras a few minutes after midnight on the day of the party,' Theo said. 'It was heading through Bainbridge on Halldale Road.'

'How come we're only finding out about this now?' Isabel said.

Theo shrugged guardedly.

'Was it Ross Allwood behind the wheel?'

'The images aren't good enough to tell us the identity of the driver,' Theo said. 'Sorry.'

'Allwood reckons he stayed at the party until twelve-thirty,' said Dan.

'That's what he claimed,' Theo said. 'And we have got footage of him leaving through the front entrance at 12.34 a.m. However, we've checked all of the CCTV footage from the factory, and there's no sign of Ross on any of the surveillance cameras between midnight and twelve-thirty.'

Isabel felt her pulse quicken. 'Let's bring him in again,' she said. 'And get Forensics to examine his car.'

***

Still conscious of the dressing-down she'd received from the Super, Isabel decided to let Dan and Theo conduct the interview. She was watching from the observation room.

This time around, Allwood looked a lot less cocky. As he sat alongside his brief, his body language was that of a wary and defensive man.

'Regarding your movements on the night of the party,' Dan said. 'In your previous statement, you said you stayed at the party until about 12.30 a.m., and that you were given a lift by your colleague, Evie Browell.'

Dan tilted his head, waiting for a response.

'That's correct.' Ross Allwood picked at his thumbnail in a show of indifference. 'Actually, it may have been a few minutes after twelve-thirty. Ask Evie. She'll be able to tell you.'

'Was there a particular reason you had a lift with Evie?' Dan asked. 'Why not get a taxi, or drive your car?'

'Evie offered,' Ross replied. 'She's good like that. Kind.'

'And the reason you didn't drive yourself home?' Theo said.

'I would have thought that was obvious.' Allwood was staring at Theo reproachfully. 'I'd been drinking. Driving home wasn't an option.'

'So, you didn't drive at all that evening?' Dan asked.

'I drove *to* the party, and got a lift home.'

'You also said in your earlier statement that the party was pretty much over by midnight, but you stayed on and were one of the last people to leave.'

'That's right.'

'Tell us what you were doing between midnight and twelve-thirty,' Theo said.

Ross scratched the side of his face. 'I honestly can't remember. Mingling probably.'

'Whereabouts?' said Theo. 'You weren't on the dance floor, or within sight of any of the other CCTV cameras at the factory. Where did this *mingling* take place?'

Ross squinted. 'In my office,' he said. 'I was with a woman.'

Theo let out an exasperated sigh. 'Why didn't you say that then?' he said. 'Why pretend you were mingling?'

Ross laughed, his brash confidence returning.

'I'll have you know she and I were mingling very successfully. I suppose I was trying to be … what's the word? *Gallant.* Yes, that's it. I was trying to protect the lady's reputation.'

'Very chivalrous of you,' said Dan. 'If a little misguided. Will this *lady* be able to confirm that you were together?'

'I'm sure she'd be willing to back me up, although I'd prefer not to give you her name.'

'You don't have any choice,' Dan said. 'We need to speak to her. She'll need to corroborate what you've told us.'

Ross pouted, pushing his lips sideways as he considered his answer. 'Naomi,' he said, eventually. 'Naomi Gregory. *Mrs* Naomi Gregory.'

Isabel watched as Dan made a note of the name.

'Let's recap, shall we?' he said. 'You're stating you didn't drive your car during or after the party, and that you were with this Naomi Gregory in your office at Allwoods between midnight and 12.30 a.m.'

'Yes.'

Dan edged forward. 'If you're telling the truth, perhaps you can explain why your car was picked up on traffic cameras just after midnight.'

Observing on screen, Isabel watched as a smile slid across Allwood's face.

'There's a simple enough explanation. My mother used my car to get home.'

'Your mother?' Dan said, sounding unconvinced. 'Your mother went home in your car?'

'Yes.'

Dan crossed his arms defensively. 'Why? Why didn't she drive her own car?'

Ross Allwood seemed bolder now, more assured. He sat back, his body loose and relaxed.

'She parked behind me earlier in the evening, and then someone came along and left their car right next to hers. She was boxed in. Mum carries a spare set of keys to my motor, so she used it to get home. She said it was easier than shuffling our cars around in the dark.'

'And Mrs Allwood will be able to confirm this, will she?' said Theo.

'Of course.'

'As your mother, I guess she'd say anything to protect you,' said Dan.

'Detectives, if you have something specific to ask, then I suggest you get on with it,' said the solicitor. 'So far, you've disclosed no evidence to suggest that my client is guilty of any wrongdoing. It's my view that this interview is nothing more than a fishing expedition.'

Dan paused.

Keep going, Dan, Isabel whispered, even though she knew he couldn't hear her. *Ask him if he knew Anna Matheson was Barry Allwood's daughter. Put him on the back foot.*

'As part of our investigation, we've been running some DNA comparisons,' Dan said, as if he'd read Isabel's mind. 'It's our belief that Anna Matheson was Barry Allwood's daughter. Did you know that, Mr Allwood?'

The look of complacency on Ross's face evaporated in an instant. It was obvious from the way he recoiled that this was unexpected news.

'What are you talking about?' he said. 'That's impossible.'

Dan let out a short huff of air. 'Far from it. Not only is it possible, it's true. DNA doesn't lie.'

The solicitor was getting agitated. 'Barry Allwood passed away eighteen months ago,' he said. 'Would you care to explain how you've managed to compare the DNA of a dead man?'

Ross slammed down his hands, his face contorted with rage.

'I've been taken for a mug,' he said, glaring at Dan and Theo. 'You've used my DNA, haven't you? When I volunteered a sample to prove I wasn't Benedict's father, I was told it wouldn't be used for anything else. Now you're admitting you've used it to … what? Prove that Anna Matheson was my half-sister? Are you allowed to do that? Is it even legal?'

Keep going, Dan, Isabel said. *Keep piling on the anguish. He'll break eventually.*

'The DNA sample we took from you was used only as agreed … for the purpose of establishing or disproving your paternity of Benedict Matheson,' Dan said. 'There was no match.'

Dan paused.

Waited.

'Do you understand the implications of what's being said here, Mr Allwood?' said Theo. 'You and Benedict Matheson aren't related.'

'Anna Matheson's paternity has been confirmed independently,' Dan said. 'We used familial DNA from another branch of Barry Allwood's genetic family, and that confirms information disclosed to us by Anna's mother.'

Ross Allwood stared at them, silent and ashen.

'We've established that Anna Matheson was Barry Allwood's daughter, and that your DNA isn't a match with Anna's,' Dan continued. 'I'm afraid that means that Barry Allwood wasn't your biological father.'

Ross Allwood blinked rapidly. When he opened his mouth to say something, no sound emerged.

The solicitor stirred himself. 'In view of this information, I'm sure you'll appreciate I'd like some time alone to talk to my client,' he said.

'Of course,' Dan said. 'That's understandable. Let's take a break for now.'

***

The team reconvened in the incident room.

'He didn't see that coming,' said Theo. 'The bloke was stunned.'

'I agree,' Dan said. 'He had no idea about any of it. I'd put money on it.'

'Let's leave him to stew for a while and turn our attentions to Faye Allwood,' Isabel said. 'Because if Ross is telling the truth, *she* was the one driving his car along Halldale Road after the party. You said the vehicle was heading north at the time, Theo? Are you sure about that?'

Theo bobbed his head. 'Definitely. The opposite direction to the one she'd have been driving in, if she'd been going home.'

'But the correct direction if she was heading up to Brightcliffe Woods,' said Isabel. 'Let's bring Faye Allwood in for questioning.'

Chapter 52

'I've rung Evie Browell, boss,' said Theo. 'The woman who gave Ross Allwood a lift home?'

'What did she say?' Isabel asked.

'Unlike Ross Allwood, she was stone-cold sober after the party, so she was able to remember everything very clearly. She was annoyed with Ross because they'd agreed to meet in reception at twelve-thirty, and he was a few minutes late. She told me she didn't appreciate being kept waiting when she was the one doing him a favour. When he eventually rolled up, he had a woman with him.'

'Did Evie say who that was?'

'Yes, she confirmed it was Naomi Gregory, a production supervisor at Allwoods. Ross asked whether Evie would be willing to give Naomi a lift as well.'

'And she agreed?' said Isabel.

'Reluctantly. Naomi Gregory's house is on the opposite side of Bainbridge, which meant Evie had to drive right across town.'

'Were you able to confirm what time Ross got home?'

'Evie dropped him off at the Allwood house just before one o'clock. I asked whether she remembered seeing any cars at the property, and she said not. There was no sign of Ross's Merc, or any other vehicle for that matter.'

'Faye Allwood could have parked in the garage,' said Isabel.

'They don't have a garage.'

'You've got to be kidding?' she said. 'I thought you said the house was massive.'

'It is,' Theo replied. 'Which is why I was so surprised there was no garage ... at least, I didn't see one when I was there.'

'Perhaps there's one round the back somewhere.'

'Possibly, although when Dan and I visited the house, both Ross and Faye's cars were parked on the big turning circle out front.'

'Thanks, Theo. Little details like that could be worth their weight in gold when we interview Faye Allwood. First though, I'd like to take a crack at Ross Allwood. Want to sit in?'

'Me? What about DS Fairfax?'

'Dan won't mind,' Isabel said, ignoring her badgering shoulder angel, who was cautioning her not to interfere. 'He can listen from the obs room. Come on. Let's see whether Ross Allwood has changed his tune now that he's had time to mull things over.'

***

Isabel's first question to Ross Allwood was blunt and to the point. 'Did the DNA results we shared with you come as a surprise? Based on your reaction, I'm assuming you didn't know that Anna was Barry Allwood's daughter, or indeed that Barry wasn't your biological father?'

The suspect had adopted the solemn demeanour of a worried man. He glanced at his solicitor before answering.

'No, I didn't know,' he said. 'It's fair to say the revelation has knocked me sideways – although, in some ways, it does make a strange kind of sense.'

'How's that?' said Isabel.

'My dad and I never properly connected. He wasn't what you'd call a supportive father – in fact, quite the opposite. He was dismissive of me, and now I realise why. He must have known I wasn't his son.'

'Do you think your mother told him?'

Ross lifted his shoulders half-heartedly. 'That's something you'll have to ask her, but I guess she must have done. It would certainly account for Dad's aloofness over the years, and his treatment of me. He was never encouraging, and I know he didn't rate my chances of taking over at the factory. More recently, he's had far more faith in his protégé, Anna. Now I understand why.'

Isabel felt a flicker of sympathy for Ross Allwood.

'You had no idea that Anna was Barry's child?' she said.

'None whatsoever,' he said, a scowl rumpling his face. 'Why would I? How do you even guess that kind of thing? Did Anna know?'

'Yes,' Isabel said. 'Her mother told her a couple of years ago, shortly after Anna started working at Allwoods.'

'Is that why she was given the job?' Ross said. 'Did my dad's ex-lover call in a favour?'

Isabel held up her hands. 'You're in a better position than me to understand Allwood Confectionery's recruitment policy.'

'We've spoken to your father's solicitor,' said Theo. 'He told us Barry Allwood was planning to meet him, to discuss a legal matter.'

'Mr Allwood died before he could keep that appointment,' Isabel said. 'However, we suspect he may have wanted to change his will … to include Anna as a beneficiary.'

'Pure supposition,' said the solicitor. 'Unless you can substantiate that point, I suggest we move on.'

'You're right,' Isabel admitted. 'We'll never know for certain what, if anything, Mr Allwood had in mind. He may have been planning to change his will … he may not. Even if he was, it's a moot point. He wasn't able to implement those changes – although that doesn't rule out the possibility that Anna Matheson was planning to make a claim on his estate.'

'Again, pure conjecture,' the solicitor said.

273

'Perhaps.' Isabel nodded. 'But you see, Ross, if that *was* Anna's intention, it would give you and your mother a motive for her murder.'

Ross scowled. 'If I'd known about it, maybe. But I didn't.'

Isabel studied him carefully. His body was tense, and he was flexing his fingers. Classic signs of nervous stress. On balance, and based on his earlier reaction, Isabel concluded that Ross Allwood was telling the truth.

But he wasn't completely off the hook. Not yet.

'You say you were unaware of all this,' she said. 'What about your mother? Do you think she knew about Anna?'

'I've no idea.'

'Not to worry. We'll be speaking to her shortly, so we'll find out soon enough.'

Chapter 53

Isabel and her team had gathered in the CID room, waiting to hear from the front desk that Faye Allwood had arrived at the station. While they waited, they took the opportunity to review the facts of the case.

Isabel was at the whiteboard, chewing the end of a marker pen. A few minutes earlier, a message notification from Nathan had popped up on her mobile. With sweaty palms, she had picked up her phone and read the two-line message preview.

Had a phone call from Bainbridge Veterinary Practice.
Someone found Nell in …

With fear twisting in her gut and a trembling finger hovering over the screen, she'd willed herself to open the message and read it in full – but she couldn't do it. Instead, she had closed her eyes and buried the phone in her pocket.

She didn't want to know, not while she was at work. She couldn't face it, couldn't bear to think about what might have happened to her gorgeous little dog. So instead, she did what she always did: compartmentalised.

She had been dividing home and work into discrete categories for years. It was her coping mechanism, her way of dealing with the horrendous things she had witnessed as a detective. Keeping her two lives distinctly separate wasn't easy, and not always successful, but it was a strategy that had saved her sanity more than once during her career.

Today, she was applying her usual strategy in reverse – shutting away her personal troubles in order to function normally at work. She had a case to solve. There were interviews to conduct. She couldn't, *wouldn't* allow herself to read Nathan's message. Not now. Not yet.

She banged the marker pen against the whiteboard to get everyone's attention. 'OK, folks. Let's review the facts. Summarise what we know.'

'That won't take long,' said Lucas, who had reappeared at his desk ten minutes earlier, smelling faintly of beer.

'Try not to be defeatist, Lucas,' Isabel said. 'Based on the DNA results and Christina Matheson's statement, the one thing we are sure about now is that Anna Matheson was Barry Allwood's daughter.'

'But we're not sure who was aware of that,' said Zoe.

'True,' Isabel said. 'But we do know that Barry and Anna were cognisant of their relationship to each other. We also know that Barry was planning to see his solicitor shortly before he died, and – before she was murdered – Anna also made an appointment with an inheritance lawyer. We'll never know for certain what legal advice they were seeking, but it's possible, if not probable, that Barry wanted to make Anna a beneficiary in his will.'

'Do you think he told Anna that?' Zoe asked.

'It seems likely,' Isabel replied. 'And as he didn't get around to setting things in motion before he died, perhaps Anna was looking for advice on how to make a claim on the estate.'

'That would give Ross and Faye Allwood a motive,' Dan said. 'Kill Anna to take her out of the picture before she could make her legal move.'

'The timing of the murder … two days before Anna was due to meet with a lawyer,' Zoe said. 'That would tally with the Allwoods being under pressure to take action.'

'The other big surprise in this case – based on DNA analysis – is that Ross Allwood doesn't appear to be Barry's biological son,' Isabel said. 'Having said that, Ross was a named beneficiary in the will, so there's no question he was entitled to receive his fair share of the estate. What else do we know? Come on, you lot, I'm doing most of the talking here.'

'Faye Allwood used her son's car to get home,' Theo said. 'We know she left around midnight, and that the car was picked up on the ANPR heading in the opposite direction to her house.'

'Towards Brightcliffe Woods,' Lucas added.

'I've spoken to Naomi Gregory,' Theo said. 'She's confirmed that she and Ross Allwood were together, in his office, between midnight and when they left the party. Evie Browell also told me that when she dropped Ross off at one o'clock, there were no vehicles parked at the Allwood house.'

'And what do we deduce from that?' said Isabel.

'Anna Matheson's body could have been hidden in Ross Allwood's car, and his mother drove to Brightcliffe Woods to dispose of it,' said Zoe.

'I'd say that's the most likely scenario.' Isabel nodded. 'We've seized the car, and the CSIs are examining it for evidence.'

Dan folded his arms. 'In a nutshell then, we're thinking either Ross or Faye Allwood killed Anna Matheson sometime after 11.15 p.m., put her in the car, and then Faye drove to Brightcliffe Woods and dumped the body.'

'It sounds simple when you put it like that,' Zoe said, 'but that kind of murder would take a lot of planning.'

'I agree,' Isabel said. 'This wasn't an impromptu act. Someone thought everything through carefully: the CCTV camera coverage; the need to delete the key card data. They worked out in advance exactly how they were going to play it.'

'Who's your money on then, boss?' Dan said. 'Ross or Faye. Or both of them together?'

'If you'd asked me that a few hours ago, I would probably have plumped for Ross,' Isabel replied. 'But that was before I saw his reaction to the news that Barry Allwood was Anna's father, and not his. He was genuinely shocked. If he's telling the truth and he *was* blissfully unaware, he had no reason to kill Anna.'

'Which puts Faye Allwood firmly in the frame,' Dan said.

'My mum never liked her,' Lucas said, stretching his arms above his head. 'And my mum's instincts are usually sound.'

Dan was pensive. 'Putting your mum's gut feeling aside for a minute, Lucas, there is something here that doesn't add up.'

'Go on,' said Isabel.

'Let's put ourselves in Faye Allwood's shoes,' Dan said. 'The worst-case scenario was that Anna Matheson would make a claim against Barry Allwood's estate. I mean, how much money are we talking about?'

'I've no idea,' Isabel replied. 'Whatever the amount, they're not short of cash. Anna's claim would hardly have left the Allwoods destitute.'

'That's the point I'm trying to make,' Dan said. 'It begs the question: would Faye Allwood have committed murder just to avoid handing over a chunk of dosh?'

'People have killed for less,' Isabel said. 'But I agree. Allwood Confectionery is doing well, and the Allwoods have a luxurious lifestyle to match. Why put all that at risk simply to avoid making a modest financial settlement to Anna Matheson?'

'Exactly,' said Dan. 'It doesn't make sense.'

Chapter 54

Faye Allwood was regarding them with eyes as sharp as flint. She had been cautioned and was now sitting with her solicitor in one of the interview rooms. Isabel assumed her brief was from the same top-notch law firm that had provided Ross Allwood with legal representation.

Isabel had disclosed details of the DNA tests, as well as the images of Ross Allwood's car being driven northbound through Bainbridge shortly after the party.

'In an earlier statement, you told DS Fairfax that you drove yourself home after the party on Saturday night,' Isabel said. 'Did you use your own vehicle?'

Faye Allwood licked her lips. 'No, I drove home in my son's car.'

'Why didn't you mention that when you were questioned?'

'No particular reason,' Faye said. 'I didn't think it was relevant.'

'So, it was a genuine oversight, was it? Not a lie by omission?'

'I had no reason to lie. I just didn't consider it important.'

'Can you explain why you took your son's car, rather than your own?'

Faye nodded once. 'Certainly. I'd parked my car directly behind his at the side of the factory. Someone came along later and left their vehicle right beside mine.'

'So, someone hemmed you in?' Dan said. 'Do you know who?'

'No, I didn't recognise the car. Rather than wasting time finding the owner of the vehicle, it was easier to use my son's car to get home. It was directly in front of mine, and I have a spare key. I'm fully insured to drive it, so no crime was committed.'

'We've not brought you in to talk about a driving offence,' Isabel said. 'We're investigating a far more heinous crime here, Mrs Allwood. I think you'll agree that murder is about as serious as it gets.'

Faye fixed her mouth in a stubborn line and stared back at them.

'I'm going to outline a scenario,' Isabel said. 'Please go ahead and correct me if I get anything wrong.'

Faye lowered her eyes and said nothing.

'We're aware that your husband was Anna Matheson's father, and we believe you knew that too,' Isabel said.

She studied Faye Allwood's expression, watching for a reaction – but her chiselled face was inscrutable, showing only the tiniest flicker of emotion.

'It's also our belief that Anna was planning to make a claim against your late husband's estate.'

Isabel leaned in, closing the gap between herself and the suspect. 'You didn't want that to happen, did you, Mrs Allwood? You were vehemently opposed to the idea of Anna sharing your inheritance, isn't that right?'

Faye's hand swatted the air, dismissing the allegation. 'I've no idea what you're talking about,' she said.

Despite the denial, Isabel ploughed on.

'I think you arranged to meet Anna on Saturday evening, after the speeches were over. Do you want to tell us what happened? Did you kill Anna in your office, or did the two of you go outside?'

The solicitor leaned in and whispered in Faye's ear.

'No comment,' she said.

'A forensic team is currently examining your son's vehicle.

Believe me, if you used that car to transport Anna's body to Brightcliffe Woods, the forensic investigators will find evidential links ... DNA ... hair ... fibres from Anna's clothing. No matter how careful you've been, how much cleaning or scrubbing or hoovering you've done, there *will* be something you've missed.'

'We're expecting the results of the forensic examination shortly,' Dan said. 'As DI Blood has pointed out, there *will* be evidence – and when we have that, we'll formally charge you with murder. But why wait until then? Why not do the right thing and tell us what happened?'

'You're bluffing,' Faye said. 'There's no proof that I killed Anna.'

'Is that right?' said Isabel. 'In that case, perhaps we've got it wrong. Maybe we should be considering another possibility ... that you're covering for your son ... that Ross killed Anna and asked you to dispose of the body.'

Faye's face twitched. 'Leave my son out of this,' she said, her words gritty with suppressed anger.

Aware of Mrs Allwood's protectiveness towards Ross, Isabel pressed on, hoping to extract a slip-up, or an admission of guilt.

'This is one situation you can't shield him from,' she said. 'You and your son both have motive and opportunity. If Ross is guilty of murder, neither you nor your money can protect him. You do know that, don't you?'

'You're whistling in the dark,' Faye said. 'My son may not be the wisest of young men, but he wouldn't harm anyone. Not even Anna Matheson.'

'You make it sound as if he didn't like her very much,' Dan said.

'That's something else you're wrong about. Despite the fact that she was a cow to him, Ross respected Anna. God knows why, but he liked her.'

'That must have irked you,' Isabel said. 'Knowing that your son was in awe of someone who was a thorn in your side.'

'Your words, not mine,' Faye said. 'I'll admit that Anna and I

281

didn't always see eye to eye but, as her employer, I was more than satisfied with her work. She was good at her job.'

'But you didn't like her, did you? Is that because she was your late husband's daughter?'

'I know absolutely nothing about that,' Faye said. 'Although you're right, I didn't like Anna. She could be nasty, critical of the people she didn't think were pulling their weight.'

'By that, I take it you mean your son?' Dan said. 'We know she wanted him removed from his position as head of sales. That must have rankled.'

'Of course it *rankled*. I mean, who did she think she was? Anna was our marketing manager – that didn't give her the right to tell me what to do.'

'On the contrary,' said Isabel. 'I'd say Anna was in an ideal position to call the shots. Is that what happened? Was she putting pressure on you? Asking for her rightful share of the company?'

'No comment,' Faye replied, exchanging a look of complicity with her solicitor.

Isabel smothered a frustrated groan. She felt as if she was chasing her own tail. What she needed, *right now*, was the forensic report on the car. She was desperate for something ... anything that would provide solid evidence and give them useful leverage. What the hell were Forensics playing at? Why were they taking so long?

The solicitor glanced at his watch. He was getting restless. Isabel filled her lungs, priming herself to come up with a penetrating, mind-blowing question – something that would bamboozle Faye Allwood, keep the interview going and buy them some time. The trouble was, the heat was turning her brain to mush.

The stretched silence in the interview room was becoming increasingly uncomfortable. Isabel looked at Dan, and he looked right back at her. They were saved by an urgent knock on the door.

When Theo leaned into the room, Isabel released an inaudible sigh of relief.

'Sorry to interrupt, ma'am, but I need to have a word.'

At last, something from Forensics. Isabel stood up and, leaving Dan to pause the interview, she followed Theo along the corridor.

***

When the interview resumed twenty minutes later, Isabel was buoyant, filled with renewed energy, and confident she could bring the investigation to a swift conclusion.

'The forensic team have finished examining your son's car, Mrs Allwood,' she said. 'Hair and traces of DNA have been recovered from the boot. They're currently being analysed, but we have every reason to believe they will be a match to the victim.'

She paused, letting the information sink in.

'I put it to you that Anna Matheson's body was placed in the boot of your son's Mercedes, and you then drove the vehicle to Brightcliffe Woods, where you disposed of the body. You've admitted you used your son's car after the party, and we know you didn't drive straight home. The vehicle was clocked on traffic cameras heading north, in the direction of the woods. That's where you were going, wasn't it?'

'The traffic camera images you've shown us are extremely indistinct,' the solicitor said, verbally brushing aside Isabel's theory. 'Whilst the registration plate is clear, there is no photographic image of the person driving the vehicle. You have no proof that my client was behind the wheel of the car.'

Isabel raised her hand. 'Save it, all right? Mrs Allwood has already admitted she was driving the car at that time, and traces of hair and DNA have been found in the boot of the vehicle. All that remains now is for us to establish who murdered Anna Matheson. Was it your client, or was she disposing of the victim's body on behalf of her son?'

'I've already told you,' Faye said, speaking through clenched teeth. 'This has nothing to do with Ross.'

The solicitor placed a cautionary hand on her forearm.

'Does that mean you acted alone when you killed Anna Matheson?' said Dan.

Faye stared silently ahead, her face impassive.

Isabel cleared her throat. 'As I'm sure your solicitor has explained, it's in your best interest to co-operate with our inquiry. If your son had no involvement in Anna Matheson's murder, the best way to avoid dragging him into this investigation is to answer our questions fully and honestly.'

Faye glanced at her brief before turning back to Isabel. An internal debate seemed to be raging inside her head, her eyes flicking nervously between Isabel and Dan. Would she keep talking? Or would she fall silent and go 'no comment'?

Eventually, Faye nodded. She had reached a decision.

'Ask away,' she said. 'What is it you want to know?'

'Did you murder Anna Matheson at or around 11.15 p.m. on the night of 7th August 2021?'

Faye closed her eyes. Took a deep breath. Nodded.

'Yes,' she said. 'I did.'

When her eyes opened again, she stared intently at Isabel. 'For the record,' she said, 'I acted alone. My son knows nothing about any of this.'

'Why did you do it, Mrs Allwood?' Dan said. 'Was it because Anna was threatening to make a claim on your late husband's estate?'

Faye laughed bitterly, throwing back her head. 'The only beneficiaries named in Barry's will were myself and my son. Yes, Anna was his daughter and if she'd engaged a good lawyer, she may – I repeat, *may* – have been able to make a financial claim. I've no idea how much she would have got if she'd been successful. Perhaps a small, annual allowance, or a lump sum of ten or twenty thousand? Fifty thousand, maybe? Whatever the amount, it would have been nothing in the great scheme of things.'

'From what we've been told, Anna was struggling financially,' said Dan. 'Ten thousand pounds would have been a lot of money to her. Fifty thousand would have seemed like a small fortune.'

Faye slapped her hands on the table.

'If she'd come to me and asked for a hundred thousand, I would probably have given it to her,' she said. 'I didn't kill her just because of the money.'

'What other reason did you have?' said Isabel. 'If money wasn't your prime motive, then what was?'

'Self-protection,' Faye said. Lacing her fingers together, she pressed her hands into a praying position. 'Everyone thought Anna was a lovely girl … an absolute delight … and, in many ways, she was. What people didn't realise is, she also had a mean streak. There was a cruel ruthlessness about her, a self-serving side that few people saw. In that respect, Anna was an exact replica of Barry.'

'Can you explain what you mean when you talk about *self-protection* as a motive?' Dan said.

'Self-protection. Self-preservation. Call it what you like,' Faye said. 'There are some things in life more important than money.'

'Health?' Isabel suggested.

'That's one of them,' Faye said, inclining her head to acknowledge the point. 'Money can't buy good health. The other thing you can't put a price on is freedom.'

'Are you saying Anna Matheson was threatening your freedom?' Dan said, his expression hovering between sceptical and quizzical.

'That's precisely what I'm saying.' Turning sideways, Faye tilted her head and addressed her solicitor. 'What the hell. I may as well be hung for a sheep as a lamb.'

'Go on,' Isabel said. 'Tell us what you mean by that.'

Faye turned back to stare at them, face-on. 'Killing Anna was risky. I knew I might get caught, but I was desperate – a frenzied gambler betting everything I had on one final throw of the dice.

I was frantic, trying to hold on to something that Anna was threatening to take away.'

'And what was that?' said Isabel.

'My liberty,' Faye said. 'The thing is, Anna knew. Or, should I say, she guessed correctly.'

'Guessed what?' said Dan.

'That I killed Barry.'

Chapter 55

The atmosphere in the interview room was instantly tense and silently expectant. Faye Allwood's unexpected confession hovered like a ghost.

From outside came a low rumble of distant thunder. The weather and the case were breaking simultaneously.

'Barry inherited the same heart defect that killed his father,' Faye told them. 'In Barry's case, the condition was under control. He took digoxin, to regulate his pulse rate. I was in charge of Barry's pills and he relied on me to remind him when to take them. I'd been doing it for years, since his heart problem was first diagnosed. I knew far more about my husband's medication than he did.'

'So, what did you do?' Dan said. 'Did you use it to kill him?'

'Before I talk about that, I want you to understand about me and Barry. We were together for a long time, but we were never what you'd call a loved-up, devoted couple, especially in the early years. We muddled along, hanging in there by our fingernails at times … but eventually, we reached a stage where we were comfortable together. We were happy enough in our own way … satisfied with our lot, you know? That's how things would have continued, if it hadn't been for Anna blundering into our lives.'

'That was two years ago?' Isabel said.

'Yes. Christina Matheson contacted Barry out of the blue, begging him to give Anna a job. Obviously, she had to explain her reasons for asking.'

'You mean telling him that Anna was his daughter?' Isabel said.

'Yes.'

'How did he respond to that?'

'He was fuming, infuriated that Christina had kept Anna's existence a secret all those years. It put him in an extremely difficult position, and he didn't take kindly to that.'

'Difficult position?' Dan said. 'How do you mean?'

'Barry was very conservative and horribly old-fashioned. He was a member of the Chamber of Commerce and Chair of the Rotary Club. He liked to think he was respected … had a certain standing in the community. He adored all that stuff … the kudos it gave him. He was worried what people would say if they found out about Anna. He was embarrassed. Not about *her* exactly, more the fact that he'd been kept in the dark by Christina. He thought she'd made a fool of him, and he found that humiliating.'

Isabel shook her head, incredulous.

'Don't look at me like that, detective,' Faye said. 'Like I say, Barry was old-fashioned. Misogynistic in his attitude and outdated in his thinking. On top of all that, Christina threatened to call me and tell me everything unless Barry gave Anna a temporary contract. As it happened, the company was planning a review of its marketing strategy, so – reluctantly – Barry agreed to take her on.'

'At what point did you find out who Anna was?' Dan asked.

'Almost immediately. I'm not stupid, and Barry was shrewd enough to realise that I'd work things out for myself soon enough, so he decided to fess up. He told me what was happening and confessed his little secret.'

'And how did you take the news?' Dan said.

'I was livid, naturally,' Faye replied. 'Although, I suppose it did balance things out a little. As you've already worked out, Barry wasn't Ross's biological father. I had an affair early on in my marriage ... more than one, actually. Barry knew about that, but he was in no position to judge, given that he was pursuing a string of women himself at the time. The truth is, back then, Barry and I led separate lives. During that period, we never had sex – at least, not with each other. When I told him I was pregnant, he was fully aware the baby wasn't his.'

'What was his reaction?' said Dan.

She gave a sardonic smile. 'We talked about divorce, but it wouldn't have done either of us any good. Barry and I were bound together by more than marriage. After our wedding, my father made a huge investment in Allwood Confectionery. The business was as much mine as it was Barry's, although never officially – at least, not until after Barry's death.

'When I got pregnant with Ross, we agreed that divorce wasn't an option. It would have been too messy. If we'd split up back then, my father would have expected his investment to be returned ... called in the loan, as it were – and that would have put Allwoods out of business. Barry and I were far from the perfect couple, but we knew we were on to a good thing, so we stayed together. Barry agreed to bring Ross up as his own, and our marriage slowly evolved into something more conventional.'

'Tell me what happened when Anna Matheson began working at Allwoods,' said Isabel.

'Barry was dead set against the arrangement at first. Initially, he did everything he could to keep out of her way. The feeling was mutual. Initially Anna didn't know that Barry was her father, but after a few weeks, her mother must have told her. I think Anna was wary, and angry, but she survived by keeping her head down, getting on with her job and side-stepping Barry as much as possible.'

'Did anyone else at Allwoods know they were father and daughter?' Isabel asked.

'No. Barry told no one but me. Ross had absolutely no inkling.'

Another rumble of thunder cracked like a sonic boom directly above the station, and heavy raindrops began to slap against the small, ceiling-height windows on the far side of the interview room.

'I'm assuming Barry and Anna's relationship must have improved during the period of Anna's temporary contract,' Dan said, when the thunder had ceased its growling. 'Why else would your husband give Anna a permanent job, and a promotion?'

'I asked the self-same question. Initially I assumed that Anna was putting pressure on him to give her a job, tightening the screws – you know? – but I was wrong. Barry said she'd genuinely impressed him. During her temporary contract, Anna managed to devise and implement some very effective marketing activities – and a few of them were beginning to reap dividends. I can't deny that Anna was good at her job, but I was livid when she was taken on permanently.'

'Because you didn't want her around?' said Isabel.

'It wasn't that. I could have lived with her doing a sterling job for Allwoods … what I couldn't stand to see was how proud Barry was of her. It sickened me. In the space of three months she'd gone from being an unwelcome interloper, to the factory's golden girl. My husband saw Anna as someone in his own image … savvy and hard-working, with a head for business. In other words, all the things Ross wasn't. And then, as he got to know Anna better, Barry started making noises about acknowledging her as his daughter.'

'And you objected to that?'

'I *loathed* the idea, but that wasn't the thing that concerned me the most. What really bothered me was, the fonder he grew of Anna, the more Barry seemed to push Ross away. They'd never been what you could call a close father-and-son team, but Anna's presence drove them even further apart. Barry was growing increasingly frustrated with Ross, and their relationship was becoming untenable.'

'And you wanted to protect your son's position,' said Isabel.

'Of course I did … although not necessarily at Anna's expense. I was willing to tolerate her presence at Allwoods … until she announced she was pregnant with Barry's grandchild. That's when things began to unravel.'

'How did her pregnancy change the situation?' said Dan.

'Barry wanted to give Anna a more senior role in the company, and he told me he was also thinking about including her in his will. Instead of leaving everything to me and Ross, he was considering leaving a share of the company to Anna.'

'How big a share?' Dan asked.

'I don't know. He didn't say.' Faye shrugged. 'I persuaded him not to make any rash decisions. *"Please be cautious,"* I said. *"Let Anna prove herself first. Don't do anything you might regret."* I reminded him that it was my family's money that had kept Allwoods afloat over the years, and I suggested his will should reflect that. He told me I was being self-seeking and overprotective of Ross's interests. Then he accused me of being unfair to Anna, said I was trying to disenfranchise her. *Unfair?* You can imagine how that made me feel.'

The bolshie indignation Faye had expressed earlier had dissipated. She seemed wearier now, dejected, displaying a bleak but remorseless attitude to what she'd done.

'Had your husband made up his mind about changing his will?' Isabel said.

'Oh, definitely,' Faye replied. 'I did everything I could to stall him, but he'd decided to go ahead anyway. I'd worked at Allwoods all my life and I couldn't bear the thought of Anna getting even one share in the company. My main concern was that Barry would side-line Ross. He complained constantly about my son's poor work ethic, his drug taking, his attitude to life. *A privileged, arrogant little shit* was how Barry described him. Ironic, given that those were traits Ross had learned from Barry.'

Isabel felt sure Faye Allwood had been equally influential in the parenting of Ross Allwood, but she made no comment.

Instead, she sat back and listened as Mrs Allwood continued with her statement.

Chapter 56

The storm broke as Zoe was driving over to see the Talbots. As she negotiated the winding lane near Bellbrook House, fat raindrops hit the car – slowly at first, and then with increasing velocity. She switched the wipers to high speed, peering through the windscreen, not wanting to miss the turn-off.

Bellbrook House stood at the end of the Talbots' driveway, defiant against a backdrop of grey sky and wet fields. It wasn't yet five o'clock, but heavy clouds were already obscuring the daylight. A flash of lightning splintered the sky as Zoe parked the car in front of the house. Seconds later, a deep crash of thunder rumbled overhead.

She smiled. Zoe liked storms. As a kid, she had loved to listen to the awesome sound of thunder. *It's just God having his coal delivered*, her mum would say. As a millennial, a member of Generation Y for whom gas central heating was the norm, Zoe had only understood the comment because her mum regularly told tales of her own childhood, growing up in a time when people had relied on coal fires.

There were lights on in Bellbrook House, and two vehicles were tucked under the carport. Zoe sat inside her own car for a few minutes, listening to the hammering rain, waiting to see if it would ease. When it became obvious there was to be no let-up, she fixed her sights on the house, opened the door and made a dash for it. Despite the overhead canopy above the front door, she was soaked by the time Edward Talbot answered her knock.

He stared, clearly not expecting to see her.

'Do you mind if I come in, Mr Talbot?' she said. 'I'm getting drenched out here.'

He took a grudging step back and let her in.

'My wife's in the kitchen,' he said. 'I've told her about Benedict.'

Zoe stepped inside, her clothes dripping. 'How did she take it?'

'Not well.' He closed his eyes, as if to erase the memory. 'She's upset. Distressed.'

'What did you expect?' Zoe said, unable and unwilling to muster any sympathy for the man. 'You're lucky she's not thrown you out.'

'There's still time,' he said, his face a picture of self-pity. 'Our marriage is hanging by a thread. My parents are looking after the kids for a few days, to give us time to talk. I'm hoping we can sort this out, and that Lauren will forgive me.'

'Your wife is the innocent party in all this,' Zoe said. 'If it's absolution you're looking for, that can only come from her.'

'I guess I'll have to be patient then.'

'Instead of begging for forgiveness, how about focusing on the things you have the power to do something about?' Zoe suggested. 'If you're serious about wanting your marriage to survive, you need to address some of your own behaviours.'

She knew she was out of order. The Talbots' marital problems were nothing to do with her – and they certainly weren't police business – but she wasn't willing to stand by and watch Edward Talbot act like the injured party.

'Don't worry,' he said, looking suitably scolded. 'I've learned my lesson.'

She followed him down the hallway and into the kitchen, where Lauren Talbot was nursing a glass of white wine. Her eyes were red and puffy, and her hair was a tousled mess.

'How are you, Lauren?' Zoe said.

'How do you think?' she said, her voice slightly slurred. 'I assume you already know about Edward's little secret?'

'Your husband came to the station yesterday and made a statement. So, yes, I'm aware that he's Benedict Matheson's biological father.'

'*Biological?* You make it sound as though he's a million miles removed from the whole fucking mess … as though none of it is his responsibility. He's Benedict's *dad* for Christ's sake.'

She held up her wine glass and waved it around for emphasis.

Zoe stood with her hands together and her feet apart. 'I appreciate this situation has presented you with a dilemma, but it's not my place to comment. Whatever happens now is for you and your husband to decide. The reason I'm here is to give you an update on the case.'

'You'd better sit down then,' Lauren said, as she guzzled her wine. 'Have you caught Anna's killer yet?'

'We have a suspect at the station. We're in the process of questioning that person, but no formal charges have been made … at least, not yet.'

'Who is it?' Edward said. 'Is it someone Anna knew?'

'I'm not at liberty to disclose that information. We'll update you further as soon as we're able.'

'Is that it?' Lauren sneered. 'Not much of an update, is it? Not if you can't even tell us who killed my friend.'

'Lauren, you're behaving rudely,' Edward said. 'You've had too much wine.'

'Oh, shut up!' she said, spinning around to face him. 'Right now, a whole case of wine wouldn't be enough to drown my sorrows. And don't lecture me on my behaviour, *Eddie*.'

Zoe cringed. Clearly, a change of subject was in order.

'I also wanted to make you aware that Christina Matheson is in hospital,' she said.

Edward gasped. 'What?' he said. 'What's wrong with her? Is she going to be all right?'

'She was hit by a car yesterday afternoon. She sustained several fractures but, thankfully, she's expected to make a full recovery. However, it may be a while before she can look after Benedict again.'

Lauren sat up, instantly alert. The news seemed to have had a sobering effect. 'Where is he now?'

'At the moment, Benedict is in temporary foster care. He's in safe hands.'

'Foster care?' Lauren repeated, making a face. 'Why?'

'That's how it works, I'm afraid. Don't worry, he'll be all right.'

'Why can't we look after him?' Lauren said.

Zoe hid her surprise. Despite everything, Lauren Talbot obviously still cared deeply about the child's welfare.

'That probably wouldn't be possible at the moment,' Zoe said. 'Your husband doesn't have parental responsibility for Benedict and, as far as I know, Anna hadn't appointed anyone as Benedict's guardian in the event of her death. The court will have to decide – but, once Christina Matheson has recovered, I would imagine she'll be appointed as her grandson's guardian.'

'I'm sure Anna's mum will do her best for him,' Edward said.

'He'd be better off here, living with us,' Lauren insisted.

'What are you talking about, Lauren?' Edward said, a baffled frown appearing on his face. 'You've spent the last twenty-four hours berating me ... furious with me, and with Anna. You said we'd betrayed you in the worst possible way. How can you now say that you want Benedict to come and live with us?'

Lauren stared at him, tears flowing from her eyes. 'I can say it because I love that little boy ... and, despite what she did to me, I loved Anna.'

Zoe noticed that Lauren had said nothing about loving her husband.

'Anna's dead, Eddie,' Lauren continued. 'You may not like it, but you're Benedict's dad. You can't walk away. Not now.'

'What about Christina?' Edward said. 'I can't imagine she'll want me involved in Benedict's life.'

'She might,' Lauren replied. 'We need to talk to her … work out what's best for Benedict … for all of us. We can't turn our backs on him, Eddie. He's your son.'

Chapter 57

Faye Allwood had found her second wind. She was becoming animated, her voice taking on a persuasive tone, as though trying to justify what she had done.

'I was incensed when Barry told me he was going to make Anna a beneficiary in his will,' she said. 'What maddened me the most was the thought of him side-lining Ross, but I knew I had to keep a lid on my anger, and go along with the idea. I cautioned Barry ... told him to think things through. I said if he felt the same way after a couple of months, he should go ahead and make the changes. I thought I'd bought some time ... time to change his mind, or turn him against Anna ... but I soon realised that was never going to happen. I had to find a way to stop him, and I knew I'd have to take drastic action. But I didn't intend to hurt him ... not then.'

'What did you do?' Isabel said.

'I stopped giving him his daily dose of digoxin. I gave him vitamin D tablets instead. They looked almost identical ... little white pills. Barry didn't have a clue.'

'What were you hoping to achieve by substituting the pills?' Isabel asked.

'Digoxin makes the heart beat stronger, with a more regular

rhythm,' Faye said. 'By taking his pills away, I assumed it would bring on a heart attack. I didn't want him to *die*. I thought if he was incapacitated for a while, he'd be unable to follow through with his plans. I was trying to buy more time.'

'You must have realised you were only postponing the inevitable?' Dan said. 'In fact, if your husband had suffered a heart attack and survived, wouldn't that have increased the urgency for him to change his will.'

'DS Fairfax is right,' Isabel said. 'And although you say you didn't intend to kill your husband, you must have known you were putting him in mortal danger. You deprived him of his medication, fully aware that the resulting cardiac arrest might be fatal.'

'Except, that's not what happened in the end,' Faye said. 'Barry didn't have a cardiac arrest because he wasn't getting his medication, he had one because he took too much.' She flipped her hair over her shoulders and stared at them.

'He called me into his office one morning and told me he was going to make an appointment to see a solicitor. He said he would make everything watertight, so that if I tried to challenge the will … after his death … I'd forfeit my own inheritance.'

'Could he have done that?' Isabel asked.

'I've no idea, but I had no intention of putting it to the test. I was out of time. I couldn't let him make that appointment.'

'What did you do?'

'Barry had been feeling ropey for a week or so … probably because he wasn't taking his proper meds. I still had his digoxin tablets, and the instructions were very clear: they should only be taken in accordance with the prescribed dose. That evening, I made a spicy casserole for dinner, and crumbled a handful of tablets into his portion. He died in his sleep that night, of heart failure.'

There was a cold callousness in the way Faye was describing her actions, a shocking lack of remorse.

'And did Anna find out what you'd done?' Isabel asked.

'She guessed, although she couldn't prove it,' Faye said. 'In the weeks before his death, Barry had dropped hints that he was going to include her in his will. He'd also told her that Ross wasn't his real son. That's why she was so suspicious, after Barry died.'

Another clap of thunder sounded outside, more distant this time.

'Anna bided her time at first, waiting to see if she'd been named in the will,' Faye said. 'When she found out she hadn't, she confronted me ... said she knew she was Barry's only biological child, and that she was willing to take legal action if I didn't put things right. She was highly dubious about the timing of Barry's death and accused me of manipulating the situation in some way. I thought she was bluffing. There was no evidence of what I'd done. Barry's doctor had been treating his heart condition for years. He signed the death certificate, and Barry was cremated. After the funeral, the only person who suspected anything untoward was Anna.'

'If she had no proof, then why did you take her threats seriously?'

'I didn't, at first. I denied any wrongdoing, but it was obvious she didn't believe me. She refused to drop it ... told me she'd go to the police and create a stink about Barry's death. *"If I throw enough mud, some of it will stick,"* is what she said. Anna had a knack for drawing attention to things, and I suppose I was scared the police would somehow find out what I'd done.'

'You could have denied it,' Dan said. 'As you've already pointed out, there was no evidence of your guilt.'

'Anna had thought of that. She swore that if the police didn't bother to investigate, or if they couldn't prove anything, she'd find another way to discredit me ... that she'd go out of her way to sow the seeds of doubt in people's minds.'

'And yet Anna never did report anything to the police,' Isabel said. 'We'd know about it, if she had.'

300

'In the end, she didn't have to. She thought her coercion had worked. After piling on the pressure and using what she thought she knew as leverage, I let her think she'd won. I told her I'd give her whatever she wanted.'

'And what was that?' Isabel asked.

'A share of Allwood Confectionery. She reckoned she was entitled to it, that it was her birth right.'

'And you agreed to that?' said Dan.

'I played for time. I told her I'd cut her in, but said I needed to consult with my lawyers first. I agreed to make her a company director and give her half of my shares when she came back from maternity leave. When she returned to work, I bought more time by telling her I was waiting for the legal documents to be drawn up. I kept her sweet by putting her forward for a hefty pay rise. I promised I'd sort everything else out in time to make an announcement at the sixtieth anniversary party.'

'But you had no intention of doing that?' said Dan.

'Of course I didn't,' she said, shaking her head to dismiss the point. 'I had no intention of consulting with my lawyer either. Instead, I used the extra time to work out how to get rid of Anna.'

'Talk us through your plan,' Isabel said. 'Why did you choose to kill her on the night of the party?'

'I knew there'd be lots of people around … a multitude of possible suspects.' Faye smiled. 'I told Anna I'd had legal papers drawn up, giving her a twenty-five per cent share of the company. I arranged to meet her in my office after the speeches so that she could sign them. I used the app to switch off the door tracking, and when Anna showed up at my office, I told her the documents were in the car … that I hadn't wanted to leave them lying around in case someone saw them. We went through Ross's office, out the rear door. I'd been outside earlier to check on everything. That's when I discovered I was blocked in. I had to move everything from the boot of my car to Ross's car.'

'So you led Anna to Ross's car, rather than your own?' Dan said. 'Didn't she ask why?'

'She didn't even notice. Ross and I have identical Mercs. Anna was hardly going to check the number plates, was she? It was dark, and her mind was focused on signing the documents. She was full of nervous excitement, under the impression we'd be going back inside to make one final announcement … that I'd be introducing her as Allwood's new director and shareholder. In fact, she was annoyed that we hadn't sorted everything out earlier in the evening, and told everyone during my key speech.'

'Is that what the two of you were seen arguing about?' Dan asked.

Faye nodded. 'She wanted me to announce her appointment before I presented the long service awards, but I told her I wanted her to sign the documents first. She was thoroughly pissed off that I'd left everything until so late in the evening.'

'Tell us how you killed her,' Isabel said.

'When we got to the car, I opened up the boot, handed Anna a legal document, and asked her to sign it. It was pretty dark out there, and when she glanced through the papers, she suggested we go back inside so that she could read them properly. As she turned away, I put on a pair of gloves, took the length of cord I'd left in the boot, and wrapped it around her neck. I took her by surprise … She struggled a little, but she didn't have a chance to scream, or call for help.'

'And after you'd strangled her?' Dan said. 'What did you do then?'

'I'd lined the boot with a ground sheet and I pushed her body onto it. Then I locked the car, and went back to the party.'

This woman is callous, Isabel thought. *Cold. Calculating.*

'At midnight, I said my goodbyes and left,' Faye continued. 'Instead of going home, I drove to Brightcliffe Woods. I know the area well, and I'd already done a recce. I wrapped the ground sheet around Anna, tied it at both ends and dragged her body into a dip in the woods. I thought she was well hidden. I didn't expect her to be found as quickly as she was.'

'And afterwards?' Isabel said. 'You drove home?'

'Yes. When I got to the house, Ross was already back, dead to the world in a drunken slumber. I was wide awake … adrenaline, I suppose. I cleaned out the car boot and shredded the fake documents, and then I wiped down the ground sheet and the rope.'

'Did you get rid of them?'

'No, I put them in one of the stone outbuildings at the back of the house. My plan was to get rid of them later.'

'And did you do that?'

'No, they're still there!'

Isabel exchanged a look of relief with Dan. Once retrieved, those items would provide them with the rock-solid forensic evidence they needed to confirm Faye Allwood's account of the murder.

'You told us earlier that your motive was self-protection,' Isabel said. 'But having listened to your confession, I don't believe that's true. There may have been an element of protecting your *son's* interests, but all along your true motive was money, wasn't it? You killed your husband to prevent him giving away shares in what you saw as *your* company. You murdered Anna to cover up those actions, and to prevent her claiming her inheritance. No one tried to take your freedom away from you, Mrs Allwood. You were completely free to make the right choice – you could have given Anna a share in Allwood Confectionery, but you didn't want to, did you? It was all about the money.'

'Perhaps you're right.' Faye lifted her chin defiantly. 'There was probably an element of pride at stake as well … I wasn't going to be held to ransom by my husband's by-blow. You say my actions were driven by money, but let's not lose sight of the fact that Anna was guilty of the same sin. If she'd truly cared about what happened to Barry, she would have gone to the police anyway. Instead, she used her position and her knowledge to gain financial advantage. Everyone thought she was a sweet, honest, hard-working girl – but the truth is, Anna was no better than me.'

'That's your opinion,' said Isabel. 'But I don't think the judge will agree with you.'

Chapter 58

'I wonder what will happen to the factory,' Dan said, once Faye Allwood had been charged, and the investigation team had gathered in the incident room for a debrief.

'I've absolutely no idea,' Isabel replied. 'It'll be up to the lawyers to fight it out. Hopefully, Ross Allwood will do the decent thing and arrange some kind of financial settlement for Benedict. As for the future of the factory, I imagine they'll get someone in to take over at the helm. It doesn't sound as if Ross is up to running the place. They'll probably appoint one of the senior managers as temporary CEO … and it doesn't take a genius to work out that Fenella Grainger will be eyeing up Anna's old job.'

'What about Benedict?' Lucas said. 'What's going to happen to the little lad?'

'There is some news on that front,' Zoe said. 'I visited the Talbots this afternoon to give them an update. Edward Talbot has told Lauren that he's Benedict father.'

'How did that go down?' said Isabel.

'Like a lead balloon,' Zoe replied. 'But I do think Lauren genuinely cares about the baby. If she and Edward can salvage their marriage, I think she'd like to be involved in his upbringing.'

Isabel turned to Lucas. 'How are you feeling?' she asked.

'All of this must have been a bolt from the blue for you and your family?'

'You could say that,' Lucas replied. 'Knowing what I know now … what Faye Allwood was willing to do to keep her hands on the factory … let's just say I'm glad my mum didn't challenge my grandad's will back in the day.'

Dan looked at his watch. 'The night's still young,' he said. 'Anyone fancy going for a pint and a bite to eat at the pub?'

'I'm up for that,' Theo said.

'Me too,' said Lucas.

'I need to get home, so I'll give it a miss, if you don't mind,' Isabel said. 'But well done, everyone. You've all done a cracking job. Enjoy the pub, and make sure you're in early tomorrow with clear heads.'

Chapter 59

After the DI had brought the debrief to a close, people began to drift away. Zoe stayed where she was, her back against the wall, arms folded, staring into space.

'You OK, Zoe?' said Will Rowe, who was standing next to her.

She shrugged. 'I'm fine. Just reflecting on the case … thinking about the victim, and baby Benedict, and how unfair life can be sometimes.'

Will folded his arms, his feet apart. 'I'm not going to argue with you,' he said. 'But what I will say in life's defence is that it's not all bad. There are fun times to be had as well, if you know where to look.'

Zoe smiled and stood up straight. 'If you say so.'

'With that in mind,' Will said, doing his best to sound casual. 'I was wondering … are you going to the pub? I'll buy you a drink if you do.'

Zoe pulled a face. 'I don't think so. Pubs aren't really my thing.'

'Right. No worries.' Red-faced and crestfallen, Will turned and began to walk away.

'I do like food though,' Zoe said. 'If you're willing to forego the pub, we could go for a pizza.'

She watched as a beaming grin emerged from Will's beard. 'Sounds good to me,' he said.

'We could have a bottle of red wine with it, if you want?' Zoe said. 'Or some beers.'

'Oh, so you do drink then?'

'Yeah. Course. Just not in pubs.'

'I'll remember that for next time,' Will said.

She laughed. 'What makes you think there's going to be a next time?'

He smiled. 'It's just a feeling I have.'

Chapter 60

Isabel stood on her driveway and breathed in the earthy, petrichor scent of the rain. The storm had passed. The heatwave was over, and so was Operation Zebra. In theory, she should have felt happy and relieved – but instead, she was petrified. Paralysed by fear.

She still hadn't mustered the courage to read Nathan's message. Instead, she'd driven straight home after the debrief to discover first-hand what had happened to Nell.

She walked towards the house on legs that felt like jelly, her emotions seesawing between hope and trepidation. Slipping her key in the lock, she opened the door and paused. Dread was squeezing the breath from her lungs. She listened.

At first, she thought she'd misheard – that she had somehow conjured the sound in her imagination.

Claws.

Nell's claws, skittering across the wooden floor in the living room.

And then, there it was. Her little grey face, ears flapping as she pelted into the hallway, racing towards Isabel. A sunburst of joy.

With a shudder of relief, Isabel dropped to her knees and swept Nell into her arms, burying her face in the dog's scruffy black fur and breathing in the scent of doggy shampoo.

'Where have you been?' she said, laughing as the dog licked her face. 'You've had us all worried to death, you little scamp.'

Nell wriggled, wagging her tail before breaking free and spinning round excitedly. She looked exceptionally pleased with herself and none the worse for wear.

'Now that you've had a taste of freedom, I hope you're not going to make a habit of this, Nelly.'

As if requesting forgiveness, the dog came back and licked away the tears that were spilling down Isabel's cheeks.

'It's good to see you, girl,' she said. 'I'm so glad you came back to us.'

As the dog scampered along the hallway, Isabel pulled out her phone, touched the screen and read Nathan's message in full.

Had a phone call from Bainbridge Veterinary Practice. Someone found Nell in their garden and took her in. The vet scanned her microchip and contacted me through the phone number on the database. He says she's a bit smelly and very muddy, but otherwise fine. I'm on my way to collect her now. I'll give her a bath before you come home. As you might imagine, Ellie is overjoyed, and Bailey is mightily relieved. See you later. ♡ 🐾 *xx*

She stood up, following the same route the dog had taken – through the living room and into the kitchen. Nathan was in there, chopping cucumber for a salad. The aroma of herby roast chicken was drifting from the oven, and a pan of minted new potatoes was boiling on the hob.

He turned and smiled, his face beaming. 'I take it you got my message?'

'I got it,' she said, 'but I didn't read it until a few seconds ago. I couldn't bring myself to. I was too scared.'

Nathan opened his arms and she moved in, hugging him tightly.

'In that case, it must have been a lovely surprise to find Nell here, safe and sound.'

'*Lovely surprise* doesn't even begin to cover it.' Isabel tipped back her head and looked into Nathan's eyes. 'I thought we'd lost her. For good.'

'I must admit, I was really worried myself, although I was putting on a brave face for Ellie's sake.'

'Where is Ellie?' Isabel asked.

'Upstairs, talking to her mates, telling them the good news.'

'And Bailey?'

'At Kate's. He went with me to the vet's though. When they brought Nell out to us, he got very emotional. I've never seen him like that before. It was the relief, I suppose. We stopped off on the way back so he could buy you a present, by way of apology.'

Nathan pointed towards the table, where a large opuntia cactus sat in the centre, a purple ribbon tied around the pot. Isabel picked up the handwritten note that was propped up against it.

A prickly present from your prick of a son. Sorry I messed up. I promise I'll be more careful in future. xx

Lifting it carefully to avoid the barbed, bristly spines, Isabel examined the flat, pad-like stems of the cactus and smiled.

'As peace offerings go, it's an unusual choice,' Nathan said.

'Much appreciated nonetheless.'

'He got it from that new florist on the high street. He's been picking spines out of his hand all afternoon.'

Isabel laughed. 'What time will he be back?'

'Not until later. He's staying at Kate's for dinner.'

Isabel smiled wryly.

'He bought his plane ticket today, Issy.'

'I see.' She pulled out a chair and sat down. Nell came over and lay at her feet, and Isabel bent down and stroked her ears. 'He's definitely going then?'

'It looks that way.'

'I'll miss him,' she said.

'Really? Even though he's been acting like a reckless teenager?' Nathan said.

Isabel remembered the way her blood pressure had skyrocketed when Nell went missing. She thought about the way Bailey hogged the sofa, his habit of leaving smelly socks in random places around the house, and the knack he had for filching every last piece of cheese in the fridge. And then she thought about Christina Matheson, who would never see her beloved daughter again.

'Yes,' she said, her heart filling with an overwhelming sense of love and gratitude. 'In spite of everything, I'll miss him.'

Nathan smiled. 'There's no need to be sad. He'll be back.'

'I know he will,' she replied. 'I know.'

Acknowledgements

I do hope you've enjoyed reading *Last Seen Alive*, solving the case alongside Isabel, and discovering what her family and her team have been up to. It seems like only yesterday that my debut novel, *In Cold Blood*, won the 2019 Gransnet and HQ writing competition. Now here I am, writing the acknowledgements for book three in the DI Isabel Blood series. Time really does fly.

As always, huge thanks go to the team at HQ, especially my brilliant editor, Belinda Toor, for her intuitive feedback on the book, and the help she has offered to me as a writer. Being an HQ author is a lot like being a member of a big, supportive family – you know they are there for you when you need them, and that someone always has your back! A special shout out to fellow HQ authors Helen Yendall, Jenny O'Brien and Amanda Brittany. Thanks for your online camaraderie and friendship, ladies. I hope we all get to meet in person one day soon.

Special thanks to Stuart Gibbon of the GIB Consultancy, who once again helped me navigate the complexities of policing as I worked through my fictional investigation (if there are any errors, they are my own). I can heartily recommend Stuart's books and consultancy service to crime writers in need of advice on police procedures.

Love and thanks to my wonderful family and friends – your encouragement means a lot. I'd also like to thank the bloggers and reviewers who have taken the time to read and recommend my novels. It's wonderful to know there are people out there who truly 'get' and enjoy my books – their feedback gives me the impetus I need to keep on writing.

Several people have asked whether the fictional town of Bainbridge is based on a real place in Derbyshire – and I can reveal that it is loosely based on Belper, where I grew up (although I've taken liberties with the setting, for plot purposes). Belper is a beautiful town, located along the Derwent Valley Mills World Heritage Site, halfway between Derby and Matlock Bath. It is packed with lovely shops, cafés and places to eat – so if you're ever in the area, it's well worth a visit. You can learn more about the town on lovebelper.co.uk.

Last, but definitely not least, I'd like to acknowledge the man who is always there when I need him – my husband, Howard. Thank you for encouraging and supporting me in whatever I choose to do, and for the cups of Ringtons you deliver with a smile during my writing stints. I'm sure it's those three o'clock servings of strong tea (with 2ccs of love) that keep me going! I'm looking forward to sharing lots of exciting adventures and holidays with you in 2022 and beyond.

Keep reading for an excerpt from
In Cold Blood …

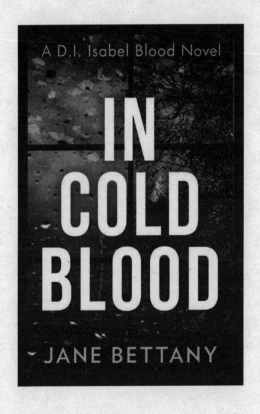

Chapter 1

The pantry was musty and airless and smelt faintly of curry powder and something that Amy couldn't identify. It was a tiny space, crammed with out-of-date food, a battered collection of saucepans, and containers filled with dried fruit and breakfast cereals. She emptied the shelves doggedly, thrusting everything into a heavy-duty bin bag.

Reaching into the corner of the highest shelf, she retrieved the last items: a jar of pickled onions and some homemade blackberry jam. Strictly speaking, she should throw the contents away and wash out the jars for recycling – but sod that. She had better things to do with her time. Instead, being careful not to break the glass, Amy placed the jars in the bag and tied it with a double knot ready to take to the bin.

It was as she turned to switch off the light that she noticed the marks on the wall. Height marks. Just inside the door.

A child grew up in this house, she thought, as she traced the pencilled scratches with her fingers. *An only child. One set of marks.*

The first measurement appeared in the lower third of the wall, alongside a date – 15th January 1965. The marks crept higher with each passing year. The last was dated 15th January 1977 and recorded a height of 5 6 .

Perhaps the 15th of January was the child's birthday, Amy thought. *There must have been an annual ritual to record his or her height on the pantry wall.*

She wondered why the marks had stopped in 1977. At 5 6 , a teenage girl would be fully grown. A boy might have gone on to gain a few more inches.

The measurements were a part of the history of the house that would soon be gone forever. When the new kitchen was installed, the pantry would be removed and replaced with tall, sliding larder cupboards. She and Paul had chosen a range of expensive, glossy units that would provide the kind of high-quality finish they hoped would sell the house.

Planning permission had been granted for a huge extension that would more than double the size of the existing kitchen. Amy's vision was for a light-filled, open-plan living space with shiny work surfaces, top-of-the-range appliances, and a vast dining area. There would be skylights and bi-fold doors opening onto the rear garden. Once completed, the bright, airy room would be the redeeming feature of the otherwise unremarkable 1960s house they had bought at auction eight weeks earlier.

Grabbing the bin bag, Amy took one last look at the height marks before switching off the light and closing the pantry door. It was cold, so she flicked the kettle on to make a hot drink. Paul had been outside for most of the day, digging out the foundations for the extension. He would be ready for another brew.

As she waited for the water to boil, the back door opened and Paul came in, shivering. He was pale. Unsmiling.

'What's up?' Amy said. 'Has something happened?'

'You could say that. I've only gone and found a fucking body.'

Amy tutted. 'Yeah, right. Very funny, bro.' Paul had been a wind-up merchant all his life. It was a trait he should have grown out of by now.

'Seriously. I'm not kidding, Ames.'

318

'Course you're not. What is it? A cat? Dog? Someone's long-dead hamster?'

'It's an animal, all right. Of the human variety.'

Dread tugged at Amy's stomach muscles. 'You'd better be joking,' she said.

'Come and take a look for yourself if you don't believe me.'

She followed him outside. They skirted the partially excavated foundation trench and stood next to what would eventually be the far corner of the extension.

'Down there.' Paul pointed at something protruding from the soil.

Leaning in closer, Amy realised it was the upper part of a human skull; the forehead and eye sockets jutted out from the damp layer of earth at the bottom of the metre-deep trench. If it had been buried a few inches lower, Paul would never have known it was there.

'Shit!' She blew air through her cheeks. 'This is awful.'

'You can say that again. It's going to delay everything. There's no chance of getting the extension finished before the new year now.'

Amy wrapped her arms across her body and glared at her brother.

'Paul! Are you for real? A body, *somebody*, has been lying here for God knows how long and all you're bothered about is the extension?'

'Come on, sis, don't give me a hard time. Our inheritance is tied up in this house. We need to get the work finished, sell up and move on to the next project. That' – he pointed into the trench – 'is a bloody disaster. The delay it'll cause is bad enough, but if word gets out, it's going to knock thousands off the property value. No one will be interested in buying this place, with or without a swanky kitchen. Who wants to live in a house where someone's been murdered?'

Paul's usual flippancy had vanished, replaced by a demeanour that was uncharacteristically sombre, almost hostile. He was obviously worried.

'Do you think that's what happened here then?' Amy said. 'Murder?'

'Of course it is. Use your nous. The body didn't bury itself, did it?'

'It could have been here for hundreds of years,' she said. 'A body buried during the civil war or something.'

'Civil war?' He scowled, shaking his head dismissively. 'What are you on about, Amy? This isn't an ancient battlefield.'

'OK. So maybe it *was* buried a lot more recently. Either way, the local paper's going to have a field day.'

Paul trailed the fingertips of his right hand along his jawline and studied the trench thoughtfully. 'Only if they find out about it,' he said.

'What do you mean?' She narrowed her eyes, staring at her brother in disbelief. 'Of course they'll find out.'

'Not if we don't report it.'

'What?' she said, incredulous. 'No way!'

'Think about it. If I hadn't dug such a deep trench, or the body had been buried a few inches further down, we'd have been none the wiser.'

Amy lifted her hands and locked her fingers across the top of her head. 'You're not seriously suggesting we keep quiet about this?'

'Why not? If I pour the concrete foundations now, this little problem will stay buried forever. No one will know but us.'

He leaned back and let the muscles in his shoulders relax. Just talking about a solution seemed to have calmed him. Paul's proposal offered a quick fix, an easy way out – but Amy was horrified by the idea.

She spun away from the trench, groaning with exasperation. 'Firstly,' she said, 'this is not a "little problem". Whoever it is lying down there was once a living, breathing human being. Don't you think they deserve some kind of justice, or a proper burial at least? And secondly, what if the person responsible for this is still around? They know what's hidden here. If they get away with it, what's to say they won't do it again somewhere else?'

'Bloody hell, sis.' Paul rubbed the back of his neck and kicked irritably at a clump of soil with his work boot. 'Why do you always have to be such a goody-two-shoes?'

Amy peered down at the skull – into the empty eye sockets from which someone had once looked out at the face of their killer. *Every house has its own secret history*, she thought, remembering the height marks scratched into the pantry wall. *Some things are best left hidden, but this definitely isn't one of them.*

She pulled out her phone and dialled 101.

Chapter 2

Detective Inspector Isabel Blood gripped the steering wheel of her car and drove through the streets of Bainbridge as fast as the speed limit would allow. She was heading to the secondary school where her youngest daughter was a pupil. At Isabel's age, attending a parents' evening should have been a thing of the past, but life had ricocheted off in an unexpected direction when Ellie was born.

It was damp and starting to get dark by the time she pulled into the school car park. She'd promised to meet Nathan outside the main entrance at five o'clock and she was already five minutes late.

There was no sign of him as she ran towards the school. He must have gone inside already. Pushing through the revolving glass door, Isabel dashed down the central corridor towards Ellie's form room. Nathan was waiting outside.

'I didn't think you were going to make it,' he said.

'Sorry. Something came up. You know what it's like.'

'You should have taken the afternoon off. They owe you enough hours.'

Isabel pressed her shoulder against a wooden locker and smiled. 'It's not always possible, as well you know.'

A door opened behind them and Ellie's form teacher, Miss Powell, beckoned them into the classroom.

They sat down and listened as the teacher began to deliver her verdict on how their fourteen-year-old daughter was doing in her lessons.

'Ellie is highly intelligent, self-assured, eloquent …'

Nathan was unable to contain a grin.

'However …'

Nathan's smile evaporated.

'Although Ellie is extremely capable, I'm concerned about her recent behaviour. She used to be a model pupil, but she's been acting very negatively since the beginning of term. She's become argumentative and she wastes a lot of time messing around with her friends.' The teacher paused to let her words sink in. There was a note of frustration in her voice as she continued. 'She's studying for her GCSEs now and she really needs to take her schoolwork more seriously, otherwise she'll fall behind. So far this term, she's handed homework in late on five separate occasions and she's not engaging in class like she used to. More worryingly, she's been turning up late for school in the mornings.'

'Late?' Isabel leaned forward, a sense of unease rippling somewhere beneath her ribs. This didn't sound like Ellie. Not at all. She'd always been a good kid.

'She's been catching the school bus, hasn't she?' said Nathan. 'Perhaps it's been running late, or she missed it.'

Miss Powell was unswayed by his line of defence. 'There have been no problems reported with the school buses. Besides, when I spoke to Ellie, she told me she'd been walking to school. That's fine, of course, if it's what she wants to do, but the school is a long way from where you live. If she's going to walk, she needs to set off earlier and get here on time.'

Isabel looked at Nathan, who appeared to be as baffled as she was.

'We had no idea she was walking to school,' Isabel said. 'We'll ask her about it.'

'Perhaps you could also find out why she's stopped coming to the after-school book club,' Miss Powell added.

Inexplicably, it was this final revelation that shocked Isabel the most. Ellie's love of books was legendary. The possibility that her love affair with literature might be over prematurely saddened Isabel inordinately.

'She still does plenty of reading at home,' Nathan said.

Miss Powell smiled. 'That's reassuring to hear, but I'm worried that Ellie is losing interest in her work here, at school. I'm disappointed. She could do so much better.'

'We'll talk to her … find out what's wrong. Won't we, Nathan?'

Although Nathan nodded supportively, Isabel knew that she would be the one who would have to deliver the reprimand. As far as her husband was concerned, their youngest child could do no wrong – and nothing the teacher said would change his opinion.

Having delivered the negative elements of Ellie's report, Miss Powell allowed herself a tight smile. 'There is one subject in which Ellie has been excelling …'

Nathan nudged Isabel and winked.

'Her art tutor is very impressed with the work she's been producing.' The teacher picked up the written report and read from it. 'He says … *Ellie is creative and talented and has a natural gift.*'

'She gets that from me,' said Nathan.

Isabel gave him a sideways glance and focused her attention back on the teacher.

Miss Powell put down the report and leaned back. 'There's an exhibition of artwork in the main hall,' she told them. 'Please take a look on your way out. Several of Ellie's pieces are on show.'

Isabel had switched her phone to silent, but she felt it vibrate in her pocket. Pulling it out, she glanced down at the screen. It was her colleague Dan Fairfax, her sergeant. He knew where she was. He wouldn't be ringing unless it was important.

'I'm so sorry.' Isabel stood up. 'Technically I'm still on duty, so I need to take this.'

She answered the call on her way out of the classroom. 'This had better be important, Dan.'

'It is, boss. I wouldn't disturb you otherwise. We've had word that a body's been found. I thought you'd want to know.'

Nathan had followed her out into the corridor clutching a printed copy of Ellie's report.

'Hang on, Dan. I need to have a quick word with Nathan.' Isabel turned to her husband. 'There's a body. I have to go.'

'Can you spare a couple of minutes to look at Ellie's artwork on your way out?'

'I'd rather not rush it,' she said, shame clawing at her conscience.

Nathan sighed, disappointed. Over the years, he had reluctantly accepted that sometimes her job had to take priority over family commitments. It was a regrettable reality they'd both come to terms with, but that didn't stop Isabel feeling guilty. Occasionally, being a good copper meant being a bad parent, or a rubbish wife. Mostly, Isabel loved her job, but there were times when she hated the way it screwed with her life.

'It's better if I come back another time and have a proper look,' she said, suppressing a flush of self-reproach. 'Sorry, Nathan. I'm needed urgently.'

She planted a swift kiss on his cheek before hurrying back along the main corridor towards the exit, the phone clasped to her ear.

'I'm on my way, Dan. Tell me where I need to be and I'll meet you there.'

'The property's on Ecclesdale Drive. Number 23,' Dan said. 'It's on that big, sprawling estate on the eastern side of town. Head for Winster Street and then turn left—'

'It's OK.' She cut him off. 'I know where it is.'

Isabel didn't need directions. She knew it well.

***

Ecclesdale Drive sliced through the centre of a housing estate that had sprung up in the early 1960s and had grown every decade since. The outlying fields that Isabel remembered from childhood had burgeoned into a confusing network of streets and cul-de-sacs, each one crammed with showy red-brick properties.

The houses in the original part of the estate were plainer, but built on bigger plots, with long gardens filled with well-established trees and shrubs. Isabel turned onto Winster Street, driving past the recreation ground she'd visited frequently as a child. The old slide was still there, as well as a vast climbing frame and a new set of swings. The flat wooden roundabout the local kids had called the 'teapot lid' had been removed on safety grounds in the 1970s, as had the conical swing that had been shaped like a witch's hat. Isabel smiled as she recalled the wild, spinning rides she had taken on that pivoted swing.

She took the second left into Ecclesdale Drive. The street was long and crescent-shaped, curving down towards an infant school and the newsagent's shop at the end. It was years since Isabel had been here. Ecclesdale Drive held lots of memories, but not all of them were good.

She pulled up behind two police vehicles that were parked halfway along the road. Her hand trembled as she switched off the engine, her fingers quivering involuntarily like the blue-and-white police tape that was fluttering around the outer cordon of the crime scene. Battling a growing wave of unease, Isabel took a deep breath and got out of the car.